Mustard's Last Stand

Kathy McIntosh

Dogged Kat Press
ISBN-13: 978-0615954707
Second Edition

DEDICATION

To my daughter, Caroline Tinker, for introducing me to the original Roadkill and for taking such delight in the release of my first novel.

To my husband, Mark Timmerman, whose belief in me rarely wavers.

And to Mother Earth.

One
Where's the Map?

Ed Mustard figured his life must be a geography lesson. Peaks, valleys, and no topographic map. He slogged on. Up? Down? Who knew? For sure, this jaunt to his ex-wife's wake at the home of his former mother-in-law hit close to bottom.

Time to leave. Past time.

He elbowed toward the street, through the small contingent of reporters. Most accepted his "No comment" reply to their questions and let him pass. Most. Not Con Lawrence, the persistent television anchor whose garlic and gin breath announced his presence before his intrusive question.

"What's the *real* story, Ed? I heard you're leaving Los Angeles. Is it true?"

"Watch out!" The high-pitched, frightened voice of Alexis Margolis, Ed's literary agent, rang out over the din of the paparazzi.

Ed whirled at Alex's cry. Not fast enough to catch the bright yellow plastic jug that sailed at him, striking his shoulder and head. He winced and jerked away from the blow. The jug bounced off his head, its already loose lid popping free. Despite Ed's effort to catch it, the jug fell to the ground in front of him, its gritty gray contents spewing over him and Con Lawrence.

His mother-in-law's distinctive cackle broke the silence that had fallen after Alex's shout. "Here you go. All that's left of the 'incomparable young actress Lise Clanahan.' She's all yours."

The door slammed behind Marliss Clanahan, allowing her return to the remnant of guests celebrating the short frantic life of her famous daughter.

"Oh, gross." Con Lawrence brushed at his clothes and backed away from Ed.

A trace of a smile came to Ed's mouth. *Hooray. Finally, a way to get rid of pesky reporters.*

Bob Gilman, Ed's lawyer, moved in front of Ed. In his large, dark-skinned hand he held a short-handled whisk broom and a dust pan. "These might help. Keep 'em in my car."

"Of course you do." Ed's smile broadened. Everything about Bob was impeccable—his clothing, his haircut, his car, his home. Count on Bob to have a broom in his trunk.

Ed knelt and swept the ashes of his ex-wife into the plastic mustard jug. He tuned out the clicks and whirs of cameras and the low-pitched murmur of reporters.

Not the way Lise hoped to be remembered.

❧

Into the Unknown, But Not Alone

Ed popped the trunk of his ancient Camry and enjoyed another fleeting smile at the wrinkled noses of his companions. Despite his efforts to clean the car, the trunk retained lingering and not-so-faint odors of the belongings of its previous owners. One of them may have delivered pizza or at least hauled a great many greasy boxes home. Another, like Ed's brother in Idaho, might have collected dead animals—the trunk wafted out an unappetizing metallic odor of dried blood.

"Holy crap." Alex stepped back.

"I don't think so," Bob said. "There's nothing holy about that stench."

"Excuse me," Ed chuckled as he tried to act seriously affronted. "That's my car you're insulting."

Alex widened her incredible green eyes. "Taking a few steps down in lifestyle might be appropriate right now. But this ..." She gestured at the run-down Camry. "What kind of statement is this?"

Ed sighed. "Not a statement. Reality."

"Jesus. The reality is, you've lost your mind. You sold the McMansion, not a bad decision considering it's so incredibly ugly. You hand that screeching witch," she tilted her head back toward the Clanahan home, "a pile of money she obviously appreciated—not—and you've stopped writing."

"I haven't stopped writing." Ed rearranged the boxes in the trunk to make room for the plastic jug. He slammed the trunk. "Took a break. I'll have the treatment to you soon." He'd promised his agent the narrative version of his next film script weeks earlier. He'd yet to write a word of it. He moved to the driver's door, faced his lawyer and his agent. His friends.

Bob's face held sympathy and concern. "No one could have saved Lise. Stop blaming yourself."

"Nobody else to blame."

"I think it's moronic that you won't tell me where you're going." Even so, Bob walked forward and extended his hand.

Ed grasped Bob's hand and pulled the taller black man into a hug. "Don't know."

Alex crossed her arms. "I'm pissed at you. I'll find another writer and you'll be looking for a new agent if I don't get something in three weeks." She grabbed him in a close hug. "Even so, I love you, sweetie. Take care."

❧

The cremains of Ed's ex-wife stayed in the trunk of the old car for two hours and seventeen minutes. Not that Ed timed it.

Outside Barstow, he pulled off Interstate 15 at a rest stop and extracted an envelope stuffed with state maps from the side pocket.

He'd spoken the truth to Bob. When he left Santa Monica, his only intention was to drive. To escape. Since heading west would be a short drive, he'd turned east. He took freeways to avoid familiar landmarks in the city he'd lived in for nearly a decade. He'd said his goodbyes in a long bike ride the previous week, before he'd sold his beloved road bike and his BMW convertible.

Peering at the California map, Ed decided to take I-40 to Needles, following Route 66 as much as possible. No more signs for Route 66, but he'd look for The Old National Trails highway turn-offs.

After a pit stop, Ed paused at the trunk, opened it and retrieved the yellow plastic jug of ashes. He tightened the lid and put the jug between his laptop case and yet more boxes in the back seat. How was it possible he had enough stuff to fill the Camry? He'd spent the last weeks ridding himself of the baggage and memories of his life since leaving North Idaho.

He settled into the driver's seat. "Don't worry, Lise. I didn't throw away your photos and awards. I knew you'd haunt me if I did." *Not that she didn't, anyway.* "Only gave away your furniture. The thrift shop is planning a special auction."

He took a sip of water now stale and tepid. "I always wanted to follow old Route 66. You killed that idea. No way were you going to stay in ancient, moldy motels in small towns where people might not even recognize you."

No response.

"If you have any objections, best voice them now."

Nothing but the sound of wind-blown gravel and the muffled idling engine of a nearby 18-wheeler.

Ed turned the key. "Could be a long journey."

Two
Call Me Mr. Roadkill

Clifford Mustard, forest name Roadkill, squeezed his handmade leather stress balls until his knuckles and forearm ached.

It would be so simple to forever wipe that patronizing smirk from Vincent Naismith's face. But he should not, could not, would not give in to his anger. He hadn't reached his thirties without learning the dangers of allowing his temper free rein. He could visualize Gina and Feather lecturing him once again that a good activist was a calm activist. Oh, yes.

So calm he would be, despite the annoying little man's condescension, despite the uninspired way he was paving, plowing and rebuilding Roadkill's childhood home. He willed himself not to look beyond the ranch's new owner. That view would only enrage him more. But his rebellious eyes focused past Vincent Naismith, to where a broad new deck protruded with obscene vigor and a weird combination of pre-fab decking, steel and cedar from the Mustard family home.

"I'm sure you see my point, Clifford," said Naismith with a curl of the lip. "May I call you Clifford?" the little prick added.

"I prefer Roadkill." He forced himself to return his attention to his host. If he didn't let up on the stress balls, his knuckles would crack. Roadkill willed his lips into a smile of goodwill on a face that wanted to scream obscenities. "But names aren't that important. Just as you've renamed the Rolling M, Camp Destiny. It's still the same land, right?"

Naismith appeared uncertain as to how to respond to Roadkill's comment, unsure whether he was being goaded.

Roadkill's smile turned real and his fingers relaxed. Yes. Keep the bastard off-kilter. Friend or foe, Naismith. Friend or foe?

Naismith cocked his head, intent on Roadkill, and then apparently opted for the good buddies approach. He beamed back a return smile, no doubt

4

as false as his own. After all, the guy used to sell cars in L.A. Probably figured he could sell anything to some hick environmental activist in Idaho. "As you saw in our brief tour of your former property, I'm making changes. All good. We're employing a lot of your neighbors, which is good for the economy, good for the community." He clasped his hands together like a preacher. "I'm sure you agree."

"I don't agree, Vincent. If one of those exotic animals escapes, it could put a spanner in the entire ecosystem. Not what I understood you had in mind."

Naismith's smile tightened like he had one of his new plastic fence posts up his butt. "I was not aware the sales agreement gave you rights to dictate how I run my property. Besides, my security, the animal housing, the holding ponds are all state of the art."

Roadkill looked away from Naismith's prissy face. Doubts jumped on his shoulder and chattered in his ear like pesky chipmunks. He'd seen the ponds, and they were well-designed. Environmentally sound. Did he oppose the man's plans simply because he found Naismith an annoying, controlling, pompous, overbearing, rich asshole, who spent more on his custom cowboy boots than Roadkill's net worth?

Or was it the way the man had paved over Mom's garden spot, and dug up the old spruce tree she decorated every Christmas?

Pain slogged a wicked path from forearms to shoulders and up Roadkill's neck. He tossed a leather ball from palm to palm, calming himself with the memory of making them, the slow process of soaking the leather strips, wrapping them into a tight ball, waiting for them to shrink and dry and harden. Like the dead earth beneath the pavement.

So much for calm. So much for doubt.

An image of the animals trapped in Naismith's state-of-the-art barns gripped his mind—the wide-eyed, cowering gazelles, the springboks darting back and forth in their pen, slamming their delicate forms against the steel bars, again and again and again. And the cats, massive, graceful, crowded into cages, some screeching their outrage, others, silent, despondent.

Nope. Not Mom's garden, not Naismith's ridiculous boots. "The animal waste from all those critters penned up in a small area could still affect the groundwater, no matter how many precautions."

For a second, an instant, maybe, Naismith's expression became wary. He breathed in, his nose pinching. "Preposterous. I've thought of everything."

"Impossible. A dozen things could go wrong, a hundred. I warn you, a few phone calls from me and you'll have a protest the likes of which you've never seen. Trust me, it would be easier for you to sell me back the property."

"Your threats don't frighten me." However, Naismith took a step back and Roadkill detected a nervous tic in the smaller man's left eye. "I'm not selling Camp Destiny. If I were, I doubt you could afford it. Consider all the improvements I've made." His thin lips curled up in a condescending smile as he took in Roadkill's long straggly hair, his tattered T-shirt and his hand-tanned vest and pants.

Roadkill contemplated yanking Naismith by the bolo tie he was fiddling with until the man choked. *Nice thought, bad strategy.* He counted backward from 15. "My brother Ed's a hot shot screenwriter in California. We agree on a price. I call him. Deal's done, that simple."

"Ah, yes, Ed Mustard. I did see his name on the sales documents. Not much interest in a little parcel in a small town he left behind years ago. I can't think of a reason he'd want to buy back, at a significant premium, property he's only recently sold."

If leather balls could screech, his stress balls would be hollering for him to stop before they disintegrated. *I can't either. But I can convince him. I have to.* "Ed's interested in environmental preservation. He's often contributed to my causes." *Right. Like bailing me out when I get arrested. That counts as support.*

Naismith crossed his arms and frowned. His thinning red hair cut in a no-nonsense military brush, showed pink scalp. His crisp khakis and blue work shirt were new. This man was no hands-on, working boss. "A deal's a deal. Camp Destiny is not for sale. No reason for you to speak to your brother. Hancock is my home, now. My plans benefit the entire community, and they will not change."

"If you'd mentioned your plans, I never would have sold you the ranch."

Naismith chuckled, a chuckle that chewed at Roadkill, tightened neck muscles already taut. In the man's laughter he heard arrogance and a bloated sense of self-importance. The irritating laughter echoed the many timber company mucky-mucks who'd mocked Roadkill and his fellow activists over the years. God, why hadn't he recognized that Naismith was a crazy little prick when he made that first offer? *Greed, buddy, pure and simple greed.*

"We all have our dreams. This," Naismith spread his arms, "is mine. My father was a hunter. Always wanted to go to Africa. Heart stopped at age 53, never even got to shoot an elk. I vowed one day I'd make a place where people could live out their dreams, yet remain in the United States of America."

Roadkill spared a moment's sympathy for Naismith's father, and for the son left without his dad. He knew what that was like. Still, he thought it a pity Naismith had elected to live out his dream on the Rolling M. Because, dammit, the dream sucked.

"I know it's hard to let go of your heritage, your legacy," Naismith continued. "So I'll tell you what. I'll spring for a plaque to be mounted at the front entrance with the name of the ranch and the Mustards who settled and built here. Men with vision, who followed their dreams. Their dreams and your name will be here in perpetuity."

Roadkill ground his heel into the mud, tried to will his temper down through his body into the earth. A plaque? A fucking plaque? Another blight on the landscape.

"A dream? This is going to be a goddamn nightmare."

Naismith reared back, his nose and lips pulled tight. "At Camp Destiny, we do not take the name of the Lord in vain. Leave my ranch. Or I shall ask my men to escort you out." He pointed toward the front entrance.

The command tore the last tattered edge of Roadkill's control. He shot a quick glance around for any of Naismith's many henchmen, cocked his arm and clocked his no-longer-gracious host on the jaw. The man toppled like a cut lodgepole pine. A short one. Even with the occupant flat on his back, unconscious, the man's khakis kept their crease.

"Not my idea of western hospitality, Vincent."

Roadkill made a casual retreat in the direction of his truck, parked in that barren lot that had once given Mom such joy.

He heard Naismith's groaning call to his men, but he didn't look back. He heard footsteps behind him and quickened his pace, but he refused to run, didn't look back. A man shouted, "Stop." He didn't pause, didn't look back.

He heard the unmistakable click of the action closing on a shotgun.

Oh, Brother

Ed ate at the Roadkill Steakhouse on Route 66 in Seligman in honor of his brother Clifford. After a root beer at the infamous Delgado's Sno Cap, he spent the night in a motel named for a local Native American tribe. Even with its recent renovations, Ed doubted Lise would have enjoyed the motel. He loved it.

At first glance, Seligman was nothing like Ed's hometown. Plopped in the Sonoran Desert at a crossroads on the way to the Grand Canyon, Seligman made the most of its Route 66 roots, milking tourists and nostalgia buffs, but still barely scraping by. As he walked the road and visited the gift shops and watering holes, a twinge of nostalgia for Hancock jolted him. Like the Hancockians Ed remembered, the citizens of Seligman knew each other's business and never hesitated to send tourists to investigate someone else's shop. Some of the storekeepers chatted so much Ed's ears clogged. Others grunted a response only when forced.

Ed's shoulders relaxed. He rubbed his jaw and wondered if he should let the day-old beard grow to—who knew, his shoulders?

His cell phone rang, a surprise this far from everywhere. He pulled it out and looked at the screen. "Oh, crap." Roadkill. Who never called unless he needed a favor from his rich, successful brother. Only Ed was not a success, and no longer was he rich.

Ed put the phone back in his pocket after putting it on Silent.

Three
I'm Carrying

Lacy Ponder bent forward and shook her boobs into the DDD cup. She reached back to fasten the bra's four hooks, but the band must have twisted because she couldn't get it hooked.

"Double damn." Her back ached from her shoulders to her waist and today the mere act of reaching hurt.

She'd stayed in bed too late, repeating her mantra, adjusting her attitude for her new job. *Quietude, strength, peace. Quietude, strength, peace.* She bent over and tried to adjust the bra's wide band, backing up as she struggled. Her mother walked into her bedroom and ran smack into Lacy, splashing hot coffee on her bare back. Lacy jumped, stuffing down the curse she knew would only set her mother off on a rant.

"I brought you coffee. I know how hard it is for you to wake up. And you don't want to be late for your new job." Her mother dabbed at her back with a towel. "Hope that didn't burn you."

Lacy straightened. "Ouch. Thanks, Mom, but I prefer my coffee by mouth."

"Always a smart comment. My, my, girl, you need to get a move on. Want some help with the bra? It's all tangled up."

Lacy clenched her teeth and took a breath. "Yes. Please." She took the coffee mug and turned so her mother could mess with the damn bra.

"There. Now hurry up so's you'll have time for breakfast, hon. You need your strength. I fixed eggs for brain power."

"I don't think being a security guard at Sears is going to stretch my mental capacities." *Still, it's a job.*

"None of that negative thinking, Lacy Anne Ponder. It sure the heck beats being a night guard at that retirement home."

"You're right." Lacy donned her new outfit, navy blue Polo shirt and khaki slacks, and slipped a rubber band onto her wrist. She looked in the mirror and hoped the large shirt hid her "gifts." Gave the rubber band a snap. *No negative thinking, girl.*

But how could she fulfill her life's purpose when she spent half that life fending off horny co-workers? Or ignoring totally stupid sexist comments about the size of her "weapons" and the "big load" she packed?

If she won the harassment lawsuit the first thing she'd spend the money on would be breast reduction surgery. Maybe, maybe, she could make it in law enforcement if she had the proportions of a normal woman instead of those of a pole dancer. She knew she had plenty of brains.

Marjorie Ponder hovered in the doorway. Without warning she swooped in on Lacy, her hands cupped, and ran her fingers upward through her daughter's thick black hair.

Lacy sidestepped away. "Stop with the fluffing. I hate fluffy."

"With your face, you need some soft curls."

She snorted and jerked her head backward. "I need to have it like it was." Flat, smooth, chin-length. Orderly.

Ignoring her daughter's request, her mother again fluffed. "There. You have such lovely hair. You got it, flaunt it."

She tensed from gut to cheeks and reached for her hairbrush. "Stop. I'll flaunt what I want to flaunt, dammit."

A frown revealed her mother's disapproval of the curse that slipped out despite her best efforts. "Fiddlesticks. Now hurry up, hon, or you won't have time for breakfast."

No way would food stay in her churning stomach. "I didn't ask you to make breakfast."

"Nonsense. You need sustenance. Whatever am I going to do with you?"

Lacy placed her brush on her dresser, careful not to slam it down, careful not to scream, careful not to lose the peace she'd worked so hard to achieve. "Leave me alone?" *Oops. You lost it.*

Her mother's shoulders sank a good three inches. Her eyes seemed watery, her complexion like the classy parchment paper on the diploma framed above her dresser. She rolled her lips together, licked them. She reached a hand toward Lacy and snatched it back. "Well, excuse me for trying to be a good mother."

Lacy picked up her belongings and braced herself. Mom's rising pitch told her not to waste the effort to respond.

"Lord knows," her mother continued, "you've been moping around this house like a cat with hair balls ever since you lost your j—" Mom's mouth clamped shut mid-word. Her face went red and her hand flew toward her mouth. "You have every right to be upset. I didn't mean—"

"Yes, you did." Lacy lifted her chin and looked at her mother. "Go on. Finish your damn sentence. Maybe add something about being so ashamed, or maybe try the 'why any daughter of mine' approach."

"I'm not ashamed of you. Never." Mom might have been striving for reassuring, but all Lacy saw were tight cheeks forcing a reluctant smile. "That job wasn't right for you. And way down in the corner of the state. I'm glad to have you home. So many more job options in Spokane."

Do not answer. Don't let her get to you. Lacy gritted her teeth and inhaled the aroma of strong, fresh coffee. *Quietude, strength, peace.* "Dammit, Mom, I didn't *lose* my job. I *found* myself against the lockers with my supervisor paying extremely close attention to my uniform. Like trying to get it off."

"You need to shrug those things off."

"Shrug them off?" Lacy could almost feel her supervisor pressing against her. Smell his breath. Feel his hands on her neck, her chest. Tiny, chilling footsteps walked the skin on her torso.

Lacy grabbed her purse from the dresser and brushed past her mother. "I'm out of here. I won't be back for dinner. I'll be looking for an apartment."

Ed's Carrying His Own Burden

Ed emerged from the Bright Angel Trail sweating and smiling. He hadn't been alone—far from it, but the majesty of the scenery on the day hike, combined with the antics of the squirrels, chipmunks and children scampering down and up the trail, had soothed a soul worn ragged in the past months.

Back in the car, he considered the map. He could head south for Phoenix, Tucson, even Mexico. He could go to Flagstaff and the north rim of the Grand Canyon. Six or eight more strenuous hikes and maybe he'd get back the urge to write, a sense of where he was going. He could follow old Route 66 to Chicago.

It almost appealed. The surge of interest in the historical route surprised him, both because he'd set most of his screenplays in the present or future and because he'd had no interest in anything other than his rose garden and a six-pack of Negra Modelo since Lise's death.

He took in a breath. Turned on his cell phone. Three calls from Roadkill, another two from area code 208. None from L.A. Weird. Now that his recent past had ceased to haunt him, Ed had to confront a few ghosts from further back. Maybe he could do it. The thought surprised him. Perhaps merely escaping L.A. and the scene of too many crimes of omission had been enough to improve his attitude.

First he'd have dinner. The box lunch he'd taken down the canyon was a long time ago. Next town of any size was Williams. Better than eating at another national park concession. Roadkill could wait a few hours.

Or could he? Maybe something serious had happened to his brother. Although Cliff considered himself invulnerable, Ed knew better. "You could tell him something about courting death," he told the ashes that now rode shotgun. "Sometimes it accepts your proposal."

He pressed speed dial for voicemail. The first was left by Roadkill the day after Ed left Santa Monica, two days ago. "Hey, bro. Once again the guardian of justice in our fair town has nabbed me. Some trumped up charge of assault and damage to private property. Need you to wire bail, ASAP."

He'd added the information Ed would need to wire the funds and hung up.

Ed smiled. Situation normal for Roadkill.

Roadkill's second voice mail, left yesterday, urged his brother to "cough up the cash, fast. This place is a dump."

This morning's message from his brother held a faint conciliatory tone. From Roadkill it was epochal. Cliff Mustard didn't apologize. "So Myrna told me your ex-wife's mother did a number on you. Not far from the tree, I guess. Said you'd disappeared from the L.A. scene. Hope you're not out of the country. You can still send the cash, wherever you are. Need some help, here, Ed." A long pause made Ed believe Cliff had ended the call, but then he heard his brother clear his throat.

"I know you're still hurting about Lise and I know you did everything you could, 'cause I know you. You can't turn that one around. But," and his voice returned to normal Roadkill high volume arrogance, "I'm working on something important up here. Critical to Hancock and to you and me. Might cost a little, but I can't explain. Trust me. Send the bail money and then we'll talk."

Roadkill's last message was followed a few minutes later in the deep voice of Byron Warnock, the sheriff of Hancock, Idaho. "Myrna tells me you may be evading calls. Hope you got the request from your brother. Cliff doesn't do well in jail. However, no one else is available to provide bail."

Ed tensed. No one except his attorney Bob Gilman knew Ed was seriously broke. He didn't wish his brother an extended stay in jail, but he couldn't keep spending money as he had in La La Land. What had before seemed equivalent to a meal or two at a four star restaurant now loomed as a big slice of the cash he'd squirreled away after selling the house and settling a sum on Lise's mother that Marliss spat at as blood money.

The final message came in a woman's voice, one he had not heard for nearly a decade. Myrna Warnock, wife of Byron and mayor of Hancock, said, soft, low, totally not Myrna, "Your brother needs help. He needs you,

Ed. Maybe more than he needs your money." Then her tone switched back to vintage Myrna. "If he doesn't get out of jail, someone, maybe me, maybe Byron, may shoot your brother. We're losing our world-renowned patience. How can one man be so annoying?"

Rage surged through Ed's body like steam from Lise's high-end espresso machine. How could his brother assume Ed would go his bail? How could Myrna assume Ed would or could help his quixotic idiot of a brother? He had failed to help Lise and failed to salvage his career.

And yet.

The familiar voices—Cliff, Myrna, Byron. Memories of Myrna's cooking, sometimes inspired, sometimes mundane, occasionally inedible, came to him. Memories of the shaded silence in the old growth forest that edged his parent's land followed. Maybe he could help Cliff, while he proved to himself he wasn't a total screw-up.

"Hang on, Lise. This road trip just took a new direction. North."

Four
The Brothers Schramm Go Shopping

Roger Schramm wondered if anything topped an afternoon at Sears. Sex, maybe. In Sears you didn't have the hassle of dressing up or worrying about saying the wrong thing, spending the night or heading home. Meandering the well-stocked aisles, nodding away friendly employees, eased the tension in Roger's shoulders.

Best of all, Dean was shopping for clothes and Roger didn't have to watch over him. What kind of trouble could his dufus brother get into at Sears, for heck's sake?

Roger ogled the tidy shelves and bins of tools. He reached out a work-worn, muscled hand and stroked a 10-inch pair of Vise-Grips. He let out a sigh of pure bliss, and ignored that little ping of anxiety about Dean that forever rode on his shoulder. *Dean's downstairs. I told him I'd meet him there. No worries.*

Roger gave their boss points for sending him and Dean to Spokane for supplies. Almost made up for shoveling wild animal crap and doing carpentry work on one of Naismith's crazy construction projects. Christ, did the guy plan to cover up every inch of dirt on that ranch? Given enough time and money, the old man would have the place a copy of his old stomping grounds in L.A.

He guffawed, then stifled his laugh. A car sales lot, only with tigers and zebras and gazelles instead of Cougars and Jaguars and Vipers.

Funny how the people in Hancock thought Naismith's plans were great for their little town, while most of the men who worked there joked about trying to bring the jungle to a pine forest.

Roger forced himself to take his time, to make a check by each item he found on the list of supplies. He inhaled through his nose. Even the smells were all Sears: the scent of floor wax mingled with the motor oil and rubber from the lawn mowers and small tractors.

When he finished with Naismith's list of supplies, he headed for Automotive. He remembered how Dean had spent the trip here popping pills from his stash in his backpack in Roger's truck, scoffing at Roger's protests. If Roger threw them out, Dean would find more. Maybe steal to fund their purchase. *I can't watch him every minute.* Yet a prickle of nerves worked its way up his spine. He shrugged it off.

He picked up some all-purpose terry towels for washing the truck, an American-made brand of car wax and a baseball cap, then made his way to Sporting Goods and chose a couple of free weights. Staying fit mattered.

He headed to the register to pay and stepped aside to let a shortish young woman with dark hair pass. She smiled up at him and Roger almost registered that it was a nice smile before his eyes took in her enormous breasts. Gorgeous breasts that swelled proud and high, even hidden as they were under a loose navy polo shirt. The Sears logo jiggled high on one boob. On the other her nametag said "Welcome to Sears. I'm Lacy."

Roger moved his eyes back to her face quick enough to catch her frown before she passed. He shook his head in wonder. Some knockers. He moved to the cashier.

The girl at the register peered up at him through lashes thick with mascara. Through her flirty smile, she chattered like a chimpanzee. "Nice tattoo," she said. "I'm saving up for a gecko."

Roger's left hand reflexively covered the tattoo of a bear claw on his right forearm. Usually he wore long sleeves. "Surprises me that Sears allows them tongue studs." That shut her up and turned her sullen. People didn't understand the importance of following the rules.

He switched hands on the heavy shopping bags and headed down the escalator to check on Dean's progress finding clothes for his so-called date. Clothes, hell. Dean's time would be better spent getting his greasy blond hair cut and washed.

What a world. If that woman kept her date with his freaky, drugged-out brother, she qualified for the loony bin. *Well, duh. Who but a nutcase would accept a date with Dean?*

Downstairs, he stood by the escalator and scanned the various departments. When he didn't see Dean in Men's, his nerves began an anxious beat in his temples. He told himself his brother could still be trying stuff on. Above, a fluorescent light hummed and flickered. He shook his head and turned to take in the rest of the floor.

He caught sight of Dean, hunched over a shelf, intent on something. In Housewares? Uh-huh. Dean Schramm, Mr. Happy Homemaker.

Roger headed for his brother. Dean seemed to be admiring himself in a mirror, God alone knew why. Not much to admire in that skinny, pockmarked face with a red nose that dripped snot most of the time. The shopping bag on his arm said Dean had bought something. In one hand, he held some sort of metal object.

Roger paused. Might as well let Dean find him, not let his brother know he doubted for a minute he could do his own shopping. He'd wait here by the towels and bedspreads.

A guy with a black long-sleeved Tool Department employee shirt headed toward Dean at a deliberate pace. Jesus, had Dean swiped something from Tools? What the hell for? Why hadn't Roger seen him and stopped whatever trouble he was bound to get in before he got into it?

He mentally slapped himself for assuming the worst. Probably nothing.

The black-shirted man, tall and broad-shouldered, approached Dean. "Son, that's not a good idea."

Dean looked up at the man and preened, so proud he'd like to bust. "'Course it is. Couldn't have Earleen see that snaggly tooth," he said. "And I ain't your son."

Dean ducked to take another peek in the mirror and tilted his head up to speak to the big clerk. His mouth dripped blood and he gestured with something in his right hand. "This ugly old tooth scared the hell out of some kid in the dressing room. Screamed to his momma about a monster in there. Me. Can't have that."

Behind Dean on the shelf several mirrors reflected him and the big clerk.

Dean pumped the arm wielding the pliers in the air. "So I borrowed your tool here and I plucked that sucker out." He grinned.

Jesus Christ. Dean had pulled his own tooth. With stolen pliers. Roger chuckled, low, maybe some shock in the sound. Nothing predictable about his little brother.

"Very bad idea," said the clerk in a quiet, strangled voice. He crumpled to the floor.

Roger's chuckle curdled in his throat. Exhaustion poured down his body and weighted his feet. Maybe he could walk out the door, alone, unburdened by his brother. Instead he stared, frozen.

Dean peered down at the big man in black. "Well, now, I would of returned these here pliers. No need to excite yourself." Blood dripped from his mouth to the man's shirt. "Oh. Sorry." He took another look in the mirror. He muttered something, a worried expression on his face.

Dean's befuddled gaze focused on a display of kitchen towels. When he crossed the main aisle toward them, a small, dark-haired woman holding a cell phone to her ear marched up to him.

Dean gawked. Roger swallowed. Damnation. It was the woman he'd noticed upstairs, the one with the huge set of melons. She said, "Sir, you'll need to come with me. I'm Lacy from Sears Security. We have first aid equipment in the back."

Roger's breath hitched and he hiccupped up acid. Shit on a shingle. Half an hour in Sears and Dean's got himself tangled up with the store cops. Should he barge on in? What could he do? *Something, idiot. You gotta stop Dean from getting in deeper.*

He ran toward the pair. His legs wobbled like a newborn foal's and the heavy bags snarled up between them. The free weights banged against a shin. Roger winced and jerked to a stop. If only he could reverse time, or freeze it. He couldn't, so he waited, poised for flight, not sure which way to run.

The big clerk groaned and shifted on the floor and Dean and the woman stared at him. The woman glanced around her, wiped her forehead with the back of one hand, knelt beside him and felt for a pulse. She talked into the cell phone, her voice high-pitched and quivery. "I'm going to bring him in. I'm in control, but send some backup. We need first aid on the floor. Housewares."

"Hold on a minute," Dean protested. "I didn't do nothing to him. He fainted or something. I'm fixin' to return these here pliers." He waved the tool aloft and now Roger could see it held the stump of Dean's broken tooth. "You don't mind me mentioning it, ma'am, you could get a better job at Hooters."

The woman stiffened and Roger saw color claim her cheeks. She crossed her arms under her boobs. "I mind." She took a breath. "Let's talk about your tooth and those pliers," she said. "You need first aid. If you'll come with me." She extended an arm to Dean.

Don't touch him, thought Roger. Whatever you do, don't touch him. He forced his legs into motion. If he was fast enough, he could stop him.

She grasped Dean's free arm.

Roger wasn't fast enough.

Dean hauled back the arm that held the open pliers, gripping them like a cop's baton. Behind him was a display of wire whisks and plastic spoons, innocent little kitchen implements.

The woman's mouth opened. Dean swung his arm down, toward her head.

No, Dean, don't. The words died in Roger's head, as useless as they would have been said aloud.

Why didn't she duck? Cover her head?

The pliers connected with her shiny black hair. Roger knew he'd never forget that sickening thud. A thud he heard even at a distance.

Roger held his breath. Bit his bottom lip. The woman crumpled, knees, hips, torso, shoulders, head, all aiming for that linoleum floor. Roger hoped she'd go down chest first. Plenty of protection there.

The woman toppled to her side and landed on the clerk from Tools.

Dean hung over her, mouth open. His blood and spit trickled onto her still form.

Roger's heart pounded in his ears so loud he wasn't sure he'd hear a siren beside him. He scanned the area. For the moment, no one seemed to have noticed the little spat.

There was a chance no one would. A chance they could escape. A chance she wasn't badly injured. He forced himself to move toward his brother instead of hightailing it out of the store alone.

Roger's stomach pulled in on itself. How had his adorable little brother, who had once galloped the living room on an imaginary horse firing his toy gun, turned into a drugged up moron who waded into trouble faster than a Labrador retriever found a scrap of food?

Jesus Christ, Mom, why did you ever make me promise to watch out for this lowlife piece of pond scum that in no way could be a Schramm?

"Dean," he said softly as he neared. He didn't want to join that pile on the floor. "Time to get out of here."

Dean's head turned toward his brother's voice in a stiff, robot-like motion, the rest of his body stock still. His gaze darted from the downed employees to his brother. "It wasn't my fault."

"Let's go home, little buddy," Roger said. He rummaged in one of his Sears bags and pulled out a terry towel and the ball cap. Handed the towel to Dean. "Drop them pliers in the bag."

"I didn't pay for them. I borrowed 'em."

"Least of our problems. Drop 'em in."

Dean dropped them in. He listened to his brother, once he got in hot water. Never before.

Roger plunked the ball cap on his brother's greasy head, tucking the tags inside. Together, they strolled out the door, just a couple of guys after a shopping trip to Sears.

❧

Schramms on the Lam

Roger's pickup reeked with the combined aromas of oil of cloves, b.o. and blood. His own body stank of fear, rank and nasty, instead of the familiar smell of healthy hard work or exercise sweat. Thank God his breathing finally approached normal.

They'd strolled out of Sears, casual as can be, and he'd almost relaxed, almost convinced himself they'd made their getaway. With Dean's record, he'd not catch easy county jail time for this one. He'd end up serving hard time.

Roger thought they might be home free when the cop cars had wheeled up to the curb and four cops ran toward the store. Right at him and Dean.

He'd moved in front of Dean and murmured, "Keep walking, slow and easy. Follow my lead."

For a second, maybe less, he considered turning his no account brother in. Serve the lamebrain right to have to pay for his dumb ass move. But no. Brothers took care of brothers. Their momma had pounded it into Roger. He'd moved on toward the lot, glancing at the cops with the same interest any good citizen would, then glancing away. One officer gave him a slow look-over, then must have decided clean-cut Roger didn't fit the description, and besides, there were two of them, not one squirrelly guy who'd attacked the security chick.

He didn't breathe until they reached the truck. Made Dean slide down onto the floor while he drove out of the mall parking lot, sedate as a drunk Sunday school teacher on a Saturday night. Told Dean to stay on the floor while he stopped at a drugstore and ran in for the oil of cloves and some gauze.

When he got back to the truck, bloody drool and snot decorated his leather car seat like some kind of weird, thin icing. Dean, whimpering, shame-faced, whined that Roger should of bought ice for his swelling face.

"What kind of a wimp was that big guy to faint, anyway?" Dean mumbled after he'd stuffed gauze and cotton in his mouth. "So he saw a little blood. Man, I sure as hell pulled that old snaggle tooth clear the heck out of my mouth. Not many folks could do the same."

Roger drove. "Not many folks could." His focus danced between the road and the rear-view mirror. He saw no problems in either direction. The problem crouched beside him in the truck. He bit back so hard on his rage he figured he could break a tooth as large as the one the moron yanked out.

"Hurts like hell now. Didn't then," Dean said.

"Odd place to pull a tooth, middle of Sears," Roger said, his tone mild. No point in hollering.

"Hey, man, I was flyin'. May not have been thinking straight. You know. I'm sorry, Roger, but that little kid started in crying at the sight of me. No tellin' what Earleen would think." Dean rocked back and forth, back and forth in his cramped little cubbyhole on the truck floor.

Roger changed lanes and headed for the next off-ramp. "We're heading back."

"To Sears? No way, man. You wouldn't turn me in, would you?"

Roger had to laugh. "No, dickhead. I'm not going to turn my own brother in. Back to Camp Destiny." He'd been so angry, so upset he'd headed to the first on-ramp and now they were driving west instead of east. "God, I hope you didn't kill that little black haired woman from Security. Why the heck you have to thump her like that?"

"She was going to call the cops on me, man. All's I was doing was some personal hygiene, for Christ's sake. A man deserves a little privacy. Wasn't my fault that guard wouldn't listen."

"Right. Never your fault."

"Oh, man, don't you go being Momma. Aaaah. This hurts like a mother." Dean reached out a hand and put it on Roger's thigh. Roger jerked and his foot came off the accelerator. "I sure could use some ice."

"We'll be in Idaho soon. I'll stop then. I want to keep movin', for now." His eyes cha-cha'd between the rear mirror and the road.

One thing about Dean. He had a pulse on his older brother's feelings. Roger guessed that was so he could take advantage of his good moods and be wary when he was short tempered.

"Sure, bro. Whatever you say. I can hook up with Earleen another day. My mouth's too sore for action, anyhow." He removed the clove-oil-and-blood-and-drool-soaked gauze and patted his swollen cheeks with dirty fingers. "Look, don't you go worrying about that guard lady in Sears. She'll be fine. Sure, I pack a wallop, but she'll be fine. Hair protected her and them Vise-Grips wasn't that big."

"I sure as hell hope so. Mr. Naismith won't be happy, he finds out."

"You see that set of melons on her? Love to get my hands on those little girls." He made the universal male gesture for cradling a woman's boobs.

Roger shook his head. Politically incorrect? His brother would be booed off the stage of a redneck bar.

His brother crawled up the seat and rummaged behind it, chattering to himself.

Roger reached out with his right hand to swat at Dean. "Hey, I told you to stay down."

"I … Yesss. Come to papa, baby." Dean tilted his head back like a baby bird and dry-swallowed some pills. When he swallowed, his Adam's apple jerked in his scrawny chicken neck.

"Christ on a biscuit," Roger said. "Hasn't that shit got you in enough trouble today? Chuck it out the window."

"This pain's about to kill me. I need this stuff. 'Specially since you won't stop for ice." Dean scrunched back down on the floor, his head on the seat like some yellow-haired mongrel dog. He wiped his running nose with a bare forearm. "I stay off the pills back at the compound. Almost always."

"Old man Naismith catches you on drugs, we'll both be out of jobs."

"Chill. Mort smokes more'n Marlboro's and I've seen him popping some working man's cocaine. Naismith's too busy setting up that freakin' Camp Destiny to worry about how his employees get their jollies. You gotta admit the guy's a nut case. Who in his right mind would try to set up a game preserve for Af-reekin' animals in North Idaho? It snows, for chrissake. It gets cold. Cold enough to freeze the balls off them poor lions."

Roger had a sudden mental image of lions running around clutching their privates with their back paws. He turned to the side so Dean couldn't see his smile. "The boss is building that heated barn. He's thought a lot about it." Roger wasn't going to admit he shared his brother's doubts about Naismith's plans. He'd never hear the end of it.

"Ask me, it's some crazy version of Noah's Ark."

"Noah's Ark? When you start quoting the Bible?"

"That long-hair who decked the boss shouted it when the cops hauled him off. Got to admit, he had a point. Jesus, we gotta be in Idaho by now. Pull over at the next mini-mart. I need ice."

Roger shot his brother a surprised stare. "You were there? Why the hell'd you let that tree-hugger hit Mr. Naismith? You never—"

Dean crawled up on the seat and peered out the window. "Take the next off ramp. I gotta pee and a gas station's sure to sell ice."

"I'm not stopping till you tell me how you let that guy get to Naismith."

Dean giggled. "Me and Mort came over when we heard them hollering, but it was too late. We grabbed the guy and called the cops, and Naismith told us not to talk about it." He laughed and moaned. "Shit, that hurts. Guess Naismith was embarrassed that the guy had the nuts to pop him one with all of us within calling distance. Now will you pull off? I'm about to piss all over your truck."

Roger turned off the Interstate at the cutoff to I-95 and headed for a gas station. No cars followed. Looked like they'd made a clean getaway from Sears. He rolled his stiff shoulders. Maybe his brother's luck was changing.

And his.

Maybe this time they'd made a clean escape from trouble.

Five
Help Me, Universe

Gina Cosentino raised her glass of raspberry iced tea. She clinked it against Feather's. Beside her, Sondra and Juanita performed the ritual in the elaborate way Sondra dictated, twist hands around each other, hook pinkies, pull, release, swig. Not a drop of tea spilled.

To Gina, the tea was too sweet, the day too hot for late September, the celebration way too soon. She couldn't bring herself to spoil her friends' buoyant mood with reality. And who knew, maybe they were right. Maybe their luck would hold with their water.

She inhaled the sweet flowery aroma of the tea, seeking a calm she didn't feel. And struggling to ignore the mildewy funk that hallmarked their temporary lodging.

"Woo hoo," said Feather. "Another town council meeting, another win for the good girls. My kind of politics." Red circles highlighted her cheeks and Gina wondered if it was excitement or artifice that colored Feather's pale complexion. In the past, knowing how her eco-activist feminist friend scorned make-up, she'd assume excitement. However, pregnancy affected not only your appetite, your profile and your blood pressure, it sometimes changed your personality, at least for those months of gestation.

Women who formerly railed against the "rapacious, manipulative cosmetic mega-industrial complex," saw their pregnant reflections in the mirror and dashed to raid the shelves of the nearest drug store for blusher. So far, Gina had not succumbed, but feeling like a tumorous pumpkin might lead to surrender.

Pregnancy's "healthy glow" had bypassed Feather. Her alabaster skin had dulled to beige and her glossy dark brown hair had lost its bounce and shine.

Gina forced a grin she hoped appeared genuine. "Good girls? I'm not sure there's unanimous agreement on that in Hancock. And what's with 'your kind of politics?' Last I knew, you were into anarchy."

Sondra snorted. "Not any more. Feather's a power-to-the-people woman now. I been gettin' to her with my 'down with honky' 'black is beautiful' message."

"You think," said Feather. "Truth is, I have a disguise to fit every situation. Flexibility is my watchword."

Across the table, Juanita's thin face warmed with her smile. "Uh-huh. Not so flexible this morning. I thought we'd need a winch to hoist you out of bed."

"It's the damn mattress." Feather gazed around the battered, grungy trailer. "This place," she declared, "is a dump."

Gina stood and downed the dregs of tart-sweet tea. It left a tacky residue in her mouth and a craving for a cup of real, caffeinated, iced coffee. "But our dump, until we get The Flat Italian remodeled." *Or forever, if Naismith convinces the council to revoke our permit. Or persuades all the contractors in town to shy away.* She clunked her plastic glass on the Formica tabletop. *Think positive, girl. That's what you're always preaching.* "Let's change and see what can be done."

Three women stood, three bellies jutting out beneath tautly stretched knit tops. "The tide is turning," said Feather. "I can feel it."

"Hunh. You're feeling the baby move," said Sondra. "More likely than the feelings of the Hancock homies."

Juanita rubbed her tummy and gently patted Feather's. "Think positive, *amigas.* That's what Gina tells us. It's good for the babies. Soon the universe will reflect our positive, powerful thoughts."

Gina told herself the universe had listened when she yearned for a child. Had listened when she sought that grant. These women trusted in her guidance. *Hear me again, universe. Not much time before the current building permit expires. Where's Roadkill? Where's anyone who'll help?*

They had to finish. *Come on, universe, do I have to shout?*

Not That Kind of Help

Joseph Graham tossed the last of his belongings in the back of the humble white van. The humble, unassuming, nondescript, dull, dull, dull, white van. He hated it. No, you couldn't hate something with zero personality. Damn, he'd miss his sparkling blue, dashing Mini Cooper, but it wouldn't survive Idaho potholes. Plus it didn't pass the "wholesome new pastor" test. He threw the CD carrier full of religious CDs onto the passenger seat. He hummed a few bars of "Shall We Gather at the River?"

A new flock. Ready to fleece.

A frown tightened his forehead. Nothing to worry about. One more scam in a lifetime of scamming. Spend a little time in the wild and perhaps head east or south after stockpiling a nest egg. Key West sounded good.

Taking a last quick tour of the apartment, he stopped at the bathroom mirror. "Damn!" Another grey eyebrow hair jutted out. He spit on his forefinger and tried to smooth it down. No such luck. In fact, he spotted another one.

He retrieved his toiletry kit from the van and used his tweezers to extract the offending eyebrow hair and a couple protruding from his nose.

Holy Hannah, was he starting to look like his father? Slivers of silver scattered through his hair added that distinguished, prosperous touch. Nose hairs and out of control eyebrows added up to scruffy old fart.

He patted cool water on the ever-so-slight puffiness beneath his eyes. He appraised himself. Good. Joseph's Filipino mother and English father had borne striking children whose looks far surpassed their own. Uniquely shaped hazel eyes, tawny skin and dark hair with a russet hint led to frequent inquiries about his ancestry.

To Joseph, his appearance was part of his arsenal and had to be maintained, ready for action at any time. He turned sideways. "Looking good, Brother Graham," he told himself, patting an almost-flat stomach. Thank the good Lord for whoever came out with the Mirdle. His male compression body shaping underwear helped him create that oh-so-important good first impression, without all those god-awful sit-ups.

He did a 360 for the mirror, checked his buns over his shoulder. Yes. Hair, torso, expression all added up to the sincere, you can trust me appearance he'd need in Idaho. With sex appeal. Not bad for a man in his mid-40s. Forty-seven still counted as mid in his book. In anyone's.

He pulled out his cell phone. Dialed. Waited. "Brother Naismith, Joseph Graham here. About to take off on my long drive north."

He listened, peering into the mirror, tilting his neck upward. No way could that be the start of jowls beneath his chin.

"Yes, I agree. The Lord is definitely smiling on our new venture. As I told you, I've been in North Idaho a few times, and it is God's country. The trees, the grasslands, the people, all are symbols of our Lord's bounty." *All deadly boring, all predictable.*

"You're right. It will be cooler. Even here by the Pacific Ocean, it can get hot. Beastly hot." *Especially when your mark gets cautious and tightfisted.*

"I'll see you in a few days then. I plan to take my time, meditate, pray, prepare myself to take on Destiny's flock."

He exchanged more inane pleasantries with his future employer and ended the call. He'd definitely need the drive time to transform from investor and suitor to humble, fervent Reverend Joseph Graham. He sighed. These days, it took more and more energy to re-invent himself. And provided less adrenalin.

Sitting on the front steps, Joseph considered his recent failure. Not failure, never failure. Setback. He'd seen it coming. Still, it stung to lose Penny. And her money. He'd misjudged her, pushed too fast.

Was he losing his touch? She had a sharp tongue and demanded much of him, yet he'd grown fond of the woman. He'd miss her. *Not smart, Joseph. Never fall for your mark.*

He pushed fast dial 7 for Penelope. Definitely not the jackpot he'd been hoping for. "Sorry, Penelope, my dear. I've been busy."

"What kept you? I've left six messages."

He lowered his voice. "Gathering a reliable and committed group of investors takes time, Penelope. I assumed you would have plenty to entertain you in Palm Springs."

"Plenty to worry about. You know I had some doubts about your plans, Joey. I talked to an old friend here and he's not sure your investment consortium is a good idea." She paused and Graham heard her take a breath. "I want my money back, Joseph."

Graham forced himself to lighten his tone. He'd known it was coming, but hearing the abrupt demand gnawed his pride like termites. "If that's how you feel, darling. I wanted you to be in on the ground floor of this one. I'll have it ready for you upon your return tomorrow."

"Good. And, uh, I'd appreciate your returning the money I loaned you for your rent last month. I think a relationship works better when we're on even footing." Penelope giggled. "Not that I stay on my feet for long when I'm around you, sweetheart."

"I can't wait to see you, either, Penny-heart."

"You won't have long. I couldn't wait, so I'm home."

"Home? Now?"

"Yes, goose. Home, now. Why don't you come over? Maybe bring that champagne you've been promising me."

Graham didn't answer. Couldn't answer.

"Or shall I come to your place?" Penny continued. "Joseph?"

Graham inhaled a sharp breath. Where was that adaptability, that flexibility so essential to the game? "You've surprised me, my love. A terrific surprise. I'll come to your place, with champagne and a check."

The giggle vanished and a harder woman spoke through the cell. "Take the time to stop at the bank. Cash would be best."

"I'm on my way, my love. On my way."

Maybe it wouldn't be that hard to get over Penelope. Somehow he doubted she'd shed as many tears over him as she would her money. Even though the sums he'd borrowed were miniscule compared to her net worth. "Penny ante." His attempt to smile failed.

Graham began the long drive north, sounds of Steppenwolf bouncing against the metal walls of his van. Plenty of time for hymns.

Six
Recovery's First Step

Marjorie Ponder hovered in the bedroom doorway. She kept her hands behind her back, no doubt hiding another of the little surprises meant to restore her daughter's spirits. Lacy couldn't imagine what it would take to restore her spirits, but she could bet her mother didn't hold it behind her back. Lacy sat up in bed, not feeling too bad physically, unless you counted the dull pain in her head and neck. She would heal. Her hair would grow back. Eventually.

But dammit, Sears was letting her go. That had to be a record. Fourth day on the job. Still officially a trainee. Which, of course, was why they couldn't keep her on. "You should never have confronted the assailant on your own. That's why we have two security people on duty plus the ability to call on the mall security forces." She'd been in training when the guy decked her. Strolling around the store, getting to know the lay of the land, the feng shui of Sears.

So she was history. No one had any reason to catch the damn nutcase who had decked her with the same Vise-Grips he'd used to yank out his tooth. Gross enough to raise goose bumps.

Lacy's injuries weren't grievous. Harold from Tools had recovered from his fainting spell, if not from his acute embarrassment. Accounting had written off the stolen pliers. No problem for them.

Big problem for Lacy, once again out of work. Out of a security job that had led many to the police academy and the Spokane PD. Now here she was, moping in the bed she'd slept in as a child, in her mother's home, while her mother tried yet another scheme to cheer her up.

Her mother minced to the bed, hands still behind her back. Before Lacy could put up a protesting hand, her mother whipped hers around and dropped something red on Lacy's head. "Now don't take it off until you've

27

had a chance to see it. I brought a mirror." She brought the mirror out from behind her back.

Lacy looked and grimaced. The hat wasn't bad. A red baseball cap, festooned with sequins and beads. Normally sequins and Lacy gave each other space, but given the bare patch on her scalp, the hat proved a decent alternative. Her mother pouted. "I thought it was cute. Kind of girly-slash-gutsy, like my baby girl."

She couldn't stifle her amusement. "Baby girl? Please." She tilted the brim of the cap to one side. "I like the hat. It's my face that scares me."

Her mother's expression relaxed. "The swelling's already down. You're young and healthy. Give it a day or three and you'll be like new."

"Uh-huh. Except once again, out of work." Lacy paused. "I swear on this hat and the hole in my head that I'll find that asshole and bring him to justice. Right after I beat him senseless."

Seven
Do All Roads Lead To Hancock?

Ed urged the ten-year-old Camry to its top speed, medium mosey. Whatever oomph, if any, the car had once boasted had drained out with 140,000 miles and dozens of quarts of oil.

He wriggled his aching butt against the sprung seat back. "I give it 45 minutes, Lise, and we'll be strolling the mean streets of Hancock. That is, I will."

Strapped in the passenger seat in the plastic jug, the ashes of his ex-wife remained silent. Not a big surprise. Not a word in the nearly 2000-mile drive.

The road became a shadowed tunnel between soaring Ponderosa pines. Then the Camry burst free, tiny clouds spritzed like paw prints on the deep blue sky, meadows of late harvest hay falling away on either side. Ed rolled his shoulders, stretched his arms over the wheel. Optimism buoyed him, surged in his blood.

"Pity I couldn't ever drag you back home after that first visit. It might have grown on you. Friendly folks watching out for each other, living their lives in peace." *Except of course for Roadkill's penchant for stirring up trouble.*

Silence.

He passed the Tidy Scots Motel, with its signboard stating, "Serving you s nce 1955." Probably only had one I in the bargain letter kit.

He tried to picture perfectly groomed Lise slipping her satin peignoir between the grayed sheets of the Tidy Scots or either of the motels where Ed had spent the past two nights.

Couldn't. It made him smile.

He recalled his Grandfather Mustard grumbling that no self-respecting Scot would lay claim to the motel's dusty drapes and dingy sheets. That was twenty years earlier. Ed shuddered. Not even an "Under NU management" sign would dissuade him from trying to find someplace else to stay.

Not that there was a sign announcing new management. In Hancock, not much changed.

"Well, Lise, you won't have to talk to Cliff. You never could abide old Roadkill and his passion for clothes tanned from dead roadside treasures. I fear he won't miss you much, either, sweetheart. Thought you were a phony. For God's sake, you were an actress. What did he expect?"

It was time for some live human companionship. Had he just heard a snort?

Set My Brother Free

Ed parked the Camry diagonally in front of the Hancock City Hall and Justice Center. Newly erected since Ed's departure, the structure seemed large and perhaps too shiny bright for Hancock. Not hard to track down, though, since downtown Hancock still spread no farther than four blocks either side of the highway, and no more than a mile north and south. No new supermarkets. Empty storefronts and For Lease signs dominated Main Street, yet Belmont's General Store remained in place. If he didn't want to head south to Sandpoint or Spokane for food, he'd have to brave Darlene Belmont in her store. Maybe she'd forgotten him. *Dream on.*

He mounted the two broad concrete steps to the government facility and turned to look across the street at the Blind Chukar Café. Memories swam to the top of his mind, and he shoved them under. *Later, maybe.* The café and bar was a good place for him to tell Cliff the money bags were squeezed empty, as soon as he got his belligerent brother out of jail.

He took in a breath, then another, and aimed for the door. A tall, substantial woman brandishing several garbage bags charged him. Ed threw his arms up to stop from being trampled. The huge trash bags blocked the woman's vision but didn't slow her.

In his struggle not to tumble backward down the steps, Ed pushed against the bags. His actions didn't go down well with the bag-toting female. "What the Sam Hill do you think you're doing?" she bellowed.

They both remained upright, if immobile. Ed peered over the bags and recognized the woman. Relief fought with concern and ended in a draw.

"Ms. Hapwood, I mean, Mrs. Warnock. Myrna. It's me, Ed. Ed Mustard."

Myrna Warnock, Mayor of Hancock, current garbage collector, former high school teacher, and she-who-does-not-tolerate-fools-lightly, lowered the bags and stared at him. Not a welcoming stare.

"Holy apple pie, it's the prodigal son, returned to the bosom of his family. If we can use the word bosom in reference to Roadkill." Myrna was in better shape than a lot of retired teachers, in better shape than most California fitness coaches. She wore her gray hair long, bouncing against muscular shoulders. Her blue eyes behind glasses trendy for a small Idaho town held deep intelligence, and indignation.

"I think we—"

Myrna rolled right over Ed's response. "You never bailed him out in person before. Planning to stay around awhile or just long enough to plop some of your largesse on the poor suffering peons in Hancock?"

Ed's face reddened and he smiled a false, tight smile. "Howdy to you, too." He deserved the attitude, but he'd be darned if he'd bow down and whimper.

"Thank the high heavens you're going to spring him." She gulped. "You are, aren't you? I take him food and receive nothing but gripe, gripe, gripe for my efforts. How your sainted mother raised such a whiner is a mystery to me. And the trouble he's causing this time. Well. He may have gone too far." She scowled at Ed.

Ed risked a scowl back. After all, he was a grown man. "A whiner and a traitor...thank the good Lord she's not here to see her sons."

Myrna squinted. "I never called you a traitor, Ed Mustard. However, it was a shame the way you sashayed out of here for Hollywood and never looked back." She hoisted the bags, shook one at Ed. "Now you go on in before Albert commits police brutality on Clifford. Totally justified, but still … I need to take this recycling home."

Ed entered the jail-now-known-as-justice-center and heard a raucous and boisterous rendering of "We Shall Overcome," in his brother's confident baritone.

"I'm here to spring the warbler," he said to the guard. He nodded toward the door at the rear of the office.

"Praise be," said the balding man at the desk. He shook his head and grinned at Ed and then stood, holding the keys in one large hand.

Ed couldn't place the man's familiar face. Welcome home, he thought, remembering that every visit entailed the embarrassing rite of running into old friends and acquaintances and having absolutely no recall of who they were. He handed the paperwork from the bail bonds place in Sandpoint and said, in a voice loud enough to be heard over Cliff's singing, "I'm Ed Mustard. Roadkill's brother, much as I hate to admit it."

"Sure thing." The deputy grinned. "Don't recognize me without the long hair, do you?" He, too, was forced to yell over the serenade. Unlike most people, the deputy skipped the humiliating guessing game. "Al Fernley. Couple of years behind you."

Ed hoped he hid his astonishment. No way could this balding, potbellied male be younger than Ed. He probed his memory. "Al. Marching band? Drama league?" How did these people get so old?

Al's whole face animated with what Ed read as pleasure. "Trombone. You played sax, right?" The singing ended abruptly. Al led Ed through the doorway.

"Alto."

"Do I hear the voice of freedom? Hallelujah, brother." Roadkill rattled a metallic object against the bars of his cell.

Roadkill marched from the rear of his cell, hands on hips, and glowered at his brother. Cliff wore his dark brown hair in a ponytail tied back with a leather thong. His face might have been a little thinner than Ed recalled, a little paler, but the orange jail jumpsuit flattered no one.

"About time. What's with coming here in person? Not necessary, you know."

"Maybe they think someone should supervise you, tiny brother."

Albert guffawed. "Tiny brother? He's got thirty pounds on you." He led them through the entrance door and paused at a locker against the wall.

"Family joke," Ed said without explanation.

"Great idea to keep an eye on him. Always in trouble, is our boy Roadkill. Becoming famous throughout the Northwest. For trouble with a capital T." Albert pulled the locker open and extracted a bulging paper grocery bag. "Here's your stuff, man. I'll need you to sign for it."

Roadkill pawed through the bag, finally signing the paper Albert offered. "That's me. Regular Jesse James."

Ed wrinkled his nose and moved a few paces away. "You smell as rank as a dead bison. Wouldn't they let you shower?"

"Protest. Plus I had no clue I'd be here this long." He shot Ed a sour look. "I'm going to change."

Roadkill emerged from the lavatory with wet hair. He pirouetted in front of Ed and Albert, arms above his head. "Am I not gorgeous? Shiny clean. Although you could improve the level of your cosmetics, Albert, my man. The soap chaps my skin." Roadkill was again in his typical attire, vintage, if wrinkled, roadkill, hand-made from the skins of animals he found dead by the side of the road. Today he wore deer hide pants and, over a T-shirt, a patchwork vest from who-knew-what and no-one-wants-to-know.

"I'll add your complaint to your list," said Albert. "Your long, long, list. I hope you have the brains to keep your backside out of jail for a while."

"Hadn't of been for the Edster here, my stay would have been much, much, shorter. What was that about, brother of mine?"

Ed took in Albert's interested expression. "I'll explain later. Let's go home."

Clifford leaned his butt against the wall, and extended his legs, arms crossed in front of him. "And what home would that be? I don't think there's room for both of us in Rosinante."

The front door of the jail slammed shut and boots clomped on the vinyl floor. "Well, well. The poster boy for the old growth forest is finally departing. Can't say I'm sorry to see you go." Sheriff Byron Warnock entered the office, crossed the room with barely a nod to Ed, and confronted Roadkill. "Myrna told me Ed was here to spring you. Wish I thought this time in the cooler had worked."

"I'm cool, Sheriff. Way cool," said Roadkill. Ed thought his brother's dialogue dated. *Cool?*

"You're a hothead, son. When you gonna learn you can't haul off and pop someone when you disagree?" The Sheriff, a slender man of medium stature whose hairline was receding, thrust his face at Roadkill's. Roadkill didn't draw back.

"Pop someone?" Ed asked.

Neither Roadkill nor the sheriff acknowledged his question.

"You and I both know that's not how it came down, Byron," Roadkill said.

The sheriff crossed his arms and jutted out his chin. "That's Sheriff Warnock to you and the other scofflaws."

Roadkill took a step forward. "That better include your hero Mr. Vincent Naismith. Talk about flaunting the law."

"Oh, for Christ's sake, Roadkill. We've been over this too many times to count. Mr. Naismith is subject to the same laws we all are. And all includes you, dumbhead. It means you can't waltz onto his property and assault him." He walked to the coffee pot on a table to the left of the room and filled a mug bearing the word, "MINE."

"Who's Vincent Naismith?" asked Ed. He coveted that coffee but it didn't seem the right time to ask.

His brother strode to the coffee pot and rummaged on the shelf above it for a mug. "You'd think a big Hollywood mover and shaker would read his contracts." He poured out the last of the coffee, coffee Ed craved, might have killed for had he not been in the jail.

"I do," Ed replied. "However, we movers and shakers have a lot to read." *Like eviction notices.*

Roadkill, scofflaw and coffee snitch, grabbed three packets of sugar and methodically dumped them into his mug. "FYI, Film Guy, Naismith is the asshole who bought the Rolling M." He took a gulp of coffee. "He's destroying what Mom and Dad struggled so hard to create."

Ed's stomach growled even as he felt it tighten with the tension his brother's presence always brought. "His place, his choice. We knew the risks when we sold it."

"We didn't know the horse's patoot would pave it and bring in goddamn animals from all over the world for him and his rich friends to slaughter."

"You're kidding." Ed glanced at Byron Warnock as if he would deny his brother's bizarre statement.

The sheriff avoided Ed's eyes. "He's within the law. That's all I have to care about. It's all I can care about." He seated himself at his desk and nursed his coffee.

"What you should care about is what those animals can do to the whole population up here if they're diseased," Roadkill said. "Or if one of 'em escapes and starts to take over. Or—"

Sheriff Warnock placed his coffee mug on his desk, pushed back his chair and stood, hands on the front of his desk, leaning toward Ed's brother. "Enough already. We've hashed this over and over. You're wasting your time fighting Camp Destiny."

"Camp Destiny?" Ed echoed. "What the hell is Camp Destiny?"

Roadkill swallowed the last of his coffee and grabbed his sacked belongings. "You mean I'm wasting my time fighting Naismith's money. This isn't the end, Byron. Nobody in this damn town has the balls to stand up to Naismith."

He breezed toward the door, brushing past Warnock's desk, his belongings knocking over Warnock's coffee cup.

Roadkill stopped at the door, spun around. "Nobody but me. I have the balls. And I will stop him."

Ed pushed the barstool back and rubbed his stomach. He wanted to relax, to enjoy this time with his brother, but guilt threatened to ruin his digestion. How could he find the courage to tell his brother he'd failed in Hollywood? And that his deep pockets had been sealed shut, that there'd be no more brother bail-outs?

Roadkill belched. "Admit it. You missed these finger steaks when you were down in La La Land chewing sushi and sipping champagne." He downed his beer.

"They're sitting pretty heavy, but I'll admit I missed the occasional finger steak if you'll admit North Idaho's gone upscale. Dark beer? Unknown in these parts when we were kids."

"And if beer existed, we sure as hell found it."

Ed smiled. He tilted his beer in his brother's direction. "To memories. The fond ones."

Before his next sip of beer made it to Ed's stomach, memories that weren't fond assaulted him. His smile fell off. He remembered the way he'd avoided visits home, first blaming school, then work, then Lise.

He glanced at the plastic jar on the stool next to him. Somehow he couldn't abandon Lise, or what remained of her, in the car, while he celebrated his reunion with his brother.

Roadkill followed Ed's look. "Can't believe you're dragging her poor ashes all the way up to Hancock. Not her favorite place, as I recall."

"Nobody else seemed to want them," Ed said. Which seemed a pretty sad testament to a topsy-turvy life.

Don't go there, Mustard. Stop with the self-pity.

"Hauling her ashes everywhere you go seems macabre, but who am I to judge someone's sanity?" Roadkill, seeming oblivious to his brother's bout of melancholy, or maybe ignoring it with the male's perennial assumption that emotions fade if you don't poke at them, wiped his arm on his sleeve. His T-shirt was standard store-bought cotton, no animal parts. "To memories. And to the future. I'm telling you, Ed, if we don't stop this Naismith character, Hancock will go to Hell in a hand basket."

"You sound like Dad. 'To Hell in a hand basket.' I never really knew what a hand basket was, did you?"

Roadkill shook his head as if warding off mosquitoes. "Not important. What's important is stopping that man and his damn fool excesses. I'm heading out there tonight to see what he's up to. I heard Albert mention that some big politicos were asking directions to Camp Destiny yesterday. He's buying them off, I know it."

"Camp Destiny. Odd name. And the idea of a hunting preserve is kooky. But as long as he's within the law, Cliff. You heard the sheriff. You get caught out there again, you're in big trouble. Why court disaster?"

"Why not?" Clifford put bravado into his staccato laugh. "It's what I do. You write and scoop up money, I court disaster while fighting the bad guys." He sobered. "Come with me. See the animals. See what he's done to the ranch. If you stay in Hancock for more than a day, you'll find out the man has practically taken over the town. Plus, he's a religious fanatic."

Ed stood, saw the tab his brother obviously expected him to pay. *Tell him, Ed. Tell him you're broke. Tell him you're homeless.* "I'm not going with you. And I'm not bailing you out again if you get caught. This one's your battle."

Roadkill jerked to his feet and his barstool fell to the floor. "And you're the same namby-pamby city slicker you've been since you left this town. You make me puke."

Ed grabbed his shoulder. "Puke all you like. No more bail money."

"Christ. You are not my father. I wish to hell you weren't my brother."

Eight
How High Can You Pronk?

Vincent Naismith tried not to stare at the sweat that oozed down John Merrill's face. He failed. He hoped his attempt to hide his disgust worked better.

Not wise to let those who held the cards you need know they revolted you.

The gubernatorial assistant wiped his face with a stiff new camouflage bandana he'd purchased at the Cabela's in Post Falls. "Now this is what I call honest sweat, good sweat." Merrill flapped the bandana before him, gaining the attention of Vincent's Cairn terrier Arlo, nestled in Vincent's lap. "Unlike the sweat it took to get Cabela's to locate their stores in Idaho," Merrill continued. "Kissing-butt-nervous sweat. Wondering if the arrogant mothers' sons will bless our poor 'backward' state. Most of them Harvard MBA types never had a use for camo in their short lives."

Vincent mentally reviewed potential responses, not one politically astute. He wanted to wipe away his own dealing-with-assholes-sweat, but he wouldn't, couldn't let them know he had any qualms. He wanted to slap the ridiculous smirk off that pudgy face, remind him his body was a temple he was defiling with fatty foods, drink and inactivity.

But this man held power. Power Vincent needed. Curse it, he hated this part of the game. But a man did what he had to, to get what he wanted.

Merrill's bandana matched his long-sleeved tee from the same prestigious outfitter. Camo. Unnecessary for sitting on the deck at Camp Destiny, the long sleeves too warm for this unseasonably hot September evening.

Ah, well. Perhaps camo helped create the illusion of Africa for city-bred Merrill.

Vincent made a mental note to stock a variety of suitable clothing to sell his guests at Camp Destiny. He'd offer them at a price his guests could afford and appreciate. High.

In the meantime, he enjoyed watching the sleazeball political hack sweat. Not a Christian thought, but no one knew those. Thank God. Okay, the Lord knew, but he'd forgive Vincent if he knew anything of John Merrill.

They'd spent the late afternoon touring Camp Destiny, ending with a few rounds of skeet shooting. When dusk settled in, they retired to the deck. Vincent's hands stroked Arlo, an always comforting rote act. Vincent had adored the dog since its birth. More faithful than any human friend, far more affectionate than his first wife, the dog had more brains than his three guests put together. *But a lot less political clout. Suck it up and smile.*

Vincent smiled, his lips curving upward as if starched, the smile refusing to enter his eyes. He leaned forward and hefted the pitcher of margaritas on the table beside him in Merrill's direction. "Another margarita?" Vincent asked.

"Wouldn't say no," Merrill said. He extended his glass and Vincent refilled it. It irked him that he had to stand to reach the tall man's glass, but Vincent Naismith knew success relied on doing things we don't enjoy. And success, huge success, was within his grasp. With patience, persistence and the willingness to kiss a few asses.

Vincent Naismith did what was necessary to get the job done. No matter how sweaty, hairy or smelly the ass he had to kiss.

He offered refills to his other, less voluble, still sober, guests. "Carl? Fred? As soon as I get the pool and the lake in, we'll have other ways to cool off," he added. No need to remind his guests that all of them were instrumental to his obtaining permission to divert the river to create a lake on his property. Then all he'd need was the blind eye of a few feds, and that shouldn't cost Emily much.

"I would surely love to see that little African antelope jump some more," said Fred Cantwell, county commissioner and avid hunter. "Can't wait till you're ready for the first hunt."

Vincent turned his head away to hide a snigger. The permits were his. *His* hunt was successful, no shots fired. Bagged his limit of politicos. If indeed there was a limit.

Each of his guests had his gun beside him, in case a hunting opportunity arose. He could let them have a springbok or other small animal. But he'd make them wait. Anticipation was half the fun in big game hunting. As in sex. Of course, with sex you usually scored only one trophy. Hunting, sky's the limit.

"Sure thing, buddy," he said to Fred. He attached Arlo's lead and took a firm grip on it. The springboks were tiny, but so was Arlo, and the feisty terrier knew no fear when it came to protecting his territory. All evening the little guy had seemed anxious and extra alert, trotting to the edge of the deck, ears pricked toward the forest, whining and returning to Vincent's lap.

Vincent radioed down to the stockade, where Mac awaited his command. "Let one springbok loose."

In moments, a small graceful animal bounded across the fenced compound that lay only yards from where the men sat. Less than three feet high, it still resembled the much larger pronghorn antelope that scattered the sagebrush country of southern and eastern Idaho.

From his hiding place in the forest, Roadkill watched Naismith's guests knock back their margaritas. So powerful were his binoculars that he could see Naismith's tongue run around the rim of his glass, greedy for the coarse salt. The earphone from his video cam told him everything it picked up, from the terrier's whines and sharp yips to the slurred conversation on the expanse of redwood deck that replaced Mom's cozy covered porch.

Roadkill sat cross-legged, silent, watchful, a position he often maintained with ease for hours. He observed the tour, every offhand comment Naismith made about the "improvements" he'd made to Roadkill's family home another painful scissors cut. "Improvements, my ass. Defiling. You'll pay for this, asshole. I swear it."

He sensed motion in the woods across from him. A small dog-like predator trotted into the clearing.

Roadkill's ease left him, replaced by taut muscles ready to react, a throat suddenly dry and quivering. "Run, little feller," he whispered. He weighed the risk of revealing himself. But from his position across the clearing, he wouldn't frighten the animal, but would definitely alert Naismith.

He couldn't see a way to assure the little guy's safety. Lord, he hoped Naismith had the sense to prevent its slaughter.

"I wanna see it pronk," yelled Merrill, his voice a clear indicator of the number of margaritas he'd downed. Naismith wished he'd served the cheap stuff instead of the Porfidio Plata. Oh, well. Emily could afford it and Vincent deserved it, even if his drunken guest did not.

Merrill let out a loud rebel yell and was rewarded by the sight of the springbok leaping straight into the air, back bowed, and landing in the same spot.

The animal continued to jump, and Naismith stifled his concern about its well-being. These were valuable beasts that wealthy customers would pay through the yin-yang to hunt, and he didn't particularly want to see one injured.

He reminded himself if the men on his deck tonight weren't happy, there would be no hunting preserve, no customers.

Arlo whined. The ruff on his back rose.

Vincent scanned the clearing and noticed something trotting out of the forest from west of the fenced compound. He soothed his dog with a pat, but the hair on the back of his own neck prickled.

This was not one of his captive beasts, imported from one preserve or another or even in some cases, the remnants of a traveling circus. This was truly a wild animal, but young, very young.

A wolf.

Vincent's heart thrummed faster, harder, pounding at his temples, his wrists, his throat. The wolf pup trotted toward the fenced enclave, intent on the springbok, potential prey it thought within its youthful abilities.

Some thirty yards behind the pup, Vincent made out another wolf, this one fully grown, at the edge of the clearing, almost invisible in the dusk against the brush. Wary of entering the clearing, it observed the pup.

Vincent froze. His first wolf sighting in Idaho. He'd heard them howling in the night, read about the success of the reintroduction, worried some that they'd get into the ranch and slaughter some of his exotics. But he wasn't prepared for the goose bumps that traveled over his entire body or the dryness in his mouth or the tension in every muscle in his legs.

"Goddamn." Next to Vincent John Merrill spoke in what he must have thought was a hushed whisper. Instead his voice filled the meadow and bounced back at them.

He would have thought the little springbok would race for cover in the brush but the wolf scent or the human scent or Merrill's voice kept it in a jumping mania.

Merrill surged to his feet, reached down to the deck beside him and brought his shotgun to his shoulder. As he swung to focus on the wolf pup, the shotgun's barrel almost smacked Vincent in the temple.

Merrill fired. The pup fell to the ground.

It happened so fast. In the instant after the pup fell to the ground, Vincent acknowledged that he couldn't have stopped the drunken shot. Acknowledged and regretted it. And wondered how the fool's aim had held true.

Even with skeet shot, the 12 gauge carried enough firepower to down the small wolf.

The guardian wolf held its ground, alert, watchful.

In Vincent's lap, Arlo whimpered and cringed. Vincent smelled the pungent odor of dog piss, felt the wet warmth on his khakis. His dog nuzzled his crotch and scrunched down against the wetness. Tarnation. The otherwise fearless Arlo was already gun shy, despite Vincent's efforts to gradually familiarize him to the loud noise. This wouldn't help. And punishing the dog would only make it worse. Son of a bitch. So to speak. In the next few, long seconds, silent save for Arlo's whimpers, Naismith concluded that not sharing his companion's blood lust might indicate disapproval. He couldn't afford to alienate one of his biggest supporters in the state capitol. Ignoring his wet crotch and thighs, he stood, strode the few feet to the sliding glass door of his home and thrust his wet, quivering dog inside, slid the door home and grabbed his own shotgun and fired. Too late, he realized that his 20-gauge loaded for skeet would not down a full-grown wolf.

The wolf yelped, turned and staggered into the forest, disappearing.

Nausea clutched at Vincent's belly. He bit his lips shut, afraid even a belch would erupt with chips, salsa, margarita. He could have fired wide, missed it. *No. No regrets. No time. Damn. Hell.*

Vincent picked up his radio. He said in an undertone to Mac, "Call the bunkhouse and tell the Schramm brothers to follow the wolf. You saw what—yeah. Get rid of the pup and get the Schramms on the big one ASAP. Tell them to bring the carcass back." He cut off further questions by pushing the button on the radio.

Meanwhile, a drunken John Merrill had swaggered down to where the wolf pup lay and had hoisted the animal by the tail. He swung it in a circle above his head, yipping like a fool.

Vincent turned away from the other men, certain his revulsion showed on his face, fearful he would vomit if he spoke. He bit the inside of his cheek and breathed through his nose. *This is another situation that a strong man can handle. I am a strong man. I can handle it. I can control it. I will turn it to my advantage.*

He made himself face the other men, saw them groping for an appropriate reaction, confused. His chance to demonstrate, to lead.

"Darn dog spilled my drink. I'll go in and change in a minute." He hoped his tone came across strong and assured, because the dog piss that soaked his khakis reeked. "Don't know where those wolves showed up from, but they sure as heck are wiping out our elk population. Like rabbits in Australia, getting out of control. They get inside my barricade and they'd wreak havoc on the imports. Thank the good Lord and our governor we've got a season on the devils." He made a whistling noise. "If not, 'Good-bye big game hunting.'" He paused, shifting his focus from one to the other of the men. "Of course if we get Fish and Game riled up over a little untagged, out of season hunting, they're sure to slow things down."

Naismith could tell from their expressions that these men were as eager as he for Camp Destiny to open on time. They'd keep quiet.

Cantwell gave a brief affirmative nod. "You're right. Let some bleeding-heart wolf-lover find out about this and the publicity and investigation could slow progress." He pursed his lips, letting some of his distaste show.

"Damn liquored up city boy."

Cantwell's companion smiled at his assessment of Merrill. Carl Douglas, a Hancock City Council member, laid the new foundations for the barns at Camp Destiny. "Won't be me leaks anything about this." He spat off the deck. "But can't say as I liked what I saw." He eyed Naismith's wet slacks with contempt, as if he knew more than a spilled drink wet his crotch.

Naismith felt violated by the man's contempt, but relieved that they'd keep quiet. He'd avoid the delays that meant more expense. Too much expense meant failure. Failure, to Vincent Naismith, was not a possibility.

Vincent joined Merrill, his wet slacks chafing against his thighs at every step. He wanted to change clothes, to get back to his dog, give the poor frightened little guy some comfort, not deal with a drunken lunatic. "Let my men bury this critter," he said. "Fish and Game might not take it too well."

Merrill frowned. "I suppose. Plenty of time for trophies later. For now, we'll abide by the old rule … 'Shoot, shovel and shut up.'" Merrill's arrogance bubbled out in his crowing laugh.

The things I have to put up with, thought Naismith. *How warped do you have to be to consider that baby wolf a trophy?*

Nine
Brothers Brave the Forest

Following the trail of the big wolf got harder as the Schramm brothers tramped farther into the dense shrubs and the sunlight faded. Roger reflected on why Mr. Naismith had sent him and Dean when Mac and Mort and some of the local crew had better tracking skills.

He reckoned Naismith didn't know this. With a mental shrug, he concentrated his effort on the hunt. The waning light gave up trying to get through once they hit the forest. Huge Ponderosa pines soared skyward. Beneath them the smaller pines, Doug fir, maybe, squeezed in. Grasses like fescue or wheatgrass formed little clumps that snagged their boots, and clutched at their stumbling feet. Puny shrubs sprouted everywhere, a lot of it blooming with tiny white or pale blue flowers. Mortensen called some of them kinnickkinnick, bearberry. Who the hell knew if that was what they trampled?

Roger didn't and his brother sure as heck didn't. If it wasn't poison ivy and if it didn't hide a rattlesnake, it didn't matter. Red and Mort told him they didn't have rattlers up here, but if one wandered in, Roger figured Dean would be the first to meet up with it.

The woods smelled musty and sour, like three-day-recycled socks.

A few yards ahead Roger saw a flattened fern, its long fronds broken. Maybe the wolf squished it. Roger headed toward it. He glanced over his shoulder to be sure his brother followed.

Dean dawdled behind Roger, his flannel shirt buttoned crooked, his jaw swollen and bruised. "That wolf could turn on us, you know. Wounded animals do. Wolves are fast."

Roger paused long enough to give his brother a look. "Point that rifle away from me, for God's sake." Then he smiled. "With two of us out here, least I don't have to run faster than the wolf."

Dean clutched Roger's arm, forcing him to stop. "You can't leave me out here. I'm in pain, and you've always been in better shape. And you're bigger, too, taller, with them long legs."

Roger gave his brother's skinny shoulder a fond pat and pried off his grasping fingers. "I'm kidding. You oughta know by now I'm not going to leave you." The conviction in his voice and the warmth behind it surprised Roger. "And you'd be in better shape if you'd put something in your mouth other than those damn pills." *Shut up, Roger. Always with the waste-of-breath, waste-of-time lectures.*

Oblivious to his brother's words, Dean spat. "Will you look at that. There's blood in my mouth again. I can taste it. I'm bleeding from that hole. I could get anorexic—whatever—from the loss of blood. Or choke on it. I say we go back."

Roger avoided looking at his brother's bloody spittle. "Wuss. And it's anemic. Them actresses don't eat are anorexic. You'll be fine. A little bleeding will clean the wound." He checked the trail for sign of the wounded animal. "Let's find the damn wolf and get this over with." He struggled forward on the obstructed path, pretending to be some great tracker. As if.

"Yeah, great. We do find it, we're supposed to bring it back. We've come a long way. Look of those prints we saw, it's one big sucker. Wait up."

Roger turned to watch Dean wheeze and pant his way forward.

Dean tripped on a shrub and fell flat on that already abused face of his. "Shit. Damn bush reached out and grabbed me." He struggled to his hands and knees and cocked his head. "I hear something. I think that wolf might be watching us, waiting. There's something evil out here."

Roger dismissed his brother's concern as typical druggie paranoia. "Maybe it's a hungry bear," he said in a stage whisper, concealing a grin with his hand. That's kinnickkinnick you fell in. Mortensen calls it bearberry."

Dean jumped to his feet and did a 360-degree turn, searching for monsters. His eyes got as big as the hubcaps on Roger's pickup.

Roger laughed aloud and then tried to swallow it into a snicker. They were making way too much noise to catch a wolf, even a half-dead one. "You are so full of shit and strange ideas. If it's out there, that's great. We have a rifle. We're both good shots. Let's finish it and get back." He started up, walking zigzag, examining the ground for tracks.

"We gotta carry it a long ways, and by then it'll be full on dark. Good thing you're the strong one."

"Figured we'd share the load," Roger said.

"Didn't I tell you I wrenched my shoulder helping Mort with the new fence? I think maybe I relocated it. Shouldn't be carrying heavy stuff. Even this rifle's starting to weigh me down."

In the woods some 30 yards behind the brothers, Roadkill held his breath. Just his luck if the morons discovered him and shot him.

Christ, what a pair. Funny, if not for the fact they were tracking a dying wolf. He worked a leather stress ball in his left hand. He stood motionless, silent, and gave the men more space. They couldn't track worth shit but they weren't deaf.

He forced his tense shoulders down. Wriggled them. He'd been over-confident. Gina always told him that cocky streak would be his downfall. Embarrassing if these nut jobs shot him instead of the wolf.

Not a good day to die. Not today. Not when he was within a fox's heartbeat of besting Naismith. Not when he'd be a father in a few short weeks. Not, come to think of it, when his brother looked to be spending some time in Hancock.

His mouth curled up in a lopsided smile. Lots of surprises, lots to look forward to.

The two ace trackers stumbled on and he followed, giving them more space. Like other forest dwellers, Roadkill stayed silent and alert and wary.

Roger halted and turned to face his brother. "You are such a whiner. I'm the one carrying the pack. I'm the one doing the tracking. I'm the best shot. You think I brought you along for the entertainment value? Or the conversation?"

To Roger's astonishment, Dean stood his ground. "I'd argue that 'best shot' crack."

Roger made a long slow assessment of Dean's hands, hands that trembled darn near all the time these days, and rolled his eyes. "Maybe five years ago your argument worked."

"All's I'm saying, think about it. All we gotta tell the old man is that we shot the damn wolf and buried it out here where nobody could find it. Then we can head on home, no one's the wiser and we're not having to haul some stinkin', bloody, vermin-covered carcass clear the hell back to Camp Destiny."

Roger thought. For once Dean the doper made a point. Half the time when the brothers hunted, they left the damn carcass, avoiding the effort and mess of hauling them back. With no one to cook it for them, once Mom passed, why bother? Roger rubbed his neck and focused on the ground. *Were they still on the animal's trail?* "It's not what the boss wanted. I like to follow orders."

Roger stilled. For an instant he hated Naismith. Hated stupid Camp Destiny, hated the wild animals, hated his role of his brother's forever caretaker.

"Lord knows that's the truth." Dean snickered. "Okay, here you go. I order you to turn around, head back and tell old man Naismith we shot and buried that sucker way out in the woods."

Roger let his brother wait for his reply. "Deal." He stuck out his hand. "Shake on it. And promise we won't tell anyone the real story. Never."

They shook. "Deal," said Dean, his skinny face dazed but triumphant. Not often could he change his brother's mind.

Roger let Dean think he'd won. No need to tell him he'd lost the trail.

Mercy or Murder?

The so-called wolf trackers passed within 10 feet of Roadkill's hiding place. When they decided to retrace their steps, he'd lunged off the trail and thrown himself prone behind a fallen cedar. His face landed in an outgrowth of mushrooms that sprouted from the fallen log. Silent, covered in red sawdust and Old Man's Beard, holding his nose to forestall a sneeze, he watched Naismith's finest blunder by.

Much as he'd love to trail the two men and video any other mischief they were up to, ethics compelled Roadkill to track down the wounded wolf. His confidence was such that he didn't doubt he'd find the wolf, only the when.

Dwindling light made it hard to track the wounded animal, but the animal's injuries slowed it. Roadkill followed the signs: broken boughs on a serviceberry bush, the occasional drop of blood, a four toed paw print. Eventually he heard the animal making its way through the undergrowth. The noise revealed the wolf's grave wounds. A healthy wolf traveled in silence.

He confronted the wolf in a grassy glade beneath aspen trees. Head lowered to the earth, its front legs splayed, its body swayed. The animal's pain-ridden gaze drilled into Roadkill's soul. Somewhere in those dark eyes lay acceptance, as well. Possibly gratitude.

He shot it with his .38, through the head of the once powerful, now spent beast. Roadkill carried the handgun for finishing animals struck by vehicles.

Roadkill bowed his head to mourn the magnificent male wolf and the innocent pup that had preceded it in death. He said a Native American blessing honoring the spirit of fallen prey. But he felt like a hypocrite. This was no honest hunt. This was slaughter for no reason save human whim.

Rage rose in his body higher than the temperature gauge on his old truck at high altitude.

He wrapped the wolf in a plastic tarp and fashioned a sling for the body from the rope in his pack. He hoisted some 70 pounds of dead wolf to his back and started the long trek to his truck.

Anger provided the fuel the first few miles. Sheer stubborn determination powered the next several. The last miles dragged every aching muscle through hell.

Ten
What's Happening In Hancock?

Ed awoke hung over, disoriented and mourning something. Not Lise, a surprise. Something else.

The smell of mildew, the cramp of legs curled into a too-short space and the down that skittered up from his shoulders when he turned over reminded him he was in his sleeping bag. On a lumpy, disreputable mattress crammed into the end of an ancient trailer in a trailer park notable only for the inattention of its owners.

The current owner being Vincent Naismith, Roadkill's latest target.

Ah, yes. He remembered. Roadkill insisted Ed help him vanquish Naismith. Ed declined. Same story, different decade, different opponent. Roadkill, seemingly the same headstrong activist, Ed, feeling decades rather than three years older than his volatile brother. He wished he could forget the fight, forget the way Cliff had stormed out of the bar, forget his own stubborn refusal to follow him, to patch together a truce.

His hand sent him pinpricks of pain. His stomach instant messaged, "Feed me now." His bladder hollered, "Where's the head?" He rose, took care of necessities and left the trailer. In search of breakfast. In search of answers. In need of peace, but he imagined that would come harder, and after he discovered for sure whether Roadkill was once again tilting at windmills or whether this guy Naismith presented a true threat to Hancock and the environment.

Myrna. Mayor Myrna would know. And Lord knows Myrna would share her opinion. Possibly she'd add a muffin.

No sugary cinnamon smells wafted from the compact bungalow where Myrna Warnock had lived since Ed could recall. Instead, loud rock music and metallic clangs greeted him.

He headed around the house toward the racket.

Bassett baying added to the symphony and a stumpy-legged hound raced toward Ed, almost tripping on his floppy ears.

"Squirt. Get back here." Myrna Warnock trotted after her dog and stopped when she saw Ed. "Go ahead and bite him," she told the dog.

Ed squatted to greet the wriggling canine. The pup squirmed and yipped and strained to reach Ed's face with its tongue. Then it grabbed hold of a shoelace and tugged.

Ed scratched behind the dog's floppy ears, pulled his lace free and stood. "Most excited welcome I've had since coming home to Hancock."

"Heard you and Roadkill got into it at The Chukar last night," Myrna said.

Ed met her eyes, kept his face neutral. "No fists, no feet, no fault. Hardly counts. Hey. Nothing says you're back in Hancock like the speed of gossip." He tilted his head to one side, tugging at his ear lobe. "Except maybe Myrna's famous Morning Glory muffins."

"That little maneuver lost its appeal when you turned ten," Myrna said. But her frown had resolved into a half smile. "Come on back."

"I gather Barley's gone to his reward."

Myrna raised an eyebrow. "Died two years back. Nice of you to care."

"Cheap shot." Ed cocked his own eyebrow, ready for combat. *Dueling eyebrows?*

Myrna had the grace to appear ashamed. Her eyes, an odd pale blue, made Ed think of his old Australian Shepherd. "I gather your ex-wife passed on," she said. "Pity."

"Thanks. Contrary to public opinion, my life isn't all sunshine and margaritas."

"Imagine not. Come on. I'll see what I can scrounge up." She headed into her workshop. Ed followed.

The workshop had grown since Ed's last visit. It housed sculptures of found art of varying size. A few pieces stood colossal and ungainly against a back wall painted pale lavender. In one corner an aluminum trashcan had sprouted legs of bicycle wheels cut in half and a head of baling wire. Its eyes, crafted from huge cans used by restaurants, stared, cock-eyed, at a handmade loom. Smaller sculptures, from garden and farm tools, many bound with bright colored wool, lined shelves.

Myrna moved to the tiny kitchen area. In the swift, efficient Myrna-style Ed remembered from high school, his former teacher withdrew homemade preserves from the small refrigerator, uncovered a butter dish and removed two muffins from a bag on the counter. "Room temperature," she said.

"Microwave turns them into gooey gunk."

"So long as the coffee's hot."

Without voicing the obvious retort about beggars not being choosy, Myrna poured a mug of coffee. Ed slathered a muffin with butter and jam and took a bite that consumed half.

For a moment, Ed was eight years old. Close to heaven, savoring the sweet muffin with its cinnamon-nutmeg aroma, the tart-sweet huckleberry jam, the smooth, rich butter.

Myrna returned to her welding.

He finished the first muffin and prepared the second. Butter, jam. It called to him but he set it aside. His hunger staved off, he had to find out what was going on. "What's up with Cliff? This latest caper seems bizarre, even for Roadkill."

Perched on a tall metal stool at her workbench, Myrna appeared to have forgotten Ed. When he spoke, her head snapped around, her expression annoyed. "He's your brother. Ask him." Myrna flipped down her eye protection from where it rested atop her head. Pulled on heavy gloves.

Ed crossed to the counter holding the CD player and turned the volume down. "He dashed off last night before I could hogtie him. Byron, Cliff, you, even Al, seem on edge. What's with that? Is it this Naismith character Cliff keeps ranting about? Is he really trying to take over the town?"

She selected an old garden tool from among several on the bench top. Turned her back, clearly dismissing him, willing him gone.

Not until I have some answers.

Myrna's reticence surprised Ed. He decided a few judicious compliments couldn't hurt. He touched her forearm. "You're the mayor, Myrna. Anybody knows what's going down, it's you."

Myrna laid the welder and the garden implement on her bench. Shoved the goggles atop her head and focused those Aussie eyes on Ed. "Don't try to butter me up, boy. I'm not one of your Holl-ee-wood bimbettes."

Okay, so maybe compliments *could* hurt.

"Not a bimbette, no," he said. "But my friend, I thought. Why the cold shoulder?"

A flash of anguish passed over Myrna's face, so brief Ed almost didn't see it. "Not a cold shoulder, Ed. Cold reality. Something your brother refuses to accept." She might have turned back to her work, but Ed's hand on her arm prevented it.

"I'm out of touch. Make me understand."

She heaved a ponderous, put-upon sigh. "Vincent Naismith's a wealthy man, bringing a chance for prosperity to this town."

"According to Roadkill, that's not what the town needs."

"As if *he* knows. Camp Destiny guests will spend money in Hancock. Naismith's already providing jobs. None of that arrives in Hancock on the wings of Roadkill's notions."

"But what if—"

Myrna's deep voice mowed over Ed, in full politico mode. "Folks around here see a chance, finally, to make a little money, either in a job or by selling their property." Her hand swept out in a broad gesture. "Look at Hancock. People barely making do, kids leaving town for work."

"You've always done okay. Teacher, garbage collector, artist."

"Right. Three jobs and Byron and I barely squeak by."

Ed moved to the shelf that housed the smaller sculptures. Fingered one of the pieces. He peered through the smeared glass of the four-paned window into the sculpture garden outside. "Rustic gone graceful. These smaller pieces could bring plenty in L.A. And the big work outside…I hope you have it all online."

She punched his shoulder. "Whacko Californian." She glanced around with disdain at her workshop, but when her eyes focused on the small piece Ed had complimented, he saw her tentative pride. And maybe a hesitant desire to ask him more about potential buyers. Instead she said, "I ever tell you your folks posed for that big one out there, the couple embracing? Cliff likes it."

"He's got good taste." He smiled at her. "You were such good friends with Mom and Dad, and have always been good to Cliff and me. Thank you."

"Nice manners," she scoffed. "Loved them, love the two of you, even if at times it's not so easy."

"If what Roadkill says is true," he mused aloud, "if the guy's destroying the water, wrecking the environment—"

Myrna slapped her workbench. "Oh, for pity's sake, you bleeding heart. You sound like Roadkill."

"I'm proud of Cliff. He sticks to his principles." Despite of, or maybe because of, their argument the previous night, sibling loyalty tugged at Ed.

Myrna stared out the window, refusing to return Ed's gaze. "Principles, shminciples. Use your brain. Byron won't let the man do anything illegal. Nothing's wrong with Naismith. It's your stubborn, quixotic brother who's breaking the law."

And nobody cared this much, up till now. In fact, people admired Roadkill's commitment to his causes, even when they disagreed. "Laws get broken other ways," Ed said. "Or bent or bought."

"Don't start spouting his theories." She turned from the window to face him. "Now you're here, keep him in line. Not that you'll hang around for long. Never do." She rubbed at her eyebrows.

Ed ignored her jibe, even though he recognized she was accurate about his urge to escape, to avoid involvement with his brother's issues. But something niggled at him about Myrna's attitude. What wasn't she telling him? Her feistiness covered something. "I think there's more to it. I don't think Cliff's that far off the mark on this one. I came to you for the truth, for the real story."

"You think there's more to it? Since when do you care so much about the fortunes of Hancock?"

Ed fought to keep his voice steady, to project a calm he didn't feel. "I've been busy."

"Oh, busy indeed. Shedding a murder rap, fighting the good fight against your old in-laws. To think we considered you the well-behaved brother."

Ed's fists clenched. Try as she might, he couldn't let Myrna distract him. He licked his lips. "This isn't about me. It's about Vincent Naismith and what's happening to Hancock. It's about my brother."

Myrna rested her head on one palm. "Yes. It's about your brother. He's in up to his nose hairs this time, Ed. You've got to stop him. A lot of people around here rejoice that Naismith has come in with new ideas, new money…and now Roadkill threatens the whole thing. He's in trouble. Trouble with a capital T."

She yanked her goggles over her eyes. Threw them back again. Her hair sprouted up behind it like a palm tree with an Afro. *Would that make it a dated palm?*

Ed put a restraining hand on Myrna's arm. "Cliff edges toward fanatical, I know. But he's not stupid. If he says Naismith is up to something, then he—"

Myrna wrenched her arm away from Ed's hand. "Leave it. Nothing's wrong but Roadkill's rantings."

Rantings. The word sliced through Ed's hung-over brain. He paled, tried to relearn the art of breathing. He'd accused Lise of ranting, of posturing. But sometimes, sometimes, the truth is inside.

"My brother doesn't rant. He sees stuff others don't."

Myrna looked to heaven. Or possibly the ceiling. Hard to tell. "Why waste my spit on you? You'll be gone again before the mud dries on your bumper. Nothing can be done about Naismith, believe me. And nothing should," she added in a defensive tone.

"There's always a way to fight injustice."

She stomped across the workshop. "Oh, for God's sake. If you care about the people of Hancock, maybe you ought to inquire after your old friend Gina. Now there's someone heading for trouble."

The sucker punch hit Ed from nowhere. He inhaled through his nose. "Gina? Trouble?"

"When her parents took that fool notion about 'returning to the mother country,' they had no idea what their daughter would get up to. Now, when she needs a friend, Cliff gets himself arrested. Maybe you can straighten her—" She paused. Her long, slow scrutiny took in Ed, from sneakers to well-worn designer jeans to Tencel T-shirt.

Her laugh came out more snort-wheeze-contempt than amused. "On the other hand, you don't fit anymore. Go back home to your mansion and your money. We don't need you here." She picked up an acetylene welding torch, flipping the spark wheel.

Ed walked to the fuel tank and turned the nozzle off. The torch's flame shrank and died. He kept his voice low and controlled and hoped Myrna didn't notice the tremor. "I'm leaving now, but I'm staying in town. Not sure how long. My brother is his own man and will do what he wants. And I respect him for that. Tell me, what's the story with Gina?"

"How long are you in town?" Her voice and her expression softened.

"Like I said, I'm not sure. A while. I've got nothing brewing in L.A. About Gina?"

Instead of answering, Myrna marched to the back of her workshop where dozens of wire cages lined the wall. She grabbed two cages, each about two feet square, and strode to Ed. "Here. I understand you're staying in one of those old trailers. Nothing can hurt them. These critters need attention, and you need to do something worthwhile." She thrust the cages at Ed.

Ed peered down at the cages. In each a bushy-tailed squirrel cowered. Each squirrel wore a cranky expression, if Ed's guess was right. Each sported a bandage. Ed crossed his arms. "Nuh-uh. No way I'm going to spend my time up here babysitting squirrels."

"They don't take much time." She grabbed a printed sheet of paper and a full paper bag. "Instructions. Food. They need help. You can handle it."

"Of course I *can*. The question is, do I want to? The answer is no." Ed didn't share Myrna's optimism about his ability to care for the squirrels but wasn't about to admit that. After all, he'd done the 4-H thing, even a stint in Future Farmers of America. He could handle a couple of squirrels. Sure he could.

Myrna directed The Look at him. "Your mother would be so disappointed to hear you couldn't spare a few minutes a day to care for two of God's innocent, wounded, creatures."

Ed thrust his arms out. "The only creature I should care about right now is nicknamed Roadkill. Hold your disappointed Mom card for something more important. Give me the damn things."

"Thank you, sweetie. Points for you." She placed the cages in his arms, the bag atop them.

"Now tell me about Gina."

"Find out for yourself. But before you do anything rash, I'd advise you to think about your history, her history. For a Mustard boy, that would be a remarkable accomplishment."

Eleven
Revenge, By All Means

Lacy Ponder slouched in the car seat and yanked the mirror lengthwise. She removed the cute red baseball cap her Mom had given her and replaced it with a boring beige sun hat to match her boring beige skirt and the boring beige jacket worn over a boring high necked blouse.

"I vow this will be worth it," she told her mirror self. "I will track down that freak and I will nab him before the cops do and prove I am an investigator, I am police material."

Step one: get the list of shoppers for the day of the attack. This get-up and a few adaptations to her walk and body language, and no one will recognize the security geek who was in and out of the employ of Sears faster than a kid can walk backward up the down elevator.

Could she convince Brad to help her find the dumb-ass monster who caused her to lose her job? Oh, and knocked her out with a pair of Vise-Grips he hadn't even paid for?

Yes, she could. No time for self-doubt.

Out of the car, she headed for the Mall's Food Court, knowing she was too early, perspiring and shivering while she waited for Brad to arrive. Hoping nothing delayed him.

Dammit, Lacy, you've faced down armed criminals with less sweat. Did that tweaker knock out your courage with one blow of his pliers?

She scanned the Food Court for Brad. One of the friendliest guys in Security during her training, Brad had asked her out after she was let go. She'd turned him down. Brad seemed too eager to please, too sweet. The kind of man her mother wished she'd bring home some Sunday.

He'd accepted her invitation to meet her for lunch with open pleasure.

You, Lacy Ponder, are a conniving witch.

53

He entered the Food Court, his eyes roving. He didn't notice her until she stood and waved. The disguise worked.

"Let's sit over there," Lacy suggested once they toted trays filled with lunch. "It's more private, if you can find privacy in a food court."

Brad led them to a table and Lacy surprised herself by noticing his butt and strong arms. Bad timing. "I'd hoped our first date would be more intimate," said Brad with a hopeful smile. "But I'll take what I can get."

You're a shit, Lacy, a selfish, obsessed witch.

She smiled at Brad. Her palms, drenched with sweat, made her fear she'd lose her grip on her plastic fork and send it flying across the table to stab Brad. Her heart thumped way too fast for the non-exercise of sitting down and eating.

Brad brought her up to date on Sears' gossip while they ate.

"I'm glad you've recovered so well," Brad said. "I gotta tell you, I barely recognized you out of the old Sears security polo and khakis. So, what's your employment situation these days?"

"Somewhere between bleak and un." She opened her fortune cookie and read it to herself. "You are a happy, sociable person with many friends who trust you."

Oh, crap. She started to shove her chair back. This was so not a good plan.

Brad didn't notice her withdrawal. "Have the cops had any luck finding the s.o.b. who attacked you and Harold? It's a lucky thing he didn't go ballistic earlier, like when he was in the dressing room with that little kid." He flushed to the tips of his protruding ears. "Not that your getting hurt was lucky. Or fired. I mean—"

"I know what you mean, and you're right. The guy's a nutcase, totally unpredictable." Lacy gripped the table so hard her fingers hurt. "I went downtown yesterday and the cops said they don't have anything so far."

"Stan faxed them a list of people who bought stuff in Men's Wear that day. That should help."

Lacy leaned forward. "Yes, but it's painstaking and time-consuming work. The kind of work I'm good at. It's not their top priority, it can't be. To me, it is. I saw him, saw his eyes. At any moment, he could go on a rampage and really hurt someone else, maybe kill people. He's a nut, an unpredictable fruitcake."

"Which makes your jumping up and running after him, trailing blood behind you, even harder to understand."

Lacy's injury, almost healed, thrummed with pain. She wished she could stop the rush of color to her face, hoped Brad attributed it to anger. "Head wounds bleed a lot. My injuries were minor."

"And you were pissed ... I mean, mad."

She kept her grin to herself. Brad was a good guy. "Well, duh. If I'd have run faster, I might have caught him."

"God, Lacy. That's why Sears let you go. Our jobs aren't to chase down madmen. We call the cops. You're not a cop, anymore."

"I'm not anything anymore." She noticed Brad's eyes, nice chocolate brown eyes, eyes that could make a woman forget her objective. She forced her eyes away from his. "If I can track him down, I promise I'll bring in the cops for the arrest. I want to catch him, yes, but I'm not crazy. That's why I need your help."

"You want me to help you track the guy down? This is me, Lacy. Security guard by day, student by night, carpenter in the off hours. Not much time to spare."

"You had enough spare time to ask me out," Lacy countered.

"Yes. You turned me down flat." Brad waved his arm as if dismissing that old news. "I'm pleased you see me as your partner in rubbing out scum, but I'm not sure what I can do for you. You're the ex-cop. I'm the wannabe."

Lacy tried not to pout.

Brad leaned forward. "What the heck. I like you. I'm good at shuffling my schedule. Tell me what your plan is and how I fit in. Could be fun, you and me as partners."

Lacy gulped. *Once again, things are not going exactly as planned.* "Uh, I had something smaller in mind. Shorter term. Like … today?" Her voice squeaked on the word *today.*

Brad crossed his arms and leaned back in his chair. "I knew it. You haven't suddenly become convinced I'm hot. Not ready to partner up." He leaned back further, cradled his head in laced palms. He let a smile sneak its way out and curl up one side of his mouth. "Oh, well, I had a few minutes to dream. What do you want? Will it mean my job, too?"

Lacy let out a breath. He was being a sport about this. And not asking for anything in return.

"All you have to do is let me in the Security room and keep yourself distracted while I run the tape for that day. I've got to find him."

"Hell, let's do it. If I think about it for more than five minutes, I'll come up with 15 reasons it won't work and another dozen ways I'll get fired. What's your plan?"

Even on a weekday, Sears processed a lot of transactions. Lacy sat at the Security register and waited while the narrow tape spewed out the report. Nervous, she rolled the tape into a tight ball as it exited the printer.

Across the small enclosed room Brad sat at a desk with several monitors showing different departments in the store.

The printer ran out of tape. Lacy stuffed the first tape into her purse.

"Where do you keep the extra rolls?" she asked Brad in a low voice.

Brad spun his chair around and bent to retrieve a new roll from a bookcase shelf. When he handed it to her, she noticed the dampness on the roll. Good. She wasn't the only one whose nerves jangled.

The door opened and after a moment, closed.

Stan.

"Lacy Ponder. Didn't know you still worked here."

Brad rose. "She doesn't. I convinced her to meet me for a movie when I got off shift."

"Uh-huh. I'm thinking your shift suddenly got shorter, son. Escort her out. Then come back and we'll talk."

Lacy stood beside Brad. "Don't blame Brad. It was my—"

"I invited her to wait with me."

Stan looked from Brad to Lacy, his skepticism as obvious as his disapproval. "I believe I asked you to escort Ms. Ponder out of the security room and the employee area."

He leaned over the security register. His eyes flicked back to Lacy. "Want to open your purse?"

Lacy clutched the boring beige handbag in front of her boring beige blouse. "I do not. It's private property. I'm leaving, like you asked." She headed for the door. Brad followed.

She waited for Stan to call out to her to stop, wondered if she would run or cave. He remained silent. She moved, measured pace followed by the next, from Security, to the hallway, past the receptionist, through the doors, to outside. Brad paced behind her.

How many transactions had she retrieved before Stan entered? Half? Three quarters? She prayed that somewhere on that tape fragment lay the name of the asshole who'd hit her. Otherwise, Brad would lose his job for nothing.

She halted. "I never should have asked you. I am so, so sorry."

"Don't be. I knew what I risked."

Lacy couldn't read Brad's face. "How can I thank you?"

Brad's eyes crinkled. "Don't tempt me, woman. I am a mere mortal man."

"How can you joke? You lost your job." Lacy watched an ant drag a crumb, drop it, back up, nudge, nip and haul again.

"It's not like I lived a lifetime yearning to be a security clerk at Sears." Brad lifted Lacy's chin so she had to look at him instead of the ant. His smile held forgiveness and encouragement. "Find that jerk. And take care he doesn't kill you, this time."

"I'll let you know what happens, I promise."

His smile broadened. "Call me if you need help. Looks like I'll have more spare time than I expected." He tilted the front brim of her sun hat back and bent to place his lips on her forehead. "I don't need payback. I'm not that kind of guy."

She cleared her throat. "I know." She checked the ant's progress. Not much, but forward. She looked again at Brad. "Stan could have searched my purse. He must have known—"

Brad put his fingers to her lips. "Find that jerk."

Twelve
A New Approach To Saving the Wolves

Exhaustion dragged at Ed like a cranky toddler and wouldn't let go. The bed, that grungy, lumpy excuse for a mattress, drew him like dog food drew ants. He deserved a nap.

He should be writing.

A nap boosts creativity and energy. *Escaping into oblivion again? No way.*

He stashed the squirrels, one cage on the kitchen table, the other on the electric stovetop.

What was Myrna hiding? Other than her talent, of course. God, the statues that woman made from spare parts should be on display in a gallery instead of hidden in her shop or her backyard. The big one, the one she said his parents had posed for? Perfect for his rose garden in Santa Monica.

Whose rose garden? You're broke, Mustard. No house, no roses, no statues.

He forced his attention back to the squirrels. "Be good or I'll turn up the heat," he said. The squirrel didn't answer but it gave him an evil look that said "put your finger in here and I'll have it for dinner."

"Thank God you're not hamsters. I couldn't tolerate you running on those tiny tin treadmills." The racket would match the one in his brain.

He should be writing.

He wondered if talking to squirrels made him less certifiable than talking to Lise's ashes.

He lay on his back, and worked to force his worries down from his brain to the core of his body and out his feet. He imagined them as heat and pushed the heat down and out, down and out.

The odd ritual had proved to be the most effective method for relaxation and sleep he'd ever discovered. Useful before and after the divorce and while Lise headed through meltdown to destruction.

He should be writing.

Two deep relaxing breaths followed by another. And another.

Followed by pounding on the trailer door. Loud pounding.

Ed barefooted it to the door, opened it a crack.

His brother poised ready to enter. Relief that his brother seemed to have forgotten last night's argument warred with Ed's desire for sleep. But he knew his brother, recognized the obstinate expression. "Come on in, Cliff."

"Call me Roadkill. Everyone else does."

Roadkill loomed large and pungent in the trailer's gloom. "I need your help."

"I bailed you out of jail yesterday. That's not help?"

Roadkill ignored him. "No one's around. Good timing. Get your shoes on."

"Let's get something straight. I am not your errand boy, not your bank, not your private slave, not your sounding board, not your flunky. I *am* your brother. I am going with you right now because I want to, not because you're telling me to."

Roadkill's smile combined innocence and love and joy. *Why do I suspect it?* "Of course you're my brother. My older, wiser, brother. That's why I came to you. But we've got to hurry."

Ed doubted he'd won that round. Still, he retrieved his running shoes from beside the bed.

Roadkill rummaged in the tiny fridge. "This is a disgrace. You need to go shopping. Shouldn't take long. You have to promise me you won't tell anyone."

"Tell anyone I've shopped?" Why couldn't his brother have arrived even 20 minutes later? Ed needed that nap. His brain needed that nap. His entire body needed that nap.

"Not even any fruit? You used to be a health nut."

"Still am, on occasion. But I promise I won't tell."

His brother's head and his attention left the refrigerator and he noticed the squirrels. "Whoa. Furry charismatic mini-fauna."

"I call them squirrels."

"Activist lingo. Myrna admire the trailer?"

"Myrna wasn't here. I went there. They came back with me. They're recovering."

Roadkill scraped a finger along a cage. The squirrel backed into the opposite corner and chattered at him. "Aren't we all? So Myrna told you Naismith is Hancock's hero."

Maybe I'm still asleep. "Where'd you go last night? I wanted to talk. Needed some answers. Had to drink alone."

"Follow me now and we'll drink later. And talk." Roadkill held the trailer door open for Ed. "Got to get this done before more rigor sets in."

Rigor? Ed bit his lips against a refusal. He didn't want to comply with Roadkill's arrogant orders, but rigor? He followed.

❧

"Tell me I am not doing this. *We* are not doing this." Ed peered into the depths of the freezer, where, nestled among freezer bags filled with dried remains of ancient unidentifiable foodstuffs, a huge wolf leered up at them.

Roadkill gave him a look. "Be grateful you're not the wolf. 'Come to Idaho and we'll shoot you and stuff your poor dead body into a decrepit freezer in a decrepit trailer park in a dying town.'"

Ed's stomach burned. The shame, of the death of a beautiful wild animal, and his own participation in its temporary interment, gnawed at his gut. Or was it hunger?

Roadkill bent over the other end of the old box freezer. "Stuff that leg in. It still has some bend in it. We can discuss my IQ later. God, he was a big feller." Although he hid it in his focus on the task at hand, Ed could tell his brother mourned the animal.

"How far'd you haul him?" Ed doubted *he* could carry the wolf across the trailer park, much less for the miles he suspected his brother had lugged the animal. His brother might be nuts, but he had muscles and determination to back his convictions.

"There." Roadkill slipped his left arm out of the freezer and slammed the lid down, barely missing Ed's hand. "We should weight it down. He'll stiffen up more before he freezes."

Ed tried and failed not to imagine a huge wolf paw, claws extended, reaching out from beneath the freezer lid. He grimaced. "Christ. Let's not open it again. We can stack stuff on it randomly." Ed kept one arm on the lid of the freezer and spun around so he could scan the little carport area. *Yes.* "Hold it down." He trotted to where a large bag of dog kibbles slumped. He heaved it over his shoulders and dumped it onto the freezer. The dust that had covered the bag remained on Ed's shirt, along with a lot of spider webs. He brushed at it with both hands.

"What happens when the owner wants a nice roast?"

Roadkill grinned. "Mistake a wolf leg for a leg of lamb? It's not gonna happen. You saw the dust on the lid. You saw the ice crystals on the stuff in there. The caretaker eats out since his wife died."

Ed examined his filthy hands. He smiled, a relaxed, who-the-hell-cares-what-I-look-like, I'm enjoying myself, smile.

He remembered the good times with Cliff. The brothers, working together to cover up some prank of one or the other. Cooperating. Conspiring against the world.

"Don't move." Roadkill edged toward Ed and flicked something off his shoulder. "Live spider. Didn't like being disturbed."

Ed froze. His shoulders pulled together, and he ducked his head. His burning guts threatened evacuation. Snakes he could handle. Bears. Wolves, that is, the dead ones. Film company executives. Not spiders. Not spiders.

He gathered his courage and forced his mind away from arachnids. "It's about time you told me where you found your friend."

Roadkill's lips twitched. He knew how Ed loathed spiders. "I did tell you. On your shoulder."

"The wolf, smartass." Shivers crept up Ed's spine and out his right scapula. He turned his back to his brother and asked, "You sure there's nothing else crawling there? I can feel—"

Roadkill brushed at his shirt with enough vigor to smart. "Dust and webs, nothing more, honest. You ask where I found the wolf? You ask where I went last night?"

Roadkill faced Ed. "While you," he pointed at Ed, "sucked down beer and savored your Hancock homecoming," Roadkill spread his hand over his heart, "I gathered evidence that will bring the enemy to his knees."

"Thought you wanted him to leave town. Could be difficult on his knees."

"Speaking figuratively, writer brother." Roadkill leaned back against the freezer. "Although I like the image." He frowned. "One of Naismith's bastard guests shot a wolf puppy that wandered onto Naismith's land, drawn no doubt by the scent of all that tame game he's got penned up."

Ed stared at his brother, shocked into silence. People don't—

Oh, yes, people do.

"Naismith shot the adult wolf that was with the pup," his brother continued, his expression a misleading calm, "used a shotgun and wounded it. Sent a crackerjack team to track it down. Once those bumbling bozos gave up and hightailed home, I had to find the wounded critter and finish it." He pulled one of his leather stress balls from a pocket and began to roll it in his right hand, a monotonous movement he found soothing. Ed found it annoying and usually teased his brother about his Captain Queeg balls.

Ed shook his head, now cleared of any sleepy fuzz. "Two questions: First, you said a guest shot it. I thought the place hadn't opened yet."

"Politicians he's wooing to clear any potential obstacles."

"Got it. The bribe that isn't a bribe. Next question: why bring its body back? Why not bury it?"

Roadkill's grin flashed, cocky, confident, exultant. "The corpse, along with a video I hid, proves Naismith is breaking the law out there. Plus it adds shock value, always useful in a battle."

"But the town's all for—"

Roadkill faced Ed, arms extended, palms up, like a preacher begging Ed to come to Jesus. "P.R., man. Public relations. Naismith might wiggle out of the legal part, he might convince Hancockians he's a good ol' boy, but the video, man, that shows what he's really like."

Recalling Myrna's tirade, Ed wondered if his brother could possibly succeed. Wondered who was right here, and if right or practical trumped. "You care to tell me where you hid this video? Or let me see it?"

"You'll see it soon. And it's safely hidden, somewhere," he dragged his lower lip between his teeth and stared into the distance, "somewhere near and dear to the heart of Mustard." He touched his heart.

Ed's face pinched in a frown. "You know how much I love your Roadkill riddles." He shrugged, assuming his brother would show him the video on his schedule, regardless of Ed's wishes.

"Listen to me," Roadkill said. "I told you Naismith's guests were politicians. Local, state. We click on the fluorescent spotlight of public scrutiny and we snare him. We have to. The man is out of control."

Ed backed a step away. "Interesting choice of words. Myrna told me you were out of control. That the town needs Naismith."

Roadkill spit out a guttural hah. "Uh-huh. Typical Myrna." He paced the breadth of the carport, spun around with arms crossed over his gut. "Everybody's got an agenda. Something they care about. Something, vital, valuable, essential. To you right now it's that plastic jug of ashes you can't part with. To Myrna, it's the town. Hancock's her fucking Holy Grail. Camp Destiny is Naismith's. Like they forget these places are all on borrowed time, borrowed from Mother Nature, warts and scars on what used to be pristine. One good fire would wipe the whole batch of us out and Mother Nature would simply start again."

Lord God, I've come home to Hancock and found a battleground. He stared at his brother, considering what he might say. Still uncertain who, if anyone, was right in this conflict.

Roadkill absorbed Ed's confusion. He drew near enough that Ed smelled the coffee sourness of his breath, the earthy pungent musky mix of sweat and leather and dust and pine. In a low urgent voice he said, "Thanks for the help. The battle is on. You decide whose side you're on. But Naismith's got a mission and it's all about him. Not about the land, not about Hancock. He's whacked."

"And you're not?" said a female voice behind Ed.

Ed knew that voice. He jumped forward and tripped on a concrete block Roadkill had stacked in front of the freezer. He fell, chin first onto the freezer top, ending up spread-eagled in front of it on his knees.

Calm, cool, Ed Mustard, a man in command of himself and the situation.

Roadkill roared. "Smooth, big brother. Got any similar moves?" He offered Ed a hand.

Ed hauled himself up with Roadkill's help. Caught. Say hello to your best friend from high school as she catches you in a stunt dumber than most you tried 15 years ago. Had she seen what they were up to?

Roadkill's smile stretched across his face and erased its earlier tension. "Hell-oh, Gina, you gorgeous thing. You grow lovelier every day."

Ed faced Gina, yearning for clean hands, a clean shirt, and a clear conscience. Or to be somewhere else. He realized now was his opportunity to explore Gina's problem that Myrna had mentioned. If he could control the mortification that threatened to overcome him as if he were still in high school.

His heart, thrumming already from the fall against the freezer, pounded louder, in his ears, his temples, his chest.

Gina stalked toward them, a tight bright green T-shirt cupping a protruding belly leading her attack.

Oh, Christ. A bulging belly. A pregnant, bulging belly. Nothing but a baby could cause that bump. *Brilliant observation, Mustard.*

Gina ignored Ed, targeting Roadkill, hands on her hips. "I grow *larger* every day, you mean. I thought we agreed you'd stick around these last weeks."

Roadkill backed against the freezer and ducked his head like a kindergartner caught with his hand in the teacher's drawer. "You've got plenty of time. Besides, I was nearby."

Gina growled, her lips curled over white teeth. "Arrrr. Right. What could be more nearby, more convenient, than the town jail? I'm sure Byron would set you free if I happened to go into early labor." She glanced over at Ed, whose mouth still hung open. "What, you think I simply got fat?" She shook her head. "I can see that your brother has kept you up to date, as usual."

Must … say … something. Ed shut his mouth, feeling like a puppet with its strings crossed. He managed to choke out a weak, "Congratulations, Gina."

Gina's frown turned to a smile. Curly brown hair sprouted from her head in every direction with no discernible style. No, make that Gina style.

She rubbed her belly. That pregnant, bulging belly.

Ed knew the questions, knew the drill. He dreaded asking them, especially the big one. Yet, despite Myrna's mysterious comments, Gina did not appear to be a woman in trouble. She appeared beatific. Earth mother joyful.

"Uh, when are you due?" he asked.

Why did Ed get the feeling Gina delighted in his discomfort? Her words were innocent, but her brown eyes sparked with mischief and pleasure. "Not for another six weeks."

She grabbed Roadkill's hand and placed it on her tummy, under her thin T-shirt. "What do you say, Poppa? When do you think our baby will peek its little head out?"

Poppa? Ed rode in the front car of the roller coaster, at its lowest loop. Breathless, unsure if the trip up was worth the next frightening descent. Not wanting to continue gaping at Gina, he focused on his brother. Poppa.

Was Cliff proud to be the father-to-be? Ashamed, for God's sake? Why hadn't he told his brother, his only living kin? Or did he doubt Gina's claim he was the father?

Gina didn't lie.

Ed's focus moved from the face of his brother to the woman beside him and back. "So, Cliffie, more secrets? Do I owe someone a wedding present?"

Shit. His brother's expression, shock merged with amusement, revealed his blunder. Ed staggered back a pace. He wanted to suck those words back with his next breath. Or slap himself. Where had he discovered this absolute, unerring skill at saying the wrong thing?

And when did he become so old-fashioned and judgmental?

Gina's face remained serene. *Serene? Make that smug.*

"No wedding," she said. "I wanted a baby, seemed time. And despite his many flaws, Roadkill has a good brain and a healthy body."

Roadkill finally returned Ed's look. "Gina made this into a 'no big deal' thing between the two of us. I didn't see why I should inform you."

Nothing Ed could do banished the mental image of Gina and his brother conceiving their child. He tried not to choke. On a laugh or on bile, it was a toss-up.

"Well, no," he drawled. "Since it didn't require asking me for money, why would you tell me?"

Gina gasped.

Roadkill gave him a not-so-light cuff on the chin. "Low blow, bro."

Ed refused to show the pain, screaming first from striking the freezer and now from the power of his brother's fist. "Sometimes the truth hits hard, *bro.*"

Gina waved her arms at the brothers. "Excuse me. I didn't come to watch you two brawl. I want to know if you intend to live up to our agreement," she said to Roadkill. "If I have to go to Spokane, I might have to ask you for help. You said you would."

Ed heard the panic underlying Gina's words and wanted to offer his help. But he kept quiet. This was not his business. Not his business. *Jesus. Gina and Roadkill. Parents.*

That sharp stab near his solar plexus? He suspected it was envy. He knew it ached.

Roadkill squared his shoulders. "My word is good." He lifted his chin. "I've been working on issues that will affect the quality of life of our child. Issues like ecology, and—"

"Spare me your pompous lectures." Gina cast her eyes skyward.

Ed yearned for the splendor of the world's tackiest trailer. Better still, he ached to be back in his car headed south. But still... If he hadn't left Hancock, hadn't been so hot to become some famous scriptwriter, would he have stayed with Gina? Been the father of this child, maybe others?

"Uh," Ed started, but had nowhere to go. He clamped his mouth shut.

Gina glanced at him for an instant and returned her focus to Roadkill. "I can believe a lot of things about you, but I find it hard to grasp that you'd lie to me."

Roadkill's lips pressed together. He thrust them out, in. Ed thought he might scuff his shoe in the dirt. He almost enjoyed his brother's dilemma. Almost.

Roadkill clapped a hand to his forehead. "Now that Ed's here, he can help, too. You'll stay till Gina pops, right, Ed?" He threw his arm over Ed's shoulder. "I mean, you guys have been friends longer than even Gina and me."

Ed's insides felt like an angry sore, a hole that nothing could fill. He knew he blushed, couldn't stop it, couldn't cover his face with his hands like some heroine of an old romance. Why couldn't he simply disappear?

Gina crossed her arms atop her stomach. "Don't bother. I can take care of myself. The other women are here for me. Mom's coming after the baby is born. She can help. You've done all that was biologically required."

Ed stepped forward. "I don't mind."

"*Really.* I'll be fine. I'm sure Mr. Big shot Hollywood screenwriter won't be staying long in boring Hancock, Idaho."

"Not boring," Ed replied, keeping his tone mild and his eyes on Gina's face rather than more prominent parts of her anatomy. "I'd already been planning to spend some time here." He couldn't bring himself to admit to his brother and Gina that his other options were few. Make that none.

When Ed left Idaho, he'd thought he'd be such a big success. Right.

"Well, gee," Gina said. "That's swell."

Ed detected the aroma of not-so-faint sarcasm but only smiled back.

"Stick around and you'll get to see Hancock Days," she added. "Remember that momentous annual event commemorating old Horace Hancock?"

Ed nodded. He had of course forgotten about Hancock Days. "Looking forward to it."

Ed returned their blinks of disbelief with an innocent half-smile.

"As to this baby thing," Roadkill said. "I'm out of jail now and I'll be around, I promise. Spit in my eye, hope to die, if I'm not."

Ed smiled for real. His brother had dredged up their ancient childhood vow. But, a promise was a promise. And a brother a brother. "Me, too, Gina. Even if you don't need me, I'm here."

Gina tossed her head, curls flying. "We'll see." To Ed she said, "Good to see you. It's been too long."

She fired a smile at him and Ed couldn't tell if it was meant to wound or to warm or to warn.

The two men watched Gina saunter out of sight. Despite the weight gain of pregnancy, she still had legs that didn't quit and a great ass.

Cliff gave a small shake of his head and seemed to dismiss all thought of the woman who bore his first child. "You've got to see this damn Camp Destiny Naismith has built on our land."

"No, I don't. Plus it's not our land anymore."

"My bad, I admit it. I regret not investigating what he planned. Most of those fools who come up from California want to commune with nature, stare at the pine trees and breathe the clean air. How was I to know this asshole had delusions of Africa in North Idaho?"

"You didn't. I don't blame you. I signed the papers, too." Ed scanned the covered patio that housed the box freezer. "We through here?"

Roadkill did a circuit of the patio, scuffing away their footprints in the dust. "Through." He rubbed his hand on his leather pants. "We can stop him. If people around here see that video, see the wolf body, and if we can find it, the body of the pup they shot, they'll consider the impact of all that imported wildlife on our native stock." He observed the sky, his watch. "I suppose it's too early for a beer?"

"It's not even noon." Ed headed for his rental trailer. "Coffee or beer, your liver, your choice." Over his shoulder, he said, "People in Hancock won't care. Don't care. What they care about is that Naismith is buying property that nobody else wanted and hiring people who haven't been able to find work in years. Like Myrna said, you're the only one fighting this battle."

"She doesn't like him, either. I can tell by her face. She's only saying what she does because she's the mayor."

Ed mounted the shaky trailer steps. "Okay. Then the mayor is telling you to butt out. As spokesperson for the town."

Roadkill elbowed past Ed and grabbed a can of beer from the refrigerator. "Beer in aluminum for the famous screenwriter?" He popped the tab and took a gulp.

"Don't see it stopping you." Ed took a Coke from the fridge.

"I'll come by for you around 12:30 or 1:00 a.m. Dress warm. Nights are cool. If you can manage it," he gestured to the urn of Lise's ashes, "leave Lise at home."

"Again with the dictates? I'm not your slave, not your flunky—"

"I got it the first time. What you are is my brother."

"You get caught, you'll wind up in jail. Don't do it."

"Mom and Dad would have despised what he's done. Despised him. You have to see it."

Using the Mom and Dad card. Christ. Twice in one day? *They know your buttons.* "You promised Gina."

Roadkill's smug smile reeked triumph. "Exactly. I need you to see what he's done. And watch my back."

Thirteen
Not Old MacDonald's Farm

The old lion took Ed's measure through the wire mesh of his cage.

Ed read disdain in the cat's gaze. After all, Ed's role tonight was to watch out for his younger brother. He who had been unable to save his ex-wife, unable to rescue his ailing career.

Disgust works better than mere disdain. I'm really here as a voyeur, to see if it's as bad as Cliff said.

The lion continued his silent assessment. The animal's tawny eyes sagged in deep sockets and matter dripped from one. The dim overhead light revealed a stringy, sparse mane. If this was the king of the jungle confined before them, he was a tuckered king, well past his prime, his fiercest attribute his rank breath.

Ed imagined the lion had considered, but discarded as too much effort, the idea of a roar. Sort of like an aging movie star who had for years sucked in his gut when women passed, but had given up. So not trophy material, Ed wondered why Naismith had bothered with it. Maybe part of a package deal.

The lion turned around, paced no more than eight feet to the rear of his cage and lay down.

Ed exhaled the breath he'd been holding. Had the lion roared, Camp Destiny would have become Camp Go-straight-to-jail-if-you're-not-shot-in-the-process for the brothers Mustard. Naismith's men who weren't standing guard slept in the nearby bunkhouse.

When the brothers had entered the barn, the animals alerted, and Ed heard shuffling, snorting and assorted rumblings. So far, none had sounded the claxon that would bring Naismith's men running.

Ed cursed himself for letting his brother drag him out here. Now he was losing sleep to stare down a desiccated, approaching toothless lion.

"What now, bwana?" he whispered to Roadkill.

Roadkill had insisted their first stop be the animal barn. "I've seen the outside," he said. "Although we need to scout out there for signs of the wolf pup's grave. We'll head out after we see what they hid inside those hell-for-stout barns."

Naismith had reinforced and re-sided the old barn, extending it with some 1000 feet of covered cages of varying sizes. Each cage opened to a hallway that led to a large fenced corral behind the barn where animals were let out for exercise. Ed gaped up and could make out stars above them through the large, closable roof vents that were open on this pleasant fall night. Even though the barn was well-ventilated, it reeked worse than an animal shelter.

The combination of animal excrement and animal fear nauseated Ed.

He nudged Roadkill and pointed upward.

"Yeah, yeah, I saw," Roadkill whispered. "Damn good construction."

Some of the pens, like the one housing the elderly lion, had gates that opened directly into the outer enclosure, no hallway herding required. Huge bins held a variety of feed. The sour smell of rotting meat harmonized with the grassy freshness of hay.

Wild animals, my ass. With room service and daily fresh bedding?

Next to Ed, Roadkill also released a breath. Even in the poor light, Ed saw his brother's anger, in the taut muscles of his neck and jaw, in his clenched fists, in the vein pulsing at his temple. "Enough to make you puke," he murmured. He waved his arm over his shoulder in a "follow me" gesture and moved ahead of Ed.

Ed could almost hear the ominous music that accompanied suspense movies.

Moving with quiet stealth, they passed another wire covered cage that held several nervous springboks. Roadkill had told Ed that the video he shot included Merrill's drunken request to see springboks pronking. They skirted the barn and the empty exercise corral.

A waxing moon and a shaded light on the barn provided minimal visibility, but Roadkill kept his flashlight off. Ed was grateful for that bit of prudence from his headstrong brother, even if it made walking difficult.

Ed stepped in something soft and gelatinous. He stifled a curse. A pungent smell assaulted his nose. His stomach rebelled.

He'd seen enough and they'd been there less than a quarter hour. He reached out to grab his brother's arm. Roadkill twisted away and jerked his arm upward in defense. Startled and off balance, Ed fell forward. Into the soft, ripening scat. With his right hand, he grabbed his brother's ankle and yanked.

Roadkill toppled, twisting to protect the camera equipment he carried. He landed on his side on the muddy, manure-covered earth, rolled over and sprang to his feet. He reached out a hand to help Ed. He brought his face next to Ed's, so the menace could not be missed. "Are you crazy?" he hissed. "We don't have time for that kind of shit."

Ed wanted to ask what kind of shit it was, but thought better of it.

They proceeded, accompanied by a distinct, grassy aroma. Ed deduced that the poop came from an herbivore. *Guardian of his brother, naturalist, scat analyst. So many roles.*

Ed's night vision kicked in, and it appeared to him that the corral ahead was empty. Roadkill must have thought the same, because he scaled the fence. Ed followed suit, with misgivings.

Entering a corral without dead certainty it was empty was not, in his opinion, a brilliant plan, but neither was wallowing in unidentified animal crap with his brother. He stifled the snort of amusement threatening to burst out.

They advanced into the murk. "Slow down," Ed whispered.

"No way," Roadkill hissed.

Ed planted his foot in yet another soft pile. He stopped and scraped his foot in the grass. More shit. This meadow had been occupied recently. Or still was. He trotted up to Roadkill. And smelled a strong, equine smell. Maybe this was the horse pasture, Ed hoped. Or maybe…what?

"Do you smell—" Ed started to ask.

"Hush. There's something near. I can sense it."

Like Roadkill was some kind of naturalist genius. Anyone with a nose could tell they were near a presence. A strong presence. No doubt a large one.

"What is that?" Roadkill asked. He turned on his flashlight.

Dead ahead, a horse-like form caught the light. The animal stared at them. White teeth like those of the Cheshire cat grinned at them.

The shit keeps getting deeper, Ed thought. *What have we here?*

Roadkill cast the light away from the animal. It trotted toward them and let out a muffled bray reminiscent of their old mule. With a slight difference. The animal snorted and tossed its large head on a thick neck.

A striped, thick neck.

Jesus. A zebra. Correction. Zebras, plural. Several other smaller striped animals flanked the first beast, all staring at Roadkill and Ed. Suddenly, as if to assure the herd behind him, the stallion grinned again and let out a bellowing bray.

Perfect. The alarm that would summon Naismith's heavily armed men, who would be more than justified in shooting the intruders on their boss's property.

The zebra stallion trotted toward Roadkill and turned its back. "Oh, no, you don't," Roadkill growled. He backed up, waving his arms and shouting in a controlled, low tone, "woo-woo-woo."

Like his brother spoke zebra. Ed backpedaled as fast as he could amid the humps of meadow grass, zebra dung—no more appealing for being identified—and thistles. He bumped into something huge and warm, shot forward and again fell to knees. He turned around and stared into a broad black face framed by curved horns. The animal snorted and nudged Ed's face. With the tiniest twist of its massive neck, Ed would be skewered.

The animal let out a low snuffling noise, nudged Ed with its wet nose and ambled away.

No air. Ed had stopped breathing. He willed himself to breathe, in, out, in, out.

Roadkill turned from attempting to woo the wild grass-eaters. "Why the hell are you sitting down? That guy may seem to be smiling, but I don't trust him."

Ed reduced the shout he so desperately wanted to an enraged whisper. "It wasn't on purpose, numb-nuts. Something pushed me. Help me up."

Roadkill reached an arm out to haul Ed up. Behind them, the zebra stallion brayed and snorted again. Ed thought the animal sounded pretty damn triumphant. Thinking he'd vanquished his enemy and thinking he'd likely be getting some from his striped harem.

They ran.

Once over the fence, Ed and Roadkill stood and listened for sounds of searchers. Nothing. Ed sighed in relief. "That water buffalo damn near made shish kabob of me."

That earned him a contemptuous sneer from his brother. "You don't know much, do you, big brother? It was an Asian water buffalo. As opposed to the fierce and fearsome African water buffalos, the Asian critters are docile, friendly even. While you played petting zoo, I faced down a herd of angry zebras."

Roadkill reached down to his ankle and freed a very large Buck Knife from its sheath. He brandished it under Ed's nose.

"Holy crap, Ed, I could kill you for tackling me out there," he growled, low, plaintive, menacing. "What were you thinking?"

Ed ignored the knife and grinned. His brother was as docile as that water buffalo. For a moment he forgot his earlier terror in the pleasure of teasing Roadkill. "Wanted to share the joy. If mud baths are good for the complexion, consider the benefits of manure."

Roadkill bent and returned the knife to storage. "People call *me* whacked. I say it's genetic."

"Is Naismith planning on letting his cronies kill those animals?"

"Not cronies. Paying guests. And yes, that's the plan." He shook his head. "First the humans feed them, build their trust, then they shoot them. Poor critters don't stand a chance."

Ed agreed. Did Hancock need economic prosperity that badly? "Let's get out of here. That particular critter made too much noise."

"Soon. First you got to see what they did to Mom's garden. And the gazebo."

Roadkill strode in the direction of the main house and stopped next to a storage shed.

Without Roadkill's pointing arm, Ed would not have recognized what had once been their mother's vegetable garden. He saw only earth, scraped bare, sculpted into a downhill slope ending in two earthen mounds. Several street lights illumined the expanse.

"Trap houses for skeet shooting," Roadkill said in a flat tone.

The gazebo that had stood since Ed's mother and father had built it as newlyweds was gone, in its place a mechanized toy for lazy hunters. The shed that hid the brothers stood not far from the main house. A strong desire for a grenade to lob in the window of the master bedroom bloomed in Ed. He rubbed his hand across his mouth, lips cracked and dry. He shook his head, shaking off the intention if not the rage.

What sort of mind created this place? Africa was Africa and Hell was Hell. Camp Destiny lay somewhere between, and Ed reckoned it was a lot more distant from Africa.

The sharp yip of a dog cracked into the cold night sky. The brothers froze.

The yapping grew incessant. A door slammed and the barking became louder, then ceased abruptly. Before Ed breathed out his sigh of relief a streak of white fur bulleted at them. The dog was silent, all its energies directed to the attack.

When it was about ten feet from the brothers, the no more than shin-high dog stopped and began to bark. For its size, it was loud. Ear-splitting, hair-raising loud. Without doubt, attention-getting loud. Soon someone would heed the warning of this tiny furry guardian of Camp Destiny.

Roadkill crouched down. He chirrucked comforting noises to the dog. At the same time he released his knife from its ankle sheath.

Ed gulped, felt his Adam's apple traverse his neck. His mouth went dry. *He wouldn't. He couldn't.*

The terrier ceased its yapping and edged toward Roadkill. Its nothing of a tail wagged with abandon. It had found a friend.

Without any abrupt motion, Roadkill reached out to the dog. It went happily into his arms. He stood, still murmuring sweet nothings to the animal. In one arm he held the dog, with the other hand, his Buck Knife.

Ed held his breath.

After the dog quieted, the night's silence enveloped them.

Then, from the bunkhouse, Ed heard the sound of men's voices. From an indistinct rumble, words soon became distinguishable.

"What's the furry beggar found this time?"

"A wood rat? A vole? Another flying squirrel? Christ, I'm tired of that pint-sized yapper."

The voices headed in their direction, growing louder. Ed stopped, immobile and silent.

"Never know. Gotta check. You know how the old man dotes on the little squirt."

"I don't hear nothin'. Think he gave up? Could you tell where he was?"

"Arlo. Arlo, come." The terrier whined and squirmed in Cliff's arms. Cliff murmured to the dog.

Ed murmured to Cliff, "We have to get out of here."

"Come on." Still clutching the dog to his torso, Roadkill faded back, putting the shed between him and the bunkhouse. Then he sped up, heading toward the forest that flanked the grounds. Ed concentrated on not stumbling, on not losing sight of Roadkill. And not thinking about why the terrier made no sound.

In moments they were half a football field into the woods and the men's voices were only occasional blips in the nighttime hush.

By the time they stopped, Ed gulped in breaths of air.

"Got to get you in shape, film guy." Roadkill sounded full of vigor.

"Too much clean air," Ed grunted.

"And as for you, small one." Roadkill squatted and set the terrier on the ground. "Think you can find your way home?"

The now content beast whined and licked Roadkill's fingers. Clueless that he'd been in the arms of his potential killer.

Ed clenched and unclenched his fists, rolled his shoulders. Had his brother changed that much? "You wouldn't have...you know..." He sliced at his throat with a finger.

Roadkill chuckled low in his throat. "This loudmouthed sweetie? No way."

Ed doubted his brother could see the skeptical raise of his eyebrow.

"You were wrong about this place. It's worse, much worse." He reflected that he had done nothing to keep his brother safe, that indeed they'd have been captured if not for Roadkill's quick action and resolve. *Chalk up another failure for Ed Mustard.*

"Better head back to the car," said Roadkill. "It's a long ways."

Fourteen
Message From a Moose

Joseph Graham upped the volume on the van's mediocre CD player. Soon he'd be in Hancock, Idaho. He hoped this would be a smooth, easy gig, no bumps in the road, no suspicious citizens. The chance he needed to build his retirement stockpile.

He pressed start and let his half-way decent tenor tussle with his favorite version of "Joy to the World."

"If I were the king of the world, I'd tell you what I'd do," Joe sang, fingers dancing on the steering wheel. "I'd throw away the bars and the cars and the wars and I'd make sweet love to you."

Joe threw his head back and belted, "Joy to the fishes in the deep blue sea." This near his destination he didn't want to take time for a nap, and singing kept him alert.

A huge moose cow trotted from the woods and sauntered across the shoulder, onto the pavement. Graham jammed on the brakes. He slowed, swerved and hit gravel on the shoulder. The van swayed, stopped, the moose no more than a dozen feet ahead. Behind him Graham's earthly belongings tumbled about, unsealed boxes vomiting their contents on the van's floor.

The song ended.

The moose stopped, faced Graham's van.

"'Joy to you and me,'" he whispered. "Don't charge. Please don't charge."

Not far behind the huge beast came a small moose, her baby. A mooselet? If he'd swerved to the left, it would have become moose mush. Moose Mama and offspring continued into the forest, unaware of their hair-raising escape from destruction.

Graham was not unaware. Sweat poured from him. He pulled farther onto the shoulder and waited for his heartbeat to slow.

A sign announced that Hancock lay seven miles ahead.

He covered those seven miles in record time, if a record existed for slow vehicle creeping with driver gawking left to right, right to left. His heart pounded at too many RPMs. Had he and the momma moose collided when he was tooling along at 65, Joseph knew he'd be singing with the angels instead of Three Dog Night.

Message from a moose. What was it?

Turn around? Danger ahead? Pack it in and head for that planned retirement in the Caribbean?

He shook his head. *Nope, Joe. You missed her and the baby. It's a good sign.* He forced himself to smile. "Thanks, reflexes. Still able to react fast. Roll with the punches." He blew into his palm to check his breath, wondering, as he always did, if that worked. He popped a breath mint for good measure, glanced in the mirror.

The stop in Spokane for a good styling had been worth it. No need for Rogaine yet, despite what the damn infant stylist suggested.

He pulled to the side of the road, rustled through his notes. Naismith had suggested his first stop be at the town's general store. A town that still had a general store. No doubt with penny candy that now cost a buck.

On the other hand, if the town still supports a general store, its residents may offer opportunity for someone like him.

Or danger. Backwaters like Hancock had given up tar and feathers, hadn't they?

He tried on the beatific smile this new gig demanded. Sent his image a cocky wink. "Are you ready for this, Hancock? Joe Graham is here and he's ready to help you understand the true meaning of charity."

Fifteen
Someone Needs Mustard

The pounding on the trailer door shook the entire structure. *I'm a little pig in a house made of straw.*

Ed rolled over and opened his eyes. "Nooo." Morning light cartwheeled through the gap in the chintzy curtains.

Ed uncurled a furry tongue from the top of his mouth.

He grabbed the little travel alarm and peered at it. Who besides his confounded brother would be pounding on the trailer door at 8:30 a.m.? Are a few hours of undisturbed sleep too much to expect? *And they call L.A. fast-paced. There I slept on occasion.*

No. Not Roadkill. Not after all the beer the two brothers had consumed earlier this morning after returning from Camp Destiny. Roadkill would still be passed out in Rosinante.

Myrna. Had to be Myrna, with another demand. More rescue squirrels? A rescue badger?

If she'd brought muffins... His stomach growled. No. Ed covered his face with his forearm. Nothing so important that he couldn't nab a few more hours of sleep.

The pounding stopped. Ed fell asleep.

"Oh, now, Ed," whispered a husky, unfamiliar female voice, "you're not going to make me crawl on in there with you, are you?"

Ed jerked upright and banged his head on the ceiling. The plastic cover for the little overhead lamp fell on his lap. His naked lap. He flipped over, yanking up the sheets he'd scrunched at the bottom of the mattress at the same time he yanked his T-shirt down with the other hand.

His attention focused on the source of the voice. A woman's head floated outside the window beside him. "Hold the damn ladder," snapped the voice, no longer sultry.

Ed shoved the curtain back and stared into the face of a young woman with hair bristling from her head in brown spikes. He'd never seen her before.

"You weigh too much for this old thing," said another female. "The limit's 300 pounds."

"I have *not* gained that … oh, for heck's sake, you—" said the woman on the ladder.

"Got you again," crowed the second female.

Beneath him, Ed heard giggles, followed by, "Is he there? Can you see him?" from a third, softer, female voice.

"Ohhh, yes, he's here and I imagine he's up. What man isn't, first thing in the morning?" said the spiky brunette. "Come on out. We need you," she crooned, back to the sultry voice.

Ed swung out of bed, the sheet wrapped around him. Then he leaned across the bed and said to the brunette, "Are you bothered that you know me and I have no clue who you are?"

The woman smiled in triumph, throwing a fist in the air and as quickly returning her grip to the ladder rail. "Introductions outside. Front of your trailer." Sultry vanished, replaced by drill sergeant. "Make it quick. We need your help."

Ed's first thought was to send the mouthy brunette away. His second thought was to wonder how she knew him, and his third was a heartfelt prayer that she had coffee, whoever she was, whatever her mission.

He grabbed a pair of dirty jeans and pulled them on. Coupled with the Pirates of the Caribbean T-shirt he generally slept in, he was decent, if in need of a shower, a shave and coffee. Especially coffee.

Outside an odd trio greeted Ed at the foot of the flimsy trailer steps. Each wore baggy sweat pants and an oversized T-shirt and flip-flops. Each held a large bath towel. Each was in an advanced stage of pregnancy.

One was black, one brown, one white.

The black woman spoke first. Tall, thick, with café-au-lait skin. "Filthy beggars turned the water off. Again. Think they can disgust us out of town. But we got friends." Her face filled with doubt. "Or so I heard."

He eyed the brunette. Despite her friend's jibes, pregnancy had not added many pounds but it clearly had not treated her well. Blue eyes above dark bags observed from a swollen, mottled face, and her stomach swelled out in a tight mound as if she'd swallowed a volleyball. The maternal glow had passed this woman by.

"Introductions?" he asked. He moved down the steps to their level instead of looming over the three women.

The brunette pointed at herself. "Feather." She pointed at the black woman. "Sondra." Next she indicated the Latina and said, "Juanita. We call ourselves Gina's girls." She paused a beat. "Some days, that is. Others, we're the First Fools."

"Yessir, that's us," Sondra chimed in. "First ones fool enough to think we could plant ourselves up here in the boonies of Idaho and be let alone to have our babies. Hell, they won't even let us bathe."

A frowning Juanita squeezed herself between the two taller women. "Are you forgetting why we are here? Gina." She gestured backward to the right with one hand.

Feather clapped both hands to her face. "Oh my God, yes. I mean, no, I didn't forget."

Juanita extended her arms toward Ed. "You must help. The water is off in our trailer and Gina tried to fix the pipes and she is, she is—" Her lips quivered. Ed thought she was crying until he realized the emotion she hid was amusement.

"She's stuck under our trailer." Sondra belted out a deep laugh. "We told her not to do it."

Ed's eyes widened. What the hell was wrong with these women? Gina, his Gina, well, not his Gina now, trapped under one of these ratty old trailers and they were standing around giggling? These were her friends? Holy crap, no wonder the woman appeared tired yesterday.

He grasped Juanita's arms. Of the three, she seemed the most sensible. "Take me to her. Now."

"Well, great," said Sondra. "Guess we have found a friend. While you're out, can we make use of your facilities?"

"Whatever. Wait. Let me get some shoes." Ed leaped over the bottom steps to the landing and ran inside for his sneakers and put them on without socks.

Sondra and Feather entered his trailer. Feather leaned against the gas stove, oblivious to the shrouded squirrel cage. She spoke to Sondra, who hovered, thick, solid, powerful in spite of, or because of, her looming pregnancy, in front of the tiny bathroom. "Be quick, so we don't run out of water. I'll make herbal tea." She held up a bag and a pot. Showing a shred of courtesy at last, she asked Ed, "How do you take yours?"

Ed ignored her. He dashed out of the trailer. No sleep, no breakfast, but maybe a step toward redemption.

❧

Have I Seen You Here Before?

Ed followed Juanita, her long dark braid swinging from side to side. She stopped at the trailer's door. Its size and its condition echoed that of Ed's trailer. Tiny and tacky and terrible. Like all the aluminum denizens of the Laughing Pines Trailer Park.

Lord, God, I'd laugh, too, if I loomed over these ridiculous excuses for homes.

"All of you live here?" he asked Juanita. *Living? More like human bumper cars.*

She shrugged. "The three of us. 'Gina's Girls.' Gina goes back and forth between the shelter and here."

Ed wanted to know more about this shelter but postponed his curiosity until Gina was safe.

He knelt to peer under the trailer, earning damp muddy knees but no sight of his quarry. "Do you know where she is? If she's conscious?"

From beneath the trailer came a loud thump. "Yes, I'm conscious. I'm stuck, dammit. Not dead. Not injured. You plan on jawing or getting me out of here?" Gina's voice quavered and Ed's gut tightened. Only a few times had he seen Gina Cosentino afraid.

She's conscious, she's talking. These are good things.

"Hang in there, Gina-feena. We'll figure out something."

"Gina-feena? I'm a little old for cutesy nicknames." But Ed heard the softness in her voice, a minute's distraction from fear.

He stood and turned to Juanita. "What about a jack?"

"The last time we tried that the floor gave out and the jack popped through."

Ed ran his fingers through his hair. "You're living in a trailer with a hole in the floor? What the hell were you thinking?"

Juanita's lips pressed together. "We were thinking we were lucky to have a roof over our head and a mattress to lie on. We put a board over the hole."

Ed gave himself a mental head slap. Why berate Juanita? The lamebrain idea had to be Gina's. It carried her do-what-works-and-deal-with-the-consequences-later attitude all over it. *Gina. Lodging issues later. Get her out. Get her safe. Then chew her ear off.*

Ed hollered beneath the trailer. "Gina, where are you? Can you move at all?"

"If I could move, would I still be here? It isn't the garden room of the Beverly Hills Hotel."

A tiny portion of Ed's tension left his shoulders and back. Gina's anger trumped her fear in his deck. "She take any tools with her?" he asked Juanita.

Juanita gazed into the distance. "I'm sure she did. A big wrench?" She gestured with her hands.

"A pipe wrench. Good."

"A hammer. I don't know what else."

"Where are you stuck?" Ed called to Gina.

"Under the damn trailer, brainiac."

The trailer creaked, a loud metallic sound. Ed tensed again and noticed

Juanita pale.

"I'm coming," he called. "No worries." To Juanita, he said, "Stick around. Might need you to bring some supplies."

She nodded. "Of course."

Ed squatted, rolled onto his back and shimmied feet first under the trailer. One advantage of its crappy condition was that no fancy skirtings blocked access.

He hadn't gone three feet before spider webs draped his head and face. He squeezed his eyes and mouth tight and wiped the webs away. What was it with Hancock and spiders and him? "Give it a couple months and you'll freeze," he muttered to any eight-legged enemy that might be lurking nearby. He forced himself to open his eyes. The morning sun shone under the trailer and highlighted spider webs of varying ages and occupancy.

If only he'd grabbed a pair of gloves. He shuddered. And scooted.

Ed made his caterpillar hunched way past broken plastic crates, cheap plastic planters drooping dead leaves, a couple of car batteries and unidentifiable relics stuffed beneath the trailer by decades of occupants. He swatted at spider webs, his head craned to one side in an attempt to see where he was headed.

His feet touched something soft, something that yielded to their advance, something that yelped, "Ouch, dammit!" He flinched, pulled his feet back and banged his knees on the trailer floor. The trailer shifted, metal moaning.

Gina squawked, "No-no-no," when the trailer creaked. Ed heard her deep breaths, followed by, "Nice you could make it." Her voice was dry, almost parched. If only he'd thought to bring water.

"Good to see you, too, Gina." He scootched around so his head was next to hers. "Now I really can see you."

Gina's reddish-brown hair was braided in pigtails, but much of it escaped, curling around her face. The curls were coated in dust, spider webs, pine needles, leaf mulch and other unclassified materials. Her muddied face showed tracks of sweat.

Ed saw a beautiful woman. Make that, stunning. Gorgeous.

"Terrific," Gina said. "Ed Mustard comes home to Hancock and our first time alone finds me stuck under a trailer, covered in filth. Nothing like being seen at my best. Particularly by the man who got away."

"Got away? Not how I recall it."

"You left. I stayed. At the least you got away from Hancock. And me."

Ed reached a finger to touch a scratch on her cheek. "I headed toward a career, not away from you." *More fool I.*

"Same result."

"Different intentions. However, I didn't crawl under here to argue with you." His finger caught in a stray curl. "You look fabulous to me." His voice caught. "For a complete idiot. Why did you crawl under this disreputable piece of tin?"

Gina put her hand to her ear. "Harsh words from the guy who didn't crawl here to argue."

"Be serious. What the hell were you thinking? In your condition?"

"Gee, let me see. Was I thinking, 'If I get myself hung up down here, some cute guy will crawl under and start yelling at me?' No-o-o. Maybe I thought, 'I'll slip under here where it's nice and cool and quiet.'" Gina sighed, long and shaky. "Is it possible you could save the lecture until after we're out?"

Cute guy? Think about it later, Mustard. And save the anger energy for figuring a way out of here.

Ed took a breath. A bead of sweat dripped between his shoulder blades. Definitely sweat. Not something crawling inside his shirt. "Possible, yes. If you're good, maybe I'll drop the lecture altogether." He squirmed back a couple of inches. "What happened?"

"Duh. I got stuck. No water to the trailer, no answer to our calls for help. I crawled under to check and…oh, I don't know. I guess I forgot how large I've grown. That is, my temporary lodger has grown. Anyway, I'm wedged in like a fox down a gopher hole."

Gina tried again to wriggle free but the movements were slight. "I'm glad you're here with me. I'm glad you came back." She inhaled as if her words surprised her.

Ed took in her belly, lodged against ancient PVC piping, then her face, eyes dilated with fear. His stomach cramped. Why hadn't he called for help from someone stronger than him, smarter, more mechanical? Someone capable?

Gina's fingers clasped his. "Don't go fainting on me, Mustard. I know how you hate spiders. We're counting on you."

Terrific. Now Gina was taking care of him. How the hell was he going to get her out? A man incapable of stringing together eight pages of a screenplay? Eight paragraphs?

You're here. You're what she's got. Suck it up.

Her fear he could deal with. His he'd postpone. He patted her arm. "We'll get you out. Not to worry. Why don't you tell the kid to scrunch down?"

"Yeah, right, that's the ticket." But her smile grew more convinced. "Scrunch down, sweet thing." After a brief silence, she said, "Kicked me. She's stubborn, already. Now, got any real ideas?"

"I'm down here battling spiders and listening to you gripe. It's distracting my creation of a brilliant plan."

Gina growled at Ed, low and throaty. Grubby face, darkening brown eyes, straggly hair. Lord, he'd forgotten how gorgeous Gina was when she was riled. He felt himself harden. *Great timing. Not even room for an erection.* He bit down on his lip, hard.

"Here's a clue. I have to pee and I don't want to do it down here. And if this trailer settles any more, I'm going to be a pancake. A wet pancake."

Ed grinned. This one wasn't fake, wasn't forced for Gina's sake.

"No worries, I have a plan. How did you get here?" Gina took a quick breath that could only have been angry and Ed hurried on, "I'm trying to figure out where and why you're stuck. Take a couple of breaths."

Ed scooted backward so he could scan Gina's torso. She lay directly under pipes that ran the length of the trailer from kitchen sink to bathroom. Her filthy maroon sweats and sweatshirt were bunched up under one pipe over her protruding stomach. "Did you start at the rear or the front of the trailer?"

"What, am I a sliver? Trying to figure out which direction I came from? Trouble is, you don't have any tweezers that I can see." Gina's voice now sounded wobbly, as if she were on the cusp of tears.

Ed swallowed, hoping to steady his own shakiness. He edged toward Gina's head and paused. A spider, nigh onto an inch long, with hairy jointed legs and tiger striped coloring, strolled across his bare hand. He yelped. Sudden wooziness struck him and he forced himself to breathe. He shook his quivering hand, but the damn thing didn't budge.

Crud. Should he swat it and risk it biting him in its tiny little death throes? Much as he feared the little buggers, he didn't wish this one dead. Just somewhere else. Life was too short as is, even for a spider. In his head he chanted, *spiders are our friends, spiders are our friends.*

"What? Ed? What's happening?" Gina squeaked. "Why are you so quiet? It's bad, isn't it? We'll have to get a crane?"

Ed took a huge breath and blew the spider off his wrist. It scurried away. "I'm right here, Gina. You're fine. I'm fine. I'm thinking."

The trailer gave a sudden creak. From quite near, Juanita shouted, "What's going on under there? Are you alive? Should I call the fire department? Or maybe get some food?"

Ed let out a low snicker and was relieved to hear Gina join him. "No catering needed. I think we can get her out without much problem. But we could use something slick. Honey? Motor oil?"

"Motor oil? What are you thinking, Ed Mustard? It's *my* tummy we're talking about. My baby. Hand lotion, maybe, or Vaseline. Honey? What would that do beside turn me into a sticky mess? Draw ants? Why not whipped cream while you're at it?"

Juanita giggled. "Got it. Something slick. I need to go inside the trailer, but I will go slow and steady. You might feel something, but remember how tiny I am."

"Tiny. Right." Gina's drawn out words denied Juanita's claim.

Ed reached out a hand as Gina's extended to meet it. "It's okay. It's not that tight and besides, you roll over on your tummy at night, don't you?"

"Not lately. Besides, it's best to sleep on my left side." The trailer shifted above them. "Oooh. It's pressing on me." She let out a loud breath. "There, if I take tiny shallow breaths I barely notice."

Ed heard her panic. He hated that fear, wanted to blow it away as easily as he had the spider. "Tell me about these friends of yours. Tell me about the shelter."

Gina squeezed Ed's hand. "When my folks decided to move to Italy, my brothers agreed I could keep our old pizza parlor and house. We're turning it into a shelter for indigent pregnant women, especially those who need to escape an abusive or dangerous environment. Sondra and Juanita fit that profile. Feather's an activist friend of mine. She, uh… She's still trying to decide whether to keep her baby or give it up for adoption."

"Quite the crew," Ed replied. "So you decided to forego the pizza parlor, one of Hancock's few remaining money machines, for this charitable venture."

Gina dropped his hand. "You're supposed to be providing comfort here, not criticism. Safe shelters for pregnant, indigent women are scarce in Idaho. Shelters lose their funding every day. People are more eager to pass judgment than pass the hat."

"Even so, you decided to launch this project." Not a surprise, knowing Gina. The surprise was the father she chose. The bigger surprise was how much the knowledge hurt.

"Yes. Been making my own decisions for quite some time."

"As we all have. Some good, some not so good."

"If you're referring to your ex-wife, I'm sorry for your loss, but you obviously had good reasons for marrying her. Some things don't work out."

Ed couldn't tell if her tone seemed dismissive or sorrowful. Nor was he certain her words applied only to his recent past. He chose a simple reply. "True. Some don't."

The trailer trembled and issued a metallic grumble, as if it were suffering a painful delivery of some smaller metal monstrosity. Ed raised his voice. "So what's with the trailer?"

"We're remodeling the old pizza parlor. My brothers offered to come up for a few weeks and help remodel, but I figure they've done enough, letting me have it for free. The grant money was enough to pay a contractor and I thought the trailer would be more convenient for the women during the work." She coughed. "Not my best decision."

"In retrospect."

"I thought we'd have our business open by now. Selling imports from women's businesses in South America, maybe some local stuff." She coughed again, longer, gasping. "This shallow breathing sucks. Feels like

I'm in labor."

"Labor?" Ed squeaked. *God, not that. Not now.*

Gina patted his hand. "*Like* labor. Not labor. It's what we practice in Lamaze. Anyway, Naismith wants me gone, so he jacked up the rent."

Ed's breathing headed back toward normal. No under-trailer delivery of baby, for now. "Wants you out? Why? And who the hell does he think he is to boss you around?"

"He *says* we'd find more support in a bigger town. *Says* he's thinking of our welfare."

"Ed? Gina?" Juanita called. "I found a jar of Vaseline. And some syrup."

"Let's start with the Vaseline," Ed said. "Don't want to waste good maple syrup. Knowing Gina, it's the real stuff."

"Let's get on with this," Gina grumbled. "I am so ready to get out from under this trailer."

"Did you fix the pipes?" Juanita asked.

"I've been hung up," Gina retorted. "Glad to know your priorities."

Ed edged toward Juanita's voice. "Can you see my hand?" He stretched his arm as far as he could.

"Si, yes, I can see you. I'm coming."

Instead of a jar of Vaseline, Ed felt Juanita's hand grasping his. "Ed, I must talk to you," she whispered.

Ed back-crawled until his head extended at the trailer's side. "This better be important. We don't have all day."

"I am aware of that," Juanita said, her whisper conveying her annoyance. "When I went into the trailer, I noticed a large crack, a gap, at a seam along the side. Behind the cupboards. It worries me."

"It worries me, too. I think you ought to phone 911."

"I already did. The dispatcher said to call my landlord." Her tone spoke of bitterness, resignation, fear.

Ed's dry mouth tasted like soap scum. "Shit," he breathed. "Then it's up to us." He spoke with a confidence he didn't feel. "I'm sure this will do the trick." He hunched his way back under the trailer, moving as rapidly as he dared, fearful he would strike a support beam.

Once again beside Gina, Ed said, "This shouldn't take long. I have to pull your sweats away, and maybe that alone will do the trick."

"If that was all it took, butthead, why didn't you try that first?" Gina asked.

"Butthead? Careful what you call your rescuer. Try Lancelot. Or Rambo." Ed rolled over and pulled his knees in, hunching his back. "I want to try everything at once, to be sure." He grasped the tops and bottoms of Gina's sweats and pulled. They didn't budge. "Inhale. Suck your gut in."

"This isn't Pilates." After a snort of despairing laughter, Gina complied.

Ed lifted up with his back, and yanked. The clothes pulled away, but the pipe still pressed against Gina's belly. It was a lovely belly. Ed patted it. Gina twitched.

"I'm reassuring the little guy," he said. "If he'd suck it in or lower that cute baby butt, you'd be home free."

"Right." A beat passed. "You mean the pipe is pressing on my daughter? Oh, God, why did I ever try this? Why do I always think I can do anything I want to?"

"Part of your charm. There's plenty of room. Stop fussing over the little guy. He'll be fine." Surprised by his confidence, Ed opened the jar and spread Vaseline above and below where the pipe crossed Gina's stomach. "Suck it in again." She did and he squeezed as much of the petroleum jelly as he could between the pipes and her tummy.

"Okay. We're going to do this together. When I say so, scoot forward as far as you can. Shouldn't take much at all." *As long as the damn trailer doesn't land on us.*

Ed positioned himself directly beside Gina's belly. If things went haywire, he might be able to fling himself over her. Ed took in a breath. Expelled it. Took in another and heaved up onto his knees, back curved against the trailer floor. "Now," he rasped. It didn't feel as if his effort had any effect at all, but the trailer shrieked in protest, louder than ever.

He strained, humping his back and stretching his arms to their limit.

Gina dug in her heels and pushed against them. Ed watched. She couldn't budge. Then she grunted, inhaled and pushed. Her belly freed itself of the entrapping pipe.

When Gina's legs were level with the pipe, Ed exhaled and lowered himself. He lay on the ground, panting, celebrating, not giving a damn about spiders or mud or centipedes. Until the thought crossed his mind.

Gina wriggled to the side of the trailer and freed herself. As she slid under, she called back to Ed, "Oops. Forgot the wrench. As long as you're there, could you do what you can with the pipes?"

Sixteen
Recruiting Rescuers, Once More

Ed stood outside his trailer, brushing cobwebs and other grunge best left unscrutinized from his clothing. He needed a shower, but doubted there'd be hot water left after Juanita and Gina finished. He ran his fingers through his gritty hair and decided cold would be fine. If they ever turned his trailer back to him. Once he'd showered and grabbed something to eat, he'd concentrate on the script. No more distractions.

He'd given up trying to repair the underpinnings of Gina's trailer. "Face it, Mustard," he said. "You've got less mechanical aptitude than that water buffalo that scared the shit out of you last night."

Roadkill rounded the corner of Ed's trailer. "Don't malign the poor beast. I'd say it smells better than you at this point."

"Where have you been? I could have used your help under Gina's trailer."

"So I heard. However, I was working on important things. I have learned that our sworn enemy Vincent Naismith is planning to further desecrate North Idaho by subdividing Thompson's Woods into, get this, 'ranchettes.'"

"Sworn enemy?"

"We have him dead to rights."

Ed's back ached. He didn't need Cliff's histrionics. "Look. I'm not keen on Camp Destiny or captive lions. But we never owned Thompson's Woods. If Naismith bought the land, it's private property and up to him to decide what to do with it. Well, him and the county commissioners."

"Exactly. We have to mount a concentrated campaign with the commissioners to oppose his development. Ranchettes, my ass."

"Sure this isn't a diversion?" Ed asked. "You never could focus on one thing. Last night your target was Camp Destiny. Today, 'ranchettes.'

Tomorrow?"

"You are so not an activist," said Roadkill, tossing a leather stress ball from hand to hand.

"True, I'm not. I'm supposed to be a writer. Writers write. They don't fix plumbing, they don't wage fruitless battles."

Roadkill continued as if Ed had not spoken. "If we can divert his attention, and some money from the ranch, we might slow him down. Then he might miss opening his little hideaway for hide-hunters during Hancock days. And who knows, lose a backer or two or three."

"You're handier than me. Take time out to help with their plumbing."

Before Roadkill opened his mouth to no doubt spout more activist propaganda, Gina and Juanita came out the trailer door. "Ed's got a point. It's your child that threatens to be born of a dirty woman if that shower isn't fixed," Gina said.

"You're clean," Roadkill said, taking in Gina and Juanita in terry robes, their hair damp around their shoulders. "Besides, Americans are too focused on germs. A little dirt strengthens the immunity."

"You go change," Gina suggested to Juanita. "I need to help my friend re-order his priorities."

Juanita snorted, a soft, almost genteel snort, but still disrespectful to Ed's thinking. "Good luck with that. Thanks for the shower, Ed." She walked away.

Gina moved between the brothers, and Ed caught the scent of herbal shampoo. "Yes, thanks, Ed." She focused on Roadkill. "Your brother tried to help us, more than I can say for you."

"You're thinking small. What's a little plumbing issue when we face the loss of yet more forest land?" Roadkill said. "Talk about priorities."

"On principle I oppose the subdivision of a second growth forest. However, today plumbing is my priority."

"You're getting finicky in your old age. Abandoning your principles for a shower." He stuck out his lower lip and scowled at Gina.

She laid a finger on Roadkill's lips. "You're pouting. Not pretty. I hope our kid doesn't inherit that trait."

Ed gritted his teeth. He didn't need reminding about the father of Gina's child. On the other hand, the child would be related to him. Carry Mustard blood. His jaw relaxed.

Roadkill crossed his arms. "The easy answer is you women move into the old Flat Italian and get things fixed up. Maybe turn the old pizza ovens into cute little baby bassinets."

Gina threw her arms up in mock surprise. "Oh, brilliant. If only I'd thought of that."

"Ed can loan you enough to finish remodeling. Shouldn't cost more than ten or twenty thousand."

Ed swallowed as if to force the rising blush down. "The thing is—"

"The thing is," Gina interrupted, "Ed isn't about to become the benefactor of my harebrained shelter, and I wouldn't ask him to. I appreciate your help this morning, but it's always been clear that tackling demons like Naismith or charging into battle for women in trouble is not your thing."

Ed wondered what exactly Gina thought his thing was, but he refused to ask. "What exactly do you think my 'thing' might be?" he asked her.

Gina's nostrils flared. "I'm not sure what your current passions are, but you made it clear when you left Hancock that you had no interests here. In fact, you couldn't get out of here fast enough after graduation."

"Whoa-ho-ho." Roadkill shouldered his way between Gina and Ed. "Seems like old times. As much as I'd like to watch the skirmish, you need to remember who started this conversation. And why."

Gina pushed Roadkill's arm aside and gave his lip an upward tug. "Zip it. This isn't about you." Again she went nose to nose with Ed.

Roadkill pressed his fingers against her lips. Ed admired his bravery. Had Ed done the same at this moment, he reckoned he might have one less digit.

Roadkill's broad smile combined triumph with a hint of mischief, as if his secrets might be theirs, if only they'd listen. "Peace. Okay. Now do I have your attention?"

Ed nodded. Gina took a deep breath, rolled her eyes and gave the tiniest nod to Roadkill.

Roadkill leaned against the trailer, heels digging into the earth. The trailer shuddered beneath his weight but didn't topple.

"We need to talk about stopping Naismith. I have some ideas to slow his progress with this cockamamie petting zoo he's setting up."

Gina rubbed her hands up her cheeks and through her hair. "That's no zoo. It's a slaughterhouse."

"Exactly. I have a few ideas on how to turn the slayers into the slain." Noticing the shocked expressions on Gina's and Ed's faces, he added, "Metaphorically speaking, of course."

"Legally speaking, too?" Ed asked. "I can't keep bailing you out forever."

"Wuss. Relax. I'll start well within the law. We'll make old man Naismith push the boundaries. You coming with me now, Ed, or later?"

"You're out on bail. Byron has his eye on you. Naismith, too. The man's got power. All you've got is your wild-ass convictions."

Roadkill glowered at him. "And here I thought my brother had my back."

Ed glowered back. Where had this throwback dolt come from? Nothing stopped him. "I had your bail. Not so sure about your back."

A hand lighted on his arm like a butterfly. Gina's. "It's easier to hear him out," she said. "Sometimes his ideas aren't as lame as you'd expect. If they are, then it's a way to keep an eye on him. Dinner, maybe?"

Ed relaxed his stiff stance. "If you join us. Keep me from choking him."

"As if you could," said Roadkill.

"I'm not promising my help but I will listen. Convince me you're not loco."

Roadkill frowned and shrugged. "Not a problem. Not much of a show of faith, but whatever. Be ready to roll, because what I have will shock your pansy ass into motion."

Gina reached out to swat Roadkill, but it was clearly half-hearted. "He said he'd be there. Me, too. Kilgore's? Eight o'clock?"

"Works for me," Roadkill said. "Now I have places to see, people to do. So little time."

He dashed off, looking way too much like the White Rabbit, his belly bulging over leather pants instead of a vest.

Ed felt a lot like Alice falling through the hole.

Not In My Town, Pardner

Ed shivered in the cutting breeze as he trotted up the steps of the city building. No Indian summer in Hancock. After a cold shower that not one part of his body or mind believed was bracing, he'd headed into town. He didn't have money to help Gina, but he still had words. He had to try.

He shivered again. He also needed to find some long johns. He sighed with self-pity. Oh, for the days when he'd taken seconds to fire up his laptop and search for the latest innovation in performance gear, with no attention to price. He wondered if the Methodist church still ran its thrift store. And wondered if scoring something great there might be more fun than shelling out big bucks for whatever was trendy and hot with the L.A. crowd.

"Quit your whining, Mustard," he said.

Behind him, Sheriff Byron Warnock's deep voice asked, "Why do that? Next to hunting, whining's the favorite pastime of folks around here."

Ed opened the door for the sheriff, who held a mug of coffee in one hand, the newspaper tucked beneath his arm.

Seated in his office, Ed in a cold, hard metal folding chair opposite him, the sheriff asked, "What can I do you for?"

"I'm renting one of the trailers in the Laughing Pines Park," Ed announced.

The sheriff nodded. "Yup. So I heard."

"Gina Cosentino's rented one, too, while she renovates her parents' place."

Another nod, another John Wayne affirmative. What was it with Byron today?

"The place is falling apart. My trailer's a sardine can with rust holes like Swiss cheese. But it's a palace compared to the one Naismith rented Gina. Their plumbing keeps going out. I'm surprised they haven't fallen through the flooring."

A shadow of a frown crossed Warnock's placid face but bowed to placid and kept going. "Darn tootin'. Place should have shut down years ago." Warnock took a pull from his coffee.

Darn tootin'? Ignoring Byron's attempt to play the dumb small-town cop, Ed leapt to his feet. "My point exactly. Vincent Naismith should either repair or replace every last one of those tin tubes."

Warnock rubbed his chin with the back of a hand. "Can't say as he shouldn't."

"So you'll give him the word?"

The sheriff placed his cup on the desk and leaned back, arms crossed above his belly. "Got to start jogging. Myrna warned me I'd go to fat once I crossed fifty."

Ed couldn't decide whether to laugh or commit assault on an officer of the law. He chose silence.

Byron put his feet on some paperwork on his desk and leaned farther back. "S'pose you belonged to one of those fancy schmancy gyms in L.A. Ever see a movie star working out?"

"The big names have personal trainers." He returned to his chair and scooted to its edge, hands on Warnock's desk. He'd force the sheriff to listen to his concerns, force him out of his laid-back yokel act. "Naismith's making Gina's life hell. Surely, as sheriff you could tell him to lay off."

Byron shifted his focus from the ceiling to Ed, cocked an eyebrow. Sighed. "Maybe it's something the health department would care about. Dunno. But I don't see how Naismith's breaking the law. Not till you tenants file a claim against him or take him to court. All's I'd do is tick him off and he'd likely take it out on Gina and those women. Or you, Ed. Best leave it alone. There's a nice Bed and Breakfast in town. Probably room for all of you."

As if I can afford it. Ed slapped the desk. "There's got to be an ordinance against the conditions at that park."

The sheriff reacted to Ed's action by stepping out of his hick sheriff role for a moment. "Maybe. Maybe not. The point is, we might be able to have it declared illegal, but then where'd you be? Might as well move before you stir up a fight."

Ed removed his hands from the desk and forced himself to appear calm, relaxed and in control. Should he whistle or lean back in his chair? Neither seemed the right move, so he laid his palms on his thighs, fingers spread open, the picture of reason. And wondered if maybe Byron made a reasonable point.

"Not wise to piss off Vincent Naismith," Warnock continued. He's brought some much needed employment to this town. Lot of big money. Why get on his bad side?"

Ed bounded up. "I have a right to get on the bad side of whomever I choose. This guy's totally off base, yet nobody dares challenge him."

Warnock stood, all traces of backwoods cop erased. "You're starting to sound like your brother. He ended up in jail. But he lives in Hancock, has a vested interest in what happens. You're a visitor. Don't wear out your welcome."

"I was born here. Raised here. I care about my hometown being sold out to some stranger."

Warnock leaned toward him. "Figure you know a lot about selling out."

Ed stepped back. His knees hit the folding chair and it collapsed backward. He walked toward the door. "Good point. But I'm getting tired of it. Damn tired."

Seventeen
Brother Graham Gets the Scoop

Joseph Graham finished his meal about the same time he completed his mental valuation of the antique furnishings of Darlene Belmont's living and dining room. Impressive. Spacious. Comfortable. Not what you'd expect to find in a home situated behind Hancock's general store.

"I'm blessed that Brother Naismith suggested I see you upon my arrival in Hancock, Sister Belmont. I'd expected only that you provide directions to his home, not a delicious meal and your wonderful company."

The widow simpered at him while she brushed some crumbs onto her palm. "My pleasure, Pastor. I don't get the opportunity to cook for guests much anymore."

Her manner, warm, a shade too eager, spoke of too many hours alone, too many meals for one. Graham recognized the value of befriending her. Not only could she introduce him to other potential parishioners, her demonstrated willingness to share local gossip could prove essential to his success.

Not to mention that the owner of a prosperous business should be considering buying a retreat north of town. Actually, the question was, *when* to mention that the owner of a prosperous business could get a great deal on said retreat by working with her honest, friendly pastor. Naismith's invitation included a generous kickback on sales of parcels Beyond Destiny.

Graham leaned back, placed his hands on his stomach and observed his hostess. Darlene Belmont eyed him the way a schoolteacher eyes the door at end of day. That told him her bed as well as her supper table had been lonely since her husband's death.

His full stomach threatened rebellion. Generally he found beauty in every woman he met, but this one's face carried the stains of long held malice and the tightness around her mouth and eyes told him that the Almighty she worshipped called for retribution and smiting, not charity, gratitude and love.

He ignored the wattles beneath her chin and saw instead a voluptuous body that strained under the lacy apron and sedate blouse and slacks. Another body yearning to be freed. Graham could be its liberator. He wondered if he had the stamina. If he could rise to the occasion.

He used the heavy cotton napkin to make a delicate pass at his lips. The napkin smelled of detergent and a sweet sachet. Freesia, maybe? He smiled, projecting satisfaction with the meal and a burgeoning interest in his hostess. A big burden for one damn smile, but Graham had practiced that particular smile for years.

Darlene Belmont sent him a questioning, almost timid smile back. "My dear departed Ardell loved my chicken fricassee. I hope it wasn't too rich for you."

Graham's face ached. *Come on, Joseph, this is what you do. Flattering this woman should take no effort.* Then why did he feel like a tired Shakespearian actor who'd made one too many trips to the stage? "Too rich? Never, Sister Belmont. A delicious meal, with a charming companion, in a sumptuous setting."

"Let me take your plate. I think what I have in mind for dessert will tickle even your sophisticated Southern California palate." She leaned forward to pick up his plate, and her modest blouse gaped between the buttons, revealing ample breasts. As she moved away, she let one breast brush his shoulder.

"I'm sure I'm up for whatever you have in mind." He forced his smile to full face width. And hoped none of his dinner remained between his teeth.

Darlene blushed. She used no makeup to hide her wrinkles and her dated hair style could have benefited from coloring other than the one she sold in a box in the General Store. Graham calculated her age at no more than ten years older than he, maybe early fifties.

"Brother Graham, you have no idea what's on my mind." She cocked her head, a rakish, flirty tilt.

If only I didn't. He opened his eyes wide. "Chocolate cake? Strawberry shortcake? Cobbler?"

She arched her brows. "It's huckleberry cobbler. You peeked, didn't you? Naughty."

"Me? Naughty? My dear woman, I'm a man of the cloth." He let his eyes deny the pious words.

"Even men of the cloth have trouble resisting my … cobbler. It's warm and sweet."

"I'm sure it is. I'm looking forward to it."

"Well, then, I won't make you wait." She put her hand on his shoulder, let it linger a moment longer than was proper. She bustled into the kitchen.

Skilled seductress or eager amateur? Graham couldn't be sure where to slot Darlene Belmont. Cripes. *When you can't accurately assess your mark, it's time to quit the game.* He called out, "Let me help, Sister Belmont."

"No, no, you rest. After all, you had a brush with death. I simply shudder to think what might have happened had you struck that nasty moose. I'll just be a moment."

When she returned, bearing two large bowls of cobbler topped with vanilla ice cream, Darlene sat at the end of the table rather than across from him. Her knee brushed his. "I do wish you'd call me Darlene."

"Sister Darlene it is. And you must call me Joseph." He leaned forward to inhale the sweet, earthy richness of the cobbler's bubbling berries.

In the kitchen the screen door slammed and they heard the clonk of footsteps. The swinging half door flipped open and a tall man dressed in skins strode to the table.

Darlene Belmont shoved her chair back so fast it scraped the broad wood floor. She fixed narrowed eyes on the man. "We're closed. Can't you read?"

The man's eyes scoped the room, the table, the cobbler, Graham, in seconds. His knowing smile, a smile oddly familiar, created an itch of worry on Graham's neck. His hand crept up to rub it.

"Too busy entertaining guests to take my money?" the man asked. "My, my, Ms. Belmont, that's not like you."

"*Mrs.* Belmont. How many times must I tell you that, Clifford?"

"How many times must I request that you not call me Clifford, ma'am?" The intruder turned his attention to Graham. And Graham recognized him. Lunch threatened a fast upward exit.

"What a fascinating surprise to see you in our fair village," Roadkill said to Graham. "You *do* remember me?"

Graham swallowed. He returned the man's smile. "Of course I do." He stuck out his hand and introduced himself, hoping to hell he'd used the same name in Missoula when he'd met Roadkill. "Joseph Graham. Good to see you again, Roadkill."

Darlene's befuddled expression might have amused Graham in other circumstances. "You know each other? But I thought you were from Califor—"

"An itinerant preacher travels many roads, my dear woman. Our paths crossed in Missoula, as I recall?" Graham gave Roadkill an innocent look of inquiry.

Roadkill's returning look held mischief in place of innocence. "I believe you're right. Your confidence in seeking converts to the Lord simply amazed me." His emphasis on the word confidence didn't miss Graham's notice. With luck it bypassed Darlene's.

In fact, Darlene's expression held only exasperation and impatience. "What do you want? Can't it wait? I should be open later this afternoon. As you can see, I have company." She sent a demure smile Graham's way. "Brother Graham is our new pastor. Mr. Naismith is sponsoring him."

Roadkill's left eyebrow rose and Graham thought his hopes in Hancock fell in inverse relationship to that cocky brow raise. "Fascinating news. You've got yourself quite a flock." To Darlene he said, "Can't wait. Need some batteries and a few snack bars. You wouldn't want me to starve, would you? Not a Christian wish."

"As if a heathen like you knows what's Christian. For Heaven's sake, go on in and leave me a note about what you take. Close the front door behind you. Remember that I keep a good inventory."

"I'm sure you do. We all need good records. Never can tell when they'll come in handy. Right, Brother Joseph?"

"Absolutely." Graham thought even that weak response an accomplishment.

Before he pushed through the door that led to the store, Roadkill gave the two of them a flutter of his fingers in parting—an odd gesture from the rugged outdoorsman Graham knew the activist to be. No doubt it held irony but Graham concentrated on regaining his composure enough to deal with the Belmont widow.

"Oh, pooh. Our ice cream's about melted. That man is such a bother. Always has been."

"Softened ice cream on your fine cobbler is like ambrosia to me. A gift from above." Graham refused to ask about the activist. No need to let Darlene see his interest. Although he'd give a great deal to know why Roadkill was in Hancock.

"Brother Joseph, you are precisely what Hancock, Idaho, needs. The Lord knew what he was doing." She raised her spoon and tapped it lightly on his wrist. "Now eat up."

"You'd think you were preparing me for battle, my dear. I'm only a simple pastor, here to do the Lord's will." *And Vincent Naismith's.*

Darlene Belmont's expression tightened. "I fear the Lord has a battle of sorts in mind for you. Clifford Mustard has caused havoc since the day he was born, I swear. Now he's up to no good, upsetting poor Mr. Naismith. Striking him."

Graham's spoon stopped mid-trip to mouth. *Hellfire. I do not want to battle Roadkill. The man possesses the energy of the righteous and the brains of a good con man. Drat.* "Striking him?"

Darlene sniffed. "I'm sure Mr. Naismith will inform you, if he feels it necessary. Far be it from me to gossip. Clifford will get what he deserves. The Lord will see to that." She ate a few bites of cobbler, licking the spoon with obvious pleasure. She pointed her spoon at him. "The battle I spoke of is of a more delicate nature. We have a nest of vipers in Hancock that I'm sure you will want to cast out."

"Vipers?" *Jesus. Could nothing be easy?*

"I assume Mr. Naismith informed you of the so-called shelter that Gina Cosentino is trying to establish."

"No. We haven't had much time to talk." The woman was as eager to spill this dirt as she was to get him between her freesia-scented sheets.

Darlene laid her spoon beside her bowl and pressed one hand to her bosom. Her ample bosom. "I'm not one to speak ill of others. It isn't Christian. But Gina's brought harlots to our town."

"Harlots? Someone's setting up a brothel?" Graham strove to put a shocked expression on his face instead of pleasurable anticipation. Hancock could be more interesting than he'd expected. Maybe he'd be forced to bring those women to Jesus ... after assuring himself that they were indeed sinners.

"Worse. Gina and her friends have gotten themselves pregnant and intend to give birth to their little bastards right here in Hancock." With her narrow lips pursed together in self-righteous outrage, not even Darlene Belmont's voluptuous figure or her luscious cobbler could make her alluring. Graham's stomach backflipped.

Tread lightly, Joseph. "I'm not sure I understand. Someone is opening a shelter for unwed mothers?"

"That's what she calls it. I call it bringing fornicators into our peaceful haven of Hancock. These girls are outsiders. Foreigners. One of them is a Negro and another a Mexican."

Graham hid clenched fists under the table. Huckleberry cobbler puke would stain his slacks. Besides, he needed this woman on his side. Naismith had sent him to her general store, told him she would be a turnkey parishioner, provide foundational support for the new congregation.

A community in turmoil created difficulties for Graham's work. This Gina might have to go. "Perhaps the young woman, Gina, you called her, thinks she is providing a service."

Darlene clenched her fist and triceps and biceps grown strong from hefting products for the store bulged. "Service? Turning a perfectly good pizza parlor into a haven for sinners? Bad enough the hippy hussy helped force the sawmill to stop operations. Now she's trying to force Hancockians to share the streets and what few jobs we have left with these, these—"

Graham placed a calming hand on Darlene's wrist. "Forgiveness is mine, sayeth the Lord. As a straying, sinning mortal, I hesitate to pass judgment on others."

"Passing judgment is your *job*. We need you to clean out the temples, cast out these sinners. Their behavior is disgusting, if not criminal. I declare, if my poor late husband could have seen them strutting around in those tight T-shirts and shorts, he would have died ... well, of course, he did die, but if he were still alive, it would kill him to see their skimpy clothes, the way they *flaunt* themselves. Not only do their belly buttons show through that thin cotton, th-their *nipples* protrude."

Graham thought seeing these particular sinners flaunt themselves might be more entertaining than watching Darlene Belmont cast her sharp edged stones at them.

Darlene tilted her head at what Graham assumed she considered a coquettish angle. "Perhaps you can convince them to seek forgiveness in our Lord." She lowered her voice to a throaty pitch. "I definitely find you most persuasive."

Graham toyed with the remains of his cobbler. He couldn't let her see his confused emotions. The woman's earthiness, her voluptuous body and thinly disguised lust drew him, but her judgmental attitude, which he figured stemmed in large part from jealousy, repelled him. Except he understood and even shared her envy of the women's youth, their arrogant display of their fecundity.

Of two minds? His twisted like a homemade pretzel. "Perhaps I could persuade you to exercise a little Christian charity toward these young women? I'm sure Brother Naismith wants us to get along with the community."

Darlene's flirty expression crisped into annoyance. "Brother Naismith wants a pious, pure and prosperous congregation. I should think his new pastor would have a care for our spiritual cleanliness. If it weren't for the fact that Gina grew up here, and that I need the business, I'd bar them from my store." Her lips curved upward, and her face softened, as if remembering good things. "When she was tiny, she'd run through the store, giggling, hiding from her mother or her brothers." Her face tightened. "Always a troublemaker."

Graham realized that he'd have more luck moving a moose than he would changing Darlene Belmont's mind. Perhaps opposing the shelter would prove a good rallying cry to grow his congregation. Not particularly fair to those women, but life blessed the strong of will. "I'll talk to Brother Naismith," Graham murmured. "Perhaps we can encourage these women to find a more welcoming community for their shelter."

"Better be quick about it. Vincent's anxious to get things in top shape for when his wife arrives."

"He mentioned she hadn't yet made a permanent move here." Graham let his statement turn into a question. Knowledge had value, whether your goal was fleecing your flock or shepherding them.

"Yes, he wants everything perfect for when his precious Emily arrives. It will be her first visit to Hancock. In time for Hancock Days." The venom in her tone made Graham suspect that Darlene had made an unsuccessful advance on Vincent Naismith.

"Ah, yes. You must tell me about Hancock Days." He let one hand stray to her knee. "I'm relying on you, Sister Belmont, to be my guide as I come to know every little thing about my new community. Every ... intimate ... detail." He licked his spoon, a slow, sensuous movement. "You are a miracle worker in the kitchen. Your cobbler is ... captivating."

"I will do everything I can to make you feel welcome. Anything and everything. It will be a joy to have you ... in the pulpit. Now let me get you some coffee."

When she returned from the kitchen with their coffee, she said, "I'm sure Mr. Naismith explained that I'm a widow and it wouldn't be proper for you to stay in my home. I've arranged lodging at a local bed and breakfast owned by a like-minded couple. Until your new parish home is ready, I'm sure you'll enjoy your time at The Osprey's Nest."

Graham nodded. "I doubt they can make me feel as welcome as you already have."

She eyed him. "If there's anything, any little thing, I can do for you, you let me know. I'm here to help you feel right at home." She leaned forward, her arms clasped under her bosom, pushing her breasts up and out like an offering plate at Sunday service.

Graham felt the warmth from her body enveloping him, drawing him to her. He stood. "If I could make use of your phone to call Brother Naismith?"

The woman rose beside him, thrusting her chair behind her and her body toward Graham, so that he could see the little hairs above her lip. "Of course." She licked her lips. "You're certain you need to phone him right this minute? I do so want us to get to know each other."

"Amen, Sister Darlene, amen," he breathed. "I do believe Brother Naismith can wait." He banished his worries about Roadkill to a far corner of his mind.

"I'm not sure I can," she replied.

Eighteen
An Activist's Ultimatum

Vincent Naismith spritzed the glass with cleaner and polished the glass-topped coffee table with a special micro-fiber cloth. He opened the curtains and scrutinized it once more. Even in bright sunlight, the table gleamed. Acceptable. Four passes, but acceptable. He puffed out a relieved breath.

With Emily arriving, he could brook no mess. Everything must be perfect. Not that he'd ever heard Emily voice a complaint. Still, all must be in order for the Grand Opening of Camp Destiny. He tugged the string of his apron up to his shoulder. Once again, it slipped loose from the ring. He yanked on the strings and jerked them into a knot around the ring. Someone should invent a better system.

He gave the dining table a good going-over and knelt beside it to inspect it. Passable. His housekeeper's dusting bettered a dog's tail only by a fraction, but her cooking almost made up for it. He buffed the brass portion of the dining table's claw feet, wishing he'd brought the metal polish down under with him.

The intercom crackled alive and one of Vincent Naismith's men cleared his throat. Vincent thumped his head beneath the table.

He crawled backward and staggered to the intercom. He turned his eyes to the heavens, pushed the button and said, "Mort, let me remind you *once more* not to clear your throat into the intercom." He took a breath. "It is most annoying. And when my dear wife is present, it may startle her."

"Sorry to startle, you, boss," Mort said, "but—"

"You didn't startle *me*. I referred to Emily being startled. Potentially."

"We got us a visitor here. Thought we'd whump him and send him on his way but Roger said we should check with you. He's got a mouth on him, he does."

Naismith tiptoed his fingers through his scalp and found a sore spot. He'd have a bump for sure. "Got a mouth? Roger? I consider him one of my most loyal—"

"Not Roger. This fella Roadkill. You know, the guy wears skins, the one what we got arrested the other day."

"I know who Roadkill is. You say he's at the gate?"

"Yup." Mort hawked a goober right next to the intercom mouthpiece, an unmistakable sound. Naismith's stomach quailed. The necessity to employ uncouth goons had not figured in his dreams of Camp Destiny. "Want I should send him on his way? He says it's imper-imperia—he's gotta talk to you."

Would the eco-pest never give up? "Escort him to me here at HQ ASAP. I shall meet with him. We are a civilized, God-fearing organization. Have Roger bring him."

Naismith gave his scalp one last painful exploration. *No blood.* He knelt to retrieve his dust rags and feather duster from beneath the table and started for the kitchen.

He heard a knock at his door, followed by the sound of boots crossing the oak-floored hall. Two men entered the room. Roger Schramm wore an apologetic expression. "Wanted to wait, sir, but this feller just barged on ahead."

The maniac known as Roadkill stopped a few paces from Naismith and eyed him up and down. His face opened into a broad smile, as if he'd discovered a fresh carcass to make into a bath robe. "Nice apron."

Naismith flushed bright red, his entire body heating. He willed his body to cool, but his body wouldn't cooperate. *His words can't hurt me. His contempt can't hurt me.* A glance at Roger Schramm caught Roger's mouth snapping shut, his expression closing. Naismith let a breath out. He trusted that no other of his men would hear of Mustard's insult from Schramm, a good man. Naismith aimed what he hoped was his least flappable expression at his unwelcome guest. "This is my home, my business." He resisted the urge to add, "Not my apron," and continued, "I agreed to see you. State your business."

Roadkill gave Naismith a hard look, ignoring Roger. "Your men didn't want me to bother you. Bother, hell. When I'm through with you, you'll be well-acquainted with bothered."

Schramm pulled his chin in and puffed out like a cat on a cold day. "Watch how you talk to the boss, man."

Naismith tried to slip the frilly pink apron over his head, but he'd tightened the straps too well and it moved only halfway, snagging on his nose. He shoved it back down and pushed it behind him, eyes tearing from the pain. He said, "Don't concern yourself, Roger. I've dealt with far worse. Why don't you head into the kitchen and get a cup of coffee. Tell Marlena to bring some for my guest." Vincent raised an eyebrow at the scruffy activist.

"Delightful." Roadkill raised his hand as if hoisting a teacup, pinky high.

Schramm appeared reluctant to leave Vincent alone with the smart-mouthed visitor. "You need anything ... " Again Naismith blessed his foresight in employing a loyal, strong man like Roger. Vincent waved his man toward the kitchen, where he knew he'd still be in easy earshot, able to return in an instant. He shook his head, and worked to avoid rubbing his jaw. A jaw that remembered well the pain inflicted by the man who now stood in his home.

Naismith rubbed his hands together. "What would Sheriff Warnock think of your visit?"

"No need for him to know. I came to warn you. Shut down this stupid-ass hunting preserve and get out of town." Roadkill approached, his voice and body language cocky. "You and your guests got a tad sloppy the other night. Call it off. This isn't Camp Destiny. It's Camp Disaster for you, from here on."

Naismith's stomach left its normal place on the digestive tract and plummeted. His bowel gurgled. "I have no idea what you're ranting about. The fine citizens of Hancock have made me welcome." He leveled a gaze at the big, long-haired man. His arms twitched and he clenched his fists. "Except you."

"Video cameras these days are remarkable. Do some of their best work at dusk. And after dark." Roadkill pulled his lips into a smug smirk, a smirk that said the man expected Naismith to fall to his knees and beg for mercy.

Naismith let Roadkill's words hang in the air while he marshaled his thoughts. They hung heavy as unpleasant farts. He could not allow Roadkill to know he was getting to him. What the hell was on that video? Was the man blustering or could he really stop Camp Destiny?

Marlena entered from the kitchen, bearing a tray with a coffee beaker and two mugs in hands gnarled by arthritis.

Naismith steeled himself to remain calm. He wanted to snap at her to get back in the kitchen. But he refused to be intimidated by a filthy loudmouth, especially not in front of the help. The man lived in a rusting, antiquated truck, with road kill for clothing.

Naismith reminded himself that this confrontation took place in his immaculate, organized and imposing home. No. Vincent Naismith did not waver before the likes of this freak.

Marlena frowned at Roadkill and crossed to where he stood. He reached for the tray, as if to help her. Marlena shook her head with vigor. "I brought coffee."

Roadkill sighed and let his shoulders slump. He glanced from Marlena to Naismith. "Would of thought you had better taste in employers,

Marlena."

She held the tray steady in front of the activist. Keeping her voice level, she asked again, "Coffee?"

Roadkill shrugged. "Sure. Thanks." He took a mug, added several spoons of sugar.

Marlena continued to Naismith's desk and deposited the tray. "Shall I add your sugar and cream, Señor Naismith?"

Naismith rushed to snatch up the mug. "No, thank you, that's not necessary." He fussed with his coffee and its additions while he figured out how to get Roadkill to reveal more about this so-called evidence.

Marlena walked toward the kitchen, but Roadkill blocked her path, clutching one of her misshapen hands. "Like I said, I'm disappointed in your choice of employers. Gloria and Tomas would be, too."

Marlena glanced for a second at Naismith. She extracted her hand from Roadkill's, and skirted the activist. She stopped in the kitchen doorway. "I did not ask my children what they thought. They don't live in Hancock. I have a job. Mr. Naismith has brought many jobs to our town. Jobs we need."

Roadkill took a pace toward the housekeeper. "Not the right kind of jobs."

Marlena straightened her shoulders. "*Basta.* Enough. Perhaps if there were jobs, my son and my daughter would not have moved to Boise and Spokane. I never see my grandchildren. You know nothing. *Nada.*" She pivoted and left the room.

Roadkill chewed at his lips.

Naismith welcomed his returning confidence. Even people who'd known the activist for years were on Vincent's side. "One phone call will send you back to jail," he said. "Tell me what you want. No crazy threats."

Roadkill rubbed his upper lip, as if in search of a discarded mustache. "Jail's no fun, I know it for a fact. I don't want to go back, but to me, it's no big deal. No one to worry about my sorry hide but myself. Perhaps your new pastor would visit me in jail and give me a blessing. What about you?"

For an instant Naismith wondered about Roadkill's odd expression when he mentioned Reverend Graham, but dismissed it with his concern about the man's stubborn refusal to concede. Naismith had to give it to him. He was persistent. Committed to his dream. Annoying as the devil, but committed. Not, however, as committed as Vincent Naismith. He smiled, benign, confident, and serene. "I wouldn't worry about me, son. I'm not."

Roadkill scratched an ear and smiled back. "How would your backers feel if you wind up in jail? Or court? I don't think you or they or anyone would consider what's on that video as good public relations. I hear your wife's due in town soon. She might not be too happy if you're Hancock's big bad news story."

Emily loved him. She'd stick with him no matter what this blustering fool had on tape. Of course she would.

The apron strings chafed at his neck. His back dripped with sweat. Why take chances? Camp Destiny was his dream. When you have a dream you make sure it happens. You let nothing stop it. And no one.

Naismith pulled a benign expression from some unknown source of strength. "Come, come. No need to get so worked up. Men can agree to disagree, but still be cordial. Marlena has some delightful muffins in the kitchen. I'll run and get a few."

Naismith hustled into the kitchen without pausing to gauge the wild man's reaction. In the kitchen he directed Roger Schramm to have Mac make a thorough search of Roadkill's truck, without leaving a sign that anyone had been there.

In seconds, he grabbed a plate, tossed three of Marlena's muffins on it, and returned to his guest.

He took a muffin, extended the plate to Roadkill. "The Bible tells us to break bread together. I imagine you know what a good baker Marlena is."

The activist eyed the muffins with yearning and paused as if searching his conscience. Then he snatched one up and bit into it. "No argument there," he said, spraying muffin crumbs in Naismith's direction. "Wonder what the Bible says about corrupt politicians who shoot innocent baby animals?"

Naismith inhaled, wobbly from shock. *Not that. Not that.* He bit into the muffin squashed between his tense fingers, chewed, tasted nothing but regret. Roadkill had somehow taped that inept drunk Merrill killing the wolf pup. Maybe even caught Vincent firing at the other wolf. He chewed more. His stomach would not welcome food. Not with that piece of news to wash down the muffin. He told himself that now he was armed. The information was bad, but information was power. He swallowed the masticated muffin, fearful he would choke it back up.

"She's a great baker." He gave his guest a bemused look. "Politicians, you say? The Bible always has the answers. Better answers than we mere mortals can provide. But I'll let you seek on your own." He strolled to his desk, won the battle against glancing at his watch, and poured himself more coffee, stalling for time. "I gather you've known my housekeeper for many years. Employing people such as Marlena is my vision, my mission. You'd be a fool not to understand what my goals are."

Roadkill's face froze into an angry mask and Naismith hurried on. "And I know you're not a fool. Let me share something with you."

He opened a desk drawer. The activist's body jerked to full alert. Naismith smiled to himself. *Could have finished the bastard here and now, if I'd wanted to.* He smiled at his visitor. "I am pulling out a map." He extracted a file, unfolded a topo map, and beckoned the activist to join him.

Roadkill relaxed and meandered to the desk, munching the muffin. Crumbs fell to the floor and then onto the map from the slob's mouth. Naismith held his breath to keep from gagging and ducked his head to hide his distaste. He brushed crumbs from the map onto a piece of paper snatched from the printer. He tossed the mess in the trash can beside the desk.

He gestured at the map. "I own all this land and have options to buy several thousand adjoining acres. I intend to sub-divide and sell the parcels to folks like you and me, folks who care about the land." He figured counting himself and the wild-eyed eco-freak as the same kind of folks would get his attention.

Roadkill's tongue sought out muffin remains on a front tooth, puffing out his lips. He stared at the map, then lifted his head and focused his sharp eyes on Vincent. "I've heard about the ranchettes. It's a pretty safe bet you, me and your buyers don't agree on a hell of a lot."

Amen, Naismith thought. "Been up to Thompson's Woods lately?"

"Not for a few months. Why?"

"I have gone to great effort and expense to preserve the natural beauty. I think you'd like what you see." Perhaps there was some truth in that. In order to attract buyers, he'd made an effort to save as many of the old-growth trees as he could, without getting crazy spending Emily's money. Didn't matter much your religious or political persuasion these days, more trees meant more money. Who didn't like forests?

He homed in on Roadkill, stifling the urge to wrinkle his nose at the combination of body odor and dirty clothing. "For a select group, I will sell the parcels at a bare minimum, and negotiate a sale to a third party at a higher price. You could get yourself some real clothes, maybe a new camper. Or buy two parcels and build yourself a retreat."

Mustard's lip curled. "You never know when to stop, do you? That sounded like a bribe, and," he pointed to his chest, "this man doesn't take bribes. I'll check out those parcels, bet on it."

Roadkill crossed the boundary of Naismith's personal space, so near that Vincent could floss the activist's teeth. It took all Naismith's balls to stand his ground and appear unfazed as the larger man continued. "But don't think you can buy me off. Or scare me off. Plenty have tried, and plenty have failed. I'll give you a day to think about it. With what I have on videotape, I've got you by the short hairs, and every move you make is going to be painful. If I don't hear from you that you're packing it in, I'll let loose a media campaign that will make you wish you'd settled somewhere far, far from Hancock, Idaho."

Naismith's heart thumped in his chest and at his temples. Things had gone so well for him in Hancock. He told himself his concern was about disappointing Emily, not fear that she'd stop the flow of funding. This creature, this abomination, threatened to spoil everything. He could not let that happen. "I'd hoped you'd listen to reason. But why would I expect reason from a man who dresses himself in the skins of dead animals? You're in the wrong century. Progress is a four letter word to you."

The activist's smiling, silent response reeked of complacency and confidence. Naismith gritted his teeth and told himself that if he called out, Schramm would be there in a moment and make short work of the paunchy fellow. But it wasn't prudent. He had to know what evidence the man had. If Mac had found anything, he would have alerted his boss.

"Guess I'll mosey on out of here." Roadkill loomed over Naismith, forcing him to crane his neck to maintain eye contact. "Think about what I said. I'm holding all the aces this time and I don't intend to let go of even one. You, my short friend, are toast."

The arrogant giant turned on a battered boot heel and strode out the door, pausing to plunk his coffee mug on Naismith's spotless glass coffee table.

Naismith ached to get a coaster under the mug but instead raced after Roadkill and from the porch yelled after him, hoping his shout would warn his men searching the man's truck. "Make sure this is your last visit, Roadkill, or I'll make sure of it," he yelled to his opponent's back. He silently congratulated himself when the man slowed and turned back to him.

"If you think a threat like that is going to stop me, then *you're* the fool."

As Naismith had hoped he would, Roadkill took time to wander the front yard. He walked to the area Naismith had paved for his guests' vehicles. From the lot paths extended toward a cleared area where Naismith planned private cabins for those who preferred quarters separate from the lodge. "This used to be my mother's vegetable garden," Roadkill said. "Lord, but she loved to dig around in that plot of earth." He spat. "You paved it."

Even across the distance that separated them, Naismith felt the rage and sorrow emanating from the younger man. Goose bumps speckled his neck and arms, but he denied any emotion. He refused to waste any sympathy on a man proving to be a huge impediment to his plans.

Naismith said nothing. After a moment, Roadkill headed to his decrepit truck. How anyone could live in that wreck was beyond Vincent's imagination. The man had the foresight not to attempt burning rubber in the ancient, bulky vehicle. He drove off at a sedate pace. Of course, the gesture he made with his arm and finger was anything but sedate.

Naismith hurried to the pole corral. He'd failed to stop the man with threats or with bribes, but if Roadkill thought he'd won, he'd made a serious error. Everything Vincent valued swung on the success of Camp Destiny, his pride, his finances, his marriage. Mustard must and would be stopped.

Mac and Roger Schramm's useless brother Dean sat on the fence rail. The men acted casual but it was obvious they'd barely escaped being discovered by the departing activist.

Naismith bent his arms, elbows against the fence and attempted to boost himself to a seat on the rail. Halfway up, his triceps failed him and he dangled, boots flopping for a few seconds before he gave up and dropped to the ground. Mac looked away but Naismith caught a stupid grin on Dean Schramm's misuse-of-genes face.

Naismith yearned for the luxury of firing the man, but knew he'd lose his brother if he succumbed to that wish. He leaned against the fence. He smelled his own nervous sweat. "Find anything?"

Both men shook their heads. "Didn't have enough time to finish," Mac said.

"The bast—booger flipped you off," said Dean. "Lot of nerve."

Naismith raised an eyebrow. "You're right. Pride is one of the seven deadly sins. Someone needs to teach that man a lesson. I think you and Mortensen are the men for the job. The men of Camp Destiny cannot be taken lightly. Take the old orange Ford, the one without plates, and cut across that back pasture to the highway. I believe our friend is heading north."

Dean puffed his skinny chest and grinned. "Our 'friend' is cruisin' for a bruisin'. He'll be sorry he messed with you, boss."

It wasn't easy, but Naismith kept his expression serious. "Yes, I believe he will. Be sure to take the opportunity to thoroughly search his truck … a camera or other video equipment, even a cell phone, but probably something larger and more complex."

Dean appeared confused, his usual condition. "Maybe we should take Roger. Or Mac, here. They both know a lot about searching."

Naismith punched Schramm playfully on the biceps. "*I* have faith in you, my boy, even if you doubt yourself. You and Mort are the right men for this job. I want the message to be forceful. Extremely forceful. I cannot afford further problems from Roadkill." He assumed the dolt had gotten his message. "I have a different task for your brother. And of course, Mac stays with me."

Once inside, he tracked down the other Schramm, the one with a mind and a decent appearance. He directed Roger to head into Hancock and inquire as to the whereabouts of his pastor, Graham. Roadkill's comment indicated the man had arrived in Hancock. No reason to track Graham down, but it would keep the elder Schramm from deciding to help his brother.

This particular assignment was not for someone with scruples.

Off-Roading with Roadkill

Yet another jolt hit the ancient ice cream truck, throwing it into a reckless swerve. Once again Roadkill managed to hold it on the road. But for how long?

As long as it takes. I can't let that little pipsqueak beat me. Jesus H. Christ, these assholes meant to kill him. The hillside sheared off on both sides of the road. He was going to go the same way his parents had, and not far from where they had crashed. Talk about your perverse destiny.

No. He can't win. I won't let him win. He gritted his teeth and focused on the road ahead. Damn. Naismith had sent his trained tin soldiers after him. *Should have thought of that. Shouldn't have tackled him alone.*

Roadkill steadied the old truck but didn't slow his pace. If he stopped, he didn't stand a chance against two men, probably armed. His gun was hidden in the back and he'd never have time to grab it. He remembered a cut-off, an old, dirt logging road, not far ahead. If he could make that, maybe he could evade them on one of its many side tracks. His right thigh quivered as he thrust down on the gas pedal. "C'mon, old buddy, not much farther."

Another thud and Rosinante swayed wildly. "Damn. Those s.o.b.s couldn't have chosen a better place to attack. There's no shoulder along here." But the logging road had to be near. If he could make it to that road, he could escape them.

The old orange truck gained on him and swerved into the left lane. Roadkill jammed his foot to the floor and managed to keep Rosinante on the road by dint of momentum and luck.

He realized then that this wasn't yet another game, another battle he'd win with tenacity and determination. The fear struck him cold yet he smelled his sweat as he struggled with the old truck. He gripped the steering wheel so tight the tendons on his forearms bulged. "Come on, Rosinante. You can do this," he muttered.

Maybe, maybe not. The gas pedal slammed to the floor, but Roadkill couldn't coax more from the truck's weary old engine. The road climbed a good two thousand feet by the time it reached Thompson's Woods. Already he'd entered another micro climate, with sparser plant life and cooler air.

He saw a gap in the trees ahead. The logging road. He grinned and let out a maniacal shout. "Yes. Almost there. Once again, Roadkill rules."

The killing blow came without warning, when Roadkill slowed to make the turn for the dirt road. The orange truck crashed into Rosinante and the exhausted vehicle careened off the highway. Roadkill had time only to slam down the brake pedal and grip the steering wheel yet tighter.

For a moment it seemed he might make it. The wheels slowed in the thick brush. Time slowed. He heard the arms of the sagebrush grasping for the truck, clutching it, scratching its sides. He smelled the bitter smokiness of the brush. Then, nothing.

The ice cream truck flew, floating above the earth. Seconds stretched into minutes in his mind. Minutes to savor the sense of lightness, of silent, effortless motion.

Roadkill screamed and felt an instant's annoyance that he'd let fear erase the joy of flying. Then the ice cream truck plummeted to earth, landing with a cracking, crunching tumult, tilting onto its side, settling back, stressed metal groaning, finishing the descent at almost a normal angle.

Speed Freaks

"Whoa, baby," Dean Schramm shouted. "Go for it, Mort. We've almost got the bastard."

He glanced at Mortensen, working hard to keep the orange truck on the bumper of the eco-freak's ice cream truck. "Holy shit," Mortensen said. "We shove him off here, we could kill the poor stiff."

"Duh. What do you think the old man meant?"

"I don't think he wants us to kill him. Scare him off and find that stuff."

"Sure, Mort. You say so." Dean didn't believe it. He'd been there, he'd seen Naismith's eyes, his hard mouth. Knew how much the guy hated being challenged. And man, Roadkill hadn't merely challenged the boss, he'd knocked him out.

When they'd started after the tree hugger, Dean wolfed down a couple of bennies for courage and stamina. Now they mixed with the Vicodin he'd taken for his no-toothache, and his skin couldn't hardly contain his muscles. Primed to fight, primed to kill, primed to roll. And old Mort here wanted to wuss out, to hold back, to *scare* the guy. Jesus Christ on a biscuit.

"If we'd of caught him on the flats, we could of beat some sense into him and then searched his truck." Mortensen's voice, as tight as the tendons on the hands that held the wheel, raised. "We've nudged him a few times. That truck's more stable than you'd guess. Thought for sure we had him back there."

"If you'd given him a good swipe instead of a polite, kiss my ass, prissy little bump, we would have had him. Go for it, man. Hit him like he dicked your sister."

Mort tossed him a quick grin. "I ain't got a sister. Just you, bud. You're like a sister to me." He pushed hard on the old truck's gas pedal and it responded. "Hell's bells. Roadkill knows these woods better'n anybody. He's bound to find a side road and lose us."

"Then step on it, buddy. Our guts will be garter snakes if he gets away." He stared past the long crooked crack that tracked across the windshield. "You can catch him on that straightaway. Step on it." He punched Mort's shoulder.

"Christ, man, you got a death wish? I go much faster, I'll lose control."

Dean barely heard him through the buzz that revved from his head down his entire body. Better than a roller coaster ride, better than a toboggan, better than sex. "Faster. We're gaining, we're gaining. We'll have that bastard soon."

Mort caught his energy. "We're on him. He'll have to pull over now.

Christ if he doesn't, he'll go off that—"

"Pull over, hell. Slam him, man. I wanna see him slide down that hillside." Dean reached over and yanked the wheel to the right.

Mort screamed, long, loud, all the way down.

Nineteen
What Can You Do For Me?

Ed eyed the urn bearing Lise's ashes. It sat on the tiny Formica counter scarred with stains and cigarette burns. Lise deserved better.

He draped a kitchen towel between the battered counter and the urn. "Best I can do," he told the ashes. He'd for some reason decided he had to explain his decision to his ex-wife's cremains. "So that's the story, Lise. I've got to help Gina. Your fault. I'll be damned if I let someone else down like I did you."

He doled out rat chow to each squirrel cage. One of the little beasts moved toward the food while Ed served dinner. "You're brave, little feller." It was the one with a bandage Ed had struggled to replace the previous day. "Guess you've figured out I'm harmless. Clumsy, but harmless."

The squirrel didn't answer. It chewed, its eyes tracking Ed's movements and his voice. Ed re-directed his one-sided conversation to the ashes. "Bet you're surprised to see me nurturing tree squirrels. They crap like crazy and the crunching could make a sloth frantic, but they need me. Remember how I always wanted a dog, but you convinced me it was too much trouble?"

Hands jammed in his pockets, Ed watched the squirrels eat, their tiny stomachs puffing in and out with rapid, nervous breaths, their constant crunch the only sound in the trailer.

"Okay, Mustard. No more stalling." He unplugged his cell phone from its charger and punched one number to fast dial his agent.

Once over the hurdle of Alex's assistant, Ed wasted no time on pleasantries with his agent. Another call could distract her. "I'm finishing up the script, you should have it soon. I've got a couple of ideas for treatments, too, but you'll have to present them. Given my reputation, that should work, right?"

"Given your recent reputation, I'd be crazy to waste my time. Crazy I'm not."

"Two Oscar nominations?"

"Too long ago. You have something great, I maybe can get you an appointment."

"That would take time I don't have." *And money.*

"You know this business." Alex paused and Ed heard her exhale. "You also know what would sell. We've discussed it."

"*You've* discussed it. I had nothing to say then, nothing to say now."

Ed breathed in and out, trying to calm the pulse that beat in his chest, in his temples. "Look, Alex, something's come up and I need the money. Got any other treatments?"

"Yeah, I do, but not for you. I'm not going to cancel our contract, not yet. I'm also not investing any time on you. I don't need prima donnas in my stable. Especially prima donnas who don't write. Show me you can still write, and we'll talk."

Alex clicked off before Ed could launch a reply. Not that he knew what to say. Hell, Alex was right. But Ed had thought they were friends. Fat chance. *Friends* was the name of a TV show in Hollywood. A cancelled one.

The trailer walls stalked toward Ed, the cramped trailer shrinking to the size of a burial vault. A vault that reeked of squirrel shit, dirty clothes and mold. And Ed's fear sweat. How the hell could he help Gina? Down to one puny script, no other work. Burned out at thirty-six.

He staggered out the door, down the steps, onto one of the gravel pathways that coursed the trailer park. He meandered through rows of battered, faded trailers settled like the skin beneath an elderly woman's chin into the earth beneath their mounting blocks.

Ed turned a corner, panting like a caged squirrel. Why had he given away the valuable contents of his Santa Monica home? Instead of helping some nebulous needy someones, he could have helped a specific, willful someone. Someone who still held a huge piece of his heart.

He took off running. He forced his feet faster, his legs to thrust forward, pull back, but his thoughts raced faster. And in more directions. After a few miles the answer came.

One hard woman had rejected him. Surely not two in one day.

Myrna was not in the mayor's office, so Ed returned to her workshop behind her home. He squatted beside her Bassett hound and watched while she finished welding an odd shaped tool to the battered blade of a garden spade.

"No muffins today," she said once she'd turned off her welding torch.

"Didn't come for muffins or for more squirrels. Or even for a fight."

"Well, darn. Heard you were chomping for one earlier."

"Byron held his own," Ed said.

Myrna waited.

"I want to help Gina finish the remodeling since Vincent Naismith has hired away her former crew."

Myrna gaped. "You?"

"Thank you. I am not a total ignoramus at carpentry and any fool can slap on some paint."

"You're more the type to pull out your American Express card."

That stung. "Thanks again. This time I want to use sweat equity."

Myrna pressed her lower lip between her teeth. "Broke, huh?"

Ed colored. "Gina has grant money to do this, but can't find workers."

"No disgrace in being broke. From what I read in the tabloids, your ex-wife and her family put your nuts in the grinder."

"Ouch. My nuts are in great shape."

"But ... "

"You're relentless. Okay, cash is not my strong point right now. Time, willingness I have. Thought you might have some supplies you'd salvaged."

Myrna crossed her workshop in seconds and hugged Ed. "Wondered when you or Gina would ask. I've been setting a few things aside. Paint, lumber, and the like."

Ed backed away. "Were you planning on telling Gina? Everyone knows she's in trouble."

"As mayor, I can't be seen offering too much help."

"Rubbish. Gina was born and raised in Hancock. Vincent Naismith is a newcomer. Why is everyone kowtowing to him and ignoring an old friend?"

"Has to do with that little something you're short of right now. Green."

Ed examined the shelf of Myrna's found art. Beautiful things made from discarded, worthless, objects. "Gina said she's planning a business in her shelter. Selling imports, local crafts. It could work." He wondered if his doubt showed in his voice or body language.

"'Planning' and 'could' don't put meals on the table. Naismith has jobs today, has bought property from people who needed the money." Myrna picked up a small metal object and some steel wool and began buffing it. "So far all Gina and her pregnant young women have offered are views of pregnant bellies tightly cupped in knit shirts and tattoos and potty mouths. Not exactly what the citizens of little ol' Hancock are accustomed to."

"Yet you've been saving supplies for remodeling The Flat Italian. You think she should stay."

Myrna coughed up a hairball of laughter. "Not at all. I think she'd be better off moving someplace more welcoming, like Sandpoint or Spokane. But I've known Gina her whole life, like I've known you and your quixotic brother. Naismith can't make her leave but he doesn't know it."

Ed smiled agreement. "Yet." After a second, he asked, "What about a loan? Or signing for the supplies we need at the hardware store? You said that Gina's got grit. Might be a great investment."

"Not on your life. I don't agree with all of Naismith's ideas, but he's a powerful man. I can't afford to take a stand against him. And like I said, Gina's ideas are dreams right now. I can't retire on someone else's pipe dreams. Lord knows, helping her is putting my job, maybe Byron's, in jeopardy. Lot of folks want to keep Naismith happy."

Ed moved to the shelf, caressed one of Myrna's larger sculptures. "How can someone create a work of art this powerful and yet be so fearful?"

Myrna's eyebrows rose. "This from the man who's afraid to admit he's broke? You tell Gina yet? Roadkill? That you're no longer the rich, powerful, screenwriter?"

Ed threw his hands up. "I will. When the timing is right. And I'm still a screenwriter. Not a rich one right now."

Myrna scrutinized Ed until his skin itched. "There's a chance coming back to Hancock will let you find what you really value. If La La Land didn't ruin you." She ambled toward the back door. "Stuff's in the far corner of the shed. You can borrow Gina's truck to haul it. Don't go announcing to everyone where you got the supplies. I'd as soon keep this our little secret."

Twenty
Not Road Kill Yet

Roadkill opened his eyes, discovered his face wet with blood and sweat. He had been thrown toward the passenger side, jammed against and almost under the dash. Still buckled in, the old straps stretched to the max, compressing his groin with agonizing power. He had to release that belt.

With both hands, he pushed himself back and to the left so he didn't feel like a chewed piece of Blackjack. He levered himself up enough with the steering wheel to release the seat belt. *Jesus, that felt good.* He pulled himself onto the seat and peered around him. The front windshield tilted out of its frame, completely shattered, the whole front of the truck crumpled. The mirror remained unbroken, worse luck because he saw his reflection. Red streamers decorated his face.

It took a minute for his fuzzy mind to realize it was blood. Another to realize it might be a good idea to stop the warm flow. Already the metallic sweet smell filled the truck. Soon its heady aroma would draw predators and scavengers.

He spied his sweatshirt between the seats. He wadded it up and jammed it against his scalp, applying all the pressure he could bear. His arm bled, too. He applied his left hand and a sweatshirt sleeve to that wound. *Making a mess of this sweatshirt. Must remember to soak it in cold water.*

Roadkill pinched his arm, hard. Jesus, he'd seen enough animals bleed out to know he had to stanch the blood. Gravity pulled his head to the steering wheel, and gravity weighted his eyelids. A moment's rest would help.

He jerked upright. The sweatshirt fell to his lap and his arm began to bleed again. He hadn't bled out yet, still had some blood to lose. Woo hoo. He wrapped the sleeve tightly around his arm. He had to get out of here. If the assholes in the orange truck wanted to check on him, they could be here any minute. He was prey, and prey survived by instinct and evasion and flight.

"Okay, body, let's boogie." His logical, outdoors-trained mind knew if he were to survive he should take some supplies. But his terrified, primitive, let's-get-the-hell-away-from-those-pursuers mind screeched at him to run.

He crawled to the back, the truck wobbling at his every twitch. Would it begin another downhill slide? He found his water bottle and a couple of the snack bars he'd bought in Hancock. Rosinante gave a little shimmy. "Hang tough, Rosinante, old pal."

He slithered to the side door and yanked at the latch, feeling a painful tug in his arm muscles and a telltale pulsing at the site of the wound. Wimp.

The crash had jammed something. *Yeah. My heart into my throat.*

He swallowed and forced a few breaths in and out of his aching lungs. On hands and knees, he crept back to the front and peered out the driver side window he'd opened during the attack. The door had crumpled on a boulder and the passenger door was too bent to open.

"Steady goes it," he told the truck. "I'm leaving through the window. Help me out here."

Every muscle protested as Roadkill thrust his broad shoulders and thick torso out the window. Wait. He drew back inside. If his ass stuck, he'd be a sitting duck and the window would prove his final exit. He'd go feet first, preventing a killing head shot. *Whoa, baby, you are thinking like the old Roadkill.*

He reversed and angled himself out the window, feet first, pain in his head, his arms, his back keeping him company. *And how far will you get if they shoot you in the foot?* He ignored the fear and edged through, cracking his head on the steering wheel. No shots rang out. He gave a final shove and popped through the frame. As he did, a piece of metal torn loose in the wild downhill ride pierced his jeans and his butt. He yelped. Bleeding from the head, bleeding from the butt. Jesus, he was a regular fountain. The blood, warm on his cold, cold skin, felt good.

Internal bleeding's what kills. His stomach and guts contracted. *Could we think about that later?*

He scanned the brushy hillside above. That way lay the road back to Hancock and home and his brother and Gina and the dinner meeting he'd forced on them. If he didn't make it, they'd assume he flaked out, once again.

Yet that way too lay the men who'd tried to kill him, waiting to finish the task.

He peered downhill. The scree-covered slope stretched far to the south beneath the truck's nose, barren, yes, but beautiful, almost as inviting as a woman's nude form. The kind of country he'd hiked for decades. Beckoning.

Twenty-one
Profiles In Vengeance

Lacy Ponder flapped her T-shirt to cool her hot, sweat-drenched skin. The air conditioning that frosted her Mom's home downstairs had taken a holiday upstairs.

The afternoon sun beat through the glass of Lacy's south facing window, warming her room like a fish tank. Or maybe a fish kettle. *Not a problem.* This particular fish was about to snag her some minnows. Or maybe one honkin' bottom feeder.

She lifted the sweaty receiver of her phone. Smiled. Dialed.

"Brad Westfield."

Lacy's buoyant mood faltered. Brad's tone held hope, and that false confidence you inject when you think the person on the other end might be phoning to offer you a job, or an interview. Her voice had projected that tone countless times. Countless disappointing times.

"It's Lacy Ponder. I wanted to let you know I'm narrowing in on the creep."

"Good news. Unfortunately, I'm expecting a call." Brad's tone, curt trying to be courteous, cut.

"This won't take a second. I've been making phone calls for hours—"

"I hope you didn't let them know where you got their names."

Lacy's good mood lay on the floor, flattened and stomped on. "Of course not. I made up a story. Anyway, I'm down to 18 names. A few house calls and Snaggletooth will be mine."

"Snaggletooth? House calls?" Brad's voice rose on that last. "You need to bring the cops in, now that you've narrowed it down."

"I need to narrow it down, then bring the cops in."

"That's about as smart as getting up, bleeding from a whack with a pair

117

of Vise Grips, and chasing after some speed freak."

"I thought you'd be pleased."

"What would *please* me is a job, a regular date with you, and the expectation you'll live through the next month." The courteous, friendly Brad from Sears Security had turned into a pissed off control freak.

A control freak Lacy didn't want to talk to. "Guess you're in for some disappointment," she said. With icy control she did not slam the phone into its cradle, simply placed it back on the hook.

Her mother spoke from the doorway. "Oh, honey, what have you done?"

Lacy pivoted, her blood pounding so hard the scar on her head threatened to open. "Jesus, Mom. I'm 26 years old. Beyond your snooping."

"You're in my home, so you're my responsibility, as much as when you were six. No matter how old you get, you'll always be my little girl." She stretched a hand toward her daughter.

Her mother's concern, even her scolding, tickled Lacy at the same time it ticked her off. But she would not, could not, cave, or she'd lose her nerve, lose the rage that drove her. She turned her back on her mother. "Excuse me. I'm occupied."

Marjorie Ponder stepped into the room and fingered the print-outs. "You need to stop this crazy vendetta. Let the police do their work."

"Not a vendetta, a chance to prove my skill, to catch a bad guy who deserves to be caught, to stop him before he really hurts someone." Why couldn't anyone understand? *Maybe because they're right and you're wrong?*

Her mother gave her the standard how-can-you-be-such-a-disappointment-to-me look. "You said you were trying to find another job. You lied."

"I had to. I knew you wouldn't understand. This is important to me."

"And your safety isn't important to me?"

"I'm smart. I'm strong. I'm trained and capable. I have a list of addresses to check out. Some of them are across the border in Idaho."

"Even in Idaho, they have po—"

"When I have this man in my sights, I'll get help. Not until then." She went to her closet and tossed two pairs of jeans and a few shirts on her bed. "I'm leaving. Don't worry about me. I'll phone when I can. It might be a while, because I intend to find him."

"Don't do this. I don't want to nurse you through another hole in your head."

"No worries. I'll be sure to duck."

Twenty-two
Not My Fault

Dean Schramm opened his eyes, squinting against the brightness, trying to remember where he was. Dizzy. Woozy-puke-your-guts-out dizzy. He'd done a lot of drugs in his time, but he'd popped a doozy this time. He could have been hanging upside down, his head about to spill his brains beneath him and his eyes squeezing out from the weight above them.

His eyes cleared enough that he made out the back of a car seat, with torn, stained upholstery beside his face, scrunching into it. And a broken window, and above it, a door handle.

Holy smoked and scalded shit, he *was* upside down. How the hell had it happened? He groaned and moved his head a few painful degrees, and saw, next to him, Mortensen. Quiet, for Mort. At least Mort wasn't hanging upside down like some piece of beef.

He had to get down. His skin prickled all over. "Mort? Can you help me here, buddy? I'm hanging ass-backward here."

No answer.

Have to do it himself, before his brains started leaking out his ears. Hot, throbbing ears. He pushed against the seat. The seatbelt cut tight against his chest and his throat and he couldn't breathe.

He curled his head down and fumbled with the seatbelt. Breaths coming in short worthless bursts, heart racing as if he'd snorted coke, he knew he'd die if he didn't get out of the damn truck right now. "Faster, dammit," he told his shaking hands.

The hands must have heard, because the belt latch gave way and his body dropped into an upside down lump. He toppled onto his side, nudging Mort on the way, and got his feet against the front console and pushed until he was against the passenger door. He scrabbled around for the handle, everything still ass-backward.

Dean pulled until something gave. The door swung outward, wrenching him from the cab. He tumbled onto the ground, scraping his arm on grit and gravel.

"Yes. Yes. *Yes.*" Dean kissed the earth. He'd escaped.

A line of ants crawled past Dean's face. He wiped his mouth with the back of his hand and scrambled to his knees. He peered across the cab at Mortensen, still lying there, crumpled like newspapers ready to light a barbecue.

"Mort? You okay, guy?" he hollered, loud enough to wake the dead.

He reached across the cab and tugged at Mort's sleeve. Mort toppled toward him.

Dean poked Mort's arm.

Jesus. Mortensen was dead, as unresponsive as a dead elk. Eyes open but blank, nothing behind them.

"You're dead. You're dead. You can't move," Dean shrieked. He wet his pants.

"Why'd you have to die, man? It was a game, was all. Trippin' on speed."

Dean jerked away, squeezed his own eyes shut. And saw the image of yanking the steering wheel, the orange truck walloping the ice cream truck, the crashing screaming bucking bruising terrifying ride down that slope.

Mort was dead. Christ, Dean had killed him.

"Hell, Mort, I never thought it would come to this," he mumbled. He rubbed his jaw. Goddamn, goddamn, goddamn.

Why did I grab that wheel? "Dammit, Mort, you should have stopped me."

He looked away from the truck, uphill toward the road. He could see gouges where the truck devoured brush and small trees and earth on its death rush down the steep hillside. "I've got to get out of here." Nobody answered.

He struggled up the slope, *out of here, out of here, out of here,* echoing in his brain, sometimes crawling on hands and knees, terror pushing him on despite the pain in his knee. Once he reached the road, his head swiveled from side to side, and he waffled, unsure what to do next, where to go.

Roger. Find Roger. Roger will know what to do.

He might have passed the eco-freak's truck, he might have seen cars pass on the highway. *Out of here, out of here,* set the pace, kept the image of Mort's body, crushed like used toilet paper, from taking over.

Somebody shook Dean awake. His brother loomed over him. Dean tried to give a weak smile, but his mouth was still aching and he'd bet five bucks his lips would crack if he spread them. His entire body trembled. He'd give his last nickel for a Vicodin. "You gotta help me," he told his brother. "We got a problem."

Dean couldn't read Roger's face. "What the hell do you mean? Where's Mortensen? What happened?"

"Mortensen's dead."

Roger's eyes widened. "Mort? Dead?"

Dean nodded and regretted the movement. "What I said. Dead. Could have been me, just as easy."

Roger appeared calm, in control, a lot like their old man seconds before he blew up and started to smack them around. *Shit.* What had Mom called him? An iceberg, most of him hidden.

"What happened?" Roger asked.

"We chased that freak, like the boss told us."

"What freak? Roadkill? Where is he?" No expression on that stone face. Christ, not even relief his brother was alive.

Dean told Roger about the botched assignment, about Mortensen, about the empty ice cream truck. He wanted to tell him how sorry he was, how Mort's death was his fault, but how could he? Roger already thought his brother was the world's worst fuck-up.

He'd forgotten all about searching the guy's truck, but all he told his brother was, "I thought I'd better get out of there before the cops showed up, you know. We can go finish the job, together. No reason to tell Naismith, Rog. Right?"

Dean watched his brother considering it. Knew he didn't want to let the boss down. "Tell you what," Dean said. "We don't find the goods, I'll tell the old man myself what went down. No sense your taking the blame for me." He watched for a reaction, couldn't find one. His brother would go along with him, bail him out.

Because if he doesn't, you, Dean Schramm, are toast.

Dean held his breath. Put on his little brother who trusts his big brother knows all the answers expression. Watched Roger.

Roger swigged two big gulps of disgusting pink liquid chalk from the bottle. His gut ached at the same time it gurgled, and threatened to upchuck or stream out the other end. Neither option appealed.

Confessing Dean's total fuck-up to the boss appealed even less. Roger took another swallow. *Oh, well, gotta do it.*

Should he blame Dean? The dunderhead said Mortensen had been driving, but his brother's squirrelly face carried guilt as well as pain. What really happened out there?

What had the boss been thinking, sending those two after Roadkill? He veered away from that line of thought. He trusted Mr. Naismith. The man with the checkbook had to have brains.

Ah, crap. He'd liked this job, decent work, good pay, for a man he respected. Yes, Naismith held the reins tight on his crew, yes, his temper ran to the hot side, but the man had ambition. Something Roger admired. Something his younger brother couldn't imagine.

Nothing for it now but to brave it out, see what the old man says. No sense blaming Dean. His brains had turned to goose turds years ago.

Roger watched his brother, across the bunkroom. He'd been uncharacteristically quiet since getting back.

Dean huddled over the sink, patting at his face like a whore putting on makeup. But slower. A whore that slow would be out of business.

"Hurry it up," Roger said. "We have to tell Naismith and hope to hell he doesn't fire your ass."

Dean flinched as if Roger had punched him. "Look at me. I'm a bloody mess. You could have lost your little brother out there. Like we lost old Mort. No need to tell Naismith yet. You and me could go out to that old truck and have a look-see."

How would Roger's life have changed if it had been Dean, not Mort, who died in the crash? He blinked and his gut pain worsened.

He shied from whatever aggravated his gut. He went to help Dean put on a cleaner shirt.

Dean stuck one skinny, bruised arm and then the other in the flannel shirt. "If I'd been driving, we might have stayed on the road," he said. "Who knows? Mort drove like a donkey in a golf cart." He shook his head and paled. "Coulda been me, easy as that." He snapped his fingers.

"No excuses with Mr. Naismith," Roger said. "He hates excuses. Every man, he says, has to take responsibility for his own actions."

"Yeah, yeah, you been preaching to me since I got back. Naismith doesn't like surprises. We got to tell him before someone sees that truck and the sheriff comes here asking questions." Dean sighed. "Stop treating me like a completely brainless fuck-up." Then he grabbed Roger's arm. "I love you, big fella. I was never so glad to see your face."

Roger thought Dean brushed away a tear but decided it was only water left after washing up.

Naismith took the news better than Roger expected. Not to say he seemed pleased.

The big surprise, however, was Dean. He stood up straight and told the story plain. Without excuses. Roger wondered if he had some kind of head injury, a swelling on the brain that brought clarity, courage and ended in a painful death.

The boss paced his study, from where Roger and his brother stood, across to a huge stone fireplace where he wheeled around and paced back, head bent like he was thinking. Except for the tromp of Naismith's boots on the wide-planked wood floor, and the occasional sniff from Dean, nothing broke the room's silence.

The silence made Roger nervous as hell. He wished Naismith would get it over with and fire them. Maybe they'd head up to Canada.

Naismith turned to Dean. "You didn't see Roadkill or his truck," he said for the umpty-umpth time. "But you're certain that his truck went off the road?"

Dean gave the boss his most earnest look, which wasn't real reassuring, given his bloody, swollen face and overall loser appearance. "Like I said, sir. He went off the road, then ol' Mort lost control of our vehicle and we went right after." Doubt crossed his face. "I know I should of searched, but Mr. Naismith, sir, I was gravely injured."

Gravely injured, thought Roger. Where the hell did Dean come up with this shit? Perry Mason reruns, he supposed. He ducked his head to hide the grin.

Naismith stopped pacing and pulled himself to his full height, slightly taller than a midget. His face solemn, he turned from Roger to Dean and then back to Roger. "Okay. You two head out to the site of the crash. Take the big diesel and a come-along. Find that ice cream truck and haul it up and if it drives, head on over to Spokane. Take it to the dump— No, find someplace to hide the damn thing ... someplace no one will find it. Get rid of the thing. *After* you search for Roadkill or signs he walked away. If he's dead, put him in his truck before you hide it. Then go through every rusting square inch of his truck for that videotape."

Naismith peered up at Roger, so Roger muttered, "Yes, sir. Got it, sir." He exhaled and wondered how long he'd been holding his breath. Sounded like they'd kept their jobs, for now.

Naismith frowned and continued. "Take a rake to hide the fact that two vehicles went down that hill. If it's rock and shale, that shouldn't be hard. If it's pine needles, well, do your best. Phone me when you're out of the way and I'll send one of the boys out to search for Mortensen. I sent Mortensen to follow the activist. That's the only story you need to remember."

He moved his eyes from Roger to Dean and relaxed his normally stiff posture. "Be sure you remember it, men. If Red doesn't find Mortensen this evening, then Dean will help him continue tomorrow and make the sad discovery."

Dean opened his mouth, obviously puzzled. Naismith clarified. "Act surprised, but see something to the side of the road. Remember, Mortensen went alone."

"First thing tomorrow," Naismith nodded to Roger, "you and I will head into Hancock and rid the town of another troublemaker. Hancock will be a haven for right thinking people, once I have my way."

Naismith strode to the fireplace and leaned against it. He started to loop one arm on the mantle, but because he was short and the mantle was not, his elbow didn't quite reach and slipped off, causing him to fall against the big stones. He looked like a weird bug trying to sniff its armpit. Roger struggled not to smile. Dean sniggered and turned it into a cough.

Naismith pushed himself away from the fireplace and stood stiff, arms behind him. "Do your best." His eyes took in again the bedraggled sight of Dean, and returned to Roger. "This is important to me. And to you as well. If anyone finds out Dean was in the truck that forced that activist off the highway, he could be up against manslaughter charges, at the least. Murder is not out of the question."

Roger glanced at Dean. Zits stuck out on his paling face like squished raspberries. He moved to him, grabbed his forearm and muscled him out of the room before he fainted.

Twenty-three
Wifely Concerns

Emily Naismith removed a facial wipe from her purse and patted away some of the grimy residue that airline travel always deposited on her skin. She sipped at the bottled water she purchased on the way down to baggage claim.

Her gaze took in the luggage carousels at the Spokane airport and the people waiting to claim their luggage. Several people smiled at her, recognizing her from the flight from Denver and from the long winding trek from the gate. Intrepid fellow travelers. Yes, folks were friendly in the West, but in her experience people were as friendly as you let them be. Often as gullible.

She decided to pay for help with the huge suitcase she had checked and spent some time tracking down a skycap, a rarity in the smallish airport.

She planned to stay several weeks at Camp Destiny. Long enough to decide if the place was indeed the money sink she'd begun to suspect. Despite Vincent's frequent reassurances, she doubted Camp Destiny was destined to provide her a comfortable retirement. And dammit, she'd planned to retire by age 50. She'd missed that one by three years.

"I'm not letting my savings be squandered on tiger chow," she muttered.

She'd cut short the long layover she generally allowed herself in Denver and caught an earlier flight to Spokane. She enjoyed the immense, sprawling Denver airport, liked to spend time shopping and people watching. But she'd decided to get to Spokane early enough to forestall Vincent's meeting her at the airport. A rental car gave her flexibility, and Emily put great value on staying flexible. On keeping her options open.

She smiled at nothing. A contented, confident, come-hither kind of smile, the kind that warmed her inside and added sparkle to her eyes. When she'd phoned with the change in plans, Vincent sounded irked. She surmised it didn't bother him that she'd have a car, but that "the little woman" had a mind of her own.

She'd sweet-talked Vincent out of his annoyance and both of them into lusty anticipation of their reunion.

"You're cheerful, ma'am," said the young skycap. "Coming home?"

Startled, Emily moved her focus to the somewhat puny youth and hoped he wouldn't drop her expensive, tiger-striped luggage. Would Vincent find her luggage as amusing as she did? She feared not. Vincent's sense of humor could use an electrical stimulus or Viagra, to perk it up.

"More of an extended visit, pleasure mixed with business," she replied and wondered why she'd shared so much information with him.

Would anyone pay Vincent to hunt exotic wild animals on a ranch in North Idaho? Could he convince those same hunters they needed to establish second—or third—homes nearby for future visits?

Either Vincent had been one hell of a salesman or his attentiveness to her every sexual whim had weakened her ordinarily tough defenses.

She smiled directly at the young skycap and he blushed. It gratified her to realize her smile still held power.

She indicated her bags making the circuit of the carousel and the skycap surprised her with his lack of effort hefting them into his cart. Like Vincent's small frame, the skycap's gangly form held hidden surprises.

"Please take me to the car rental area," she said.

She bit her lip, anticipating a warm reunion with her husband. And bit it harder to remind herself that the trip was not a sexual adventure but a financial reconnoitering. Sex she enjoyed, but business took priority.

If she didn't think Camp Destiny would prove financially viable, it was past time to yank her support.

Twenty-four
One Of Us Grew Up

Cosentinos don't give up and they don't give in. Gina heard it enough as a child and she believed it to be true. But maybe the hereditary trait wasn't the blessing she'd always considered it. Maybe, maybe, the wiser tack would be to give in to Naismith and move the shelter to a more welcoming community.

No.

Gina grabbed a flimsy towel from the flimsy rack attached to the flimsy hollow pressboard bathroom door of the flimsy little trailer. She managed to pat herself dry and bump her elbow only twice. She sniffed. Mold grew somewhere, despite her scrubbing and generous use of vinegar. She imagined mushy clumps of green-gray and black goo behind the shower walls, emitting spores that would cause her child to have enormous ears or a tiny brain or immense, warped feet.

At this point she'd give up that child for a good night's sleep. Her eyes got wet. "I'm kidding, sweet thing," she told the baby.

Gina tossed her towel over the door handle. She took in a deep breath, ignoring the instant image of encroaching mold spores, and let it out.

She invested more than the normal two minutes on her hair and wore her best meet-the-funders deep turquoise maternity top and slacks.

Grabbing a flashlight, she waved good bye to "Gina's Girls," and headed into town to meet Roadkill and Ed.

"Tonight I listen to Roadkill," she told the baby. "He's your daddy and he's really smart and really caring and a good friend I've known forever. Tonight I won't make fun of his opinions. He gets enough of that from others. What they don't know is that without people like your daddy, we could lose all our forests."

The baby wriggled, the movement pressing on Gina's beleaguered bladder. "Sweetie, your timing's terrible. It's another five minutes to Kilgore's."

She increased her pace a little. Experience had proven that walking too fast led to backaches. She regarded the darkened sky. "Okay, universe, get me to the restaurant without peeing my pants and I promise I won't even argue with Ed." This morning's spat had rekindled memories of their constant friendly sparring in their teens. She realized she'd missed it. Missed Ed, as well.

"And if I start to ask him for a donation, give me a good swift kick, baby mine. We're not going to become the Ed Mustard Charitable Women's Shelter." Or worse, she thought, the Lise Clanahan Memorial Women's Shelter. *But a loan? Until the grant renewal comes through?*

"We'll see."

Julie, the young hostess with a perfect figure and teeth that were way too white informed Gina that one of her dinner companions awaited her.

She cursed under her breath as she waddled after the graceful girl. She'd wanted to be safely hidden behind the table so Ed and Roadkill couldn't observe her ungainly arrival.

Ed sat by himself. He'd cleaned up after his foray under the trailer. Relaxed, grinning a welcome, the lines she'd noticed earlier invisible at this distance, he appeared much the same as the day they'd celebrated his departure from Hancock.

He stood and helped her settle into a chair.

Not the same Ed. An improved, aged edition. She reminded herself that Ed's life path was distant and foreign to Gina.

"Truce?" asked Gina.

"Peace tonight?" Ed asked at the same time.

They smiled in unison and Gina's tension ebbed.

"It's Roadkill's meeting. I told myself I'd let him talk," she said.

"Me, too." He gestured at her water. "I didn't know what to order you to drink. Water, no ice, still?"

"Maybe some apple juice." Gina picked up her menu. "We'd better decide. When Roadkill arrives, he's like a tsunami washing over you."

"That's my brother."

They made their dinner choices but ordered only her juice and a Black Butte Porter for Ed, deciding to request their entrees after Roadkill came.

"Feeding me here is a waste," Gina commented. "I can't eat much at one sitting these days."

"You can take the leftovers home."

"Yeah. The starving nibblers will make them disappear in moments."

"Tell me more about the shelter." Ed seemed more upbeat to Gina this evening, but perhaps she imagined it.

She leaned forward. "Like I told you this morning, the grant covered renovating The Flat Italian and operating costs for several months. If that man hadn't lured away all the workmen I'd found, we'd have been set up, selling stuff in the shop. But now the grant money's running out."

"What will you sell?"

"Imports from a co-op in Venezuela and some hand-crafted things we make, maybe some from Idaho crafters."

"Hancock's not exactly a tourist destination."

"Are you a dinosaur? The Web, duh. Once we get the permits for importing, figure out the marketing and the website and the pricing, we'll go online, and it should bring a steady stream of income."

"Stream of income? Marketing?" Ed frowned. "Where'd you learn all this?"

"Spokane Community College. Life. Work. I am, despite your doubts, a competent adult by now."

Ed frowned. "Okay. You've learned about marketing and gotten a grant. But no competent adult would let those women stay in The Laughing Pines trailer park, soon to be known as The Fallen Pines."

Her mouth fell open. Since when did truce mean bossing around old friends? "Which Prince Charming is going to ride up in his carriage and whisk us away? And to where?" *Decide now, Gina. If he offers you money, are you going to take it?*

"Maybe Missoula. Doesn't one of your brothers live in Missoula? Missoula's a progressive place, I've heard."

If he says Missoula one more time I will kick him in the nuts. She smiled, an I-am-losing-patience-with-you-young-man kind of smile. Hmmm. Good practice for an ornery toddler. "No, Ed. Not Missoula. Not Myrna. Not moving. We're staying."

Ed let out a long slow breath. He took a swig of his beer. "Okay. I have the message. I'm slow, I admit, but I gather you're here to stay. And if Roadkill would get here, he could share his foolproof plan for getting rid of Naismith."

She glanced to the door, not willing to give up on Roadkill. He said he'd be here, said it was important. "He lives on Roadkill time. He'll be here when he gets here. You're right about the trailer, of course. We can't stay there. Two more women arrive soon. We're moving into the pizza parlor soon. I didn't want to live there while it was being renovated. Didn't want the women exposed to the paint fumes, the dust, the noise. But there's no alternative. We'll move in, we'll do the work ourselves."

"It's a lot to take on in your condition."

"Women have accomplished many things 'in this condition.' My dad taught me to handle a power tool. And the others can paint, now that they're further along. We'll use non-toxic stuff and good masks."

"I worry about my friends. I know you're a grown woman and make your own choices. It's—" Ed stopped mid-thought. He spun his beer bottle between his palms for what seemed forever. "Sounds like you have a plan. A shelter and a cottage industry. And despite Naismith's money and the fact that he has most of the town on his side, this is where you're staying."

Cottage industry? Can he be more patronizing? "I appreciate your worry," Gina said, "but it's misplaced, really." She wondered if her voice sounded as tight with anger to Ed as it did to her. "No one around here seems to remember that not too long ago Coldwater Creek was the brainchild of some silly Sandpointer. Now it's a multi-million dollar company. And Burt's Bees? Started in an eight foot by eight foot cabin."

Ed smiled, and it was not a patronizing smile, not a don't-upset-the-pregnant-woman smile, but rather a smile that brought memories to Gina that made her blush. She sipped her water. Ed should get himself back to California, where he wants to be. He's a distraction. *I can do this myself.*

"Let's order," she suggested. "Roadkill can catch up, when he gets here, *if* he gets here. He could have forgotten our meeting and taken off on some crazy tangent to snare Naismith."

"He made it sound damn important to blow it off," Ed said. "I hope he shows up for his bail hearing. I posted the bond for it."

"He will." She glanced again toward the door, trying to hide her concern from Ed. "It's not like him to skip a free meal, but the consequences of not showing up for that hearing are worse. Let's make a deal and not worry about him unless he blows that off, too."

"Deal," Ed said, but his attempt to appear concerned only about his pocketbook should Roadkill fail to appear did not fool Gina. She'd share a little attitude with Roadkill when he finally showed up. If he showed up. *When, dammit, when.*

She waved to their server. Once their orders were placed, Ed asked, "This seems an absurd question, but does Cliff carry a cell phone? Or is he too much of a Luddite for that?"

"He has one. I bought it for him and made him promise to carry it. Except it's usually off."

"Doesn't seem the most reliable guy to choose as your baby's father."

"He's not, but his role is minor. Let's enjoy our meal and not argue." She reached across the table and touched Ed's arm. "Roadkill's a grown-up. He'll be fine."

Gina hoped her words and her hope would prove correct. Because she couldn't imagine why Roadkill would have missed this chance for a free meal and to enlist his brother's help in his fight against Vincent Naismith.

Twenty-five
A Meeting At Destiny's Doorway

Emily Naismith sashayed out to the deck to greet her husband and the man he'd invited to Hancock to establish a congregation of the faithful. She needed to seize every opportunity to learn more about Vincent's plans.

To Emily, the man and the proposed "Church of Destiny's Doorway" seemed yet more pipelines to siphon money from her retirement kitty. Thus he became another puzzle piece to observe.

When she'd questioned Vincent's decision to pay someone to set up a church, he'd said their cash outlay would be minimal. "I've deeded over several of the lots to Beyond Destiny. Joseph Graham was in sales before he got the calling."

Now that she'd seen Reverend Graham, the cynic in Emily wondered precisely what called to him.

As different from Vincent's employees that she'd met since her arrival as grits and American cheese were from risotto, this smooth, suave newcomer intrigued her. Olive skin, dark hair sprinkled with gray. He wore expensive shoes totally inappropriate for tromping around Camp Destiny and a maroon v-neck sweater over a pale blue dress shirt, khakis. Minister? Salesman? What?

"You must invite our new pastor in for coffee, sweetheart," she chided her husband. "I'm sure he enjoyed your tour, but walking around out there could give anyone a chill."

"I am mightily impressed with what your husband has done at Camp Destiny," he said in a ringing voice Emily figured the zebras in the pasture could hear. "Honored to be in on the start of such an enterprise."

"Brother Joseph wants to do a blessing before we lay the foundation for our new chapel," Vincent said.

Brother Joseph? Oh, dear. Emily busied herself with the coffee.

"Worshipping with the majesty of God's creation outside the windows," Graham said. "Inspiring."

"It's part of my plan for a godly retreat in a family-oriented community. All the advertising for Camp Destiny and Beyond Destiny touts family values."

And here I thought they were coming to kill wild game.

"As it should, Brother Vincent. You're a visionary."

Vincent preened. "My prospective clients will be making a substantial investment. Hancock must be pure. For them, and for my dear wife."

Godly? Pure? Emily kept her expression bland and wondered where her attention had wandered when Vincent touted the economic mother lode that his safari camp would become. *Oh, well. She was open-minded. People could worship as they wished as long as they tithed to her coffers, as well.*

The new pastor sipped his coffee and directed a smile first to Vincent, then to Emily. "From what I've seen of Hancock, it's a warm, welcoming community. And your land Beyond Destiny will be a beacon to the faithful."

Vincent paced the room. "The whole experience, from safari, to surrounding properties, to the town of Hancock, must inspire awe. I have a vision, as you know. The shelter the Cosentino woman now plans to establish for pregnant women does not fit into my image."

Emily's spoon stopped mid-stir. *What's this? A cloud over Vincent's vision?* How could a little community program affect Camp Destiny's bottom line?

"Sister Darlene told me you oppose the concept," Graham said. "Remember that the Bible preaches charity toward all. You might gain more value, even some community good will, from assisting rather than opposing these women. After all, they have chosen to bear their children rather than abort them."

Emily thought the man had a point, but she saw Vincent's face darken. He wasn't accustomed to disagreement. "Those women are pregnant out of wedlock. Their dress is immodest. You can see their—their navels bulging out from those tight T-shirts."

For pity's sake, sounds as if they dressed like every pregnant young woman these days, except maybe Jehovah's witnesses or the Amish. Emily chose not to voice her opinion.

"Besides," Vincent continued, "other than the Cosentino woman, and possibly her friend who calls herself Feather, they don't fit the Idaho image. One is a ghetto black woman, the other a Mexican. They do not fit my vision for Hancock."

Oh, my. Vincent's "vision" began to seem myopic and bigoted. How had Emily not seen this? *Because your vision involved a new way to make money from a large pool of willing marks rather than one sucker at a time?* She told her conscience to put a sock on it.

The Reverend Joseph Graham sat silent for a moment. "I understand. Then we'll find ways to encourage them to move."

Emily took a sip of coffee to hide the unbidden curl of her lip. The man knew who held the checkbook.

"I have a few ideas," said Vincent, his face smug with the satisfaction of forcing yet another person to kowtow. "I'll be meeting with Miss Cosentino this morning. Should that meeting prove unfruitful, I'll expect you to find some peaceful way to extricate them."

Why did Vincent's words make Emily feel that he might employ stronger methods should the pastor's peaceful approach fail?

Emily scrunched up her nose in a friendly way. Time to find out about another piece of the puzzle. "Vincent's mentioned Beyond Destiny so many times." She gave her husband a friendly tap on the shoulder. "But I've yet to see any of those parcels. I feel as if I've been in a nunnery. All tied up and nowhere to go." She wondered what kind of convent restricted their sisters with knots instead of vows.

Vincent pinched his nose between his fingers. "Such a busy time, my dear. Preparations for Hancock Days—"

"We can't have you feeling a captive, Sister Naismith," broke in Reverend Graham. "I'd be more than happy to take you for a tour. That is, if your dearly beloved thinks you'd be safe in the hands of your pastor."

Vincent's expression became yet more rigid and for a second Emily thought he might be seriously ill. Then he focused on Graham and she recognized his ailment as simple jealousy. Her heartbeat quickened and she tilted her head to hide her tiny smile.

Emily giggled. "Call me Emily, please. Oh, Vincent, may I go? I know how busy you are and that you had plans today and I just hate to be a bother to you." *Could I lay it on any thicker?* "Shall I have Marlena pack some sandwiches?"

Vincent frowned. He coughed and cleared his throat. He couldn't object to her going with the man of God, even though his discomfort with the idea of her heading out with the attractive pastor mottled his face to the color of zebra dung in a water trough.

What a pity. Emily smiled, a hidden, inward smile.

Twenty-six
The Mustard Thickens

The satisfaction Ed felt seeing the huge stack of supplies he'd unloaded at The Flat Italian almost overcame his frustration with his brother and the pain in his arms and back.

He'd spent an hour or so fruitlessly searching for Roadkill in local cafés and a couple of campgrounds where he was known to park Rosinante. He felt a smidgeon of shame that his interest in finding his brother hinged more on the need for his muscle to help tote supplies than concern about Cliff's welfare, but Roadkill had been taking care of himself for years without Ed's supervision.

The previous night Ed walked Gina to her trailer after their dinner and asked to borrow her truck, lying that Myrna had asked for his help. As he'd hoped, her truck key shared a fob with the key to the pizza parlor, so he'd been able to sneak the materials in before the pregnant women insisted on helping him. Yeah, yeah, call him old fashioned, call him a worrywart, God forbid anyone would think him simply a nice guy.

Now he eased Gina's truck over the potholed roads of the trailer park to Gina's trailer. He hoped he could dig up the courage to tell her the truth about his financial situation. He'd rather wallow around under her trailer, braving mud and countless spiders than see the disappointment on her face when he confessed that he'd failed in Southern California. At screenwriting, at his marriage, at saving poor Lise's life. And now at giving Gina the financial support she needed.

A red pickup with Idaho plates filled Gina's parking space. Rather than block it, Ed pulled into an empty space of an unoccupied trailer.

As he mounted the trailer's steps he heard a man's voice. "So you see, Miz Cosentino, how inconvenient it would be for you and ... your charges to continue living in Hancock. My previous offer to take your parents' place off your hands still stands, but not for long." Ed stopped.

"I already told you, Mr. Naismith, I decline your offer," Ed heard Gina reply. "I have chosen to open my home to women in need. You've lured away the workmen I'd hoped to hire, so I'll complete the renovations myself. We're here to stay. No way can you persuade me to change my mind."

Ed didn't like the menace he heard in the laugh Gina's words evinced from the man. "That may not be the case. There are many, many ways I might persuade you. I only hope you do not force me to employ them."

That asshole was threatening Gina. Ed yanked the door open, heedless of its god-awful wail. Every head in the trailer turned his way.

Sondra, nearest the door, squeezed against the dark haired, over-muscled man who stood next to her. The sleeves of his plaid flannel shirt were rolled up, revealing a tattoo of something clawlike.

"You're threatening me," said Gina, after making the tiniest nod of recognition at Ed's arrival. "I don't like threats."

Naismith's glance took in Ed and dismissed him. His expression grew grim. "Really? In my experience threats are something you activists throw around like dog treats."

Gina swiped back a strand of hair and spoke through tight lips. "Your experience should tell you we're not easily intimidated. I suggest you and your thug leave."

You tell him, Gina. What the hell kind of person threatens a pregnant woman? Especially Ed's woman. *Not your woman, any more. Maybe never.*

Naismith glanced over at the tattooed man who was obviously his strongman. Although the man attempted to keep his expression blank, his brows knitted in a way that made Ed wonder if he had some doubts about his employer's intentions. "You forget who owns this trailer," Naismith said.

All he needs is a mustache to twirl, Ed thought.

"*You* forget we both signed a rental agreement," Gina said. "If you're here to inspect the premises, you didn't provide notice. You are no longer welcome."

Naismith sneered. "Perhaps you are not aware of the extent of my influence and the strength of my will. I will not allow you and your Godless, unclean women to remain in this community. Nor will its right-thinking citizens, I assure you."

Beside Ed, Sondra inhaled. "Only reason we're unclean is your crappy plumbing," she said.

Ed moved toward Naismith, grasping his upper arm. "Gina asked you to leave," he said. He glanced at the table where Feather sat. She rolled her eyes. Sheez, was he supposed to stand there and let the guy bully them?

"Yes, I did," said Gina, with the emphasis on the I.

Uh-oh. Gina frowned at both of them, but Ed gathered that the strength of her ire focused on him. Not Gina's the happy expression of the rescued maiden in distress. How unreasonable.

Naismith's minion with the interesting tattoo grabbed Ed's wrist. Joy and adrenalin washed through Ed. Much better than squishing spiders.

Rather than fight the guy's strength, Ed took a quick breath and relaxed into him, causing him to stumble backward a step in surprise. Ed struck out with his right leg, catching the man behind the knee. The man fell backward against the flimsy table. It cracked and buckled beneath his weight.

While Ed paused for a second, savoring his triumph, his opponent sprang back like one of those Bozo the Clown blow-up bop bags, and butted Ed's stomach with his head as he rose. Ed noticed a tiny bald spot on the younger man's scalp. *Ha! Weightlifting can't prevent male pattern baldness.*

Ed staggered back against Sondra, but she'd prepared and shoved him forward with strong arms. She leaned near his ear, and whispered, "Get Bear Claw boy, macho man." Her force propelled Ed through the tiny open space of the trailer toward his opponent's raised, moving, freckled fist. Ed parried with his left forearm and swung with his right, connecting with the guy's chin. The man jerked back and to the side, striking the corner of one of the upper cupboards. He crumpled to the floor.

Ed rubbed his right hand with his left, still high on adrenalin but already dreading the coming pain.

"Oh, my sweet Lord." Gina yelled. She pivoted and reached into the tiny refrigerator, extracting the ice tray. For an instant Ed thought she intended to ice his bruised knuckles. She dumped the ice into a kitchen towel and shoved the bundle at Naismith. "He'll need this."

She turned her angry attention to Ed next. "You have a nerve barging in like that." She sucked in air and pointed first to Naismith, then to the door. "Out. Ed, Feather, carry that man to his truck."

Naismith stepped to the door. "Every one of you will regret this." He left.

Ed leaned against a wall, trying to catch his breath. Gina rounded on him, her face inches from his. "Last night I thought you were a distraction. Now I know you're a disruption." She spun around and picked up her cell phone. Then she waved at Ed and Feather. "Go on, pick him up and get him out of here."

Ed did.

On the way back to his trailer he heard a siren. In a few moments, Sheriff Byron Warnock arrived to cart yet another Mustard to jail.

Twenty-seven
Pragmatists and Politicians

Camp Destiny had issues, despite Vincent's assurances to the contrary. Emily remembered the vows they'd taken when they married last spring. In sickness and in health. Perhaps. In debt? No way.

She had to find out the level of opposition and the odds of success for this weird hunting resort and the land development that lay to the north. If she decided the odds were stacked against her, she'd yank the rest of her money out faster than a greenhorn hauled on a horse's reins.

Soon after Vincent drove off in a red pickup with one of his men, Emily aimed her little rental car toward downtown Hancock. She walked from the quiet side street where she'd parked to the town's main drag. Even though the morning sparkled with the glittery tang of fall, foot traffic was sparse. Seeing the number of empty storefronts she passed, she realized why Hancock's citizens welcomed Vincent as an economic savior.

She got directions to City Hall from a knitting-needle-thin old man wearing battered cowboy boots. She reflected on her outing yesterday with Vincent's pet pastor Graham to the development north of the ranch. Beyond Destiny? Beyond belief. No structures, one paved road, a few clearings still clogged with the trees felled to make them.

Some of the trees in Thompson's Woods, the site of the planned land parcels, were old growth, raising, according to Reverend Graham, the risk of environmentalists opposing further development.

Graham, the man, intrigued her. She'd felt an instant connection to him, but couldn't tell if it was sexual or spiritual. More than religious fervor brought the man to Idaho and his quick assessment of the issues facing Beyond Destiny suggested a shrewd mind with an excellent internal calculator. But what was he adding up? Souls? Sawbucks?

The mayor was in, seated at a huge Mission style desk strewn with manila file folders, several newspapers, a laptop PC, an office phone; and an iPod docking station. Her desk lamp had to be a reproduction Tiffany. Beneath its multi-colored shade, several small creatures, crafted from old utensils, cavorted, a couple of them serving as paperweights. Emily thought they cried out to be picked up, but she didn't.

Mayor Warnock rose. She offered her first name and her hand. It engulfed Emily's smaller, softer hand and the woman stood several inches taller than Emily, but she sensed no effort to intimidate her. The mayor appeared alert, almost on edge.

Her well-worn jeans and hounds-tooth checked shirt suited her and the community and Emily hoped her new jeans and silk shirt in a splashy turquoise and red print didn't come across as "rich bitch, slumming."

"Heard you'd arrived. Welcome to Hancock." She waited for Emily to speak, almost like a hunting dog testing the wind.

"I thought the best way to learn about my new town was from our mayor," Emily said. "If you have time, that is." She tried out her ingratiating, humble smile.

The mayor didn't appear bowled over by Emily's graciousness, but she did say, "Let's go over to The Chukar for some coffee. You'll want to try Ardath's scones."

The women crossed the street and chose a booth by the window.

Once their food arrived, Emily asked about the town, the upcoming Hancock Days and Myrna's path to public office. Myrna's answers were polite and politic. Emily couldn't tell if they hid antagonism or jealousy or simple disinterest.

Time for blunt. "I'm concerned about the opposition to Camp Destiny," she said.

Myrna's face remained interested but unreadable.

"Vincent mentioned an environmentalist, someone with an odd name."

Myrna smiled. "Roadkill. I've known him since he ran around naked and pooped on his parent's new sofa. Always a hellion."

"Vincent didn't go into much detail about their disagreement." In fact, Emily had to pump the housekeeper and every employee she could find when Vincent wasn't around to get the sketchy picture she had.

Myrna dunked her scone in her coffee. "Told you these were fantabulous."

Emily knew her smile stretched in a taut line across her face. Trying to get information out of this woman was like milking a rattlesnake. "If there's widespread opposition to Camp Destiny … "

Myrna took too long to answer, almost as if she enjoyed taunting Emily. Finally, she said, "We have quite the gossip circuit in Hancock. I heard you're not just the little wifey. I heard you're the money behind Vincent Naismith."

Emily shrugged. "Then I have every reason to want Vincent to succeed."

"And every reason to withdraw your funds if you think his investment's a shaky one." Myrna sipped her coffee. "Roadkill doesn't have much support. Most Hancockians think Vincent is a miraculous gift. As mayor, I'm pleased he's given us an injection of capital and of hope."

A lifetime of deception gave Emily insight into half-truths. "As mayor. But?"

"Ah, yes. Takes a woman to recognize a big but." She shook her head. "You like the scones?"

Emily laughed. "I love the scones. I like the coffee. So far, I like the town. I want to see more."

"Shouldn't say this, but the shopping's better down south in Sandpoint. But we do have a general store you won't want to miss." She winked.

Emily wondered what prompted that wink. "Then I won't. The but?"

The mayor let out a breath as if she'd made a decision. "Your husband is a religious man with strong convictions about what's appropriate for Hancock. He's got it in his mind to stop a young woman from setting up a shelter for pregnant women."

Emily cocked an eyebrow. "I did hear him mention it. I gather you don't agree that the shelter is bad for Hancock."

"The young woman starting it has lived in Hancock her whole life. I'm fond of her."

"You hope Vincent will let her be."

"Never said that," Myrna said. "Elected officials try to go along with the majority opinion."

"Somehow I don't see re-election hopes driving your actions."

The mayor kept smiling and said nothing.

"I appreciate your time and honesty." *Can't say much for your information sharing.*

Emily followed Myrna's directions and found Belmont's General Store after a short walk. For some reason the mayor wanted Emily to see the store. Emily doubted it was because of its historical significance. Why, then? Maybe the store served as the gathering place for the town's old men, who'd share more than a chaw with Emily. Not likely.

She hadn't gotten much out of Myrna, but she'd gathered that the woman didn't like Vincent, despite the boost he brought to the economy. Emily didn't care if Vincent won or lost a popularity contest, as long as it didn't affect the success of his venture.

She decided her reason for going to the store would be to purchase some gloves, totally appropriate given the chill in the fall air.

Emily passed a parking lot with shopping carts but decided to skip the rear entrance to Belmont's General Store and check out the street front. Beyond the lot a residence extended from the store, its small fenced yard adjacent to the lot. At the back of the yard a huge maple tree announced fall in brilliant crimson.

She went around the side of the building, thinking she'd buy gloves and earmuffs, hoping that the owner's small town taste ran to traditional instead of tacky. *Don't be such a snob, Emily.*

The store's double doors led to a small anteroom and another set of doors, protection against cold winter gales. She shivered. She intended to be out of cold country before the snow flew, but only if she could leave confident her investment here would grow.

She held the door for a young black woman whose grouchy expression turned into a surprised smile at Emily's courtesy. "Thanks," the woman said. Two canvas shopping bags dangled from her shoulders. A dark gray sweatshirt cupped her pregnant belly.

"You're welcome. Do you know if they carry gloves?"

The woman let out a small snort. "If that old bat could make them out of my hide, you bet they would. You're better off at the hardware store."

"Oh, not work gloves. For the cold." Emily gave a mock shiver.

"She has a little of everything, so maybe. I stick to the bare necessities. In, get a few ugly looks sent my way, out." She smiled as if to indicate her annoyance didn't include Emily.

"Thanks for the warning." Before she entered she added, "You have a wonderful day."

Inside, long aisles stretched crowded and without an apparent order across the breadth of the store. Emily made her way to the register, intent on discovering what Myrna's wink meant.

Two people flanked the checkout counter, a full-bodied woman and the Reverend Joseph Graham. Neither noticed Emily's entrance. The woman's face pinched in bitterness. Emily pretended interest in the shelf to her left while she observed the couple. "You saw her. That's the kind of women Gina's brought to our town. That hussy strolled in here, brazen as you please."

"Everyone needs to shop, be they sinners or seekers."

Ooh. There he goes, golden voice and a way with words.

The woman reached out and caressed the man's arm. No other word for it.

Emily stepped back, inhaling. She'd swear that sour-faced harpy had a thing for the new minister. "You have a kind word for everyone," the woman said. "I hoped you'd save them for me." The drop in pitch, the tone, even without the yearning on the woman's face, told Emily these two were lovers. Or bed partners. *My, my, my. Reverend Graham's more intriguing than I imagined.*

Time for Emily to enter the conversation. She strolled to the counter, clearing her throat. "Good morning." She smiled what she hoped was an all-knowing smile of a wise and perceptive observer.

The man spun around and the woman backed away, widening the distance between them, her face confirming Emily's assessment.

An instant's annoyance flashed across Joseph Graham's face but disappeared when he recognized her. His bright, welcoming expression confirmed that his interest yesterday had gone beyond clerical. "Mrs. Naismith. Emily. Have you met Sister Belmont, the proprietress of this answer-to-every-person's-needs?"

Sister Belmont crossed her arms and her face took on the expression of a sullen teen. "It's a simple general store, is all."

Oh, my. Haven't learned to share, has she? Nor to hide her feelings. Emily extended her hand to the woman. "I'm so pleased to meet you."

The woman took her hand in a reluctant, quick clasp. "Heard you'd come to visit. Welcome." Not, oh so not welcome, Emily realized.

"Vincent's had nothing but good things to say about you and your establishment." *Okay, he's said nothing at all. Same as nothing but good.*

Darlene Belmont's smile wavered toward genuine then gave up and fell into tense. "Your husband is a blessing for Hancock." Her emphasis on the word husband told Emily that Sister Belmont did not believe Vincent's wife brought similar blessings.

Brother Joseph placed a hand on each woman's forearm. Darlene Belmont stiffened. "Amen to that, Sister Darlene. I am honored to have him as my patron." He directed the gaze of those tawny eyes to Emily. "I can only hope that my relationship with him is as solid and long-lasting as your wedding vows."

Emily's attention shifted from Darlene Belmont's struggles to control her jealousy to the object of the poor woman's infatuation. Joseph was mocking Emily, but oh so cautiously. He suspected her motives, as she did his. Kindred spirits.

Emily batted her lashes at the minister. "Well, now, that's a hope that I share with you, Brother Graham."

Her pulse quickened. This encounter had brought new meaning to Camp Destiny.

Twenty-eight
Roger Meets a Ghost

"Attention. Attention. Roger Schramm, report to Headquarters. A-S-A-P. Roger Schramm to HQ."

Roger jumped at the crackling announcement from the Camp Destiny loudspeaker.

Roger handed his hammer to Dean. When the boss called, you answered. Simple. "Don't know how long I'll be. See if you can keep up the momentum." Dean's expression and a goober hawked to the left of Roger's foot let Roger know his brother caught the sarcasm.

Despite the fact that it usually spooked the animals and often they heard only a mishmash of unintelligible garble, no one on Naismith's crew complained about the loudspeaker. Everyone figured the boss got a kick out of hearing his voice echoing throughout the ranch. Roger grinned. Maybe it reminded Mr. Naismith of his days selling cars in L.A.

Roger hustled toward the house. His mission these days was to keep the boss happy, to keep his nose clean, and to try his best to keep Dean's nose from getting hopelessly dirty. None of those was easy, the last hardest, but he'd promised himself to try 'cause other options weren't leaping out of the trees for either of the Schramm brothers. Maybe he'd get a piece of Marlena's coffee cake. His stomach growled at the thought.

The growl curdled when he recognized Mr. Naismith's guest.

Sucker-punched by a tiny, black-haired female. No warning. No air in his lungs, no breath to speak. Screwed. Still, something in him admired her luxurious form, her glossy hair.

"Roger, good, you heard my page." Naismith turned to the woman from Sears. The woman Dean had KO'd.

Roger nodded, frozen in place. If he forced himself to speak, he'd

142

squeak. Or babble about how glad he was she was alive. *Right, that was good news. Alive. And here. Looking for Dean. And maybe for him, too.* Not good news.

In the middle of too many nights awake worrying about what had happened to the woman in Sears, Roger imagined the police coming for Dean. He imagined himself figuring out some slick alibi that put them in another store, another mall, another lifetime. He hadn't imagined her coming, in person, seeking revenge. Trying to find his brother.

Naismith waved a beckoning arm to him. "Come and meet Miss Ponder."

Fuzz took over Roger's thought processes. His heart loped. Thank God he'd already pulled down the sleeves of his shirt to cover his tattoo. Assuming Naismith preferred his men clean-shaven and without tattoos, Roger usually wore long sleeves. He crossed the room, reaching Naismith and the woman without staggering, and accepted her offered hand. Gripped it lightly in his. So tiny. Warm. As opposed to his iced fingers. She smelled spicy, like cinnamon apples.

She appeared confused, disappointed, maybe. "Pleased to meet you. You seem familiar. Have we met?"

He ran a dry tongue over his front teeth. *Talk, dammit. Think of something.* He gulped in a deep breath. *Maybe it's time to come clean. Let Dean pay the price of his damn foolishness.* "Don't think so. Imagine I'd remember you, miss." His voice high, strained, to his ears.

Naismith shot him a puzzled look, probably reacting to the weird voice. "Miss Ponder's trying to find a shopper at Sears on the day you were there getting supplies. Tracked you here to Camp Destiny. You got some supplies, correct?"

"Yes, sir, yes, ma'am. Picked up all the stuff on your list and a few things for myself. Is there a problem?"

The woman checked him out, from work boots to the baseball cap he crushed in his sweating hands. "A customer lost control, assaulted a Sears security guard."

Naismith saved Roger, whose ability to speak had evaporated. "My goodness, that's a terrible thing. However, I assure you none of the men in my employ would lose control or assault *anyone.*"

Roger, who still showed evidence of the previous day's encounter with the Mustard from L.A., felt the color go to his cheeks. The woman's skeptical expression told him she saw through Naismith's fancy answer. Yet Naismith's answer and his expression both said, "Stonewall."

"Was anyone else with you?" asked Ms. Ponder.

Stonewall it is. Even though we all might be better off with the truth, strutting on the old man's carpet, buck naked. "Nope. Nope. All by myself. Not that big a load, as I recall." Roger didn't allow himself one nervous peep at Naismith and he reminded himself keep his answers short and simple.

143

The woman chewed on her cheek, gave him a level stare. Roger returned it. Would she argue with him about who he was with or insist on seeing every man jack on Naismith's team? Thank the Good Lord only Roger had used a credit card. He always doled out cash to Dean.

He wondered if he or Mr. Naismith could force the woman to leave. Maybe if he stared at those knockers, made a rude comment? She wouldn't like that. He rubbed wet palms on his jeans. Stayed quiet. If he riled her, she might stick around just to be argumentative.

Naismith gazed from Roger to the woman and back, his face expressionless. After a moment, he said, "Well, then, sorry we couldn't help you. Any more questions, Miss Ponder?"

"*Ms.* Ponder. No more questions. Thanks for your time, Mr. Naismith. Mr. Schramm." She headed for the door, spun to assess Roger, her expression doubtful. "You sure you were all alone that day? Didn't take another man along for company?" She seemed to be questioning Naismith, as well as Roger.

Roger shook his head. "Nope. Just me. Spent quite a while in Sears. Love that store."

She left. The way she walked—slow, steady, the way she pulled the door to—firm, not slamming it, revealed her anger better than a stalk and a slam. She knew he lied.

Roger breathed. His pulse slowed its uneven thrumming on his temples. Now, of course, came Naismith's questions.

Naismith went to the door and opened it, watched the woman get in her car and drive off. He crossed the room and refreshed his coffee. Didn't offer Roger any. Took a sip. By the time the boss spoke, Roger's bladder and his bowels threatened rebellion. "Funny, I'd swear you took your brother with you that day."

Roger smelled nervous sweat, rank, ugly. He wanted to tell Mr. Naismith the whole story, spill it and relieve the burden of guilt and responsibility he carried. Yet the knowing, almost gloating expression on Naismith's face warned Roger to stay with the lie. Even though the truth was with them, in the room, bigger than Naismith's plush couch. "Yes, sir. But I dropped him off at a video games place before I went to the mall. He loves those games."

Naismith nodded and gave that knowing little smile more leash. "I see. Glad to know there was no problem. I'm sure you and your brother realize that adverse publicity for Camp Destiny would be bad news for all of us. Solidarity, loyalty, fidelity, son."

Son, my ass. When our old man beat us, we all knew where we stood. This man's veiled threats made the pain unending and unpredictable. His grasp on Roger's short and curlies was tightening and getting worse.

Twenty-nine
The Righteous Must Stand Firm ...
Even When Their Feet Hurt

Joseph Graham's shoulders ached and the soles of his feet berated him. He moved the damned picketing poster to his other shoulder. He rolled his shoulders but found no relief.

He could, would, must make it through this gig, score big and retire. Warm places like Mexico or the Caribbean beckoned, especially given the chill in the air today. All he had to do was impress Vincent Naismith with his moral posture and encourage the poor woman who started this shelter that she'd be wise to move somewhere more welcoming. Not that hard, and no cause for the pain that divided his head into sore, splitting and excruciating segments, each screeching "stop."

Graham ignored the pain, congratulating himself for his discipline. He paced past the pizza parlor that Gina Cosentino hoped to transform into Rainbow's End Shelter for indigent pregnant women. He reversed and headed back. If he tilted the sign at the right angle, maybe no one could read the hateful message painted by Darlene Belmont: "Hancock Won't Harbor Harlots."

He shuddered. Ugly words. Hadn't these people heard of "live and let live?"

Nope. Furthermore, Joseph Graham had no time for a conscience until this game concluded.

He shifted the sign so all could see.

Darlene Belmont and the other "like-minded souls" she'd recruited marched by, each bearing signs with similar nasty messages. "Hancock is too small for your big bellies," "The Lord is Watching ... and Waiting," "Fall is time for YOU to Leave."

145

The workings of the human mind fascinated Graham. Why were Naismith and Darlene so set against these women? They were bearing their babies, not aborting them. You'd think that would tickle Vincent and his religious zealot friends. But no, the babies were maybe the wrong color or maybe not conceived in wedlock. Was that the objection?

The real issue, he concluded, was that the women weren't ashamed, weren't hiding themselves away, but rather flaunted their pregnancies in tight T-shirts. Graham thought a good God would be pleased to see these young women so happy to bring these new souls onto the earth. He sighed.

Darlene Belmont marched straight toward him, her head high, and her plain face bright with excitement and pleasure. Graham returned her smile with no effort.

Joseph Graham considered all women God's gifts. He never offended the Lord by rejecting His offerings. Joseph might not approve of Darlene's bigotry or the way she shunned these young women, but her narrow-mindedness ended beneath the comforter. And on the kitchen table, the dining room rug, and oh so many other places in her home. As she approached, she licked her lips and stared at his package, which threatened to salute her. He rearranged himself with his free hand. And winked, just as they bumped shoulders in passing.

Graham dragged his straying thoughts back to the topic at hand, wondering if it was time for another chorus of *Blessed Assurance*. Maybe *Be Not Afraid*. Probably *Abide with Me* wouldn't cut it. And maybe not *Love Lifted Me*.

He smelled Darlene before she spoke as she moved from behind to his side, a nice combination of fresh-roasted coffee, cinnamon and early-morning sex. "I'm taking a few of the picketers back to my place for a potty break." She giggled, a tinny grating little bray. "I'll bring more cookies."

"Ah, a thoughtful as well as a godly woman. What hymn do you think we should try upon your return?"

"I'm quite fond of *Bind Us Together*," Darlene said. Her pupils widened.

Graham chuckled. "Followed by *Amazing Grace*." Annoying giggle aside, the woman did have a unique talent.

Darlene pranced away and Graham caught up with another of his new parishioners, a rotund, florid-faced man bearing another hand-made sign. Bud Porter, Graham recalled.

The four targets of the picketing sauntered in their direction. Refusing to hide in their shelter, marching into battle with their opponents, like scantily clad Valkyries. Top heavy and unwieldy in their tight shirts and leggings, yet impressive and lovely. Graham whispered a little prayer of thanks for the female form in its many shapes and colors.

Next to him, his fellow picketer huffed. "Don't see why they don't head on down to Boise. Or even over to Spokane. Lord knows that town's a hotbed for liberals like them."

Graham paused and observed first the women, second, his companion. Porter's belly boiled over his jeans like the innards of a just-squeezed baked potato. The women glowed with health. The man glowered with bitterness. "Brother Porter," Graham said, "let us continue our non-violent approach. Perhaps we might discuss your opportunity to get away from the hustle of town living by purchasing acreage at Beyond Destiny. Your own little piece of heaven."

Bud Porter frowned. "Doubt I can afford it."

"We can discover some creative mortgage opportunities, I'm sure." Graham waited until the four women neared. "You did mention a desire to escape the crowds."

Porter scowled at Gina, whose lovely face appeared strained, in contrast to the mocking, defiant smiles on her companion's faces. "Look at her. Thinks she owns the dang town. Just 'cause she grew up here, don't mean she can drag in foreigners as easy as she pleases. I always knew her and her kin was trouble. Even if her momma did make a mean pizza pie. They was Eye-talian, don't you know," he added. He coughed and spat. "Her folks went back to Italy. Should of took the girl with them." He hefted his picket sign and waddled faster. He lifted his voice and yelled in the direction of the large black girl, "Movin' On Out is what you should be doing."

The woman stopped and made a long slow turn toward Porter. At the same time Gina reached for her friend, Graham placed a restraining arm on Porter. "Brother Porter, we agreed we'd avoid direct confrontations."

Mayor Myrna Warnock elbowed her way through several gawking townspeople and positioned herself in front of Bud Porter. Graham had met her the previous day when he'd gone into City Hall to find out if a permit was necessary for them to stage their peaceful demonstration.

Mayor Warnock pressed in, only Porter's paunch stopping a nose to nose confrontation. She breathed in and out, and in moments her predatory face made the man lower his eyes. Next she raked Graham with her angry eyes. She shook a finger at them. "Back off and shut your trap, Bud Porter. You have a right to your opinion, not to mouth off like some troublemaking, bigoted pissant."

"But, Myrna—"

The pregnant women halted not ten yards away, taking in Mayor Warnock's diatribe.

The mayor ignored Porter's sputtering. To Graham she said, "You promised this would be a peaceful demonstration." Despite the temperature, she wore a short-sleeved T-shirt that revealed muscular biceps and forearms he doubted were nurtured at a nearby Gold's Gym. *She must wield a wicked gavel at City Council meetings.*

Graham raised both hands, palms out. "On occasion, emotions run higher than anticipated, Sister Warnock. I assure—"

"Don't 'Sister Warnock' me. I'm not you're sister. Keep your people under control or Brother Sheriff Warnock will jail the lot of you, Reverend Mr. Graham."

Graham threw an arm around the shorter Porter's shoulders and gave him a significant squeeze. "Of course. We're not out to start a fight."

Brother Porter took a breath and might have commented but Graham continued in his strong come-to-meeting voice. "We all know violence is not the answer. Often compromise is the best solution. Surely, the grant funding the women seek isn't solely for a shelter located in Hancock. Um."

Graham stumbled over his words and cleared his throat. Emily Naismith moved into his line of sight, beyond Gina and her women, but definitely within earshot. Her head cocked, attentive to his words, frowning. He'd swear he read disapproval in that frown. The pounding pulse at his temples announced an imminent headache. He gave his head a little shake and tightened his lips. *Think fast, Joe. That's supposed to be your stock in trade.* "Brother Naismith wants what's best for Hancock, and I know you do too, Mayor Warnock."

The mayor straightened. "Of course I do. We all do. It's our home."

"And mine now, as well, thank the Good Lord." Graham nodded at Gina and shone a benevolent gaze on the three other women. "Sister Gina, I'm certain you only wish to help these young women, not demonstrate the strength of your will to the people of Hancock."

Gina bowed her head but did not respond. Her shoulders slumped. Two of her companions flanked her, whispering, yet she said nothing. Her despair had a quality you could almost touch. Jesus, he wasn't the one who wanted her to leave. He was merely following orders, Naismith's orders. *Uh huh. Guess that's what those Roman soldiers said way back when.*

Graham licked his lips with a thick dry tongue. His voice scratched when he finally spoke again. "As reasonable, loving people—" *with the exception of Bud Porter*—"let us pray together for a solution."

Emily Naismith stepped forward. Her face revealed a mixture of amusement and contempt, neither emotion boding well for Joseph Graham.

Graham's hands chilled along with his hopes for this gig.

"I think another hymn is in order," Emily said. "If we're all going to get along, I suggest 'In His Hands.'" Staring straight at Graham, she began, her voice light, luscious. "He's got the whole world in His hands, he's got the whole wide world in His hands." When others took up the hymn, she smiled, a wide, knowing smile.

He knew his ears shone bright red. Somehow this woman saw him as he was, and yet, perhaps she also saw possibilities.

Graham sang.

Gina Loses Heart and Ed Loses His Reserve

Byron let Ed out of jail after feeding him the sandwiches Myrna dropped by. Ed's gratitude for the free meal fled when he learned that Byron had kept him in jail until after Joseph Graham's protest march ended.

"Couldn't have you punching out our new preacher." Byron let a grin cross his stern face. "Myrna came mighty near to clocking him as it was."

"Dammit, Byron, I should have been there, stood up for Gina."

"You forget that's what got you locked up? My advice is, stick to what you're good at. Writing. Stay away from Naismith and his men."

If the sheriff had patted Ed on the head, he couldn't have been more patronizing. Ed forced out a tight-lipped smile and bit back the words he wanted to say. "Being locked up gave me time to meditate on the benefits of non-violence. I'll be good. But tomorrow's Roadkill's bail hearing, and I'm going, no matter who else shows. You can't stop me."

"Actually I could," Byron said, his voice mild. When Ed tensed, he added, "But I won't. You better hope your brother shows, or you'll forfeit bail."

"I hope he shows, for more important reasons than bail." Great sentiment, but you better hope you don't lose that cash.

Ed ran back to his trailer, intent on releasing his anger and cleaning up before he faced Gina. He had to apologize for butting in yesterday. Would she apologize for getting him arrested? Didn't she realize he wanted to help an old friend, couldn't hang her out to dry like he'd abandoned Lise? Sweat pooled in Ed's armpits and made its itchy way to his waistband as he mounted the trailer steps.

Gravel crunched behind him. Ed spun around, managing not to tumble over the spindly side porch railing.

Gina Cosentino stood a few feet away. Her dark hair curled about her face. She wore a long skirt that hit mid-calf, heavy-soled sandals and a baggy long-sleeved blue sweater. She looked gorgeous. Long legs. Strong ankles. Glossy hair. Smooth, Ed. Next you'll ask to examine her teeth.

Ed swiped at his sweaty face with both hands and rubbed them on his jeans. He leaned back against the trailer door, going for casual. The door he'd forgotten to lock swung open. Ed fell backward on his ass.

Smooth. Ax casual, insert ridiculous.

Ed scrambled to his feet. The last time he'd seen Gina, she tossed him out of her trailer and phoned the cops.

She walked to where Ed stood.

"Come to see me?" Ed gave himself a mental pat on the shoulder. Not "come to apologize?" or "pipes leaking again?" A friendly, non-confrontational welcome.

Gina smiled. An incredible smile. Honest, unforced. An essence of Gina smile.

Ed wanted to sweep her into his arms and promise to keep her safe forever. Instead, he waited for her to speak.

Gina's smile lost some of its bounce, as if leaking out some of her amusement, along with her normal confidence. "I owe you an apology."

Ed's mouth opened but nothing came out. Gina, apologizing?

She rubbed her palm along the stair rail, up and down, up and down. "You were out of line, but you meant well. I called Byron. Had you arrested right after you delivered supplies to the Flat Italian. Of course I had no idea, but I'm ashamed."

"Naismith's an asshole. He makes everyone crazy. The man doesn't know what he's up against if he thinks he can scare you."

Gina's left eyebrow tilted up. She had exceptionally lovely eyebrows. "He does scare me. Ordinarily, I wouldn't let him intimidate me, but today I realized I'm just being stubborn Gina."

"I don't see that. You have every right to establish that shelter."

"You didn't see that protest," she said.

When Ed began an apology, she stopped him with a hand. "Not your fault, I know. The thing is, that new minister has more support than I expected. Darlene Belmont rallied her loony friends. It hurt. Nobody carried picket signs for us." She moved away from the trailer, scuffing the gravel with her shoe.

Ed trailed behind her. "Probably no one knew. I heard Myrna stood her ground."

She cast him a look over her shoulder. Her lips twitched in a halfhearted smile. "Myrna wants to keep Hancock peaceful. She'll be glad if we leave."

"That's why she saved all those supplies for remodeling The Flat Italian," Ed said. "Makes sense to me." Ah, yes. Good old sarcasm. The weapon of choice when a Mustard wants to avoid a sincere conversation.

Gina reversed her retreat and stood before Ed. "Look. I appreciate the supplies and your delivering them, but there's no one to do the work. Naismith's hired everyone away." None of Gina's trademark animation vibrated in her words.

"I can help. I will help. I can paint, I can hammer. Working together, we can do it. You've got three other strong young women—"

Gina's tiny smile barely moved her lips. "That's sweet. Trouble is, I'm foolish to think I, we, can do this. Sure, the paint's non-toxic, and yes, they're willing. But Sondra's got some problems with high blood pressure, dangerous stuff, and it could happen to—"

Ed broke in, speaking as fast as he'd recently run. "Jesus, this is my fault. It would be so easy to pay someone, but I can't. I can't loan you anything. I'm broke, flat, busted. A failure." His voice cracked on the words.

Gina's mouth opened. Ed gently pushed it shut with one bent knuckle. Her dark brown eyes filled with disappointment. Small town boy makes good, goes bad.

"Ed Mustard, you sweet thing, you are never a failure to me. Don't even think it. I'm the one who screwed up here, the one who should have given up weeks ago. I've always been too stubborn, too optimistic. I can't ask these women to face the stress of remodeling and the hatred in this community."

Never had Ed heard Gina so down on herself. He squeezed his eyes shut, took in a breath through his nose, but couldn't hold back the fire that engulfed his body. Rage at himself, at Naismith—but most, at his damn brother. Gina needed Cliff and Cliff wasn't here. So like the time Lise needed Ed and Ed didn't show. Maybe it was a genetic defect.

Ed held Gina's face between his palms. He inhaled her scent, a mix of vanilla and cinnamon. "Promise you won't make up your mind yet. We can do this. I'm going to find that damn brother of mine. Between him and me, we'll finish the remodeling and figure out how to convince Naismith and the whole town that you and Rainbow's End are one sweet deal for Hancock."

She shook her head. "Now who's chasing rainbows?"

"Nothing wrong with it, especially when you have friends. Promise you'll give me a few days?"

She smiled, and Ed saw it reach her eyes. "Fat pregnant ladies don't move that fast, anyway."

Ed didn't move or speak. He stared into those brown eyes.

Gina colored. "Oh, for Heaven's sake. Yes, I promise. Thank you for your faith, your friendship, your muscles. We might even start with some painting. You've got my promise."

Thirty
Lacy Takes Aim

Lacy found the sheriff's office without a problem and pulled into a dirt lot, empty save for a beat-up Camry, an official SUV and a couple of pickups.

The other morning she'd left Camp Destiny certain that Roger Schramm had lied about his visit to Sears. He wasn't Snaggletooth, she knew that, but he was lying. Why? She thought she might have pushed him for the truth but his boss stopped her. Again, why? Innocent people would have asked for details. An assault in Sears by a shopper gone postal? Fascinating stuff to most folks.

By the time she entered the town of Hancock, doubt had seeded itself in her whirling brain. Schramm's face was familiar but that meant nothing; she'd been traipsing around the store before encountering Snaggletooth and could have passed Schramm anywhere. He might have been an innocent shopper.

Nevertheless something was weird at Camp Destiny. Schramm had lied. His boss had known it and covered for him. That reeked.

With only two other names on the list of Sears' shoppers to check out, it was worth pursuing anything out of the ordinary. She'd decided to stick around Hancock for a while and had checked into a Bed & Breakfast called The Osprey's Nest. Yesterday she'd relaxed, explored the town, and observed a bunch of oddballs picketing a pizza parlor.

Despite that evidence of backwater looniness, Lacy liked the town and wondered if there were openings in law enforcement. She'd spent the afternoon on her laptop, trying to find out more about Camp Destiny, Roger Schramm and the community.

According to the local paper, Vincent Naismith represented the Holy Grail to the economically strapped town of Hancock. She would have to be cautious asking about him.

She paused on the lowest steps. Sweating, despising the anxiety that sizzled through her each time she entered a police station. You'd think she was the dirtbag, dammit, instead of a sexually harassed woman hoping to get back into law enforcement.

She shook her head and charged up the remaining steps and through the door. Into an empty room without personality or a person at the reception desk.

Three doors led from the cheerless vestibule, one behind the desk, one each to the left and right. The door behind the desk was made of security glass, the others were wood doors with glass windows. Lacy concluded that the glass door led to cells and the wood ones to offices, or perhaps a kitchen. Kitchens took priority over offices for people who worked long hours and odd shifts.

She took a seat on the wooden bench against the front wall, assuming the officer on duty had taken a brief break, grateful for time to prepare her attitude and her story.

Angry voices came from a room to her left.

"So are you going to look into Roadkill's disappearance now?"

"Now that there's a bench warrant out for him? Seems likely, since it's my job. I'm still wagering he's off on a wild goose chase. Leaving you out the bail money."

"It's not the money. I'm worried about my brother. No one else except Gina seems to share my concern."

"Don't tell me I don't care. I care about your foolish brother. I've had my deputies keep a special eye out for signs of accidents along the highway, for anything out of the ordinary. I'm short-staffed as it is, and I sure as hell don't have enough people to put on a full search for him."

"You could start at Camp Destiny. It's the last place Roadkill went."

"So now you've joined the 'I Hate Vincent' club. What is it with you Mustards?"

"Dammit, the man's a maniac. Who in his right mind would bring an African safari experience to a territory where you can walk out the door and shoot an elk or a moose? Something's fishy at that place and you're afraid to check it out."

A chair scraped. "I'll let that slide because you're upset about your brother, but we're done. Before that mouth of yours gets you in more trouble."

"I believe Roadkill is injured. If he dies because no one in this town cares … "

"We care. Believe me. On the other hand, the charge wasn't that serious. If Roadkill doesn't want to be found, he won't be. The man knows the wilderness better'n anyone I know."

Slow and quiet replaced rage in the man's voice when he finally replied.

"Sorry. I … don't know what to do. I thought if he missed his arraignment, you'd go after him. Then Gina would know the truth. I feel useless."

"I know, son. It's tough when you want to help, but don't know what to do."

"Tell me about it."

The man's bitter tone chilled Lacy. She jumped up and hurried to the office door, carried by enthusiasm if not common sense. Here was a chance to spend time in Hancock, find out more about Camp Destiny and its owner, impress the local law, and do what she did best, track down bad guys.

She entered the office just as a chair clattered backward to the floor.

Lacy faced two men, the older one seated at his desk, in uniform, and the other standing in front of the fallen chair. Both stared at her, wide-eyed.

"I may be able to help." She straightened. "I *can* help."

The sheriff recovered fastest and stood. "Eavesdropping?"

The tall, slender man in his 30s moved his lips in and out. "Can't this wait?" He kept his tone flat, but she guessed he struggled for civility.

Lacy took advantage of their surprise and moved farther into the room, closing the door behind her. "I couldn't help overhearing your 'conversation.'"

The sheriff's mouth twitched. "Didn't know we had an audience."

"I'd apologize," she said directly to the younger man, "but I think I can help."

The man's eyes widened, as if he worked to prevent an eye roll. However, she saw no humor on his face. What the sheriff found amusing, this man found annoying. "So you said."

"I used to be in law enforcement and I'm good at tracking people down. I want to know more about Camp Destiny and some of its employees. I think I can help you find this Roadkill person." Lacy knew her speech raced as fast as her blood pulsed at her wrists. She forced herself to take a breath, to shut her mouth.

"Woo hoo. We got us a bounty hunter," said the sheriff, his tone expressing his lack of delight.

"No. I'm not a bail enforcement agent."

"Could be. No license required."

The man with the missing brother crossed his arms and tilted his chin up. "My brother is not a fugitive."

"Yes, he is," contradicted the sheriff. "Sit down, both of you. Might as well hear her out. If you're so set on finding Roadkill, Ed, you'll need help."

Lacy watched the guy called Ed retrieve his fallen chair. His jeans cupped a nice tush and his dark hair had a better cut than most men Lacy knew. She caught the sheriff watching her and sat, every muscle twitching. *No babbling.* This could be her chance.

Ed Beards the Lion's Owner

The ancient Camry dawdled and groaned and strained its way along the road to Camp Destiny, apparently as reluctant as its owner to complete the trip.

"Jesus, Camp Destiny, my ass," Ed muttered. "Can you spell ostentatious?"

The ashes of Lise, again strapped in the passenger seat beside Ed, made no response.

"You may be wondering why I've chosen to beard the lion, actually the *owner* of the lion, in his den."

No reply.

"I need to find out if this guy is a blowhard or a megalomaniac. I also have to find out if Cliff stopped by. If he left. Where he went."

He glanced at the plastic urn. "Yeah, I know. Why would Naismith tell me? I'm the guy who punched his employee, the guy whose brother socked Naismith. But I've got to see him, talk reasonably to him. Find out if the man *can* have a reasonable conversation."

He saw the gate ahead and stopped the car. He leaned out through the window to give his name to the guard in the gatehouse.

An olive skinned man with a bruise on his chin slid back the glass window.

Ed gulped. His stomach contracted. The guy he'd hit the other day. *Well, good. Now you can apologize.*

The man gave Ed a lopsided smile. "Come to finish the job?" He slid the window shut and stood, and Ed saw his backside as he left the guardhouse.

Oh, God. Not another fight. No way I can surprise him twice. Ed got out of the car.

The guard came around the little shack, still wearing that smile.

Make the first move. Pre-emptive strike. Ed cleared his throat. "I want to apologize about—"

The man stuck out a hand. A hand to shake. "No apologies. You got me fair and square. Roger Schramm."

The name jolted and surprised Ed. This was the guy who'd lied to Lacy Ponder. *Go figure.* Ed accepted the man's hand and shook it. Not the time to hike that trail, although he reflected it was good thing Lacy had stayed in town. "The cabinet got you, not me."

Schramm rubbed the back of his head. "Wouldn't think anything in that flimsy trailer could pack such a wallop."

Ed breathed again. "Glad I saw you. Thanks for not holding a grudge."

"Just doing our jobs, I guess." He shook his head. "Sometimes don't know where the boss gets his ideas. She seems a nice girl."

Ed's hackles rose. "She is a nice woman." *My woman. Not.* "Thought I'd apologize to your boss, see the place. Used to be our ranch before Mr. Naismith bought it."

"So I heard." The man's smile seemed apologetic. "Boss wants us to wand all visitors. Hope you don't mind."

"Not a problem. Guess us Mustard brothers have got him worried."

Something flashed across the man's eyes. Guilt? Fear? Amusement? Rage? It went too fast for Ed to recognize. "I'll let the boss know to expect you." He walked to the shack, picked up a phone, then returned to Ed with a portable metal detector.

"Tell me that's not a cattle prod." Ed hoped the emotion he'd seen had not been a thirst for revenge.

The man smiled wide.

Ed slammed his car door. Vincent Naismith strode to meet him, hand outstretched, broad smile, white teeth, the whole welcoming host routine. Ed raised an eyebrow and smiled right back, hand clasping the smaller man's, keeping his eyes wary, but his mouth smiling, always smiling.

He realized that he and Naismith had chosen the same role. Pragmatic, friendly businessmen. With an eye to their backs. Required flexibility and good eyesight.

Ed saw Naismith assess Ed's appearance, from jeans and wrinkled polo shirt to the beater Toyota, in an instant. A puzzled expression mixed with distaste flitted across his face, gone faster than a car salesman whips out the contract, replaced by the bonhomie of the gracious host. Ed's fingertips tingled. He stretched them out. He forced his fingers and hands to relax against his thighs and kept smiling.

"Well, well. Ed Mustard. Screenwriter. Academy Award nominee. Quite the honor for a small town like Hancock." If Naismith's tone held a sneer, it stayed well beneath the surface. "So, what can I do you for today? I'm assuming we've both forgotten about the little fracas in Gina's trailer."

Ed didn't believe it but nodded anyway. "I spoke with Roger at the gate. Nice guy, no grudges."

Wariness, possibly, showed in the man's expression. "Indeed. I pride myself on a loyal crew."

Ed took a long slow assessment of his childhood home. "I'd like to see the old stomping grounds. You've made some big improvements to the old ranch."

"Normally, I'd be pleased to show you around. However, I'm on a deadline, preparing for our grand opening. We'll be giving tours then."

Thus Naismith let Ed know he didn't trust him and saw no need to court his favor.

Naismith guided Ed up stone stairs to the deck that protruded like an ugly petticoat around the perimeter of the remodeled Mustard family home.

"I've made many changes. You'll like what we've done," Naismith said. The words and tone were bland, but behind them Ed sensed a challenge: *If you don't, see what you can do about it.*

Ed nodded, but said nothing. Naismith stretched an arm toward the horizon. "From here, you can see the new outbuildings we've started. Staff housing, more barns, equipment storage."

The view from the deck revealed outbuildings scattered over acres where grain and alfalfa had grown in his youth. Ed's gut tightened. He rolled his lips together, searching for a neutral response. "Lots of construction."

Naismith darted a quick look over his shoulder at Ed. "Yes. Good progress. I have a dream for Camp Destiny. Not a small vision."

Ed tried to see this man as a businessman embarking on a profitable business venture. Yet he could see only the battered old lion. Would that animal and the other exotics Naismith was importing benefit? He maintained a neutral expression and muttered, "Vision, yes."

Ed reminded himself of his objective. "We Mustards seem to be causing you problems recently. You've got my apology. Has my brother shown his ugly mug around here? He was headed to your place the other day, against my advice, of course."

Naismith's answer came three seconds too late. "Roadkill? No, no. Since that first little encounter, he hasn't been welcome. Your brother tends to violence."

"No one would accuse Roadkill of being a pacifist. He's passionate about his causes."

Naismith curled a scornful lip. "Passion's good. Extremism isn't. I'd just as soon Roadkill take his causes elsewhere."

Okay. The gauntlet's thrown. You say he hasn't been here. I think he has. I know my brother and I think you're lying. "Tell me more about your plans for Camp Destiny."

Naismith puffed up like a chukar on a chilly morning. "The thrill of an African safari with only a short plane flight and a limo drive from the Spokane International Airport."

Ed forced his eyes to widen in a fake show of interest. "Quite a concept." *Bizarre, freaky.*

The man's eyes sparked with enthusiasm. "Our guests will be in the heart of God's country, the U S of A, surrounded by congregants of the new church Brother Graham is forming in Hancock. The few, the faithful."

Oh, shit. I cannot laugh. I cannot even grin. This man is serious. He pretended to be absorbed in the surroundings, because one glance at Naismith would tip

Ed into hysterics.

The view was absorbing. Not the ranch where Ed had grown up.

Naismith pointed with one arm, hooking the other hand over it, as if sighting down the barrel of a gun. "You see where I'm aiming? That will be a circle of exclusive cabins. I've erected a gazebo as the hub of the wheel, with the spokes leading to each cabin."

No response was needed. So wrapped up was the little man in his glorious plans he'd apparently forgotten for a moment that Ed was not yet a declared fan. Naismith was like too many film executives Ed had known in L.A., narcissistic and pompous and bombastic all in one.

Across the clearing an enormous gazebo sprawled over the site of the tiny gazebo Ed's father had built for their mother as a hideaway from "all her boys." The garish, gilt-painted structure Naismith had erected loomed like a monstrous bloated tumor on the grave of its delicate predecessor.

Ed wondered why his brother had stopped at merely slugging this prick. He himself had an urge to beat him to a whimpering, slimy, gory pulp. He inhaled and exhaled until he calmed. "Hmm. I'd love to see more."

Naismith pointed to the paths radiating from the gazebo's hub. "I'm considering paving the paths for our guests who prefer golf carts."

Ed nodded. Hunting from a golf cart? Instead of "fore," what would the hunters shout? "May we shoot through?"

With two fingers, Ed rubbed his temple. If Naismith wouldn't let him tour these grounds, how else could he find out if Roadkill had been there? Or if Naismith knew something about his whereabouts.

When in doubt, prod. Especially around those full of hot air.

"My brother mentioned his concern about the safety of the wild animals."

Naismith stilled. "My stock is secure. Your brother's concerns are misplaced." His voice held an edge. Anger? Fear?

Okay. Time to push. Ed's thoughts clicked away from Naismith to Gina and her pregnant friends. He suppressed a shudder. *Push Naismith's buttons.* "He meant the wild animals around Camp Destiny. Not your tame exotics."

Naismith's eyes widened and his neck muscles pulsed. His reaction to the double-barreled attack gratified Ed. "The animals I brought in for our safari experience are not tame. They are wild. They're well-protected. There is no risk to the surrounding game. None."

Ed let his lips curl in a satisfied, phony smile. The man's strong protestations gave him away. "Not sure Cliff meant the danger's from the animals so much as your guests." *I know, asshole, and you better worry just how much I know.*

Naismith's face paled but his expression didn't change. "No guests arrive until after the grand opening."

Time to let the pissant simmer. "Well, sir, I won't take up more of your time.

Just wanted to clear the air."

"Glad you did, son, glad you did."

I am NOT your son. My father might have shot you if he'd seen what you've done to the Rolling M. Ed knew he should shake Naismith's hand, but didn't trust himself not to crush it. Instead he stared at the man for a long, slow minute, before giving him a nod. "Thanks for the chat."

He followed a gravel path to where he'd parked the car, keeping his stride measured, calm. He cast his eyes to the earth his mother had loved, ashamed somehow that he hadn't simply throttled the violator of her precious home. A round object caught his eye. He knelt as if to tie a loose lace and snatched up one of Roadkill's handmade stress balls. Proof that Roadkill had been here. He'd had them with him when they stashed the wolf. So Roadkill had been out here since then.

Of course Ed didn't keep track of how many of those little balls his brother owned.

Outside the gates and away from the eyes of guards or cameras, Ed pulled his car to the shoulder. He should be speeding back to town, meeting up with Lacy to plan the great Roadkill search. Instead he seized the plastic jar that held Lise's ashes in both hands and held it before him, at eye level.

"Okay," he shouted. "You're dead. Supposedly out there somewhere. Can you see my brother? Can you talk to him? Did that maniac and his crew of hulking retards kill him or is he off communing with a Ponderosa?" He lowered the container to the passenger seat and sat for long moments, staring straight ahead.

In a controlled, quiet voice he spoke again. "Well, Cliffie, I don't know what's become of you and I don't know how to find out. But I tell you this, bro, that man has got to be stopped. And it might be up to me." He shook his head. "Dammit to hell."

Thirty-One
Hunting Brothers

"We go slow, make sure no one's home, nobody gets hurt," Roger Schramm reminded his brother as he parked his pickup a few rows away from the trailer Ed Mustard was renting. "That's what the boss wants, that's what we want."

Dean drummed the fingers of both hands on the dashboard, in a fast, off-synch, jerky tempo. "The boss wants us to find the video, so's Mustard won't screw up his plans. That's what the boss wants. We're his fixers."

"Uh-huh." *Bad choice of fixers.* Dean's magic fingers managed to screw up most everything they touched, and Roger? Roger was damn tired of trying to clean up the messes. He rubbed his head, felt the lump he'd taken in the pregnant woman's trailer. Be nice if things went smooth and easy, for once. Be nice if his brother didn't fuck things up, for once. *Be nice if you didn't hope for the impossible, for once.*

Roger turned off the engine and Dean jackrabbitted out of the truck, slamming the door behind him. "Don't go crashing on—"

Ignoring Roger's cautionary words, Dean loped ahead and pounded on the door of the trailer. The door swung open and Dean marched in.

If we find a dead body, I'm gonna find out what Mexico's like.

Roger smiled without joy. He trudged up the aluminum stairs, dreading the task of searching through the belongings of a guy whose hand he'd shaken only hours ago. *Mexico sounds good, body or not.* Only doing his job, he guessed, but he tried to stay within the law and within his own moral code. Both were getting bent with this assignment.

"Well, lookee that," Dean Schramm said, a twisted smirk on his damaged face. "Nobody home, and he even left the door open for us."

Empty. No dead body. "His car's not here, but he might be back any time." Roger pressed his lips together, tight. "In. Search. Out. We're searching for a video, maybe photos."

"You worry too much. That Roadkill was so cocky he would've kept the video himself. No reason to give it to his brother."

"Then why didn't we find it in his truck?"

"Maybe he took it with him when he crawled off to die."

Pain shot behind Roger's eyeballs. A vision of the activist, bloody, on his hands and knees, pasted itself in his brain. He didn't like how casual Dean sounded about killing a man, but preaching would only piss Dean off, might make him head for more drugs. *Jesus.*

"Gloves?" he reminded his brother.

"Yeah, yeah, wussy boy." Dean struggled with the latex gloves Naismith had insisted they wear.

Roger slipped his on sweaty hands. He hoped they'd find something that would make the boss proud. Otherwise …

The place smelled musty but had a shipshape appearance. Roger thought he smelled something like old grass, not marijuana but the backyard kind. Where'd that come from?

Dean scuffed to the back of the tiny trailer. "Come here, looka this."

"Keep your voice down. We're not here to admire his decorating," Roger said. But he joined his brother. Two wire cages sat on the counter that stretched the width of the bed. On the floor in front of the bed was a twenty or thirty pound bag, some kind of hamster or rat chow, the unsealed top folded over on itself.

"The guy raises hamsters." Dean giggled. "Talk about your squirrelly types. He's got to be from California. He opened one of the cages and stuck his hand in. "C'm here, little critter, come to Daddy Dean. Didn't we hear about some Hollywood type who ate the darn things or … what was it? Something kinky." He bent to cage level. "Come on, buddy, I won't hurt you."

Roger put out a restraining hand. "I wouldn't just stick—"

"Ouch. Goddamn, the little shit bit me." Dean jerked his hand out and almost upending the cage. "And it ain't no hamster. It's a squirrel, a tree squirrel, I swear it."

Roger didn't even try to hide his smile. "Bright, bud. How bad is it?"

Dean's eyes narrowed. "Isn't funny. You see a first aid kit or a box of Band-Aids anywhere?" When Roger shook his head, Dean moved to the kitchen sink and wound the dishcloth around his middle finger before Roger caught more than a glimpse of the wound.

Roger considered telling his brother to wash the bite, but didn't. The hell with this constant babysitting. "We're not here to play with squirrels." He turned to scan the rest of the trailer. Opposite him was a row of closets and drawers, built-in. He rummaged through Mustard's belongings, trying not to make too much of a mess. With luck the guy would figure some kids were trying to find cash. "You start in the kitchen," he told Dean.

"Goddamn but I'm sick of your bossing me around," Dean said. But he returned to the cooking area of the trailer and slammed cupboards open and shut.

Roger searched through Mustard's clothes, mostly jeans and such, but they sure as hell didn't come from Sears. They had that same expensive air that Naismith's wife's clothing had.

He heard the water pump on the trailer and looked around to see Dean swallow a handful of pills. "What the hell you think you're doing?"

"It's for the pain. Toothache. And that squirrel had some killer teeth on him."

"You already downed a couple of Vicodin. That shit is what's gonna kill you, Dean, not a little pain or a little squirrel."

"Quit your nagging. You sound like Mom."

Yeah, and my nagging works about as good as hers. Roger sighed. He returned to searching, pulling up the mattress on the trailer's double bed, shoving aside the bag of chow and tugging at the flimsy drawer beneath the bed until it grudgingly opened. No camcorder. When he tried to shove the drawer back into place, it jammed, so he left it part open.

"I gotta take a dump," Dean announced. "Might as well use this guy's crapper." He waltzed into the trailer's bathroom.

An unopened laptop computer perched on the table beneath the trailer's front window. Naismith had made clear their target was a camcorder or a camera, not a computer. Roger stashed the laptop under the table, out of Dean's sight. His brother would want to steal it, but Roger figured Mustard needed it for his writing. "In. Search. Out," he whispered to himself.

A row of small cabinets provided storage above the window. Roger pulled open the first, and removed books and papers, going through each stack in case Roadkill had taken still photos in addition to the video. No photos, no video, no cameras.

He cocked his head toward the bathroom. Dean was taking forever in the can.

Roger repeated his systematic search in all five cupboards above the front window, finding nothing but more books. Person could read for a long time.

Roger was stretching up to feel above the cabinets when something brushed against his leg. He jerked back, and a pile of books tumbled onto the floor and his right toe. "Damnation."

He spun around. A huge orange striped cat trotted lightly toward the opposite end of the trailer, soft footed and alert. Ah, hell. He ought to stop the damn cat before it tackled those squirrels. He hoped Dean had latched the cage. He ran toward the bed.

An immense clatter announced that the cat had found the squirrels. He reached the bed. Yeah. The cat had found the squirrels and knocked the cages from the shelf.

Maybe he could—maybe not. A squirrel with one bandaged rear paw dashed over his boots, cat at its tail. Either Dean hadn't latched the cage or that was one smart, fast kitty. The squirrel headed under the table, thunked into the wall and headed straight back at Roger, jumping into the open drawer under the bed, the cat almost on it.

Before Roger could slam the drawer shut, the cat jumped into it and hunkered down, trying to force its too large body into a too small space. Failing that, it stretched its paw toward the back of the drawer, tail twitching. If the squirrel didn't move from the back of the large drawer, didn't have a heart attack from fear, it was safe. The squirrel chattered at the cat, scolding it, cussing it out for all Roger knew.

He heard a scuffling sound and saw a second squirrel from the other downed cage race toward the open front door and freedom. The cat noticed, too, and stared at the escaping rodent. Had to be a tough decision. Stick with the one you trapped or go for the moving target.

"What the hell was—" Dean emerged from the bathroom, zipping his fly, scratching his butt. The squirrel slipped between his feet. "Holy shit, why'd you let the little bastards out? They're vicious." He backed into the bathroom, making the closed door his barrier. He shouted, voice pitched at high volume and higher whine, "Get rid of them, Roger. Get them out of here."

Roger wished his ears had flaps to shut out his brother's screech. *I'm the big brother, the responsible one.* He forced himself to stand tall and open his eyes.

The cat went for the moving prey and dashed out the door after the squirrel. Or maybe just away from Dean's screaming. Roger wanted to trot after the cat, but he forced himself to stand still, to breathe in and out.

Time for the Schramm brothers to make tracks out the trailer, too.

"Squirrels are gone, Dean. Come on out." His voice came out level, calm, surprising him.

Dean emerged, peering around the door. "For sure?" When Roger nodded, he came all the way into the room.

"You and the cat and the squirrels made enough racket, somebody might call the cops." Roger took a last scan of the trailer. Unless they removed the paneling, maybe the flooring, he couldn't think of anywhere else to search. He dropped his chin to his chest. Another failed mission for the boss. Maybe they should get in the truck and keep driving, before Naismith had the chance to ream him and then fire them. What had Naismith said? "Failure is not an option," or something equally cheesy.

Dean giggled that really high-pitched giggle that told his brother the drugs were kicking in again. "I didn't find the videotape. But I found a bandage for the bite. Plus we don't got to worry about that pansy-assed Californian no more. I left him a message in the bathroom to bug out of our business."

Roger inspected the ceiling, thinking maybe his head would explode and his brains and his problems would just disappear. "Great, bro. Just great. Always thinking." No point cleaning it off. Nothing would hide the fact that someone besides a hunting cat had been in Mustard's trailer.

Dean nodded. "He'll know we can find him, even when he's sleeping."

Roger wished he were sleeping. Sleeping in the sun, on a beach, in Mexico.

Ed pulled his car forward to allow room for Lacy's compact pickup. He'd been glad of the short drive alone, so he could chill out. Why weren't any of the women he encountered of the docile variety?

After finding Roadkill's stress ball in Naismith's front yard, Ed was ready to head back there, six guns blazing, so to speak, to find his brother. If not that, he wanted to alert Byron and let the lawman obtain a warrant and search Camp Destiny.

Lacy did not agree with either plan. Lacy argued. Lacy argued loudly, so loudly that had any of Naismith's cohorts been in The Blind Chukar, they'd have reported Ed and Lacy's plot back to Camp Destiny. If indeed they had a plot.

Fortunately they'd been alone, and again, fortunately, the Chukar had closed for the afternoon, forcing the two of them to regroup at Ed's trailer. He cringed at the thought of inviting anyone into his current residence, but they realized that the fewer people who saw them together, the better.

Ed headed inside, toting the urn of Lise's ashes and a bag of groceries he'd bought before meeting Lacy. He stopped when he noticed a striped orange and white tail protruding from beneath the trailer, switching back and forth, back and forth. That huge tom he'd seen around the park must have something trapped. "As long as it's not a skunk, go for it," he called. The tail stilled for a moment, but the cat did not budge.

He opened the door to his trailer, and waited for Lacy. He'd again forgotten to lock the door. He set down the bag and the urn and called to his squirrelly charges. "Okay, little guys, your servant has returned."

Silence greeted him. He looked toward the cages. Saw first that the bag of chow had been moved, next that the cages lay overturned on his bed. The drawer beneath the bed stood partially open and when Ed squatted to shove it in, he saw a flash of movement within. Furry movement, as in the tail of a frightened tree squirrel. He put a shoulder to the drawer and pressed it shut. "We'll get you out of there later," he told the squirrel.

Lacy came up behind him. "This place is so tacky even the captive squirrels want to escape. Some digs."

"I like to think of it as charmingly eccentric."

"The smell is eccentric, if by that you mean totally weird. The charm is absent."

"What's absent are the squirrels, one of them, and—oh, shit." Ed ran the short distance to the table at front. No laptop. His throat tightened. He tried to swallow but found his mouth too dry. "My computer's not here. I almost bought that a cat could move the bag of chow, you saw his tail, he's a big mother. But a cat didn't take my laptop."

"No one took your laptop." Lacy pointed beneath the table.

Ed squatted and peered into the shadowed area where, clear in the back, his computer lay, upright, closed. His throat relaxed and moisture returned to his mouth, although a bitter residue remained. *I can still write. The journal I kept after Lise died isn't lost.* "Hallelujah." He'd aimed for a carefree tone and hoped Lacy didn't notice the tremble.

"Make sure someone didn't fry your hard drive before you give thanks. While you do, I'm going to use your toilet."

"Right." Ed retrieved his laptop and flipped it open. It hummed and sang its way to "on." Its owner wanted to hum along.

Ed took little note of the toilet's flush or the sound of footsteps. Lacy spoke in a low urgent tone. "You'd better see this."

Ed jerked at the sound of her voice. "There's a plunger beside the toilet."

"I don't need a plunger. You need to call the sheriff."

He turned away from his computer screen and took in Lacy's face. Pale, with a bright spark of red on each cheek.

"I've tried that. He won't do a thing about the condition of this place, so I doubt he's gonna cry about some spilled chow and a missing squirrel." He grinned. "Although his wife might care."

Lacy touched his shoulder. "Come here. Now."

Ed finally recognized the tension in Lacy's demeanor. He followed her to the bathroom. Printed on the mirror, in lipstick no doubt left by one of the pregnant women who'd used his showers, was the message: "Nosey peeple end up Rd Kill. Get out."

Ed froze. "Not *my* lipstick," he said. He preferred deflection to facing the message and the fear it sped through him.

"Not mine, either. You need to call the sheriff." Lacy's voice, steady and low, calmed Ed.

"You already said that, and I already told you he won't care." He checked the tiny space, noticed a box of Band-Aids on the floor. "Someone cut himself." He bent to pick it up.

"Or herself. Don't touch it."

"Doesn't matter. You yourself said it, you heard him. Byron won't get involved with this. It's up to me. And you, if you still want to help."

"That little nasty gram changes things. Makes it clear something has happened to your brother. The sheriff will want to know."

Ed's chest ached and he couldn't catch his breath. He rubbed the side of his neck. "I'll tell you what's changed. I know for sure that someone wants the evidence Roadkill has against Naismith. I know for sure someone has hurt Roadkill. Or worse."

Lacy grabbed Ed's shoulders and pulled him back into the area he called the trailer's Great Room. "Breathe," she ordered. She rubbed his shoulders and along his shoulder blades. "If you feel strongly that Roadkill is hurt, all the more reason to call the sheriff." Ed stiffened beneath her fingers. "Promise you won't dash off without our talking, and I'll promise not to ring the sheriff on my cell."

"Deal." Ed faced Lacy. "Byron will want more evidence than the stress ball and this little warning. You convinced me he's not going to search Camp Destiny without more proof. Even if he takes the message seriously, what more can he do? He's got a BOLO out on my brother. I'm going to find him the proof he needs or I'm going to find my brother."

"Make that *we* and I'll sign on to the plan."

"I wish to hell I knew where Clifford put that tape." He paced the length of the trailer, five small paces, and returned. "I need to let Gina know about this."

"Why?"

"Roadkill is the father of Gina's baby."

Lacy sucked in a breath. "You're kidding." She shook her head. "Thanks for sharing. So we need to warn her. You said they cleaned out the trailer they were living in."

Ed was halfway out the door before he spun and returned for his laptop. "Follow me."

Thirty-Two
I Will Track My Brother Down

The glass door to the women's shelter formerly known as The Flat Italian pizza parlor stood open, propped with a brick covered with a needlepoint canvas of a pizza slice. Like many of the stores on Hancock's main drag, the building was of red brick, faced with vertical redwood planking.

Ed refused to let his mind drift to the hours spent at The Flat Italian, helping Gina finish her chores so they could—*Do not go there.* Ed bit his lip until the pain diverted his attention.

He stepped inside, Lacy at his side. It comforted him that he had someone with experience in law enforcement helping him in the search for Roadkill. At the same time, he hated that he couldn't do it alone.

Even though red and white gingham curtains no longer covered the windows, the room remained dim in contrast to the bright fall outdoor light. Ed waited while his eyes adjusted. The Flat Italian had left the room. No booths lined the walls. No oilcloth-covered tables scattered the floor. The old linoleum tile had been ripped up, pieces of it still clinging to the floor in a weird patchwork.

Ed swore the aroma of pizza sauce and yeast that once filled the building wafted to his nostalgic nostrils. His stomach growled.

A woman's voice, lower-pitched than Gina's, floated down from above. "Ed. You came. Good. We need help."

Ed squinted toward the voice. Feather lay on her back on a tall, narrow scaffold, surrounded by several small cans of paint. "Call me Michaelangelina," she said in an orator's voice.

Ed snickered. Beside him Lacy groaned.

"I've brought a helper. Gina around? We need to talk to her."

"Talk, shmalk. Anyone walk's through that door better come armed with a paint brush or a hammer."

From behind them came Gina's quiet voice. "I'm right here."

Ed spun and almost collided with her.

Gina's hair was caught back in a red bandana. Her face appeared pale and freckled. A complication of pregnancy? Ed's breath caught until he realized the spots were specks from the paint roller she held in one hand.

Ed took his handkerchief from his pocket and wiped at a large streak beneath Gina's right eye. His arm nudged against her nose as he reached across. Her nose felt rough from the paint spatters, as if her skin were medium-fine sand paper. The sensation caused goose bumps to rise on his arms. And something else to rise, lower on his torso.

Lacy cleared her throat, pulling Ed's attention from Gina.

"Gina Cosentino, I'd like to introduce Lacy Ponder. She's offered to help find Roadkill, who, oh by the way, did not show up for the arraignment this morning."

A slant of a smile crossed Gina's face. "A bounty hunter?" She offered her hand to Lacy.

Lacy frowned but took the hand. "It's complicated, but I have doubts about Camp Destiny and its employees, and I think we can help each other." She turned to Ed, handing him control.

"No doubt," Gina said.

Ed caught something odd in Gina's tone but her face betrayed nothing. "Byron's put his men on the lookout for Roadkill, but he's not going to do much else, so any help we can get is great. Some recent events have convinced me something has happened to Cliff."

Gina put a hand to her mouth took a step back. "Come in the kitchen and fill me in."

After Ed and Lacy gave Gina an abridged version of Ed's and Lacy's separate visits to Camp Destiny and the search of his trailer, Gina's only comment was, "Myrna's not going to be happy about the squirrels. Did you call her?"

"Hellfire," Ed said. "I've got a squirrel to spring before it chews its way through my clothes and the drawer."

Lacy held up her hands, palms up. "On the one hand, find your brother. On the other, tackle a tree squirrel."

Gina giggled. She held her palms out in imitation of Lacy's. "Hmmm. Cliff? Squirrel? Squirrel? Cliff?"

Ed put up a hand. "I get it, I get it. Brother first."

Gina and Lacy exchanged a smile. Ed tried to understand why it bothered him that these women, his dear old friend and one he'd met today, seemed to be getting along so well, even understood each other's motives better than he could. He again wished Lacy didn't offer help he sorely needed. *Sweet, Ed. Gracious, even.*

"I'm going to Camp Destiny tonight and see what else I can find that might tell us what happened to Roadkill. If any of you has a camera with night vision, I could take some photos that we can use with the media. If people see those animals and their fear, we might be able to put enough negative economic pressure on Naismith to get him to back off."

"Optimist—" Gina began.

"I'll go with you," Lacy said.

"Someone should stay here, in case it's Naismith's next target," Ed said.

"We don't need a guardian," Gina said. "I'm surprised, however, that you're willing to break the law, Lacy. I hadn't realized the path to law enforcement was through the jail door."

"We'll be careful," Ed said. "No one will know we're there, and if they do, how likely is it Naismith will call Byron and invite him to search his property?"

"Others beside Naismith might call the cops," Gina said. "Let's see, will we have *Deputy* Ponder or *Detainee* Ponder?"

"You don't want me as guardian, you don't want me with Ed. I'm trying to help, girl. What do you want?"

Gina smiled. "Simple. I'm going with Ed. Feather has a camera that used to be her father's that we can borrow."

"Wait-wait-wait," Ed sputtered. "There's a slight chance of danger. Might not be safe for you, in your—" He broke off, knowing where that path led.

Gina leaned toward him. "And what will you have to keep you safe?"

"Stealth. Sneakiness. My incredible wit?" *Not to mention sheer goddamn stubbornness and persistence, something nobody ever seems to see in me.*

"Hear me on this one," Gina said. "If you try to go by yourself, I'll follow you. Singing "The Lion Sleeps Tonight" at the top of my lungs."

Too late to concede with grace, Ed simply conceded. "Got it."

Juanita bustled into the kitchen. "I need to make dandelion tea for Sondra. Feather says it's good for edema." Sondra trailed behind her, rubbing her scalp. Juanita spun and seized the black woman's arms. She backed her out of the kitchen. "*Dios.* I told you to lie down. No, no, you do not listen. *Idiota. Tonta. Imbécil.*" She chattered with each step.

Gina struggled to her feet. "I'll make the tea, and I'll bring some ice for her headache. Put pillows under her feet."

Ed clutched the kitchen table. "Is she in labor?"

Gina shook her head. "No, no. She'll be okay. The baby's not due for a few weeks yet. But like I mentioned the other day, she's got high blood pressure and swelling. Instead of resting, she insists on helping with the remodeling work. It makes me crazy."

"Are you sure you want to leave her tonight?" Ed asked.

"Oh, yes. All day these three have been on my case. 'Don't give up. This is your town, not his. We can't give up on Rainbow's End.' If we can't find anything to help us locate Roadkill, we can get more dirt on Naismith. And dirt is ammunition."

"I guess if you're on a smear campaign, it is," Lacy said. Her face had lost color while Gina explained Sondra's health issues. Ed empathized.

"There's plenty of time to get in some painting before Ed and I leave for Camp Destiny. Feather can get you two started."

Lacy and Ed both jumped to their feet. Two cowards preferring the terrors of painting to those of impending childbirth.

❦

Another Midnight Adventure

"Five grand? You're kidding, right?" Ed said. "Feather's a starving activist. She can't have a camera worth that."

"It was her father's. He was a wildlife photographer. He died in a car wreck in Bolivia last year."

"I can't afford to replace it," he said. "Maybe we should leave it in the car. I told you I was broke. " *And you never asked a word about it.*

Gina watched him, a tiny smile on her face. Not the Madonna, the Mona Lisa. "Banish bad thoughts. Nothing's going to happen to the camera. You need coaching in abundant thinking. You have plenty of money. You paid the rent for your trailer, you bailed out Roadkill, you paid for our dinner the other night."

Ed's mouth hung open for a few seconds until he consciously sealed his lips. When did she get so woo-woo?

"Earth to Gina. Here we have Ed Mustard, a guy who left his hometown and his old friends behind to become a famous, wealthy screenwriter. That's the image everyone has of me. Hell, that's the image *I* had of me until my ex-wife committed suicide and I went broke."

Gina moved her attention from the scenery outside to Ed. "Then change your image. As for the rest of us, maybe you're projecting." She paused, then said, her voice so low Ed strained to hear, "Believe me, when I see you, when I saw you last week, 'famous, wealthy screenwriter' isn't what came to mind."

Do not ask. Do not go there. She belongs with Roadkill.

The car's engine strained and gave an occasional burble like a fart but the interior remained silent. Except of course for the beating of Ed's heart somewhere in the vicinity of his eardrums. "And what did come to mind?" he asked. *Terrific, Ed. Couldn't keep a lid on it, could you?*

"My first feeling was joy," Gina whispered. "Then pain, for you and all you've been through recently. Then, of course, I wondered how long you'd stick around for this visit. So I felt sad."

Ed kept his eyes forward, appreciating the anonymity provided by the car and the distance between the bucket seats. He wanted to stop, to hold Gina's face between his hands, to absorb her feelings and any pain she'd experienced. Instead he said nothing.

"Right now," Gina continued, "I cherish every friend I have. Need them. Especially …"

"Especially?" God, what was he fishing for? Hoping for?

"For Pete's sake, Ed Mustard! I'm pregnant. I'm battling a madman for survival in my hometown. My hormones are out of kilter. You were the first man I loved. The first man I made love to. I felt all the old emotions. Love, betrayal, hatred, you name it. I wasn't mentally assessing your credit rating or the reviews on your latest film." She huffed out another breath. "You must think me pretty effing shallow. Or you've been hanging with shallow people." She blew her nose.

You made her cry. Great move, Mustard. He pulled to the side of the road. Reached for her arm. She jerked away and stared out the window. "You're not shallow," Ed said. "I've been living in La-La Land, where money makes the man." He swallowed. "I recall promising each other in high school that we'd call when we needed help. Yet you asked my brother."

Gina shrugged. "It seemed that the time had passed for that promise when you married the glorious, glamorous Lise Callahan."

Ed swallowed. "Point taken. I apologize. It was, I mean, I'm happy for you, but still, Cliff?" *What you really mean is you're jealous, but you can't admit it.*

"Maybe I liked his genes."

"From Roadkill?" Ed wondered about Gina's taste in men's attire.

"Mustard, dufus. As in DNA. Not J dash E dash A dash N."

"Oh." Ed smiled, somehow comforted. "Maybe we should go back. You're in no shape to be wandering around in the dark."

Gina turned on him like a cat caught in the rain. "I walk four miles, twice a week. A couple of months ago I was running five miles that often. We need to find Roadkill. We need to stop Naismith from going ahead with this wild animal farm." She waved an arm. "Now drive. And stop arguing and fishing for compliments."

Ed drove. He kept his grin inside. This Gina, the Gina he remembered, couldn't be defeated.

Ed stopped the car along the north-south highway that ran parallel to Camp Destiny, parking the Camry behind a gravel pile used by the county on icy winter roads. A logging road bordered the ranch property about half a mile west and downhill from the highway.

They reviewed their plan outside the car while they donned their skulking gear, black sweatshirts, ski masks, and leather gloves. Ed tried to think of the plan as flexible, but flimsy and vague described it better. He tried not to consider the consequences should they be unable to find his brother, locate the hidden tape, or dig up new evidence on their own. Without other evidence, without proof of who shot it, what would people think if Ed revealed the frozen wolf corpse? That his financial downturn had made him really, really hungry?

Gina fussed with the sweatshirt, first bunching it up over her protruding belly, finally stretching it over the bulge, so she resembled the Saint-Exupery boa constrictor that swallowed an elephant in *The Little Prince*. "Damn shirt's too small. I keep forgetting I'm showing."

"You're pregnant. You're supposed to be big."

"Big? You're saying I'm fat, aren't you? Insults won't help. I'm going, with you or by myself."

"We should be reviewing the plan, not arguing," he said.

"We'd be in and out a lot faster if we split up," Gina said.

"You've shared that opinion several times. Not up for debate. We're staying together. I've lost my brother. I intend to keep an eye on you."

"You think Naismith and his men chopped Roadkill into little bitty pieces and buried him? Or maybe just scattered him around?"

Goose bumps tap-danced across Ed's arms and neck. "Not funny. Don't underestimate Naismith's determination. He's obsessed with Camp Destiny, with shaping Hancock to meet his vision for it. Never underestimate the lunacy of a man who thinks he's right."

"Point taken. Especially a man convinced God is on his side."

"Absolutely. Remember our politicians."

Gina shuddered in the too-small, too-tight sweatshirt. "Please. That thought's enough to bring back my morning sickness."

Ed's stomach pitched. "You were sick? Was it awful?"

"I'm fine. Stop worrying."

He swallowed. He wanted to worry about this woman. That worried him. "Remember the plan: we go in, we get pictures, we check out the obvious places. We get out." He waited until he saw Gina nod and he jerked his head in strong assent. "Let's rumble."

Gina's low laugh warmed Ed to his toenails. He led the way downhill, across the road, to the new fencing that bordered Naismith's compound.

To anyone speeding by, the fence appeared to be one of those upscale horse fences that Nouveau Idahoans were installing at record pace around Sandpoint and Coeur d'Alene. A leisurely Sunday driver might notice the heavy-gauge, fine mesh wire that blocked the spaces between the rails. Only when Ed and Gina got to the fence did they see that the top beam of the fence also broke the norm. Shards of embedded glass and steel protruded in a seemingly random pattern.

"Welcoming, isn't it?" Gina whispered.

Ed said nothing, simply threw the heavy old sleeping bag they'd plundered from the basement of The Flat Italian over the top rail.

Gina looked like a burnt, toasted marshmallow struggling to make it over the fence without getting stuck. She backed up the rails, butt against the fence and teetered at the top. Ed reached out to steady her but she growled and he backed a pace away. At the top she swung one leg over, rearranged the grip of her hands and repeated the leg move. She lowered herself to the ground. Ed released his held breath and followed, leaving space between his crotch and that deadly top rail, despite the sleeping bag running interference.

He hid the bag a few yards inside the fence, stuffed beneath a fallen log. Wary of guards walking the perimeter, they used hand signals to communicate once they breached the fence. Stealth didn't come easily to Ed. Or quietly. With each step, his hiking boots crunched against the ground. It had been that way since he'd been a child, hunting with his father. Dad had moved silently through the forest, like Hawkeye in *The Deerslayer*. Cliff trailed noiselessly behind their father. Ed shuffled along in the rear, struggling to be silent, unable to master the technique.

Beside him, Gina carried her bulk almost without a sound.

Capricious clouds toyed with the intruders. One moment the darkness enveloped them, making it hard to avoid obstacles, but providing great cover. The next the bright moon sailed forth and shone full down on them, their shadows crisp against the earth.

They entered the compound at the end farthest from Naismith's home. They moved past the bunkhouse and the horse barn to the building that housed the doomed wild animals.

Once inside the animal barn, they risked turning on their flashlights. Ed wondered if the sight of the terrified springboks would outrage Gina into charging Naismith's house armed with only wrath and flashlight, but she stayed at his side as he took photos, once or twice leaning over the rail and chirruping encouragement to the little animals. Beyond the springboks, several gazelle peered wide-eyed at them, crowding the far pen wall.

The gazelle cage bordered a zebra corral, where one of the beasts ventured toward them, snuffling, as if it expected an apple. *Ha, wily bastard. You weren't so friendly the other night.*

A tall wood divider with double doors led to the area where the predators were caged. When they reached the old lion, it slept on, heedless of their arrival. A pen of four or five ocelots alerted to their presence immediately and crouched, ears erect, nowhere to run. Ed squatted and focused the camera lens through the cage, intent on keeping the wire fencing as well as the animals in focus.

Gina grasped Ed's arm. As they moved about the enclosure, Ed could smell the heavy, unpleasant mixture of fear and feces. The smell of his own fear-tinged sweat now joined that of the animals. Gina's fingers dug deeper. Ed shifted the camera's focus from the animals to Gina's face. Tears streaked down her cheeks and her nose dripped. She wiped it on her sweatshirt.

"Let's go," he whispered.

"I'll catch up. I dropped a tissue and someone might notice."

Ed waited a few brief moments and when Gina rejoined him they headed to the door.

Glaring spotlights surrounded Naismith's home, giving it the illusion of a spaceship that had landed in a forest clearing. Below the house, on the hillside that led down to the river, the gazebo stood shrouded in shadows.

Gina touched Ed's shoulder and stretched to whisper in his ear. Her hair smelled of vanilla or ginger, something spicy and wholesome, and to Ed's regret, desirable. "Show me where you found the stress ball."

They continued uphill toward HQ, clinging to each other to avoid stumbling and falling.

Ed heard a snuffling noise. He froze.

The sound of hoofbeats reached his ears and he knew. The zebras.

He peered at Gina, standing in the moonlight like a statue of Buddha, belly rampant. Smiling like the Happy Buddha or, more likely, the Grinch. One who let wild animals out of the bag, or the barn, instead of stuffing them in.

"Oh, shit," he murmured. "Adios, Destiny."

A chain link fence bisected the ranch property, keeping the wild animals off Naismith's lawn and out of his garden and home. Ed trotted along the fence line until he came to a gate. The gate was in the outer perimeter of the coverage from one of the floodlights. He prayed no one would see them pass through. Fortunately the gate opened silently. They left it open. Distraction might help them escape.

They skulked past the house, staying in the shadows as much as possible, alternately stumbling in the dark and silhouetted in the moonlight as the clouds swam across the sky.

And then the zebra poop hit the windmill.

Half a dozen of the striped beasts, the odors of Naismith's garden luring them, trotted past not 20 yards distant. Goats ambled by, their heavy curved horns supported by thick, sturdy necks. Behind them a group of springbok antelopes bolted away from the spotlight. Ahead a frenzied dog barked, its yapping reverberating across the meadow.

"Vincent?" a woman's voice asked. "Do you see what I see? Good Lord, preserve us. They're in your garden."

"Our garden, Emily. Everything will be fine. My men will take care—"

A whip snapped. "Yee hah." The cowboy's cry cut across the chaos. "We're on it, boss." A horse's whinny mixed with the odd vocalizing of the zebras.

Ed heard a shotgun being pumped shut. He threw himself in Gina's direction, landing awkwardly on her as she lay on her side. Her entire body trembled.

"Jesus," she whispered, "trying to crush me or put me into labor?"

"I want the little one to have a live mommy," he whispered back.

From the deck, Naismith shouted, "No shooting. That's valuable livestock."

The voices from the house continued, but Ed couldn't make them out over the racket now filling the grounds. Gina was still shaking, still silent. He heard an odd, muffled sputter.

"For God's sake," he whispered. "You're laughing. This isn't funny. We have to get out of here."

He knelt beside her, offered his hand and they stood. Ed gestured to the south, above the house.

As they approached the house, they could see three figures on the porch. Two of them moved down the steps, and Ed recognized Naismith by his small stature. Not good. If they could see the two men, the men could see Ed and Gina. They crouched, ready to run when the chance arrived.

"Have the men go easy on those animals, Mac. No shooting, unless absolutely necessary. Either somebody snuck onto the grounds or one of our men got damn careless."

"I've got it under control," said the other man.

"I need to settle Arlo and the wife. I expect a report about what went wrong in the morning. If you find something—or someone—tonight, alert me."

Naismith remounted the porch steps. The man he called Mac headed toward the heart of the commotion. He passed within yards of the two intruders but his attention was focused on the escaped menagerie. The beasts were not responding well to the attempts of two or three men on horses to wrangle them. The horses, obviously disconcerted by the almost-but-not-quite horses, crow-hopped and snorted.

As soon as Naismith and the woman put themselves and the little yipper on the other side of the sliding doors, Ed stood and hauled Gina to her feet. She clutched at her back and rotated her pelvis. "Too much weight to squat," she said.

Ed held Gina's hand and pointed toward the fence on the southern border of Camp Destiny. They'd face a long walk back to his car, but it was the farthest from the ruckus in the garden and parking areas. When they neared the fence, Ed felt as if someone had loosened a belt cinched too tight around his diaphragm. The adrenalin burst of their near-capture drained away, leaving exhaustion. The photos he'd snapped had better be worth it.

Gina sneezed. Not a dainty, girly, kitten-like little sneeze. A honking, hearty, blow it out, get-rid-of-those-damn-germs whoop.

Ed tripped and fell face forward, twisting into a tuck as he landed. His left leg caught most of his weight.

Gina knelt beside him. "You okay?"

She shifted her position so she was between the house and Ed and turned on her flashlight. As she played the light along Ed's body up to his face, she muttered, "Oh, my God, if he's passed out, what am I going to do?"

"Some sneeze," Ed whispered.

Gina yelped and clapped her hand to her mouth as if to catch it. Too late.

"Whatever happened to stealth?" Ed asked.

"Excuse me? That fall sounded like a Ponderosa falling."

"Thanks for the sympathy." Ed moved to all fours and pushed himself erect, the muscles in his left leg burning with every movement.

"Can you walk?" Gina threw one arm around Ed to support him.

They moved on, each step a mix of pain and pleasure for Ed. When he inhaled against the pain, Gina's scent comforted almost as much as it invoked erotic images.

Gina sneezed again.

"Dean, is that you?" a voice straight ahead of them called. "What the hell are you up to now?"

They hid behind a tall clump of rye grass. Footsteps came their way. "If you're out here snorting something when we're all supposed to be herding up wild animals, I'm gonna shoot you, I swear. Anybody else would have."

Gina sneezed again, more of a gurgle that escaped through her covering hand.

The voice grew closer, targeted their way. "Who goes there? I swear to God, answer me or I'll shoot."

They took off running, Ed limping, fear speeding his pace. They made no attempt at silence, just ran.

A shotgun fired. Shot pelted them from above. Gulping in air, Ed sped faster, and Gina stayed right beside him. Another shotgun blast.

Yes. The white fence beckoned. They dashed around a small grove of willows and raced for it. Ed clambered over, glad for the leather gloves, but Gina threw herself on the ground and tried to wriggle beneath. Without success. She was too big for the gap. From the other side, Ed tried to haul her through but she put a hand out in protest. "No room." She panted. "I forgot."

How could she forget she'd turned into a blimp? "Climb over."

Gina scrabbled in the earth beneath the fence rail.

The footsteps that had been pounding behind them suddenly stopped. Ed shut his gaping mouth and tried to breathe without loud rasps. He could hear his pulse pounding in his ears and wondered why the guard could not.

"Who goes there?" the man's voice boomed. He had to be within 20 feet of them.

Ed helped dig the earth away, clawing with both hands. Gina shoved him away and rolled under. He grabbed her by the armpits and they loped into the woods. They startled a deer that was grazing the buckbrush and it ran toward Camp Destiny.

When they'd run as far as they could, they stopped, leaned against two pines, and sucked air. "Maybe he'll think the deer made the noise," Ed said when he could speak.

"Right. First, the deer sneezed. Then it dug out under the fence. Then it left its camera lying around. An amazing animal."

Ed clutched at his chest. Nothing hung from his neck.

"I have to go back. I need those photos."

Gina bent over, inhaling and exhaling, holding her hips. "Not to mention Feather might notice if we don't return her camera."

Gina trudged to the car and relocated it where she and Ed had made their hurried escape from Camp Destiny.

Half a liter of water, a few minutes sit-down in the car, legs on the dash, and Gina felt renewed. "Thanks, body. You did good out there." She patted her tummy. "You, too, lamb chop."

She tried to relax, told herself Ed would find the camera, and be back soon. She squinted at her watch. *When had he left?*

Too long ago. Where the hell was he?

Gina threw open the car door and rolled sideways out of it. *Who cared about a damn camera?* She went to the back of the car, squatted and peed, then used the rear bumper to haul herself erect. It had been easier, though embarrassing, when Ed had stood behind her and hoisted her by the armpits. She smiled. He hadn't made a single unkind remark during that procedure.

"Waiting sucks." She paced the length of the car and back. Ed might need her, might need a distraction. "Too long." She'd find him. Had to find him.

Ed gripped both her arms. Her breath caught.

"Got it," he said.

Gina threw her arms around Ed's neck. "Thank God you're safe."

Ed hugged her back. "You're supposed to be resting in the car." He sounded more pleased than angry that she'd come after him. He stroked her back.

Ed held a filthy, flattened metal object. "Feather's not going to be pleased to see her camera, but I'm hoping the memory card survived the trampling."

"Better it than you."

Thirty-three
Priorities

Roadkill awoke. In an instant he remembered where he was, in a self-constructed pine shelter somewhere north of Hancock. Safe, for now, from Naismith's crazed employees. Thirst, fuzzy, burning, dry-mouthed thirst, engulfed him. His lips, chapped and cracked, ached and his mouth, swollen beyond normal size, was a tomato ripened too long in the sun.

He next noticed the smell. Stench, more like. He stank of sweat and fear and sick and anger and pain. He had to pee, good news, telling him he wasn't yet dreadfully dehydrated.

Oh, sweet Jesus. He had to get back to Hancock, to Ed, to Gina, to the sheriff.

Woo hoo, it's me, his bladder yodeled. *Pee time in the Rockies.*

He forced himself to his knees. His back scraped against the low pine branch ceiling. He answered nature's vibrant call from his knees, wishing he could move further from the shelter, but not trusting his legs to keep him upright.

"Okay, priority number one, done. Water next." With grit ball eyes he sought his water bottle. Roadkill knew he'd never leave his truck without water. Water: the outdoorsman's American Express card. He found it outside his shelter, a small plastic bottle lying in the sunlight. The warm bottle was half full, or half empty, he guessed with a little despairing giggle.

Roadkill trembled. He sat back on his heels and screwed open the top with great care. Took a few sips, enough to slake the raging thirst, not enough to make him vomit it back up.

Hell, he was conscious and concentrating, not delirious. That bottle was half full.

His next step had to be in the direction of help, of Hancock. Of course, he had no idea where he'd wandered to in his delirious, hysterical escape from Naismith's men. Not to mention his head pounded, his vision blurred, and he remained on hands and knees.

He sat back and extended both feet. His right calf swelled above his boot and his foot throbbed. Removing the boot might provide pain relief, but what progress would he make hobbling barefoot? Even if he knew which direction to head.

A welcome thought lighted in Roadkill's yet muddled brain. Cell phone. The new cell phone that Gina had forced him to carry, so she could summon him. Queen Gina. He warmed at the thought of her, smiled until his lip cracked and began to bleed. Had Gina been trying to reach him on that phone? Sweet Jesus, had she gone into labor and not been able to reach him? Would she fear for his safety or get angry and write him off for pulling a typical disappearing act?

He puzzled for a minute about where the phone had been.

On Rosinante's passenger seat.

Well, damn. Never there when you need it.

He took another sip of warm water, capped the bottle with great care and lay back down. He used his left foot to scrape some leaves and dirt into a pile to rest his right foot on. A little elevation might ease the swelling.

The Searchers' Secret Weapon

"Deer," Lacy Ponder said.

"Yes, honey," Ed replied as he braked his car. A mule doe and a half-grown fawn trotted across the road.

They shared a smile at the overused joke. Ed's cheeks hurt with the effort it took. Two days of driving isolated roads, hiking endless trails, camping when exhaustion demanded it, had abraded Ed's initial energy and optimism. He had to fight against losing hope of finding his brother. He couldn't lose hope, couldn't let Gina down.

"Give me another of those fake grins," Lacy said. "Makes me all quivery."

Ed's spontaneous grin came out real. "Oooh. When you quiver, things jiggle."

"Fuck you." Lacy twisted in her seat, thrust her shoulders back and shimmied.

After Gina and Ed's futile break-in at Camp Destiny, the three of them realized their next step had to be to track down Ed's brother. Sheriff Warnock had loaned them a detailed topo map that showed hiking and ATV trails and logging roads. Ed, Gina and Feather marked all the places they thought Roadkill might head if he was injured, or simply trying to hide out.

What had seemed too many choices that first day now narrowed to too few.

They'd found traces of campers and recent campfires but nothing that shouted Clifford aka Roadkill Mustard was here.

The car ascended a saddle in the mountain ridge. "Time to try the secret weapon again," said Lacy. "I sure wish you'd brought your lederhosen."

"You probably think you're the first woman who's wanted to see me in lederhosen." Ed pulled the car to the side of the road.

"If I'm not, you're in worse shape than I suspected. I'm thinking of your safety, though. The sight of you can't fail to scare away an amorous bull moose or elk."

"Joke if you must. I'm not anxious to get personal with a rutting moose."

"Actually I'm not joking. This is too scary." Ed glanced at her and she sent back a brave smile. "Well, maybe about the lederhosen. Keep it light and nobody asks the hard questions."

"I know that one," Ed agreed.

They jumped out and went to the trunk. From it they extracted a six-foot long alpenhorn, with its narrow birch tube ending in a bell-shaped horn. Fortunately the seat in Ed's car folded down, allowing them to squeeze the horn in with the rest of their gear. The horn had belonged to Ed's father, a gift of a friend in Boise who made the odd musical instruments. When their parents had died, Ed and Cliff had given the horn to Myrna.

Before Ed and Lacy took off on their search for Roadkill, Myrna had insisted he take it along. "You never know but what he'll recognize the sound. Lord knows it carries. Funniest thing I ever saw was your Dad out there calling the cows in the Idaho pine forest. But they came."

"I'm not going to sound like Dad," protested Ed.

Ed's initial efforts sounded like a farting bear bagpiping. However, several times a day he and Lacy hauled the horn out and Ed blew while Lacy snickered and told him, "You really blow."

After several minutes of serious tooting, with pauses to listen for any possible response, they heard a loud noise in the woods beside the road.

"Hear that?" Ed asked. "Could be a bear."

Lacy paled and her eyes grew wide. "Make more noise. Bears need to know you're there."

"That advice always confuses me," Ed said. "Do you make noise to let the bears know you're in their territory? Or is that mountain lions?" He shot her a sideways, teasing glance. "Could be a mountain lion."

Lacy crossed her arms and sent him an impatient glare. "You have no idea what's out there."

"None." He paused. The rustling grew louder. A guttural snort pitched above the rustle. The earth shook, or might have had they dared wait longer. They took off running for the car, abandoning the horn to their visitor.

From the safety of the front seat they watched a young bull elk amble into the clearing. It sniffed at the alpenhorn. It bugled, but the sound was more squeak than majestic bellow.

"What's with that?" Lacy asked. "Elks get laryngitis?"

"He's learning. It's early fall and he's young. I think he thought I was a potential challenger."

The elk walked and grazed, stripping bark from a nearby birch.

They gave the animal several minutes to leave the premises before they returned the alpenhorn to the trunk and pulled out their packs. Ed shouldered his pack. "This is one of the places I told you about. Cliff and I came up here pretty often. Found a lot of arrowheads." His shoulders slumped. "If he had to die, better here than in some hospital bed. Roadkill hated hospitals."

Lacy yanked a strap on his pack. "Dammit, Ed, stop with the past tense. You don't know if he's alive or dead. I prefer alive. Positive thinking is important."

Lacy's physicality tickled Ed, and for an instant his sexual interest was piqued. "Pull my strap and I'll follow you anywhere." Before she could follow the yank with a stomping, he grinned. "You're right. About staying positive. I am positive that jerk you described is one of Naismith's men. I am positive we will find Roadkill."

"Good. Now, repeat after me. 'I am positive Gina still cares about me. I am positive there was nothing I could have done to save Lise.'"

"Jesus, Lacy, you know more about me than I do." He squared his shoulders. "Okay, your turn. 'I am positive I will find another job in law enforcement. I am positive I will not have to live with my mother forever.'"

"Oh, God, I'd rather stay here in the forest with nothing but your alpenhorn for company. It's quieter than Mom." She bit her lip. "She means well." She shrugged her pack into place. "You know for once all this frontal mammary weight works to offset the weight on the back. Otherwise I might fall over backward."

Ed grinned. "I'm not touching that one. Or should I say those?"

"You bet you're not."

Ed folded the map and locked the car, carefully zipping his keys in a small pocket of his pack. He shouldered his. "We're getting low on food. Should have put out a snare for that elk."

"You bet. And then we could have stabbed it to death with your knife and smoked it. I love you rugged outdoor types."

"Wait until you meet Roadkill. If anyone could do that, it would be my brother."

"Which also tells us if anyone could have survived out here, it's your brother." She leaned against a huge boulder that marked the edge of the clearing. "You're pissed at him for agreeing to father Gina's kid."

"You'll make a good cop. You see people's motives."

The trail led sharply up, a tough vertical climb. They saved their breath for the hike, walked silently save for the crunch of gravel beneath their boots.

Another path branched from their trail. At the juncture, they found an area of squashed grasses and a mound of dirt and rocks. A little digging revealed the remains of a fire.

"He's been here," Ed said. "He's headed for the lake. Come on." He turned away so Lacy couldn't see the tears on his face.

"Don't get your hopes up, Ed. It could be anyone's fire."

Ed held up a scrap of red cotton. "This is from a cotton hanky, a 104 he used to call them ... for all their uses. Roadkill had—*has* a lot like that."

"So does every other hunter in Idaho and Washington."

"It's his. It's got to be. If it's not ..." He continued on the path they'd been heading. He wouldn't let her see his tears. Again. "Come on."

"How do you know this is the way he went, oh great tracker?" Lacy called to Ed's back.

He ignored her and kept walking. It had to be the right direction.

Thirty-four
Brother Graham Makes a Gesture

Gina bent to grab a rag. That was the easy part. Raising her pregnant form to standing took more effort, more muscle, more willpower. *When you finish painting the ceiling in this room and the next one over, you can take a bath. A long soak in that deep tub in Mom and Dad's—no, in* my *bathroom.*

The work and the resulting exhaustion kept her from worrying too much about Ed and his search for Roadkill. Getting help from the Ponder woman was a good thing. Young, healthy, a trained tracker, slender, stacked. *Jealous bitch. Be thankful he's got help. Not out there alone, when it could snow anytime now.*

"We're almost done," she said to Juanita, who painted woodwork across the room. "I sense it."

"You said that yesterday," Juanita said. "Also perhaps the day before, but I am too tired to recall."

"So little faith." Gina used the rag to wipe a glob of paint from her cheek. The paint roller package called it "never-drip." More like, "ever-drip." Her hands, her arms, any hair that escaped the ball cap she wore, were white with a fine spattering of dried paint. Getting it off wasn't half as easy as the label claimed. "To think at one time I worried this place wasn't big enough."

Juanita groaned. "It is plenty big."

"Woodwork's easier than the ceiling," Gina said.

"Ha. This requires skill. What you are doing, a man could do as well."

"No way." Gina's foot slithered on a fresh new drip on the tarp. She whispered a foul curse, hoping her baby couldn't hear from its wombside seat. She scrubbed at her foot with a rag, precariously balanced on the other.

She clambered up the small stepladder and raised her loaded roller to the ceiling above and a few feet ahead of her. She pictured Vincent Naismith's smug face above her and ran the roller over it. Another swipe for motherhood and freedom of choice. Another swipe against rich bastards and religious hypocrites.

A huge glop of paint dropped onto her upturned face. Thanks, Vincent.

Someone knocked at the front door and yodeled, "Hello. Anybody home?"

Gina dropped her roller. The handle fell into the paint tray, overturning it onto the tarp. Juanita yelped and backed into her can of paint, and emitted a string of Spanish curses.

The knocking persisted. Gina threw her rag at the spilled paint and stomped to the front door. She opened it a grudging few inches. Joseph Graham, Naismith's pastor in a pocket, stood at her door, his smile beseeching. She cocked her head to assure herself that he was alone. She scowled and crossed her arms over her baby. "Yes?"

Graham's smile exuded bonhomie. He ducked his head as if in apology. "I don't pretend you're glad to see me, but it's urgent that we talk." He cast his eyes downward and back up at her.

Holy shit, is he flirting? Slamming the door seemed easiest, maybe wisest. Gina pushed the door toward him and jerked her head to indicate that was the only invitation he'd receive.

Behind her, Juanita stood, her can of paint cocked backward, her eyes focused on Graham. "We don't have to let him in," she said.

"He's like a toothless old dog. Noisy, but harmless. And besides, we have him outnumbered and definitely outweighed." To Graham, she said, "Come on in."

The minister edged past Juanita. To Gina he said, "I came to see you, Ms. Cosentino." He peered at the chaos in the front room. "My, you are certainly busy. Aren't you worried about the paint fumes hurting your babies?"

What ploy is this? Bad pastor, good pastor, all in the same person? "Nope."

Juanita stalked to the window she'd been painting. "Not after the first trimester. We are all past that. Not that you really care."

Whoa. Sweet Juanita can get pissy. Way to go, girl. "There's chairs in the kitchen," Gina said. "If you stay to the outside edge, you should miss the mess."

She led the way to the kitchen and waved at a chair. She'd be damned if she'd offer this hypocrite anything to drink.

"Let me apologize for my drastic tactics the other day. I assure you I personally mean you no harm, but Mr. Naismith is funding our congregation and as such has a great deal of control."

"Sounds like a rotten arrangement to me." They stood at opposite sides of the table. The man wouldn't sit until she did. She didn't want to concede, but her feet and legs craved the rest. She sat. Graham sat.

"We all have our crosses to bear."

Oh, please. Gina said nothing. No point calling attention to a pile of horse puckey.

"I came to offer an olive branch. I made an attempt to convince Vincent to allow you girls to remain, but he is adamant." He paused. "And powerful." Another weighty pause, perhaps a pregnant one. That thought made Gina want to giggle but she remained silent, with what she hoped was a stoic expression. "And wealthy." He cleared his throat. "His wife, Emily, a lovely woman, indeed, has indicated her desire for compromise, but Vincent remains adamant."

"Why are you here? To threaten us? To convince me what a nice man he is?"

Graham extended both hands, placating. "I came to you in a gesture of goodwill. I believe Sister Emily might assist with your relocation funding."

Gina opened her mouth to protest, to insist that she would never leave. She let her mouth fall shut. Listening couldn't hurt.

"I am acquainted with your friend Roadkill," Graham continued.

"How do *you* know Roadkill? Not likely you met him in church."

Graham shook his head. "No, Roadkill in church is a hard image to conjure up. We met in Montana, I believe. An itinerant preacher such as myself covers a lot of territory, frequents a variety of places. God's word can be heard anywhere."

Gina realized she wanted to know about Graham's acquaintance with Roadkill, but didn't want to encourage him or let him think that friendship dulled her anger over the man's efforts to get her to leave Hancock. She'd find out from Cliff, once Ed and Lacy found him. So she said only, "True."

"I consider him a friend and wish he, and you, were not at odds with Brother Naismith. However, the practical reality is that I am 'Naismith's man,' and thus must make every effort to abide by his wishes, as long as they are in line with God's will."

Gina lost the battle for control of her temper. She jumped to her feet and crossed to stand over Graham. "God's will, you say? Do you think it was God's will for Naismith and his men to kill Roadkill?"

Graham jerked his head back. "What in heaven's name are you talking about? Everyone knows he's a free spirit. I'm sure he just took off on another adventure." He looked at her stomach. "Maybe the responsibility of being a father became too much for him."

Gina strode to the window, breathing heavily. "Other than fathering the child, he has no responsibilities aside from friendship. He promised to stick around and he's disappeared. Right after he went up to Camp Destiny." She turned to stare at Graham. His face was unreadable.

"I'd heard he'd been up there again, pestering Mr. Naismith. I'm told he left." He moved to Gina, yet kept a respectful distance. "I would tell you if I knew anything more. It would be my Christian duty."

Gina cast a quick glance at him. Maybe he was unaware of Naismith's implacable commitment to having things his way. Oddly, she believed Graham, even though he wore the role of man of God awkwardly. A sincere phony. She grinned. "I believe you might."

Graham caught her smile and returned it with an ingratiating one. "Don't you think you and the other women would be better off in a larger, more progressive community? Like Spokane?"

"What you and Naismith don't understand is that this is my home. My inheritance. I want to use it to carry out some good. Here, in Hancock, with the folks I grew up with. Where I want to raise my child, to make my contribution. It's my right, and if you know anything at all about me, you'd know that I believe in free will. I will not back down."

What was happening to her? Two days before Gina had been ready to capitulate, sniveling about her failure. Now she sounded like a suffragette. "My friends will hold firm with me. If Naismith wants a fight, he has one. Or you, his man of God, can advise him to live and let live."

Graham shook his head. "Believe me, I don't have that kind of power over him." He paused a beat or two. Almost to himself, he muttered, "I don't see what he's trying to prove." He cleared his throat and seemed to readjust his preacher's frock, even though he was wearing only jeans and a polo shirt.

He moved to the door. "I'll just let myself out, my dear. I had hoped to persuade you, to intervene before things get uglier, but I see you are as obdurate as my benefactor."

He disappeared into the living room. Gina heard a splosh, a thump, a male "Oh, shit," followed by Juanita's throaty giggle.

She made it to the front door in time to see a paint-covered pastor stomping down the sidewalk. Trailing down the porch and in the dripping pastor's path were the pale yellow imprints of his left shoe. Feather stood on the ladder Gina had been using, wearing paint splattered overalls and a satisfied smile.

Joseph Graham limped away from the place Darlene referred to as the "house of whores."

"Oops," said the young woman who'd dumped the paint on him.

He heard light footsteps behind him and wondered who else witnessed his humiliation. "There's a faucet and hose out back," Juanita called. "And here's a T-shirt one of Gina's brothers left behind."

Graham stopped. Juanita's expression blended amusement and

sympathy. The sympathy surprised him more than the other woman's parting "gift." Again he regretted being on opposing teams with these women. Paint oozed from beneath the top apron of his leather moccasins when he spun to accept her offering. He smiled his thanks, attempting to maintain some paternal, pastoral dignity.

Juanita grinned. She pointed down an alley that he assumed led to the back. "It's latex paint. Should rinse out."

As he stood at the faucet, stripping off his paint-soaked long-sleeved Polo shirt, Emily Naismith strolled up. She pulled off her sunglasses and eyed first the shirt, then his bare chest with interest. "Working on a 'coat of many colors,' Brother Joseph?"

Joseph Graham blushed. "More like my humility."

"Were you helping them paint?" She nodded toward the back of the shelter, where a beat-up sign still proclaimed it as The Flat Italian.

Graham's mind must have been muddled by embarrassment. He couldn't tell if Emily Naismith approved or disapproved of his visit to the shelter. He told himself it didn't matter. His reasons were easy to justify as the Reverend Joseph Graham, so why care about Emily Naismith's opinion? And why wonder if she joined her husband in wanting to rid Hancock of Gina and her flock of wounded females?

Graham didn't know why he abandoned his normal rule: When caught out, prevaricate, equivocate, pontificate. He told the truth. "They're unhappy with my opposition. I went to seek peace, and found—"

"Paint." Emily giggled.

Graham considered her giggle appealing and disturbing, because he disliked giggles from most women over 29. "You need help." She grabbed the hose and his shirt, spread the shirt on a nearby lawn chair and sprayed it, without regard to the threat to her jeans and boots.

Graham commandeered the other lawn chair and stripped off his shoes and socks. He tossed his socks toward Emily, who hosed them down, as well.

Once Graham was dressed in the borrowed T-shirt and cleaner, wrung out, but still damp socks, Emily said, "I was about to pay a visit to Ms. Cosentino. Wonder if I'll receive the same warm reception."

Graham inhaled and made a decision. He exhaled. "Don't go. I believe we need to talk. May I buy you a coffee?"

Emily's lips curled, slow, wide. "I like mine strong."

Thirty-five
The Schramms Are Back in Town

Roger worried bringing Dean to the general store was a mistake, but he didn't know what else to do. The hole where his dumbass brother had pulled out his tooth wasn't healing right. The squirrel bite was swollen and red. The pain and fever from both gave Dean an excuse to pop more pills. He chattered and moaned and complained nonstop. The other guys at the ranch grumbled and might rat on him to the boss any day. Roger didn't dare leave him alone.

Dean refused to go to the town's little health clinic because the nurse practitioner, an old, tough, leathery-skinned woman who'd lost any last bit of that caring nurse attitude about forty years back, refused to give him painkillers and ragged on him about getting off drugs.

Roger couldn't take him to the hospital in Sandpoint. They'd know he was on drugs and turn him in faster than water danced on a hot skillet. Lock him up. Keep him safe. *Sounds good. Sure as hell easier.*

Roger pulled his baseball cap lower and checked to be sure Dean was wearing that battered black cowboy hat he loved. He scoped the store and hoped it stayed empty. What if that woman from Sears had stuck around? If she sees Dean, she'll scream for the cops.

Ah, hell. Too many what ifs. Just go for it. Get in, get what you need, get out.

"Stay with me," he told his brother.

Dean giggled. "Sure, Mom."

Roger selected bandages, peroxide, antiseptic cream, and a bunch of dental washes and goo that the packaging hype swore would solve his brother's problems. *Uh-huh.*

Darlene Belmont, the dried up old widow who owned the store, stood behind the register, and greeted Roger with a grudging smile as he walked

189

toward her. From the nasty old bat who usually snarled a thin-lipped complaint about the mud they tracked in, the smile was a red carpet welcome. Her hair seemed different, softer maybe, and she wore a pink blouse with ruffles instead of the dull brown sweater Roger'd always figured was her store uniform.

"Ma'am," Roger said with a polite nod.

"Ready?" she asked, and began to ring up their choices.

Dean stood at the far end of the counter, perusing the display of magazines. Roger was pulling out some bills to pay when Dean moved toward him, waving some ladies' magazine at Mrs. Belmont. "Got anything better behind the counter?" he asked, a leer tilting up the good side of his mouth.

"No." The woman's terse reply conveyed disgust, but she didn't bother to add one of her typical digs about gutter minds.

Dean ignored her expression and leaned forward over the counter. "Well, now," he drawled, "that surprises me, given it's obvious you've been reading that there Cosmo advice on how to catch a man. You're looking good, like a fresh-laid woman should."

Roger's brain couldn't move fast enough to stop his brother's tongue. He put a hand on Dean's arm, but Dean jerked away. The Belmont woman's face turned such a bright red it matched the tobacco cans displayed behind her. Her eyes widened. Her mouth opened.

"Looks to me like you're ready for a *real* man." Dean stood straight and put his thumbs in his belt straps and eyed the woman's ruffled blouse and straining buttons. "I'm ready for you, babe, anytime of the day or night. I have a tool to satisfy your every dream."

Roger grabbed both of his brother's arms, then bent the right one, the one with the squirrel bite, behind Dean's back. He squeezed the finger, hard, and backed out of the store, dragging Dean.

Dean screeched. "Owwww. What the hell you think you're doing?"

"God only knows," Roger muttered. "You are for *sure* a tool." He looked back at the store owner. "My apologies, ma'am. He's delirious with fever."

He didn't let go of his brother's arm until he shoved him into the truck. But he couldn't lock Dean in there forever. *Mom, you asked too much. Nothing, nobody can save the kid from himself.*

Only later did Roger think maybe Darlene Belmont didn't want to hear that only delirium would drive a man to proposition her.

Thirty-six
What's Lost Is Found

A clenching from bowels to heart shot through Ed, and he knew, simply knew that they had found his brother.

Why now? During this search they'd come across other campfires, recently abandoned, still carrying the scent of smoke and grease. Why this one? *Don't question it.*

He cut a glance at Lacy. Her expression told him she shared his conclusion. Triumph shone from her eyes, along with joy. "This is it," she whispered.

Oh, God. To Lacy, this was the end of a successful hunt. She didn't know and love the man they sought. Dead or alive, they'd found their man. Probably channeling Nelson Eddy singing, "Here come the Mounties, we'll get the man we're after now."

He paused and listened. Heard nothing but Lacy's footsteps beside him. He put out an arm to stop her.

Silence, save for a pine siskin chittering in the brush beside the trail.

"I have a feeling he's here." Lacy resumed walking.

"So do I."

"We ought to make some noise," she said. "What if he's armed? We don't want to frighten him."

"Roadkill is rarely frightened." *Especially if he's dead.* He caught up to her and began whistling. Could he help it if the only tune that came to mind was that damn one about being out to get you, dead or alive?

A voice came from the side of the trail. "Never did I dream I'd be rescued by Nelson Eddy. Couldn't you try to make it to the Madonna decade, big brother?"

Ed bowed his head. His brother was alive. Here. Now. Safe. Breath filled lungs he hadn't known were empty. He could think of nothing to say.

Lacy moved toward the brush Cliff had spoken from. "Come out of there, Roadkill. I'll protect you from Ed. He might hurt you."

Cliff stepped from the brush. "Hurt me? Sheez. Get yourself run off the road, practically die and what happens when you're rescued? Some girl has to protect me from my own brother?"

Ed rushed toward his brother but stopped about five paces away. He thought he'd prepared himself for this moment but now that it was here, he realized he'd given up hope. Believed his brother was dead. But, dammit, he'd kept searching despite that. "Just how long did you think you could hide out in the woods? We needed you. Things are going to hell." The sight of his brother, his filthy, ragged clothing, a tree limb used as a crutch, pole-axed Ed.

Lacy put her hand on Ed's forearm. "Your brother's alive. Take a breath. Take two." To Roadkill she said, "We were beginning to think you were dead."

"So was I. So was I." In a low voice, Roadkill added, "Came close this time. Damn close."

Cliff's long curly hair sported pine needles and bits of other brush, with a large mass of spongy greenish brown plant life springing from one side of his crown. His grimy face, marred by a mish-mash of scabs and a scruffy beard, bore a goofy grin that Ed hoped didn't signal fever or fear-induced dementia.

Roadkill limped a few steps toward Ed. Ed erased the gap and embraced his brother. "I am so glad to see you," he said, able now to speak truth instead of sarcasm. Tears streaked his face. "Damn glad."

Roadkill returned Ed's hug. "Would have dashed right home, old chap, but I was so enjoying this little jaunt in the wilderness. Nothing like roasted rodents to tempt a man's appetite." He extricated himself from Ed's embrace. "Come see my home away from home."

He lurched toward the forest and appeared so precarious that Lacy and Ed supported him from either side.

Roadkill asked, "Bring any Oreos? I find them an excellent accompaniment to willow bark tea."

Lacy laughed. "You were right about this guy. He's nuts." She and Ed shared a smile behind Roadkill's back. Her face still held the glow of triumph at their successful search.

Ed realized then that he'd miss their time alone together. He liked this determined, stubborn, willful woman and her outspoken opinions that tickled him despite his constant worry about his brother. Without her persistence and upbeat attitude he might have given up.

Once in the campground some 50 or 60 feet ahead, they settled Roadkill on the pine needle bed he'd made. This time Ed's sleeping bag lay over the needles and Lacy covered Roadkill's torso. His right foot was elevated on Ed's camping pillow.

Lacy said, "I've had some first aid training. May I check your ankle?"

"Be my guest. Let me know if I'll live." Roadkill grunted when Lacy removed his boot. "I left the boot on because I knew it would swell. Might not be pretty."

Lacy pulled off a grubby sock. She gulped and cursed under her breath. "Keeping the boot on was a good idea. It served as a splint. You've got severe bruising."

"It hurt like hell or I'd have walked out." Cliff yelped.

"Ed's making soup. Once we get some broth in you, I'll give you an Aleve."

"Codeine's what I had in mind."

Ed moved to his brother's side. "If you're a good patient, and don't whine, you can have an Oreo."

Lacy turned on Ed. "You had Oreos? *Oreos?* And you didn't share with me?"

"They were for Cliff. His favorite."

"Used to be. Nowadays homemade pumpkin chocolate chip are my favs. Surprised Gina didn't send some along."

The bowl shook in Ed's hand and some of the soup slopped on his brother's lap. "Gina had other things on her mind," he said.

"Yeah," Lacy said. "Like why Ed was heading off into the wilderness with a young, not pregnant woman."

"An attractive young woman with a rack," Roadkill said. "Aaargh. The foot, girl, the foot."

"Don't talk about my boobs, or the pain will get far worse."

"And here I was, missing my friends and family when I should have been reveling in this time without the complications of the civilized world."

Ed smiled. Vintage Roadkill. With a thick layer of grime and blood and rodent guts.

"Let's rig up a travois and get him to the car," Ed said to Lacy.

While they built it, Roadkill filled them in on his last meeting with Naismith and the chase that might easily have ended his life. Ed and Lacy brought Roadkill up to date on events in Hancock.

"Whoa. Seems my big brother's holding up the Mustard tradition with style," Roadkill commented.

Ed tied off some rope and cut it. "About time," he muttered.

"After what you told me, I think the odds are good one of the guys who ran me off the road was the same one who clobbered Lacy in Sears," Roadkill said.

Lacy sprang up. "That guy at Naismith's place lied to me and Naismith knew it. A decent man would have asked more questions, wanted a better description, considered all his crew. His employee admitted he was in Sears but I don't think he was alone. Now your brother's saying that one of the men in that truck looked like Snaggletooth."

Roadkill and Ed exchanged smiles. "Snaggletooth?" Ed asked. "I don't recall you calling him that before."

Lacy's face went red and her lips clamped shut. She squatted and returned to her task, attaching cross beams to the travois long poles. "Because you'd tease me," she eventually spat out. "All I'm saying is that Roadkill saw a skinny guy who could have been a tweaker."

Roadkill nodded. "They pulled right next to Rosinante. I got a good look at the guy in the passenger seat. His mouth was twisted all out of shape. The question is, how do we use it?"

They lapsed into silence. Ed and Lacy worked. Roadkill watched. Ed appreciated his brother's abstaining from comment on his poor lashing skills.

A thought pinballed into Ed's exhausted mind and rolled to bulls-eye. "The statue. You hid the video by the statue."

Roadkill shifted to his side and stared at Ed. "You just now realized that? You're supposed to be the smart brother."

"I always hated your damn riddles. Besides, my brilliant mind churned with other topics, like worry about my lame-ass brother, and how I could help the woman he left behind. Did we mention things have been hairy in Hancock?"

"The woman he left behind?' You've been so jealous thinking of me with Gina you couldn't make a simple deduction."

Lacy waved her hands in the air. "Excuse me? What simple deduction are we talking about?"

"Where I hid the video."

"Lame," said Ed. "I'm not jealous of you and Gina. I left. Her love life and yours are your business."

Roadkill guffawed, loud, and so hard he winced and choked. Lacy ran to help him.

Ed stayed where he sat, his face a clay mask without expression, his eyes dry. He'd left his initial jealousy behind. *Wrong, bud.* If Lacy or Cliff even glanced at him, they'd see the pulse pounding in his neck. He unclenched his fists.

"This is priceless," Roadkill said once he'd regained his voice and blown his nose. "Gina still hasn't told you?"

"Told me what?"

"Ever hear of artificial insemination? Sperm donors?"

Ever so slowly, Ed rose from the rock and moved so he stood, gazing down on his brother. "You're not kidding?"

Roadkill put a hand up. "Swear to the universe."

"You didn't think to share that little gem with me?"

"Figured it was Gina's to share, more than mine."

"I could kill you. Pick up that rock and drop it on your smug face."

"Then I'm glad you brought lovely Lacy as a witness." He sat up, the effort it cost him obvious. "What's the plan to tackle Naismith once we get me home?"

"Naismith offered his place for the Hancock Days celebration, to coincide with the grand opening of Camp Destiny. I figure we can liven the celebration with a few surprises."

"The video," Roadkill said.

"Oh, yeah, that too," Ed replied.

Roadkill smiled so broadly his cracked lips split and began to bleed. "I'm damn glad you tracked me down. Go ahead and drag me back. We'll wump Naismith's ass and snare us a Snaggletooth, too."

Thirty-seven
The Road to Vengeance Holds Speed Bumps

Ed drove to Spokane, accompanied only by Lise's ashes. His first stop was a camera store willing to rush the production of B-rolls from the video they'd retrieved at Myrna's place that morning. Ed would give the footage to every media outlet he lured to the grand opening of Camp Destiny.

The previous night Cliff limped into the back door of The Flat Italian, supported by Lacy and Ed, who were exhausted from hauling Roadkill to the car.

Roadkill accepted the tears and joy from Gina and her guests as his due.

"You would have applauded," Ed told the ashes of Lise. "Knew he was the center of attention and milked every last tear and tender ministration."

Ed and Lacy, ignored, pouted, and agreed their sacrifices were under-appreciated. "Come to think of it," Ed said to Lise, "I should have recognized a déjà vu moment, with my brother, instead of you, basking in adulation."

"You're wondering if he was okay. Why we didn't take him to the hospital?" The ashes neither nodded nor spoke, but Ed continued as if they had. "Cliff hates hospitals, plus we want to save him as a secret weapon for Saturday, along with this video."

Gina called on the dour nurse practitioner who ran the town's clinic to check Roadkill out. "No worse than usual," was her diagnosis. His ankle appeared to be only sprained, not broken.

The manager of the Spokane camera store told Ed that his only hope of retrieving the images from the ruined camera lay in the hands of Rusty Wintersteen at Wintersteen Electronics several miles to the west. "The guy's a genius, used to work for the feds. If he's in the mood, you're in business."

Ed drove west on I-90 and found Wintersteen Electronics in a strip mall in Medical Lake. "Wish me luck," he said to the ashes. Silence, perhaps slightly resentful due to Ed's last comment.

Rusty sat behind the counter of his small electronics shop. Faded copper curls ringed a bald pate. Eyebrows that had never known a comb, let alone scissors, curled in front of and behind the lenses of his glasses.

His eyebrows might have risen a notch when he saw the crumpled camera, but Rusty accepted it without comment.

"Shouldn't be a problem. Coupla weeks. Gimme a call."

"This is urgent." Ed smiled. "Could you put a rush on it?"

One raggedy eyebrow raised into a vee. "When you have in mind?" he asked in a flat voice.

Ed leaned forward, elbows on the counter. "Tomorrow or the next day?"

Rusty hoisted himself off the stool. He towered a good three inches over Ed's six two, his belly protruding over the counter edge, orange hairs creeping out of his shirt and onto the counter. He slapped both hands outside Ed's. He exuded annoyance tempered with menace. The formerly pale face shone bright red.

Ed's smile weighed heavy and his lips fell into a flat line. He fought his urge to back off now that Rusty's moodiness had surfaced. The counter lay between them and he hoped to God Rusty couldn't spring over it to throttle him.

"Thing is," Rusty said, "I don't share your urgency. I have a lot of shit on my plate, and your flattened camera might fall off the edge." He paused and picked at a scab on his hand. Then he returned his focus to Ed's face. "Whaddya say you wait for my call?"

Ed took a deep breath. "Not good enough, Rusty." The guy's eyes opened wide and Ed held both hands up, palms out. Sweat trickled down his sides. "Hang on. Hear me out." Another breath. "Those photos might mean my brother's life. At the least, they might get him out of a jail sentence. I know the camera's not your problem, it's mine. My brother's problems aren't yours, either. But I'll tell you what. I'd appreciate anything you can do to move that camera up on your list."

Rusty crossed his arms across his chest. "Where's the big show of cash, buddy? The 'I promise to make it worth your while'?"

Ed shook his head. "I'll pay what you ask, but I'm not trying to buy you." Then he shut up. Hoped he'd read moody Rusty right.

Rusty squinted at Ed and his lips tightened in what might have been a phantom smile. "You're a piece of work. Ah, hell. I'll give you one thing, you didn't bore me with the story of what happened to the $5,000 camera." He contemplated the pile of squished metal and manure. "I'll see what I can do. I got your number."

"Thank you."

Ed waited until he got back in the car to wipe the sweat from his face.

Ed headed back into downtown Spokane, to the offices of the *Spokesman Review*. It pleased Ed to see that even with a shrinking readership and staff downsizing, the paper remained in its old headquarters, a red brick building with a round clock tower. Touring the century plus old building in grammar school had launched Ed's career in writing. Bizarre, given his current opinion of the media.

Ed bluffed his way past the receptionist and into the newsroom. He carried still photos captured from the video Roadkill shot at Camp Destiny. He smiled with confidence at the first person he met in the crowded newsroom and followed her directions to an editorial office in the back corner shared by a man and a woman.

"Who let you in?" the sharp-faced male asked.

The woman took the polite road, introduced herself and asked Ed if he had breaking news. "If so, we can hook you up with a reporter or an intern," she added, tilting her head in the direction she obviously hoped Ed would head, into the newsroom and out of her office.

"I do have breaking news, from North Idaho. We're trying to stop a private hunting reserve that threatens our local wildlife, and some adjoining old growth forest."

When Ed mentioned old growth forest, he watched four eyes glaze over and two bodies tense. As if working hard to keep their eyes from rolling. Maybe for the first time in his life, Ed felt empathy for the frustration his brother endured in countless actions fighting for the environment.

He'd always relied on words, but now Ed didn't know which words would work. "This developer, Vincent Naismith, plans to let rich guests kill wild African animals he's got penned there. It's neither humane nor sporting. It's slaughter."

A silence followed his words. The two editors exchanged a look. The woman cleared her throat and spoke. "Vincent Naismith. You're talking about Camp Destiny."

Ed couldn't read her flat tone, but he took it as good news that she'd heard of Camp Destiny. "Yes. Camp Desolation might be more like it. You need to see these photos."

Two heads shook. "No, we don't," said the man.

The woman's face showed regret mixed with sorrow. "Our publisher is excited about Camp Destiny. Excited. He can't wait until it opens and he can fulfill his dream of an African safari. Says he thought he'd never be able to afford one, but now that the animals will be in his backyard ..." She shrugged. "You get the picture."

Ed tensed. "This is news. You cover news. If one of those animals escapes—"

"*Then* it would be news and we could cover it. Until then, it's investigative reporting and sending someone out on that story would not be in his, her, or our best interests. We're into keeping our jobs, something that gets harder every day in this industry."

The woman editor stood and ran both hands through her short blond curls. "No one can stop us from reporting the news. But when it comes to deciding where to send resources on speculation, Mr.—"

"Mustard, Ed Mustard," Ed filled in.

"Mustard. Sometimes reality sucks. Bring us a real story, breaking news—"

"I have a video of Naismith and some high mucky mucks shooting an adult male wolf and a pup. That's immoral and illegal. Should be newsworthy."

The editors exchanged another look and a smile. "You're friends with Roadkill?" the woman asked.

"Roadkill is my brother. We were raised in Hancock. Camp Destiny used to be the family ranch. We despise what's happening to our home." Ed wanted to share the facts of the attack on Roadkill, but they'd agreed to wait until Saturday.

"You're *that* Ed Mustard?" the man asked.

"The Ed Mustard who married Lise Clanahan?" added the blonde.

Tiny pinpricks of light, harbingers of a headache, darted and swam before Ed's eyes like minnows. He kept his voice low, calm. "Yes, I'm that Ed Mustard." He inhaled and exhaled for a few beats. "That's not the story today. Today's story is an old lion, probably a cast-off from some traveling zoo, forced into a corral and used as target practice for drunken louts shooting from Naismith's deck. Tiny springboks hauled under who knows what conditions to a country with habitat and weather totally opposite what they're accustomed to, too terrified to move, and once they do move, becoming targets and trophies for heavily-armed two-legged predators."

The female editor reclaimed her chair, again ran her fingers through her curls. Her nails were short and a deep maroon shade. "It might work … 'forlorn, guilt-ridden screenwriter returns to family homestead to find it cleft apart by invading developer.'"

Ed groaned. "Oh, please. *I'm* not the subject. The subject is—"

"What about this?" the male editor posited. "We run the exclusive on you and Lise and the night she died, and include a sidebar on Camp Whatsis."

"No, no sidebar," Ed said, despair smashing his hopes like hard rain on a butterfly. "This story's about Hancock, Idaho, not about me. Not about Lise."

The woman waved a hand. "Listen to me, Ed. You may have a good story—greed, potential environmental devastation. But we can't run with that. However, a story that gives the real truth about the death of Lise Clanahan? We could slip in the stuff about Camp Destiny. The publisher couldn't put the kibosh on that story." She exchanged another glance with her cohort, but this time it was conspiratorial, not bored.

Maybe the story would be enough to oust Naismith, maybe not. Given the publisher's bias, Ed doubted that the dangers of Camp Destiny would be headlined. But Lise? Once again the subject of prying eyes.

Ed shuddered. *Face it, Mustard. The fact is, Lise loved being sensational. She loved the press. The discomfort is all yours.*

Ed brushed his hands down his jeans. "No, thank you. That's not why I'm here."

"Don't be hasty." The man stuck out his hand, and Ed shook it, reluctant to offend him. "We didn't even introduce ourselves. I'm Stan Fox and my partner is Victoria Douglas. We can work this out, I'm sure."

"Stan's right." The woman moved in on Ed and touched his arm. "You need media and we need a big story." She walked to the window that overlooked Riverfront Park on the Spokane River. "Your expression says you hate the media, hate our focus on celebrities. Truth is, we cover what readers want to know, and no one's that excited about an old lion, springboks or old growth forest. Everyone knows there are gaps in the story of Lise Callahan's last night. Gaps only you can fill."

"Even if I can, I have no desire to do so," Ed said. "Lise's story is sad old news. Saving those animals, saving a town from one man's greed, is much more important."

Stan Fox stood behind Victoria Douglas, backing her up. "You're a writer. You know every story needs an angle. With your name and Lise's on it, the story's sure to get carried by AP, get national coverage. A story about Hancock, Idaho, will get regional press at the best. It's a win-win."

"Let's do lunch. Talk," said the woman. "I'd like to hear all about the story. See those photos."

Ed had to try again. "No chance you can do this and leave Lise and me out of it?"

Victoria nodded upward. "The big guy would stop it, trust me."

"Then I think we're through." At the door Ed turned back to the two editors. "Thank you for your time."

Stan pressed his lips together. "Think about it. You know where we are if you change your mind."

Never Say Never

Ed drove home in silence, not even bringing the ashes of Lise up to date on his failure with the Spokane media.

As he drove, his pressure on the accelerator increased, until he might have been speeding by the time he neared Hancock, if the old car had the capacity.

In Hancock, he stopped at his trailer and dumped its contents into his car. He would not provide even that tiny income to Vincent Naismith.

He drove to Rainbow's End, neé The Flat Italian and parked in the back lot. He moved his belongings to the room Gina had offered him, next door to Roadkill, before heading for the kitchen.

There he pushed open half of the double doors without a sound. For all the revelers inside cared, he might have blown the alpenhorn.

Gina was the first to notice his arrival. She fell silent at the sight of his solemn face. If she noticed that he carried the urn of ashes, she made no mention of it. Her eyes stayed focused on his face. She sat at the kitchen table with Sondra, Feather, and Juanita in the other chairs. Lacy perched on a stepstool. Roadkill was ensconced in an easy chair someone had brought into the kitchen, his foot on a bolster.

Roadkill tilted his bottle of beer in Ed's direction. "Brother Ed, you've returned from battle. We are celebrating the completion of painting the downstairs of this little pizza palace."

Gina cut Roadkill a glance. "Shelter. No longer a pizza parlor. Now with shiny clean cheerful walls."

"I'm not in a celebratory mood." Ed went to the refrigerator and took out a beer after placing the urn on the counter beside it.

"Oh, but we are," Roadkill said. "Here's to a little paint, a little rescue from certain death." He drank.

"Myrna brought us some melons and nut bread, along with an apology," said Gina. "It's nice to know we have a few friends."

"Myrna see Roadkill?" Ed cut in.

"No, Myrna didn't see me," Roadkill said. "You do have your ears in a gnarly knot. What's the problem?"

"You say that as if there couldn't possibly *be* a problem," Ed said. "How about, *The Spokesman Review* has no interest in coming on Saturday unless it's to learn more about the night my ex-wife died. Two editors there tell me no one cares about Camp Destiny or old growth forest or, I guess, Gina, her shelter, or the fortunes or misfortunes of Hancock."

"What about the memory card for the camera?" Feather asked.

"What the fuck does it matter?" Ed said. "The guy thinks he can retrieve the images, said he'd get back to me. But like I said, what if we have photos and nobody looks?"

Gina put down her glass of ginger ale. "Darn. Wish we'd known before we painted," she said, her voice empty of all her earlier pleasure.

Feather tilted her head toward Gina's. "Not now, girl. Remember that vow to fight the bastards."

"I'm furious about this. I don't want to back down. Don't want Naismith to win. But you can't always get what you want." She chanted the last like Mick Jagger. She bit her lips together and rubbed a knuckle to wet eyes.

"We can still show Byron the video and get Naismith and Merrill arrested for taking wolves out of season, without a permit," Lacy said.

"Ouch. That will hurt them and their deep pockets. Not." Ed drained his beer. Went to the refrigerator and took another, opened it and downed half. He burped.

Gina nudged her chair back as if to rise, but stopped. "Don't go nasty and bitter on us, Mustard." she said.

Ed took in the faces around the room, saw Lacy's angry reaction to his sarcasm, his brother's amused, observing grin, Gina's dejection. "Excuse me. But I am pissed and I'm not ready to weep and back down. Not by a goddamn long shot."

Gina rose and moved toward Ed. "If we can't make a big media splash—"

Ed stopped her with one outstretched hand. "Oh, but we *can* make a splash. *Will* make a splash." He checked his watch. "I have 36 hours to write a treatment for my new film, a film that will tell the story of Lise Clanahan's life, the Lise the world didn't see, didn't know. The Lise they *thought* they wanted to know." He deposited his empty beer bottle on the counter and held the urn bearing Lise's ashes in both hands, extended before him. "Who knows if you would approve? You're dead. I'm alive, and you're not. That's the choice you made. The choice I make is to use your life and wasted death for good." He moved his attention from the urn to the stunned faces of his brother and the women. "The plan continues. We're taking back Hancock."

Sondra clapped first. Then Lacy. Then Gina and Feather.

Roadkill grinned. "Welcome to my world, brother. The world of the terminal optimist."

Thirty-eight
Is the Tide Turning or Did My Water Break?

Saturday morning dawned cold, blustery, threatening rain or snow on the 93rd annual Hancock Days parade. Gina had made a tepid effort to convince the other women, especially the ailing Sondra, to forego the parade.

"Forget it," said Feather. "We'll show this town that Rainbow's End is a beginning. And that shelter doesn't mean hidey hole."

"You got that right," Sondra said. "Activists act. Lying down is for wussies. I may be fat. I may be preggers. I may be sick. But I am not gonna hide myself away from these assholes."

"We must support Ed and Roadkill," Juanita added.

Gina stuffed down any remaining doubt and shouted, right arm in air, "Woo hoo. We're going in. Watch out world, here come the fighting fat ladies."

Feather, Juanita and Sondra had commandeered a few local teens to rig up the bed of Gina's pickup in a style befitting the parade. Bales of hay supported a beach umbrella and provided a comfortable throne for Sondra and Juanita, who refused to ride in the pickup's minimal back seat. The bales also hid Ed's laptop, plus a projector and screen he'd rented.

Feather drove. Gina rode shotgun. The wide-open back window to the pickup enabled shouted conversations with the bundled and blanketed women in the back but also let in cold air. Gina hunkered into her coat. She pulled out her cell phone and called Ed.

"Battle of the Bulge has begun. Team Rainbow in place."

"Roger," said Ed. "I always wanted a chance to say that."

"You be careful," she said.

"I'll watch out for Roadkill."

"Watch out for yourself, dammit." She ended the call.

"Aww, pillow talk," said Feather.

"You're going too fast," Gina grouched.

Feather tossed her an annoyed glance. "Fat chance."

Ahead of them, the Hancock High School Marching Band and Baton Corps stumbled their stuff. The Baton Corps consisted of two eager and talented young women and one energetic but agility-challenged young man. The band's music suffered because its members had to dodge batons gone wild. Gina smiled despite her jitters.

A mini-car darted across in front of them, halting not more than ten feet ahead. Feather braked and the old truck groaned to a halt.

Two men struggled out of the car, straightened their fezzes and doddered over to the passenger door. The youngest, Walter Feeney, published and edited the Hancock weekly newspaper, more a collection of ads, obituaries and graduation notices than a news medium. The older man, Leonard Lennart, was a retired carpenter who spent the main part of his days whittling and spitting on the bench outside the seed, feed and hardware store.

Feeney cleared his throat. Leonard hawked and spat and shuffled his feet.

Feeney finally spoke. "Gina, gal, we wanted you to know how bad some of us feel about that there protest." He swallowed, his Adam's apple bulging, making a jerky journey up and down his wrinkled neck. "And about not being more supportive ..."

Leonard Lennart elbowed Feeney aside. "What he means to say is, we're sorry we let you down. Yer folks were good people and so are you and we shouldn't never have listened to that crazy Darlene Belmont and her friend the Reverend. I don't know what's got into Darlene. I think maybe she's mentalpausal."

Gina opened her mouth, unsure how to respond. Feeney spoke. "Now, don't you say a word. We've been talking and some of us Shriners and some other old farts can help you finish up the remodeling on that shelter. Make it a real home, safe, cozy, for you and your gals and their little ones."

"I appreciate the offer, but—"

"Sweet. She'll be in touch," Feather said.

The men's responses were drowned out by the clop of horse hooves on the pavement. A horse's speckled muzzle nudged Gina through her open window. She leaned sideways.

"What's the hold-up?" asked the horse's rider. "This old tank break down?"

Gina inhaled the comforting scent of horse: hay, dust, outdoors, scratched between the horse's eyes and gently pressed his head back out the window. She peered up at the horse's rider, one of several members of the

Appaloosa Horse Club who pranced the outskirts of the parade. "We're fine," Gina replied. "Moving slow."

The two men shuffled to the mini-car, where they performed the amazing feat of stuffing their creaky, portly forms into the little vehicle.

"I knew it," crowed Sondra from the back of the truck. "The tide's turning in our direction. God has heard my prayers."

"If He had," said Feather, "we'd be riding in a convertible filled with chocolate bars, and Matt Dillon would be offering his help."

"You been listening in on my private conversations with the Lord."

Gina stared after the mini-car. "I can't imagine those two on a scaffold."

"Better them than me," said Sondra.

"Keep those prayers up. Ed's plan is complicated, and we've got to get this stuff to the ranch soon for it all to come together."

"Relax, friend. The plan is complicated and weird," said Feather. "Bound to work. I love it."

Thinking of Ed elevated Gina's temperature. Given the cold, maybe she'd think about him a lot today. She smiled. "Can you get around these kids? We've got to get a move on."

The band began what might have been a samba. Enthusiasm and volume outweighed allegiance to a tune. Sondra spoke through the open window.

Gina couldn't make out Sondra's words over the raucous notes of the high school band they followed. "Speak up," Gina shouted.

"I said, remember those prayers I'm supposed to be saying?"

Gina twisted around in her seat, not easy for someone the size of a manatee. She peered through the small back window into the bed of the pickup. Sondra sprawled, legs splayed, back against a bale of straw, her skin gray and speckled with sweat.

Gina forgot to breathe. "Stop," she told Feather. "Slow and easy," she added, her afterthought too late. Feather slammed on the brakes and Gina's right elbow hit the dash. Pain shot up her arm. She opened the door and made her way to the tailgate. Beside Sondra, Juanita knelt, clutching the black woman's wrist, praying.

Sondra's eyes squeezed shut and her cheeks bulged. Her hands clenched over her distended belly. "Shit. Damn. Hell. F—"

Juanita's fingertips stopped the obscenities. "The baby hears you."

"You wait till you're in labor. Jesus, Maria and the whole flock of saints will blush." She opened her eyes and Gina saw her dilated pupils. "My head feels like a pomegranate someone split open. I figure my brains will be spilling out soon."

Gina opened the tailgate. "Breathe, sweetie."

With Juanita's help Gina struggled onto the gate and crawled to Sondra. She placed two fingers on her neck and counted. Fluttery, fast pulse.

Dangerous. "Damn."

With Sondra's eyes fixed on her face, Gina forced a confident smile.

Sondra spoke through her pain. "Sorry to piddle on your parade, but I'm about to have a baby."

Gina wiped Sondra's wet face with her bandana. She spoke to Feather through the back window. "We have to leave the parade. I'll clear a path."

Feather called to Sondra, "Hold your horses and keep that baby inside you. We'll get you to the hospital in bunny time."

Gina looked to the front and rear of the truck. Ahead of them parade watchers lined either side of the long block, settled in on lawn chairs or blankets on the curb. A few spectators darted across the pavement in the widening gap between their truck and the marching band. Behind them was a band of riders on Appaloosas, the speckled horses dancing and shying, their riders looking confused about the delay. Two teenagers followed the horses, bearing the scoops and plastic bags and wearing T-shirts that identified them as members of the clean-up crew. A couple of antique cars pressed up behind them, followed by another band from a rival high school.

The driver of one of the cars tooted his old ah-ooo-gah horn. A horse reared. Its hooves clattered on the pavement. Its rider calmed the horse and sent Gina a questioning look over its neck.

Gina lifted one leg, then the other over the rear gate. She balanced on the rear bumper for a moment, and lowered herself to the ground, clutching the gate with both arms, dangling until she felt the earth beneath one foot. A light ripple of applause told her the spectators had been worried about her ungainly exit.

She trotted to the driver side window. "We'll have to turn around," she told Feather. "There's a side street not far back. I'll see if I can make room."

She moved toward the first horse. "Go around us. Emergency stop."

The rider nodded her understanding, waved to the others in her group, and angled her horse around the truck.

The horses edged past Gina. *Now what?* She waved her arms in a "stop" gesture and the first old car slowed to a halt. *Woo hoo.* So what if she stood in a horse dropping the teen poop patrol had missed. All she had to do now was hold back the parade long enough for Feather to reverse the truck.

Darlene Belmont moved into her path, a deep frown plowing her face.

Gina shoved past Darlene but the woman grabbed her arm, the one that had hit the dash. Pain tracked from elbow to shoulder to her neck. She wheeled about and focused on Darlene's mottled, angry face. "Let me through."

"You're slowing the parade," Darlene said.

Gina nodded her head in the direction of the pickup. "My friend is in labor. She has high blood pressure and could die if we don't get her to the hospital. If you do not move, move right now, I will grab that drum major's baton and beat the living hell out of you."

Darlene's eyes and mouth opened like popped bubbles on a pizza crust. After an instant, she said, "I can help."

Standing beside Gina, Darlene added her voice and waved her arms to clear a path. Together the women shouted, "Emergency. Out of the way."

Gina floored the old truck. It responded with a groan and a shudder. "Cra...ckers."

Feather laughed. "Let it out. Juanita can't hear you."

Gina cocked her head but kept her eyes moving between the road and the temperature gauge intent on a personal high. "Come on, you rusting mixture of tin and rubber. We don't have much time. I can't have abandoned Sondra for nothing."

"Juanita's good with her. She'll be fine," Feather said. "But maybe we should give Ed a call. Tell him we're running behind."

Gina couldn't believe fight 'em till they drop Feather was considering the possibility that they might not make it to Camp Destiny in time. That alone chafed, but the fact that considering calling Ed made Gina want to screech, wail or do both in unison totally stank. "What happened to your 'Activists Act' slogan? To 'Power to the Pregnant'?"

"I'm not admitting defeat," Feather retorted. "I resent your accusation. I'm suggesting we warn Ed. *Skilled* activists call it contingency planning."

"Yeah, yeah. You're right, but I hate to let Ed down. Come on, you bastard son of a bicycle," Gina muttered to the truck.

The truck bucked as if it had hit a fallen Ponderosa. Gina raised her right foot from the gas and as they slowed, a hissing came from the engine.

"Tell me the truck is not overheating," said Feather. "For pity's sake, it's cold enough to snow."

"The truck is not overheating," Gina replied. "It already has." She pulled to the side of the road, grateful that the shoulder was wide and flat at that point.

She put out her hand, palm up. "Give me the phone."

Fat white flakes began to fall on the windshield.

A Change of Plans

Ed hunched against the wind that had picked up since dawn. It whistled through the pines, cold, moisture-bearing, threatening rain or snow.

He hadn't spent this much time on the Mustard ranch property since his teens. Back then, his goal was to repair the fence before a horse or a steer found an escape route. Now, he, Cliff and Lacy had broken in before Naismith and his crew awoke to prepare for the Hancock Days' ceremony. After a brief, successful foray to the animal pasture, they awaited the signal from Gina to launch the next thrust in the plan Ed had dubbed the Battle of the Bulge.

He shivered. He hoped his plan worked. Dammit, it *had* to work.

The phone vibrated in Ed's pocket. He glanced at his watch. *Too soon.* He pulled off his glove with his teeth, extracted the phone, flipped it open and murmured, "Team Friendly Buffalo." Which sounded more like "Thb thb thb-thb." He spat out the glove and tried again. "Team Friendly Buffalo."

He listened. He frowned.

"Got it," he said. "Try to make it, if you can. We'll go to the contingency plan." He listened again. He squatted and spoke into the phone, his voice louder. "Of *course* there's a contingency plan. That's what planning is. Don't worry. Take care of yourselves." He flipped the phone shut. Stood. "Change of plans."

Two of his three companions appeared interested. The other continued eating.

"You have a contingency plan?" Lacy asked. "I hope it involves a fire or some other way to stay warm." She wrapped her gloved hands around her torso. "It's cold enough to snow."

"So little faith, these women," said Roadkill from the blanket where he lay, propped against the fence bordering Camp Destiny. He wriggled his eyebrows at Lacy. "Come bundle in my blanket with me and I'll keep you warm." To Ed he said, "What's up?"

"Sondra went into labor. Gina took her to the hospital. Truck broke down on the way back."

The crunch of oats between bovine teeth filled the stunned silence following Ed's announcement.

"Sondra—all of them—are okay?" Lacy asked.

"And the new plan is?" asked Roadkill.

Ed observed the water buffalo's satisfied chewing. "They're all fine. Give me a minute." *You're a writer, Mustard. Change the climax.* "No, nobody can die," he answered himself.

Lacy shot Roadkill a startled glance but he shook his head, put a finger to his lips, and tapped his head with the fingers of his other hand.

Lacy made a reverse clockwise circle gesture on one side of her head with her index finger. Ed pretended not to notice.

"Shock them, shake them up, unexpected," Ed said. He paced farther, checking his path to avoid moist buffalo offerings. He squatted down beside his brother. "You okay here alone for a while?" He re-arranged the tarp so the snow would, with luck, not drift over his brother. *What luck?*

Roadkill patted the thermos beside him. "Perfect. Go fix things."

Lacy marched over. "Anything you want to run by Team Frozen Buffalo?"

"Team *Friendly* Buffalo," Ed corrected. "Tell you in the car." He threw the sleeping bag over the jagged fence top and began the climb.

"Team F'ing Buffalo, BFD, who cares," Lacy grumbled. She followed Ed.

❧

Team Friendly Buffalo Strikes

"Some plan, Mustard," Lacy said from where she sat, nose to windshield, the passenger seat of Ed's car pushed to its forwardmost limit. "Did you consider what might happen if we get caught with a frozen wolf in the back seat of your car? Not to mention a stolen Red Flyer?"

"Relax. Won't happen," Ed said. "We'll have the wagon back home before its owner notices. The entire town's caught up in the Hancock Days celebration. They're either in the parade, or already out at Camp Destiny."

"Which just happens to be *our* destination, as well." Lacy wrinkled her nose. "I can smell your back seat passenger. Yuk."

"The wolf is frozen. Doesn't smell. And I told you I know another route to the ranch. I grew up there, as you may recall."

"Where you fell off your pony and bumped your head and have never been the same."

"Funny woman. Neither your insults nor your ridiculous worries will make me throw you out of the car."

"What if I attack your driving skills? You don't keep a steady pace, I'll end up straddling the wolf."

Ed winked. "Nothing will work. I need your help. Plus you want to be in on the action." Ed hoped they'd find Lacy's snaggletoothed nemesis among the crew at Camp Destiny. She deserved a win.

Lacy's breath steamed the car's windshield. "You better hope your car can make it on the back road, in snow," she said.

"Good driving trumps bad cars."

"Har. I was a cop, remember? We'll order that little slogan for our gravestones."

"Sheez, woman. Lise's ashes are better company than you. Stop complaining or you'll join her and the wolf in the back seat."

"My neck's getting as stiff as that beast in the back seat. How much farther, Daddy?"

"Good whine. We'll be there soon." *As soon as I find that back road to the Rolling M and assuming it hasn't washed out or been subdivided in the past decade.*

They rejoined Roadkill and the water buffalo later than Ed had hoped. He felt a stab of relief when he saw his brother, still safe by the fence, unnoticed by any of Naismith's guards.

He couldn't stop himself from saying to Lacy, "Meanwhile, back at the ranch …"

She grunted, still cranky.

"Trouble?" Roadkill asked when he saw Lacy's face.

"Good thing we had the shovel," Ed said in his cheeriest voice. "Didn't take long to dig ourselves out of that little snowdrift."

"Good thing I didn't bash your brother with it," Lacy said to Roadkill.

"You have to admit the shoveling warmed us up after the Toyota's heater called it quits." Ed said.

She crossed her arms. "I admit nothing."

"Lucky thing this damn animal didn't squish me, trying to stay warm," Roadkill said. His voice was muffled by the body of the water buffalo lying next to him, its huge head nudging his leg.

"Poor thing hates the cold weather," Lacy said. "I can identify with that." She pulled a wool blanket from the car trunk. "This should warm him up."

"What about me?" Roadkill asked, hunkering down and making a good attempt at pitiful. "I'm stuck here waiting, with only a foul-breathed animal for company. You could warm me up without a blanket."

"You got any masking tape in that car?" Lacy asked Ed.

Ed shook his head. "We're on a mission, kids. No bickering."

"Grump," said Roadkill. "Save your mean for old man Naismith."

"Point taken. Team Friendly Buffalo is moving in," he said.

He and Lacy harnessed the Red Flyer to the water buffalo. They tied the stiff wolf to the wagon. They settled Roadkill, wrapped in another blanket, atop the buffalo. The animal pawed nervously at the snow-covered ground, as if to ask what the hell the cold white stuff was.

Ed and Lacy started out, one on either side of the buffalo's head. Snow speckled them with white. Mud and gravel sucked at the wheels of the laden metal wagon, and the buffalo slipped and balked, despite Lacy's encouraging words and Ed's tugging. Every step drained Ed's muscles even as his wet running shoes came up heavier with each footfall.

Ed's stomach growled, reminding him of the breakfast he'd forgotten.

When they reached the small grove of aspen and birch at the back of the meadow where Naismith's crew had set up rows of chairs and a large, elaborate wooden stage, Ed stopped, confident they could remain there unseen.

Soaked from the inside with sweat, from the outside with melting snow,

Ed shivered. The light snow blurred his view, but he could still see familiar Hancockians and a surprising number of strangers observing Vincent Naismith as the man strutted and preened before them. The sound system broadcast his words the length of the meadow to Ed's unwelcoming ears.

"Team Farting Buffalo is in place," Lacy said.

"The comedian cop," Ed said.

"You fed this damn animal too many oats, too fast. It's not pretty."

"Be glad you're leading it."

From atop the buffalo, Roadkill said. "I've got a clear shot from here. One good sniper rifle and bye-bye, Vincent.'"

"What happened to non-violent activism?" Ed said. "We want to humiliate him, expose his crimes, not commit our own." Yet for an instant, before he shook himself to dispel the thought, he shared his brother's desire for a fast, violent solution.

"Joke, brother, merely a joke," Roadkill said. "But there's the asshole who shot the wolf pup." Ed heard a yearning note in Roadkill's voice.

The governor's aide sat on the stage among other luminaries, including Mayor Myrna Warnock and Reverend Joseph Graham. The elaborate stage rose some four feet above the audience, skirted with a red, white and blue bunting.

Watching from the audience, no doubt hoping Naismith would finish before their rumps froze to their chairs, sat most of the adult citizens of Hancock.

In the open area between audience and stage, children pirouetted, heads upturned, mouths gaping, tongues out, trying to capture the huge snowflakes.

When Ed saw his former agent Alex Margolis shivering in the front row, beside the editors from *The Spokesman Review*, the worry he had carried since returning from Spokane took flight. True, the worry flew a crop duster, capable of circling tightly and returning, but Ed chose to enjoy it, even for an instant. "My agent's here," he said, "and lots of people with cameras. The media came." *Hallelujah, the media came.*

"Tell it to the ashes," said Roadkill. "Your ex-wife has drawing power beyond the grave."

"Ed made the phone calls," Lacy said. "Ed wrote the treatment for the script. He deserves the credit, not a jar of soot and bones."

"Woo hoo, Lacy," Roadkill said. "No fear of the spirit life in this woman."

There's your cue, Ed. "Showtime," Ed said. He took off toward the stage, head high, stride purposeful, all the while telling himself it was *not* the voice of his dead wife who had given him his cue. He shivered, and told himself it was from the cold. All the while remembering why he had chosen creating stories, not starring in them, as his vocation. Every limb trembled like a bad diva's vibrato as he made his way from hiding to spotlight.

Ed's entrance didn't create much of a stir until he was recognized by a reporter. Then, following shouted instructions, photographers trailed him and darted ahead of him to film him proceeding down the long cold narrow slippery passage to confront Naismith.

Naismith stopped mid-sentence to gape when he noticed the commotion. He cleared his throat and the microphone emitted an ugly squawk. "Mr. Mustard," he said. "Welcome."

Ed didn't acknowledge Naismith's greeting. He wove through the photographers to the stage stairs.

Naismith made little effort to hide his annoyance at Ed's interruption. "If you could wait a moment. Please, take a seat."

"Nope, can't wait. You invited me, as I recall. To represent the Mustard clan?" Ed trotted to the podium. Knowing Naismith's men could tackle him at any time made his legs Jell-O.

Naismith shuffled through his papers. "Never let it be said that Vincent Naismith stands on formality. I can be flexible." Ed responded with a sweet smile and cold eyes. "Many of you know," Naismith continued, "that the land I've dubbed Camp Destiny was once called The Rolling M—"

Ed grabbed the mike with one hand and leaned into it. "M is for Mustard, not maniac, as some of you might think." The audience laughed, that uncomfortable rippling laugh when people wonder what's going on and who's embarrassing whom, and Ed stepped back and gestured to Naismith to continue.

Naismith's face reddened. Ed smiled at him, a smile that said *don't you wish you knew what the hell I was up to?* Naismith's eyes turned dark with anger and confusion. He went on, his voice tighter and higher pitched than moments before. "As I was saying, the ranch was most recently owned by Ed Mustard and his brother Clifford. I have had a bronze plaque created that will be displayed at the front entrance. The plaque honors the Mustard forebears, and of course the memory of Cliff Mustard, whom many of you knew as Roadkill."

Comments rumbled in the audience, many unaware that Roadkill was missing, let alone dead.

Gotcha, asshole. Ed smiled. He grabbed Naismith's hand as if to shake it and pulled him away from the mike.

"Well, now," Ed drawled. "That's a mighty fine gesture, but I'm wondering why you refer to my brother in the past tense." He took a tighter grip on the microphone. "Could be because you ordered your men to follow Roadkill and force his truck off the road."

The rumble grew to cacophony.

"Could be because your men left him for dead," Ed raised his voice to be heard over the audience.

Naismith leaned in to make a grab for the microphone, and yelled, "That's preposterous. How dare you? Everyone knows he's been missing for days."

Ed smiled once again, a smile that released the pent-up rage of the long search for his brother, the disgust at Naismith's plans for death-Camp Destiny, the revulsion at Naismith's bigotry against the women Gina had brought to Hancock for refuge.

He thought it might have been a scary smile, given that Naismith backed away from the podium.

"Missing?" Ed made a broad gesture toward the back of the meadow. "Tell that to Roadkill."

At the back of the audience, old Mrs. Adela Charters rose to her feet, and twisted to gape. She let out a shriek that assured her continuing post as lead soprano in the Methodist choir. "Thank you, Mrs. Charters," Ed murmured.

"Clifford Mustard, where did you get that beast?" she screeched. Everyone heard her, no microphone needed.

Behind them, Myrna said, "Holy shit."

Naismith said nothing. He stared, like the rest of the audience, at the center aisle. His men, too, froze and focused on the spectacle, not bothering to try to reach Ed or stop Roadkill.

Good thing, too. I might have hurt them.

Down the center aisle came Lacy, leading the lumbering water buffalo. A long stream of snot issued from its nose. Roadkill straddled the beast, one leg curved around its fat belly, the injured ankle protruding at an angle.

"Here comes the man you ordered killed," Ed announced.

Wide-eyed occupants of aisle seats rose and pressed back against their neighbors. Two daring pre-teens darted into the aisle in front of the animal. It let out a deep, reverberating low.

"It's Roadkill," someone shouted. "What's he got there?"

"Holy crap, it's a dead wolf," someone else yelled. "Frozen stiff. On a kid's wagon, no less."

Naismith's complexion had evolved from angry red to pasty and his fixed stare at Roadkill reminded Ed of the terror of the springboks. His nostrils flared and closed, flared and closed.

Lacy, the buffalo and Cliff paced on.

Ed shouted into the microphone. "That wolf was shot by Vincent Naismith here on the ranch, out of season. A wolf pup was also killed. We have a video of this illegal and inhumane slaughter, and copies for the media."

A man ran toward Roadkill and Lacy from the side of the audience. He stopped, and pointed a thin, shaking arm at Roadkill. The man's face was obscenely swollen on one side, with red streaks emanating up one cheek.

This isn't part of the plan, Ed thought. *Might work, though.* His insides shrank from watching someone make an ass of himself.

"You're dead, freak. You're not here," the man shouted. His eyes widened. "I saw your truck. You're a ghost ... a ghost. You're as dead as Mort."

"That's him," Lacy shouted. "That's Snaggletooth." She trotted toward the man, dragging the water buffalo and his passenger behind her.

The crazed man raised the shotgun he held in his other arm. "Stay away from me, boob lady. I didn't mean to hurt you."

Lacy stopped, but didn't back off. "Put down the gun. You don't want to hurt anyone else."

The audience held its collective breath. No sound except the buffalo's snort vied with the man's rasping, wheezing breathing. The wheezing turned into racked sobs. "The old man told us to scare him good. Then Mort had to go and die. You died, too." He spoke to Roadkill as if they were alone.

Roadkill answered the man in a flat, soothing tone. "You didn't kill me. You didn't mean for Mort to die. Lacy's okay, too."

Ed moved, fast and silent, from behind the podium and down the stairs. He came up behind Snaggletooth.

Roadkill's eyes widened when he saw Ed.

"She's dead, too. You're dead. You must be ghosts." The man raised the shotgun again. His hand was swathed in gauze and bandages, but his trigger finger extended beyond the bandaging. His arms wobbled.

Ed tackled him at an angle, pressing down on both arms, so the shotgun pointed earthward. His momentum knocked the gun from the man's arms. Ed kicked it under the stage skirting, and spun and grabbed the man's injured hand, forcing him to his knees.

The man screeched in agony, yet he fought against Ed. He bucked up and his head hit Ed's chin. Ed's jaws slammed shut on his tongue, the pain far worse than a minor mis-chew. He had to stop this maniac, whose strength belied his scrawny body. He slapped the man's swollen inflamed face, flinching as much from the pain he knew he inflicted as from his own.

The man emitted a horrific, high-pitched keening and crumpled to the ground.

Ed slipped in the mud-snow-blood at their feet and fell forward, on top of his opponent, and under the nose of the placid water buffalo. He released the sobbing man's hand, but kept hold of his forearms. They lay together, gasping. Buffalo snot dripped on them.

Roger Schramm ran up to them and knelt beside Snaggletooth. "Time to give up, bud," he said. He ignored Ed and focused on Lacy. "This is my brother, Dean Schramm. He wants to turn himself in. Me, too, I guess."

On stage, Myrna commandeered the abandoned podium. "Folks," she called to the audience, most of whom were standing, stomping their feet to stay warm, and wearing confused expressions. "Don't leave now. Ed Mustard promised the press a story and I think we all want to hear it." She aimed her best school teacher look Ed's way. "But make it snappy. The caterers are ready, even if our host Mr. Naismith seems to have taken a powder."

Ed rolled to his hands and knees and spat out blood and spit. He made an effort to stand. Not one body part cooperated. Then an arm hooked under his left shoulder, and another wriggled beneath his right. "On three," said a familiar female voice.

On "three" Ed straightened his legs and pushed upward and expectant Team Rainbow minus two hauled him erect and guided him to the stage steps.

"You missed the fun," Ed said to Gina.

"Not all of it," she said. She handed him a bandanna.

🐾

Ed Shares His Truth

Ed leaned against the podium for support. He gathered his breath and his scattered thoughts. He sipped water from the bottle he found there and swallowed, tasting blood. Then he abandoned his scripted speech, released the microphone from its cradle and untethered himself from the podium's formal confines. Heedless of his wet, filthy clothing and the way his shoes sucked against the wooden stage, he made his way front and center stage.

"Ever let anyone down?" he asked. "Feel bad about it?" He saw a few reluctant nods among the surprised faces in the audience. They'd been expecting some fancy press speech, maybe.

"I have. I gave up on Lise Clanahan. I didn't help her when she needed me. And I lost her. I was tired of the drama, tired of her mood swings, fed up with her refusal to take the medications she needed." Beyond the audience, beyond clearing skies he scarcely noticed, Ed saw Lise's body lying at the edge of the ocean that had claimed her life.

"For over a year, I listened to her threaten suicide. I raced to stop her, or called for assistance." Ed's voice fell. "Then one night I didn't answer. Maybe I thought, like the other times, it was just a threat, a plea for attention." Ed's battered mouth ached and his tongue felt three sizes too large. "When I got there, it was too late. I'd let her down."

He ignored the murmurs from the audience, ignored the video cameras focused on him, the occasional flash of a bulb. "People told me I couldn't have stopped her, it wasn't my fault, but I never quite believed them, not in my heart."

"Yeah, my head knew I wasn't responsible for Lise's life or her death."

He touched his head, then moved his hand to his heart. "But here? It hurt. It still hurts.

"When I arrived in Hancock and saw that my brother needed help, that my friend Gina Cosentino needed help, that the animals trapped here awaiting a stupid, ruthless death, needed help, I vowed I would help them. It's bad enough to lose someone when you *can't* help. How much worse would it be when you *can?*" *Enough with the lectures, Mustard. Wrap it up.*

"Somewhere in the search for my brother and the fight to get the truth to you, I forgave myself. I think Lise did, too. And my new film will not be a tale of sorrow, of a life lost to disease, it will be a story of her passion— passion for acting, passion for life, and the joy she brought to so many during her too brief life."

He walked back to the podium, replaced the microphone. Leaned forward to speak. "I think she'd like it. I hope you will."

Thirty-nine
A Place to Rest

No sentry blocked the entry to Camp Destiny. Ed drove past an empty guard shack. A few hands remained to feed the animals and clean up after them. Construction had been halted.

A phone call to Emily Naismith gained them permission for what Ed wanted to do. A breathless Joseph Graham answered her phone. Ed grinned. He could imagine the kind of energetic solace Graham had been providing to Emily, a woman whose husband was on the lam.

"You think you'll keep the name Camp Destiny?" he asked Gina as he helped her out of the car.

"Who knows? I'll discuss it with Emily, since it was her gift to us. I still can't believe she wants to be our partner."

"Guilt came late to her, but she's handling it well," Ed said. "She and the man formerly known as Reverend Graham will have a great time traveling the world, negotiating for stuff for you guys to market."

"True. They've promised honest dealings from now on, but it goes against both their natures. I'm taking the leap and trusting them." Gina rubbed her back. "I'm not sure I should have let you lure me away from the hospital. I may be occupying the bed next to Sondra soon."

Ed's eyes widened and blood drained his face. He swallowed. "Want to go back? We can do this anytime. Really."

She sent him a devilish grin. "I'm fine. A good walk might be just the thing to get me going. And believe me, I'm ready for this baby." She moved away from his clutching arm.

Ed breathed again. "I'm not. I need time."

"Doesn't matter if you are or not."

"Women."

"So, what's so important that you took me away from Sondra and that adorable little baby boy?"

Ed smiled. "You mean Sondra's kid or Cliff? My brother is soaking up attention from you and the others like shortbread in tea."

"When the judge put Roadkill in our protective custody, I thought it was

217

an act of mercy. Now I wonder if she had a grudge against me."

Ed walked to the trunk of his car and opened it. Extracted a canvas bag. "It's time, Lise," he said to the bag, realizing as he spoke that he hadn't said anything to the ashes in more than a week. "Time to say good-bye."

He turned to Gina. "I asked Emily's permission to scatter Lise's ashes in the family cemetery," he said. "Now I need to know if it's okay with you."

"As the new owner?" she asked, her face quiet, expectant.

"That, yes, but more as my friend." Ed took a breath. "Gina, I'm not going back to L.A. I'm sticking around, writing from here." He held up his hands when she might have replied. "Wait till I'm through, please. This isn't easy for me."

Gina waited.

"I was a prick to leave Hancock without you. The scholarship went to my head, maybe."

"And then Hollywood went to some other body part?"

Ed's laugh rippled up from his belly, loosening muscles clear to his shoulders. "No argument there. God, Gina, when we were kids we were soul mates. What happened?"

"Things change. People grow up. I had my obsessions, too, Ed. Activism. Activists," she added with a mischievous grin that caused a flare of jealousy in Ed's gut.

"I know we can't go back. I know this child isn't mine, it's Cliff's." He took another gulp of air. "But I want to be a good uncle. Be close to the kid. And to you. Be here for you this time."

"I think that's a terrific idea." Gina took his hand and started toward the cemetery. "Now let's give Lise a chance to rest someplace beautiful."

ACKNOWLEDGMENTS

Special thanks to Lisa Smith and the late Linda Houle, who launched my novel with love and skill through L&L Dreamspell publishing. Many thanks to my critique partners through the years: Dianne Anderson, Elizabeth Burtner, Conda Douglas, and Maureen Harty, and to first readers Cathy Carson, Marsha Davies, Bruce Demaree, Kathy Glass , Margaret Scott and Caroline "Frog" Tinker. I am very grateful to the real Roadkill, Jeff Damm. Couldn't have done it without you.

ABOUT THE AUTHOR

When she's not penning humorous stories of suspense, Kathy McIntosh is an editor, a columnist and a speaker about words and writing. She lives in Idaho with two hairy cats, one large, lazy dog and a husband who generally is neither hairy nor lazy.

Mustard's Last Stand, first in the Havoc in Hancock humorous suspense series about the offbeat denizens of Hancock, Idaho, was inspired by her love of the outdoors and her hope that we will save it. For more about Kathy, visit www.KathyMcIntosh.com.

Kathy loves to hear from readers. Email her at Kathy@KathyMcIntosh.com. If you enjoyed *Mustard's Last Stand*, consider posting a review on Amazon, Goodreads or other sites where book lovers hang out. It helps other readers decide whether they'll enjoy a book. Or share this book with a friend.

Look for the second book in the Havoc in Hancock series, *Foul Wind*, coming Summer 2014.